RAGE WITHIN

Jeyn Roberts was born in Canada and has been writing stories all her life. When she was twenty-one she moved to Vancouver with dreams of being a rock star, but instead she ended up studying Creative Writing at the University of British Columbia and then Bath Spa University in the UK. Since then Jeyn has been everything from a courier to a tree planter to a teacher – all over the world. *Rage Within* is the sequel to *Dark Inside*, her chillingly brilliant debut novel.

Also by Jeyn Roberts

Dark Inside

Praise for Dark Inside

'An intense, exciting slice of apocalyptic awesomeness'
Leanna, Daisy Chain Books

'Exciting, emotional and thrilling'
Stacey, Pretty Books

'A captivating read from the very first page. Definitely one of the best books I've read this year'
Dark Readers

'A highly intriguing debut'
Sophie, So Many Books, So Little Time

Jeyn Roberts

RAGE WITHIN

MACMILLAN

First published 2012 by Macmillan Children's Books
a division of Macmillan Publishers Limited
20 New Wharf Road, London N1 9RR
Basingstoke and Oxford
Associated companies throughout the world
www.panmacmillan.com

ISBN 978-1-4472-1790-9

1 3 5 7 9 8 6 4 2

A CIP catalogue record for this book is available from
the British Library.

Typeset by Ellipsis Digital Limited, Glasgow
Printed and bound by CPI Group (UK) Ltd, Croydon CR0 4YY

For Fiona,
a great muse and an even better friend

NOTHING

Greetings and salutations.

I know you missed me.

I missed me too.

What can I say? I've been around. I've been seeing everything. Slinking through the streets. Crawling through the train tunnels. Walking across water with my eyes alight with fire. Licking the crud off spoons and picking at the chewing gum on my shoes.

None of it really matters. They've left me alone for now but I know those days are ending. The Baggers want me back. They dropped their apron strings for a split second and the naughty child bolted into the wilderness. They won't make the same mistake again. I hear them calling me. Now they're starting to look. I'm on their radar. Eventually they will find me and drag me back by my heels.

And things will change.

In a blink of an eye, history will repeat itself. Remember, we've been through this before. From the moment mankind stepped out of the primordial ooze, they've been here to keep us in our places. Obviously a select few lived to tell the tale otherwise we wouldn't be here now. But how many of us are going to survive this round?

Tick, tock. Tick, tock.

Time is running out.

If a tree falls in the middle of the city, does anyone notice? Do they hear the creaking of the wood? Do they witness the leaves shaking above them? Do they sense the desperation or feel the sudden gush of wind against their faces?

That one great second before gravity takes over, and what was once magnificent becomes nothing but lumber.

Timber!

Or do they just go about their daily chores, continue on to work with their lattes in hand, iPods blaring, BlackBerries ringing, ignoring everything they've witnessed?

There were warnings. There are always warnings. But we missed them. We chose not to see. We didn't believe.

And now we are finished.

Game Over.

The Baggers are gathering their armies around the world. They are taking back the cities, rebuilding civilization on their terms. They have ideas. You wouldn't like them.

Now humans are considered a virus. A mutation. A disease. They need to be removed from this world. The Baggers will control those who are left to make sure humans don't go back to their nasty ways.

I wake up sometimes in the dead of night. A panic I can't explain from a dream I can't remember. Is this my life? Am I destined to spend the remaining days wondering what is real and what is a nightmare?

Who am I?

I am Nothing.

Am I?

Or am I the one they've grown to trust?

I want to be the one she wakes up to when the morning sun nuzzles her pillow. I want to walk along the sea wall with her, holding hands and exchanging gentle glances. I want to hide her away in a castle or a log cabin where she'll be safe and nothing can ever make her cry again.

But I'm more likely to be the one who holds the knife against her skin.

Tick, tock. Tick, tock.

What happens next? Your guess is as good as mine.

Three weeks before
the earthquakes,
before the world ends,
before the Baggers awaken.

THE MAN

He liked the basement. It was quiet down there. So quiet.

It made the voices that much easier to hear.

When they first started speaking to him, he tried to ignore them. He'd seen stuff on the television about people who went plumb crazy. It wasn't a good sign. He tried silencing them. Drinking heavily and popping sleeping pills. But the voices wouldn't go away. If anything, the drinking made them that much worse. They said terrible things. They whispered in his head about what was coming. They talked about the future. Earthquakes. Death. Chaos. They talked about how important he was. He didn't want to believe it.

But, as time went on, the voices started to make sense.

His role was explained to him in great detail. He grew excited when they told him what he needed to do. He would play a part in this new world. He was necessary.

The basement had always been his space. Unfinished, it was cold and dark, and his wife didn't like to go down there because she thought the place was ugly. Ugly. Her word. She much preferred her lacy curtains and bed filled with dozens of pillows that he wasn't allowed to sleep on unless he showered first.

He kept most of his tools down here. There was a shelf at the back that was covered with all sorts of wonderful things. A power drill. A chainsaw. Dozens of plastic boxes filled with nails, screws and other bits and pieces he'd convinced her he needed. He liked to do all the handiwork and she couldn't complain because he often did a good job. He enjoyed working with his hands.

In the middle was his work table, and he sat at it now. In front of him was a device, a wonderful contraption he'd built all by himself. He found most of the information on the internet; it was amazing what sort of stuff people could find on websites these days. Before the voices came, he mostly just checked his email and the occasional dirty site of which his wife would never have approved.

None of that mattered any more.

She'd been dead since the morning.

He was vaguely disappointed about this. He knew he'd be the one to kill her but he'd hoped to do it when he wasn't so pressed for time. He'd wanted to savour the kill, enjoy the moment, making her pay for all the annoying things she'd done over the years. But she'd surprised him earlier. Come downstairs into his work haven for some odd reason or another. Her eyes had widened when she'd seen his handiwork. She couldn't stop looking at the dynamite.

When she saw his eyes, she screamed. He had to silence her.

Now her body was lying in the corner. He didn't even think about trying to get rid of it. He wouldn't be in this house much longer. The earthquakes were coming and after that he'd leave to wherever the voices told him to go. They would have more work for him to do and he'd have to travel to another city first.

When he was finished here, the entire town would be dead.

Upstairs, he could hear his children arriving home from school. Three children. One boy and two girls. Twelve, ten and seven. Cursing, he looked at his watch, wondering how the entire day had got away from him so quickly.

'Mom? Dad?' His oldest son was hollering loud enough to wake the dead.

'I'll be up in a minute,' he said, pleased at how calm his voice sounded.

He picked the gun up off the table and double-checked to make sure it was loaded. Standing up, he winced a bit as his knees popped. He turned and headed for the stairs. The voices whispered away at him, a soft seduction wrapping around his brain. They knew what to do and everything they said made so much sense.

There would be no remorse.

Just another job to do.

DANIEL

'Hello, Daniel.'

He didn't look up. Instead he kept his gaze on the walls. Someone had washed them recently. He could see smears of dirt from where they'd tried to wipe it away. Cracks. Something had smashed up against it. Black cracks on white wall. Odd. Somehow he'd expected this place to be spotless but it wasn't. The tiled flooring was worn and he could see tracks in the dust from where someone had moved the desk chair a few inches closer to the window. There were scuff marks on the door, and the window blinds were bent and crooked. The janitorial staff must be slacking off.

The woman in front of him didn't wear a white lab jacket with a stethoscope round her neck. She wore a business suit, beige, and had running shoes on. Her hair hung loose around her shoulders and she didn't wear glasses.

She looked very normal.

'I'm Dr Coats,' she continued when he didn't answer or acknowledge her smiling face. 'As you know, I'm here to talk with you for a bit.'

He crossed his arms and then changed his mind. He'd read about that in psychology. It was considered a defensive position. It made him look like he had something to hide. Guilty. Instead he shoved his hands in his jacket pocket and tapped his foot against the desk. His shoelaces were dirty.

'Daniel?'

His eyes flickered over towards her. She was holding a clipboard and a pen but she hadn't started writing. She was waiting for him to talk. To spill his guts. So she could take notes and make decisions.

He didn't have anything to say.

'Daniel, do you know why you're here?'

Don't say a word. They can't do anything anyway. It'll be over soon.

But he had to say something. He didn't want to spend the next hour just gazing at the scuffed walls. Why did people always feel they needed to cover stillness with sound? Even at home his mother had the television on almost twenty-four/seven. She said it calmed her nerves but she never paid any attention to it.

The problem was he didn't know where to begin. A lot was riding on this conversation. There were countless words he could use, too many versions of everything going around in his head these days. How did he begin a conversation with such variables, each of which might lead to a different outcome?

'Daniel?'

'He started it.' There. First words. Not the best choice. He should have said something else. Inwardly, he cringed.

Dr Coats's lips curled upward. 'So you can talk. I was beginning to think you were a mute.'

Daniel shrugged.

'Excellent beginning. But, no, we're not here because he started it.' She moved over towards the side of her desk and sat down on the edge. Daniel could smell the shampoo in her hair. Or maybe it was her hand lotion. Coconut.

There was a long silence in the room while Dr Coats waited for him to speak again. He knew he should say something, but what? There wasn't any point in talking about it as far as he was concerned. It happened. He couldn't change the past.

There was no taking it back.

He wanted to take it back.

No, you don't. You want to do it again. Don't deny it. You hated Chuck Steinberg. Hated him. He treated you like dirt every single day of your life. What about the time he kicked the stray dog you were feeding? Then he told your mother you did it. What happened then? No, he deserved it.

'You told the police you don't remember doing it.' She pulled the cap off the pen and waited. 'So how do you know he started it?'

'I remember that much.'

She wrote a few things down before continuing. 'Would you like to tell me about it? The parts you do remember?'

You're dead meat, pretty boy. I'm gonna mess you up good.

He'd spent too much of his life being invisible to most adults. Now everyone knew him. In a few short minutes he'd gone from average nobody student to the one everyone talked about in the teachers' lounge and PTA meetings. Hell, this had even made the newspaper. No one came near him any more. Students actually went out of their way to avoid his locker. The group of girls who used to giggle when he walked past now turned and looked the other way. The last part he didn't mind so much. He preferred being alone.

Safer that way.

It'll be over soon.

'Daniel?' Dr Coats tapped her fingernails on the clipboard, staring directly at his face. 'Remember, everything you say in here is confidential. But I'll also remind you that we're here to talk. I can't help you if you don't help me.'

He really wished she'd stop repeating his name like that. No one liked being reminded that they existed.

He sighed. 'He came up to me after class. Slammed me into the lockers. Said I'd side-swiped his car with my bike. I hadn't been anywhere near his car. I don't even know what it looks like. When I denied it, he punched me twice.'

The room was quiet except for the sound of Dr Coats's pen as it scraped the paper. She wrote for a few minutes before looking back at Daniel. He didn't continue. The phone in his pocket began to ring. He'd forgotten to turn it off. Quickly he pulled it out. The

Ryan Adams song grew insanely loud as the guitars seemed to bounce off the walls. He turned it off.

Suddenly his cheeks flushed and he felt like he'd done something terribly embarrassing. It was as if he'd shown up for this appointment wearing nothing but a raincoat and a pair of wet shoes. He glanced up at the doctor for a brief second and noticed how she was studying him intently.

'What else do you remember, Daniel?'

His mouth was dry and he couldn't swallow. What did he remember? They told him that he'd gone crazy. Grabbed Chuck by the shirt and punched him several times in the face. Once Chuck had dropped to the floor, he'd kicked him repeatedly in the head until the maths and biology teachers managed to drag him away. Chuck had to go to the hospital and get treated for concussion. They had to take X-rays because they were afraid Daniel had cracked the bigger boy's skull. Afterwards Daniel discovered the blood soaked through his sneakers and his white socks were stained red.

But he didn't remember.

He only knew what they'd told him.

'I don't know,' he said. 'That's pretty much it.'

The doctor lowered her clipboard. 'That's all you can recall?'

He nodded.

'Has this ever happened to you before? Not being able to recollect certain events?'

He hesitated and then shook his head. Lied. Waited

while she made more notes on her clipboard.

'Head injuries?'

'No. Maybe when I was little. Nothing major though. Basic kid stuff. I think I fell off the couch once. Had to go to the emergency room.'

'So nothing recent then?'

He nodded.

'Any other fights?'

'Nope.' At least none that he'd admit to.

'What about aggressive tendencies? Have you had thoughts about hurting people?'

He'd never considered himself violent before. He was the quiet guy who went to school each day and hung out with a few good friends. The semi-popular boy who was always reading during lunch period and playing guitar on the front lawn when the weather was good. He was a lover, not a fighter. There were a few girls who would agree with that. He was the guy everyone assumed would go on to college, get a liberal arts degree and end up being some obscenely successful writer. Even his yearbook picture said he was 'the guy most likely to win a Pulitzer Prize in literature'.

But violent? No, that wasn't his style. At least that's what he thought. What he kept telling himself.

Make them suffer. They will all die.

Daniel grabbed his jacket. 'I've got to go.'

Dr Coats looked up at him in surprise. 'We've still got forty-five minutes. I'll have to report this if you leave now. You know this isn't voluntary.'

It doesn't matter. None of this matters.

'I'm sorry,' Daniel said. 'I don't want to talk any more. I've got to go.'

He grabbed the handle and was out of the door before she had a chance to say anything more.

Outside it was raining and he pulled his hoody up over his head and stuffed his hands in the pockets. Turning round, he looked back at the hospital, half expecting to see big burly orderlies running out of the door to hunt him down. But no one came after him, only an older guy in a wheelchair, his pencil-thin legs sticking out from under his hospital gown as he tried to open a can of Pepsi.

A cold trickle of water worked its way into his shoes, soaking his feet. Looking down, he realized he was standing in the middle of a large puddle. He stared at the water, mesmerized as the raindrops pelted a steady beat into the ground.

It made him want to go swimming. Maybe he could catch a bus out to Buntzen Lake and go for a swim. It wasn't that cold yet. It would be nice to float with the rain tickling his face as the mountains loomed over him. Maybe he could get a diving mask so he could hold his breath and watch the fish swim beneath his feet.

The car honking its horn from behind pulled him out of his trance. Daniel stepped over to the kerb, shaking his head slightly to try to clear it. Swimming? Now? Man, he needed to get his priorities straight.

There were far more important things to worry about.

Looking back at the hospital, he knew he was going to get into trouble for leaving early. Part of his probation was the weekly visits to work on his anger issues.

But all that seemed so insignificant.

He didn't know what it was, only that it was coming. Soon.

None of this would matter.

MASON

'It's suicidal.'

'Nah, it ain't. People have been doing this for years. My dad was talking about it last summer. They used to make the entire football team do it for an initiation or something. Told me he'd break my legs if he ever caught me doing it. But he's done it. I could see it in his eyes.'

Mason stood with his friends at the edge of the Diefenbaker Train Bridge. They'd been there for the past half an hour, trying to gather the courage to climb up into the metal girders and make their way towards the middle of the Saskatchewan River.

Although it was September, the weather was crazy warm. People were wearing shorts and it felt strange walking through the mall and seeing all the back-to-school clothing for sale. The snow seemed a million miles away.

The river was still the perfect temperature for getting soaked, and although it was a weekday everyone and their dogs were taking advantage of it. There were people water skiing and kayaking. A few minutes ago, a motor boat full of pretty girls in skimpy bikinis crossed under the bridge. They'd hollered and waved their beer bottles as they passed. Both Tom and Kurt screamed at them to come back.

All this fine summer weather. Girls in sundresses and short shorts. It really sucked being back at school.

But even he had to admit he must be missing a few extra brain cells since he was now standing under a bridge, debating the most efficient way to crawl across it without falling and breaking his neck.

The bridge was old. The bottom part was designed with steel so ancient it was dyed a permanent black from the years of train exhaust. Up above was a system of wooden boards (also stained a variety of dark colours), two long parallel steel rods and hundreds of railway ties. There was no walkway to cross to the other side. In fact, there was a huge chain-link fence round the outer perimeter to try to keep people from trespassing. Of course that didn't stop the teenagers in the slightest. There were several places in the fence where kids had cut holes in order to sneak through. Although the bridge was on the outside limits of Diefenbaker Park, it wasn't heavily monitored at night, which made it the perfect party place. Mason had done plenty of drinking here in the past.

But it was a Thursday afternoon and not a weekend evening. Thankfully none of them were hitting the bottle. Of course, Mason realized, the whole situation would make more sense if they were.

It was known in Saskatoon that the ultimate way to test one's bravery was to jump from the bridge into the river.

'Mason. Dude. Brother. What do you think?' Tom

grinned at his friend. Mason knew that look. It usually meant they were about to do something that would get them in a big heap of trouble.

'Definitely suicidal,' Mason said.

That seemed to be the general consensus. Scotty and Kurt nodded their heads in unison.

'No one said we're going to live forever,' Tom said. He pulled his shirt up over his head and dropped it into the wild grass. He took his car keys and phone from his pocket and tossed them on top of the shirt. 'Can't lose those. Mom would have a bird.'

'I dunno,' Scotty said. 'This really isn't a great idea. There was that kid a few years ago who broke his back. Remember that? It made the papers and everything. Cracked his neck on a rock or something. Water's kinda shallow this time of year. We should test it first.'

'First of all,' Tom said, 'I heard all about that. Dude was drunk out of his skull. Tried to do some sort of back flip and landed hard. It's his own damn fault he broke his back. Second, the water is deep. Look at the banks. If the water was low, we'd be able to see it. No sandbars either. Bottomless blue, baby. It's all good.'

Mason nodded. 'We had all that rain earlier this month. Our basement even flooded. It's safe enough.'

'I dunno,' Scotty said again.

Kurt stepped forward, removed his shirt and tossed it next to Tom's. 'I'm in,' he said. 'The fact some guy ended up a veggie and wearing diapers for the rest of his life isn't enough to scare me.'

Mason nodded, although that certainly was enough to scare him. But if the other guys were hell-bent on doing it he'd have to do it too. No way he'd let Tom hold something like that over him. He'd never hear the end of it. Brothers by choice, daredevils for life. If one of them did something, the other had to follow. That was the code. Even on the minuscule chance he might wimp out, the least he could do was watch and make sure no bones got fractured. And he was a strong swimmer. He'd be good to have around in case something went wrong.

'We should just head back,' Scotty said. 'It's gonna be dark soon enough. I got homework tonight.'

'Don't be such a coward,' Kurt said. 'Especially not in front of the ladies.' He pointed in the direction of Staci and Britney, who were trying to find a graceful way to crawl under the fence. Britney was struggling – some of her hair seemed to be caught in the chain link. 'How's it going, girls?' he yelled back at them. 'You stuck? I can always give you a hand.'

Staci gave them the finger.

They waited, but when it became apparent that the fence wasn't going to let go of Britney's hair, Mason trotted back to them.

'How'd you manage this?' he asked. A good chunk of hair was twisted into the metal wire. Staci was trying to unwind the strands but it only made the knot tighter.

'How should I know?' Britney muttered. 'How on earth did you talk me into this again? This is the last time we do this sort of crap, Mason. Next time we're staying at the mall.'

'Fair enough,' he agreed. 'I'm gonna have to cut it.'

'Great,' Britney said. 'Just destroy it, why don't you. Why don't I just spend the rest of the semester bald. It's not like I have a social life or anything.'

Mason pulled out his jackknife, a final gift from his father before he died. 'I won't ruin your pretty hair. Just don't move or I might take off an ear.' He grinned and twisted away when she tried to playfully smack him.

He managed to trim the hair without doing too much damage. Once Britney was free, she picked up her bag and grabbed Staci by the arm.

They returned to the group, where Tom and Kurt were arguing about how to best climb up on to the concrete pillars. The plan was to swing out on to the metal rafters and from there, carefully work their way towards the middle of the bridge. Once there, they would each take their turn jumping and then swim back to shore. The girls would judge who jumped the furthest.

Easy as pie.

'Of course you're welcome to jump too,' Tom said to Britney, giving her a wink and a kiss on the cheek. She shoved him away, half smiling.

'I've done enough damage to myself today,' she retorted, patting her hair down with her fingers. 'Besides, we're not crazy. There's no way you'd ever catch me in that river. It's polluted. You may want green skin and hair loss but not me.'

'And the undercurrent,' Staci said. 'My mom said that even some of the world's strongest swimmers have died in there. The current pulls you down and you can't swim back up. So you drown. Not me. I'm not that dumb.'

'You really believe that?' Tom asked. 'I've swum in there dozens of times and nothing ever pulled me under. That's just crap that parents tell their kids when they're little to keep 'em from taking a dip. Name one person who died. Just one. I'll bet you can't.'

'I don't remember their names,' Staci said. 'But I know they died.'

'Did not.'

'Children, calm down,' Mason said with a grin. 'Or we're going home right now.'

'Now or never,' Kurt said. He began to scale the concrete pillar, putting his feet into the cracks and pulling himself upward. It wasn't long before he was six feet above everyone else.

Mason looked over at Tom who shrugged.

'You're not really gonna do this, are you?' Scotty asked.

'If Kurt's doing it, I'm doing it,' Tom said. He stepped forward and began to scale the pillar.

'Same here,' Mason said. There was no way he was going to let the others show him up. He pulled his shirt over his head, dropped it on the grass and handed Staci his phone. He put his palms against the concrete, studying the best crack to shove his sneaker into so he could pull himself up. It didn't take long and minutes later he swung his leg over the top and dragged himself into a standing position.

From there he had a clear view of underneath the train bridge. It required some bravery, but if they could walk across the rafters to the next few pillars they'd be able to jump. It wouldn't take more than a few minutes to make it out to the middle of the river. Below him, he heard Scotty swear as his sneaker lost its grip. Scotty had decided that it was better to risk his life than stay on the shore with the girls.

'Next bit's gonna be tricky,' Kurt said as he jumped in the air, grabbing hold of the rafters with one arm and swinging back and forth like a monkey. He was showing off now, waving at the girls, who weren't even watching. Britney had her phone out and was showing Staci something. They were both giggling. Carefully, Kurt stepped out on to the railing until he was inside the tangle of black metal. Once there, he could work his way towards the middle of the river.

They watched until Kurt was a good third of the way out. Mason followed second with Tom and Scotty behind him. It was harder than it looked. The metal was rough and it bit into Mason's hands. He didn't really have to use such a death grip but his brain seemed to believe he had to hold on for dear life. There was a lot of open space underneath and it wasn't hard to imagine himself slipping and falling down into the water below.

Everyone knew that the river was only deep in the very middle; the edges were shallow enough for the fall to probably kill him. Or, at the very least, leave him crippled for life. Neither sounded very enjoyable.

So he concentrated on putting one foot in front of the other, ignoring the brilliant blue water beneath him. When he paused and looked back, he was surprised to see the shore was far behind him. Staci and Britney were tiny figures now; he couldn't even tell if they were still playing with the phone. Tom was right behind him and even Scotty was just a few feet beyond that. Mason could see the beads of sweat on Scotty's bright red face.

'What's the matter?' Tom said with a big grin as he caught up to Mason. 'Getting tired, old man? You need a nap?'

'Not even close,' Mason said. 'Just checking to make sure you don't slip and break your pretty little neck.'

'Never gonna happen,' Tom assured him. 'And if by some miracle I do die I'm gonna come back and haunt your ass for all eternity anyway. Just think, for the rest of your life I'll be there, smiling at you every time you try to make it with a girl. You'll never pee in private again.'

'Nice.'

A few minutes later, all four of them were in the perfect position to jump. It was windier out there in the open; Mason could feel the coolness of the breeze on his body. Suddenly it didn't seem as summery as it had half an hour ago. He looked longingly at the shore, wondering why he'd bothered to take off his shirt.

'Water's gonna be cold,' Tom said, reading his mind. 'We should have done this back in July or August.'

'Now's just as good,' Kurt replied. 'Just think of the stories we'll be able to tell tomorrow. We'll be kings.'

'Doubt anyone will believe us,' Mason said. 'We should have told the girls to take pictures. Think they'll do it anyway? Staci's got a nice camera on her phone.'

'Maybe,' Tom said.

A gust of wind blew up over the water, raising goose bumps on the back of Mason's neck. To the west, the sun was starting to lower itself into the ground. In half an hour or so it would be twilight and too dark for them to even consider doing this stupid stunt. They'd have to take the plunge soon or head back to shore with their tails between their legs.

'I'm not doing it,' Scotty suddenly said. 'I can see the bottom. It's not deep enough.'

Mason looked down but he couldn't see anything but dark blue water washing up against the concrete pillar. It was a good forty feet to the surface beneath him.

'It's deep enough,' Mason said but he wasn't so sure any more. 'Anybody got something we can throw in to test it?'

'Why don't we just toss Scotty in first,' Tom joked. 'If he sinks, we head back to shore. If he swims, we jump.'

'Not funny,' Scotty said.

'I think it's a great idea,' Kurt said. He swung his legs around the side of the rafter and stepped in front of Scotty. 'What do you say, coward? Heads you sink. Tails you swim?'

'I'm not going first.'

'No one said this was voluntary,' Kurt said. He reached out and tried to grab Scotty's arm. The smaller boy pulled back, almost tripping over his feet and slipping out from underneath the metal.

'Dude, watch it,' Tom said. 'You're gonna make him fall.'

Kurt smiled and lunged at Scotty again. 'That's the idea.'

Scotty stepped backwards, bringing his arms up to try to block Kurt's advance. His foot slipped off the railing, throwing his body off balance. Mason witnessed the whole thing in super slow motion. There wasn't enough time to do anything but watch. Scotty's eyes grew wide, mouth opened at the beginning of a scream. Kurt laughing.

Mason lunged forward, grabbing at air as Scotty's knee cracked into the railing. Scotty emitted a cross between an oomph and a high-pitched yowl. He managed to clutch blindly at the black metal, tightening his arms in a death grip as gravity took over and his body swung downward into the open air.

'Take my hand,' Mason shouted. Wrapping one arm round the bar for safety, he reached out with his other hand, grabbing hold of Scotty's shoulder.

Kurt was no longer laughing. His face was pale and he stood there panicked and obviously unable to do anything. Tom rushed past him, stepping carefully around Mason to try to help. Scotty was still suspended in the air, his legs kicking helplessly beneath him as he held on. Far below him, the river flowed dangerously fast.

'Don't let me fall,' he kept repeating. The words shot out of his mouth like a machine gun firing.

Let him drop.

The voice whispered in the back of Mason's mind. He blinked several times. What the hell was he thinking? Tightening up his grip, he pulled until his knuckles whitened.

'I'm not going to let go,' he said.

'I've got him,' Tom said. He'd got down on his stomach, reached down and grabbed hold of the boy's belt.

'I don't want to die. I don't want to die. I don't want to die.'

Mason dropped to his stomach, copying Tom. Wrapping both his hands around Scotty's shoulders, he was able to get a firmer grip. His palms were coated in sweat and at one point he almost let go, but Kurt suddenly reached down to help. He'd somehow managed to shake his earlier paralysis. He reached past Mason, grabbing hold of Scotty's now free shoulder.

'Relax, man,' Tom said through clenched teeth. 'Stop kicking. We can't pull you up if you're doing that.'

It took forever but the three of them finally managed to haul Scotty back on to the railing. They sat there, breathing heavily as they tried to catch their breath. Finally remembering the girls, Mason looked back at the shore where Britney and Staci were watching. He waved at them and shouted that everything was fine.

'What the hell were you thinking?' Tom finally said. 'Are you really that stupid? You could have got us all killed.'

'I'm sorry, man,' Kurt said. 'I didn't think he'd freak out like that.' He turned to Scotty who was on his knees, leaning against the railing and still trying to catch his breath. 'I'm sorry. You know I was joking, right? I'd never have actually pushed you. Don't take everything so seriously.'

Scotty glared at him for a long time before finally nodding.

'Let's get out of here,' Mason said.

No one disagreed.

Tom went first, climbing along the railings and back towards the shore. Mason went second. He'd only travelled about ten feet before he heard the splash. Turning round, he only saw Scotty. He stared straight at Mason, dark eyes glowing in hatred.

'Who's joking now?' Scotty said.

'What the hell did you do?'

He didn't wait for an answer. Crisscrossing the metal beams, he moved underneath the bridge and to the other side. He scanned the water below for Kurt but he couldn't see anything. The current was moving unbelievably fast. He tried to calculate how far Kurt might have already travelled. Searching the water out in front of him, he finally saw something moving just below the surface.

He didn't stop to think. No voices whispered in his head. He jumped.

The water was just as cold as he expected. The shock made him gasp, forcing a good pint down his throat and into his lungs. Kicking hard, he propelled himself upward until his head broke the surface. Treading water, he coughed liquid and scanned the area for Kurt. He spotted him, thirty feet away and moving fast, his head bobbing up and under the water.

He couldn't tell if Kurt was unconscious or not. All he knew was that his friend wasn't trying to swim for shore.

Ignoring the numbness in his arms, Mason immediately headed in the direction the current was taking his friend. Pumping his muscles hard, he tried not to think about what might happen if he didn't reach Kurt in time. He concentrated on putting one arm in front of the other.

Come on, Dowell! Move it.

He could hear people shouting from the shoreline but he didn't take his eyes off Kurt. Tom and Scotty were way behind them now, probably just reaching the ground where Staci and Britney waited. There was nothing any of them could do.

He pumped harder.

The next time Kurt bobbed to the surface, Mason was closer. It made him kick his legs that much harder.

He almost cried out in relief when his hand brushed against Kurt's back. Reaching round his friend's neck, he managed to pull Kurt's head up and out of the water. Ignoring the moment of panic when he saw Kurt didn't seem to be breathing, he concentrated instead on working his way to shore.

Tom was waiting for him. He'd taken the quick route, running along the edge instead of climbing back up the riverbank. He jumped into the water as they drew closer, wading up to his waist where he was able to help take Kurt from Mason's exhausted arms. Together they dragged the unconscious teen back to land where Tom shoved Mason aside and began to do mouth-to-mouth resuscitation on him.

After a few impossibly long minutes, Kurt coughed water. Eyelids fluttered and eventually opened.

'What the hell happened?' he spluttered.

Mason glanced back at the train bridge where he could see the rest of his friends slowly moving along the shoreline. The girls were in the lead. Scotty was at the back, barely trying at all to keep up.

'I'm not sure,' Mason answered.

'I wasn't doing anything,' Kurt said. 'He just turned round and clocked me.' Bringing his fingers up to his face, he winced as he touched the flesh. 'I think he broke my nose.'

'Scotty punched you?' Tom asked incredulously. 'That's impossible. He's never hit anything in his life. Dude's a wimp. He can't even kick dirt without a guilt trip.'

'Well, he did,' Kurt said. 'He clocked me and then pushed me off the bridge.'

Mason stood up and started walking towards the girls. He moved along the shoreline, ankle deep in river water, toes squishing into wet dirt. It didn't take him long to reach the girls. Ignoring them completely, he turned to Scotty.

'You punched him?'

Scotty didn't say anything. He glared at Mason with hate-filled eyes.

Mason brought his arms up, pushing Scotty backwards and into the bush. 'Answer me.'

'Yeah, fine, I hit him,' Scotty said. 'He started it. You were all fine and crap when it was me he was pushing around. How come you didn't stop him?'

Mason froze. 'Everything happened too quickly. You know that.'

Scotty didn't respond.

'You could have killed him,' Mason finally said.

'And he could have killed me,' Scotty shot back.

'He was joking,' Mason said. 'Yeah, it was a bad joke. We get it. But what you did was worse.'

'You're such a hypocrite,' Scotty said. 'You'd better remember that because it's gonna come back and bite you in the ass. Soon enough. You'll see.'

Scotty turned and ran straight into the bushes, gone before Mason even had time to respond. He stood there and stared at the spot where Scotty had disappeared until Britney came up and handed over his shirt.

'Here,' she said. 'You're all covered in goose bumps. You're gonna freeze to death.'

'Thanks,' he said.

The shirt was warm against his body.

'Do you think we should go after him?' Tom wandered over, buttoning up his shirt.

'Nope,' Mason said. 'He might be waiting at the car but I doubt it. Let him walk. Maybe he'll cool down.'

'That was messed up, man,' Tom said. 'Why'd Scotty do that? I didn't realize he hated Kurt that much.'

'Not sure,' Mason said. 'It was weird. Did you see his eyes?'

The others came over to join them; the girls had their arms round Kurt's waist. Blood was dripping down his face, staining his shirt.

'I want to go home,' Staci said.

Mason nodded. 'Yeah, I think that's a good idea.'

ARIES

Granville Street was packed with people, and not in a friendly way.

Aries and Sara had agreed to meet up at Blenz to grab a coffee before heading down to Robson for a day of shopping. Neither of them had any money but that didn't matter. Looking in windows was free and Robson was always entertaining. But shortly after they sat down with their drinks on the patio, the crowd began to gather on the pavement. Within half an hour people were starting to get a little riled up. Aries could feel the electricity in the air, or maybe it was the way the crowd was buzzing with excitement.

'Is this a protest?' Aries said.

It was hard to tell. An older man with glasses and a bad haircut screamed at the people across the street. He was holding a sign that said something against abortion. There was a picture of a dead foetus in technicolour detail along with a coat hanger. The image made Aries feel a little nauseous so she pushed the remains of her drink away. The man continued to yell and brandish his sign at a group of kids passing out Gay Pride stickers. They were giving him the finger and waving multicoloured flags. Another pack of people wore strange masks with white faces and large pointy noses.

Their bodies were covered with long black capes and robes. They bounced up and down in the middle of the street, adjusting their masks while letting their robes flutter and drag along the pavement. From behind Aries and Sara, a girl with green hair and a nose ring dropped some pamphlets about animal rights on their table. Pictures of monkeys being tortured in laboratories stared back up at Aries. She quickly turned the leaflets over, but the back side wasn't any better. She picked them up and tossed them in the garbage.

'It's weird,' Sara said. 'They're all here, but no one seems to be on the same side.'

'Whoever organized this should be fired,' Aries said.

Sara grinned. Her phone beeped and she checked it, immediately sending a text back. Aries assumed it was Colin by the way she smiled. She'd never understand for the life of her why her best friend liked the biggest jerk in school.

'Hey, the guy from Greenpeace is picking his nose,' Sara said as she put her phone back in her bag. 'Now is that any way to represent a company?'

'Seems very natural to me,' Aries said. 'Isn't Greenpeace about nature?'

Sara giggled. 'It must be environmentally friendly.'

'Still,' Aries said, 'this is weird. I've never seen a protest that protested everything before. Doesn't that kind of defeat the purpose?'

They watched the various groups standing around in the street. There were a lot of puzzled faces in the growing crowd. No one seemed to know what was going on. People were filling up the pavements and overflowing on to the streets where confused motorists slowed down and honked their horns. A bus driver pulled over and started screaming at a group of teenagers wearing black hoodies and ripped jeans. They yelled back, refusing to move.

More people showed up. A lot of people stopping now had puzzled expressions on their faces. Many of them were just hanging out like Aries and Sara. They'd heard the commotion blocks away and had come down to check things out. Several started texting on their phones. A group of German tourists wearing Vancouver tourism shirts chattered away while taking pictures on expensive cameras. Aries listened to an animated girl on her phone screaming at her friends to come down and join the fun. Someone bumped into her, and her phone flew through the air where another girl stomped on it accidently with her combat boots.

'Hey!'

Aries looked up and saw Becka Philips and Joy Woo heading over towards their table.

'This is crazy, right?' Joy said loudly. The noise on the street was growing and she had to shout. 'Can you believe it? We were just down by the SkyTrain and they've got the cops bringing out the riot gear. We saw tear gas!'

Becka nodded excitedly. 'Might be a good time to split. It's worse down there. The cops are getting upset.'

'This is so weird,' Aries said. 'Any idea what's going on?'

Someone shouted from behind the girls. Aries leaned round Joy to get a better look. Two of the boys in the black hoodies had picked up a newspaper box, and they threw it at a parked car. Glass shattered and a car alarm immediately went off.

'It's all over the news,' Joy said. 'Apparently it's a bunch of computer hackers. They sent out multiple messages on all these Vancouver forums. Just about every single protest group got email information to come down to Granville.'

'So someone made it all up?' Sara looked impressed.

'Seems like it.'

Further down the street, a homeless man held up an empty Starbucks coffee cup, begging for change. A guy wearing an expensive leather jacket punched the cup, sending change scattering into the gutter. When the man got down on his knees to retrieve the money, someone kicked him.

'Anyway, you should get out of here,' Joy said. 'We're gonna head back around. I've got my car parked a few blocks off Davie. Hopefully we can still get to it. Do you need a ride?'

Aries glanced over at Sara. They'd taken the SkyTrain down. If the police were gathered by the station with riot gear, they might not be able to get back on the train. The station might even be temporarily closed. The thought of walking home definitely wasn't appealing.

'Yeah, we could use a ride,' Sara said. 'Only if you don't mind.'

'No worries,' Joy said. 'But let's go now before it gets even crazier.'

Aries stood up and Sara reached under the table to find her bag. Aries saw the brick coming first. She managed to grab Sara, pulling her back and away before the window shattered. Glass and part of a neon sign rained down on where the two of them had been sitting. Aries could see the backs of two of the hoody-clad guys disappearing into the crowd.

'Are you OK?' she asked.

Sara nodded. Her lower lip was trembling.

'Can you believe that?' Joy said. 'Bunch of jerks. There's always someone who has to go and make things violent.' She turned and shouted at the crowd. 'Come back and do that again, you cowards!'

Sara giggled nervously.

They started making their way through the crowd and towards Davie Street. It was slow moving; there weren't a lot of open gaps to sneak through. Aries noticed that several stores were locking their doors and putting CLOSED signs in the windows. She didn't blame them in the slightest.

'At least we're moving away from the cops,' Becka said. 'I doubt my parents would be impressed if I got arrested. My brother would love it though.'

'Where are these people coming from?' Sara said. She dodged being shoved by a kid with a skateboard and wraparound sunglasses. 'You'd think it was New Year's Eve. I've never seen such a crowd. And we were down here for the Olympics. Remember? It wasn't nearly as crazy as this.'

'Word travels fast?' Aries said. She watched a family cowering in a doorway, the father trying to manoeuvre one of those fancy jogging strollers. 'It is strange. You'd think people would have better things to do with their time.'

From somewhere down the street, loud muffled blasts filled the air. Someone beside them screamed. Becka immediately covered her ears with her hands.

'That sounded like gunshots,' Joy said. 'Come on. Move faster.'

'Where's it coming from?' Sara asked.

'Behind us,' Aries said. She tilted her head forward to hear better. 'At least I think so.'

'I'm not sticking around to find out,' Joy said, pushing her way between a bewildered couple wearing matching windbreakers.

But in front of them things weren't getting any better. One of the Pro-Life people broke into a fight with a girl who might have been a Greenpeace member – it was hard to tell. She was screaming at him when he picked up his protest sign and waved it around several times before bringing it down on her head. As blood dripped from the gash in her forehead, another protester, maybe animal rights, grabbed the wooden board, and a violent tug of war broke out.

A man stood a few feet away from them with dirty tacksuit bottoms, no shirt and a Santa hat perched on top of his head. He was holding a badly painted banner, waving it high above his head.

The End of the World
is Here

He was chanting something over and over. It took Aries a few seconds to make out the words.

'From our lips to God's ears. From our lips to God's ears.'

It was so comical Aries burst out laughing before she could stop herself. Sara looked at her like she was crazy.

But it was the banner, not Sara, that pushed the chuckle back into her stomach. The way it stood out above the endless sea of heads. Something about it suddenly made her throat close, and goose bumps broke out against her skin.

The banner was right.

No. Absolute rubbish. People had been predicting the end of the world forever. And some crazy guy in a Santa Claus hat couldn't possibly know the truth about something so big. The world wasn't going to end any time soon.

Right?

He speaks the truth.

The voice was so subtle she didn't realize it was just her thoughts. She actually caught herself looking back, trying to figure out where the voice had come from.

Great, now you're going bonkers. Wonder if he has a matching hat for you.

It didn't help that the crazy guy had noticed her watching him and started making his way through the crowd. She froze. People pushed into her, shoving her back and sideways but she couldn't move.

Then Sara reached out and grabbed her hand, pulling her onward. A new wave of people passed by them, and the man and his banner disappeared.

'Come on,' Sara said. 'Or we're gonna lose Joy. I don't want to get stuck here.'

'Me neither,' Aries said.

It took them several minutes but eventually they reached the end of the block. They caught up with Joy and Becka waiting on the corner.

'Let's cross over to Howe,' Joy said. 'It shouldn't be as bad down there. I think it's just Granville.'

Aries nodded.

A sudden series of sharp banging noises filled the air. Someone had set off fireworks in the middle of the intersection. Aries was shoved from behind. Turning, she immediately recognized the green-haired girl who'd given her the animal-rights tracts. The girl screeched several times in her face before falling to her knees and covering her ears. Pictures of abused monkeys and anti-fur pamphlets fluttered to the cement.

Aries glanced up to where she could barely make out the fireworks bursting above the street lights. Too bad it wasn't dark out; it would have been very pretty to watch. People started pushing against her, shoving and shouting, trying to get away from the explosions. No one else but her seemed to realize that the noises weren't threatening. Sara grabbed hold of her hand, pulling her close and away from the mob.

'It's OK,' Aries shouted. But no one heard her.

A voice rose from the crowd. 'Cops!'

Further down the street, she could see the police officers in their riot gear, coming through the crowd. Decked out in ballistic vests, they had their batons raised. Some of them were even swinging. They marched in a single line, dispersing the crowd, forcing everyone back towards Granville. People scrambled in all directions to get away.

Nothing like a little crowd control.

She realized that Sara was still tugging on her hand, almost pulling her shoulder out of its socket. Aries turned and allowed her friend to drag her away. Several others were moving back on to Helmcken Street. Joy and Becka were about ten feet ahead of them, and Joy kept pointing to the right-hand side.

Howe Street was better. People were still running about in all directions but the crowd had thinned out. They were able to move faster. A few cars pulled out of parking spaces and drove slowly down the one-way street. The general consensus seemed to be that everyone suddenly had somewhere better to be.

Two blocks down and they reached Joy's car.

All the windows were smashed. Glass littered the ground and the leather seats.

'Oh man,' Joy said. 'My dad's gonna kill me.'

It could have been worse, Aries thought as she did her best to brush away some of the glass before sitting down in the passenger seat. The tyres could have been slashed. But she didn't bother saying it out loud. It wouldn't have made Joy feel better.

At least the car started. Joy put the car in gear and they got out of there as fast as possible.

'Well, that was fun,' Sara said as they headed on to the bridge. 'What should we do tomorrow? Rob a bank? Sky diving?'

'I've got a chem quiz,' Aries said. 'That's terrifying enough.'

The bridge was fairly empty, and as they drove across Aries glanced at the bay to where the ocean stretched past Stanley Park. She could see boats out on the water, and people walking along the seawall, enjoying the afternoon. Seagulls soared gracefully above English Bay, oblivious to the humans below them. Everything looked so peaceful. Such an odd contrast from the scene they'd just witnessed.

Funny how everything could change so quickly.

NOTHING

People behaving badly. All over the world. None of these were isolated incidents. But the majority were subtle enough that no one noticed.

Oops.

We would sit in the darkness over the next few weeks and repeat these stories, these small cautions that no one realized were warnings until after the fact. They seemed so very important, and it was as if each of us wanted to remember the tiny details so we could add them to all the history books they might one day write about us.

I wonder if people will remember me. I hope not.

It's better if they don't.

PRESENT DAY

Three Months After the Earthquakes

MASON

Cambie Street was quiet. Nothing moved.

The engine of the motorcycle destroyed all that beautiful silence.

It was late afternoon, possibly Sunday. Earlier back at the house Mason had noticed that someone had put a calendar up on the big stainless-steel refrigerator. They'd started crossing out dates with a neon pen. So many endless days had been lost. He couldn't actually remember what day it was any more. It's not like he had anywhere to be or a certain date on which to do anything. He didn't own a watch and he didn't really care what time it was. Some of the others still paid attention to the time but not him. As far as Mason was concerned, the world now worked in daylight and darkness. He'd have to assume that whoever was doing the marking actually had a clue as to what was going on. And according to the fuzzy kitten calendar it was Sunday and less than a week until Christmas. Funny how time flies. Only this year there wouldn't be any stockings hung by the chimney with care. No eggnog mixed with rum and partying in his friend's basement. Last year Tom had got so drunk he'd thrown up candy canes and mincepies all over the snow-filled driveway. Good times gone.

It was so weird living in Vancouver now since there wasn't any snow. Back in Saskatoon everything would be buried under several feet of the white stuff at this time of the year, and he'd probably be shovelling it while his mother baked the aforementioned mincepies and other Christmas treats. Not that he was complaining. Without the electricity, he couldn't imagine what it must be like for any survivors still hanging around his hometown. They'd be frozen popsicles. Was Saskatoon a complete ghost town now or were there Baggers patrolling the streets like they were doing here?

So many holidays that meant nothing any more. He'd completely forgotten about Thanksgiving and Halloween. So had everyone else. Once upon a time, 31 October had been his favourite holiday. No point in thinking about these things any more. Dressing up. Candy. Still plenty of scary monsters these days though. They didn't even have to wear costumes.

And luckily none of them appeared to be following him right now.

At the bottom of Queen Elizabeth Park, he stopped in the middle of the road. He looked around to make sure the coast was clear before cutting the engine. Tugging at the strap, he pulled his helmet off and let it hang from the handlebars. His ears strained against the silence, listening for any sign he could interpret as a warning. Voices. Cars. Psychotic nut jobs running towards him. Anything.

From above, a group of Canadian geese began to

honk as they headed north, probably over to Stanley Park where they'd be able to spend their afternoon baking in the sunlight, cleaning their feathers in one of the man-made ponds, and lounging about completely undisturbed. Not that the geese ever cared much about people anyway. They probably didn't even realize the humans were gone.

So much easier being a bird.

He turned his attention away from the sky and to the back of the motorcycle where the pretty girl with green eyes struggled to remove her helmet.

'So where next?' he asked.

Aries shifted on the seat behind him, trying to undo the strap with her fingers. Mason bit his tongue to keep from saying something along the lines of an 'I told you so'. It was impossible giving directions this way. Neither could hear each other over the engine without screaming and that would only attract more attention. It didn't help that Aries was insistent on them wearing the safety gear. Cracking his head open against the cement was the least of Mason's worries. But he went along with her because it was better than arguing.

Easier to just nod his head and agree to everything these days.

'We can turn left here or keep going up to Forty-ninth,' she said as she pulled at the tangles in her hair. 'It's your choice.'

'Not my choice,' he said. 'Remember, I'm the newbie. I know nothing about this city. As your boyfriend likes to say, I'm Tourist Boy.'

Aries frowned. 'He's not my boyfriend.'

'Then why do you keep crawling out the window to meet with him late at night?'

He was glad to see the shocked look on her face. She hadn't realized he'd seen her the past few nights. She must have thought she was being secretive and it probably worked for some of the others. But not for Mason. It takes a sneak to recognize a sneak. He'd been doing a lot of his own midnight walkabouts. It was impossible for him to get more than a few hours of sleep each night. He wasn't used to sharing a house with so many other people, and when he did drift off something always brought him back. There were too many memories being pulled to the surface when he dreamed, too many nightmares. Once the tossing and turning got to be too much, he'd sneak outside and go for a walk. He never went too far, just a few blocks. Enough space to give him room to breathe. Sometimes he'd hang out in the garden while watching the moon drag itself across the sky. He felt safer there. A guardian angel. He could watch over everyone while they closed their eyes and became utterly dependent on him.

Every single night he managed to talk himself out of leaving. Or was it the other way round? How many times could he convince himself to stay?

There were a lot of them now. A new family. So many people he felt responsible for saving. He didn't want this again. He'd failed too many times.

Too many people died as a result.

When he finally did sleep, he still dreamed of her. Chickadee.

I want you to promise me something.

He'd stuck to that promise after they'd met on the road as fellow survivors – at least for a while. So why was he still here? He didn't owe her anything. It's not like she'd asked him to go and find new people to take care of. He'd come and he'd felt the ocean and in a way it had made him feel better. But he was still empty. And she was still gone. So were the others. Coming to Vancouver hadn't changed anything. Reaching into his pocket, his fingers closed around the small glass vial he now carried at all times. A bottle filled with sand. A little token he'd taken from the morning when he'd kept his promise to Chickadee and given his legs a good soaking in the ocean water. It comforted him. His good-luck charm, not that he believed in such things.

'Let's go up to Forty-ninth,' Aries finally said. 'Take a left there and then we head down a few miles.'

'You're the boss,' he said.

From somewhere not far enough away, a recorded voice filled the air.

WARNING. WARNING. THE CITY IS CLOSED. NO ONE IS ALLOWED IN OR OUT. THERE ARE GUARDS POSTED. TRESPASSERS WILL BE SHOT. DO NOT TRY TO LEAVE THE CITY. DO NOT STAY IN YOUR HOMES. IT IS NO LONGER SAFE. SURVIVORS ARE INSTRUCTED TO GO

TO THE PLAZA OF NATIONS IN THE DOWNTOWN CORE. THERE ARE PEOPLE THERE WHO CAN HELP YOU.

WARNING. WARNING. THE CITY IS CLOSED . . .

The recording started in on its second loop.

The Baggers were more organized these days.

Scary.

Mason grabbed his helmet. 'Time to go. Come on or they'll see us this time.'

Aries wrapped her arms tightly round his waist as he started the bike.

The recordings were coming from white vans with tinted windows. There were several of them touring the streets. No one knew who was driving but they had a good enough idea. It was almost as if the Baggers had gone in and cleaned out the entire inventory at Budget Van Rentals.

And the Baggers were looking for them.

Not just them. Any survivors in general.

He didn't want to imagine what they might do if they caught Aries and him taking this particular joyride.

Mason didn't know if the recordings were true. He hadn't tried to leave the city. But he didn't doubt for a second that they would try to kill anyone who didn't take the warning seriously. They'd already destroyed most of the world. What were a few more people?

What was even scarier was the bit about sending people into the downtown core. They were rounding up the survivors. And Mason was positive there were enough scared, exhausted and confused people who would willingly walk into their trap. It was a clever ruse, offering help and salvation to those still alive despite all the odds. What were the Baggers planning?

He figured in the next few days he'd have to go down and check it out for himself.

Half an hour later Mason pulled the bike over to the side of the road and killed the engine. They were parked in front of a two-storey house in the middle of what once might have been a nice neighbourhood. The street was quiet and lined with skeletal trees with leaves rotting on the grass beneath them.

Mason glanced down the road, checking for signs of life. It was hard to believe no one lived here. On any other day he could picture people. Teenagers grudgingly raking up leaves or doing some other sort of weekend chore. People would be out talking to their neighbours or cleaning the debris out of the gutters. Mothers might be chasing after their children or pushing babies in strollers. Others might be taking the family dogs for walks or getting ready to do some grocery shopping.

But this street was dead. No amount of wishing could change the eerie empty feeling that curled along the base of his spine as he climbed off the bike and put the kickstand in place.

Aries wasn't paying attention to the street; her attention was set on the house in front of them. It was a split-level house with a wrought-iron fence round the front. There was no car in the driveway.

'Are you sure you want to do this?' he asked. 'You don't have to.'

'Yes, I do,' she said. 'I should have done this ages ago. But I couldn't bring myself to. And time just kind of flew by. But now I have no excuse. I'm here. Might as well go in.'

They left their helmets on the bike and walked towards the gate, which squeaked when Mason pulled it open. Their feet echoed on the concrete as they moved along the path towards the door. He could feel the waves of stress pouring off Aries's back. He wondered if he would have felt the same way if he was back at his own house in Saskatoon. But that wouldn't happen in a million years. He'd burned the house down before he'd left so many weeks ago. Part of him was glad he'd done it. At least now he'd never have a reason to go back.

You can't ever go back. Never again.

Aries had a keychain with a little stuffed toy of a dog with buttons for eyes. She had pulled it out of her pocket before realizing she wouldn't need it. The front door was open a few inches. Both of them raised the police batons they now carried wherever they went. Michael and he had taken them from some dead cops they'd found sitting in a car in Kitsilano. They'd been searching for guns, but those had been long gone. At least batons were easier to carry than baseball bats. It was a shame they hadn't found enough for everyone to use.

Good weapons were hard to find. It seemed that someone had already claimed all the guns.

'They've been here, haven't they?' she asked, referring to the fact that the Baggers had been doing house-to-house searches. Aries herself had witnessed the results when she and her friends had hidden in a garage in the early days of the change and watched as the Baggers forcibly removed people from their homes, killing them in the streets.

'I don't know,' he said. 'Maybe. It's pretty clean. I don't see any blood. But that doesn't mean anything, right? It's been raining lots.'

Aries's shoulders hunched forward and he instantly realized he'd said the wrong thing. Up until that moment she'd still had hope that she'd come home and find her parents waiting for her. There would be hugs and tears and things would return to the way they were supposed to be. But seeing the open door and Mason's casual words had crushed that particular fantasy.

'I'm sorry,' he said.

She turned to look at him. 'Why? You didn't cause this.'

'You may not find what you're looking for. Just remember that certain things you see . . . you can't take them back. And no amount of wishing will make them go away.'

She paused, looking him straight in the eyes. He held the gaze as she studied his face. 'Is that what happened to you?' Glancing downward, she studied his hand, the fingers of which had been broken by one of the Baggers. 'Does it still hurt?'

He flexed his hand a little and dull pain shot up his arm. There hadn't been much he could do. It's not like he could have gone to the emergency room and had it fixed up. In the end, Clementine strapped it with some bandages they found at the Safeway pharmacy. 'Yeah, a bit. Usually when it's raining. Guess it didn't heal properly.'

'Do you want to talk about it?'

He shook his head. What had happened that day was between Daniel and him. The important thing was they'd stopped the Baggers long enough for everyone to meet up and stay alive. They were safe for the time being. Aries was a tough girl and he had no doubt she'd understand what they did to survive. There was blood on everyone's hands. There had to be, otherwise they never would have made it this far. But he wasn't ready to share. She knew nothing about his past and he intended to keep it that way. No one would ever know about his background, what had happened to his mom and most definitely not about Chickadee.

'I understand,' she said. But he could tell she didn't.

'Do you want me to wait out here?' It seemed like such an invasion of privacy. He never would have allowed someone to come with him. He'd have to do it by himself.

She shook her head. 'No, it's not safe. And I'll be OK. You don't need to worry. I'm not going to fall apart and drop to the floor or anything. I'm just as strong as you, you know.'

'I may not know you well but I know that's true,' he said.

'Let's do this.' Turning back to the door, she gave it a soft shove. Immediately the blast of foul decay hit their faces. Now that was a bad sign.

But Mason could tell Aries was determined not to let anything stop her. She held her head high and stepped past the entrance. He paused and then followed her into the house.

Inside, Aries lost some of her control. She tore down the main hallway and disappeared round the corner. Mason followed her, his police baton poised and ready. The living room was dark and cold, dust particles floating in the small slivers of light that beamed through the closed blinds.

'Mom? Dad?' Aries's voice was barely more than a whisper.

No one answered her call. The room felt empty. Unused. Wherever Aries's parents were, Mason was one hundred per cent positive they weren't there.

At least not in any shape that would be considered alive.

In front of the fireplace, a not-so-fresh splatter of dried blood stained the fine cream carpet.

Aries turned and pushed past Mason, running round the corner. He heard her feet on the stairs as she climbed. Sighing, he walked over to the blinds and opened them a crack with his fingers. The street was still clear. A good sign, but they couldn't spend much more than five minutes in the house. The motorcycle may be small, but it still made noise and that attracted not-so-nice people. There was a good chance they were already being watched.

Safety first.

He went up the stairs carefully, listening to Aries as she opened doors and checked out bedrooms. At the top, the long hallway branched out in several directions, each blocked by a white door. He wasn't sure which one she was in so he started by opening the first. Inside he found a master bedroom and more carnage. A torn and rust-stained shirt. A bloody handprint on the wall. A series of drips that led through another door that opened up to a small peach-coloured bathroom. A broken mirror.

But no bodies.

He found Aries in what used to be her room. She stood in the middle, close to her dresser, holding a hairbrush in her hands. Posters on the wall, a laptop on the desk, a large bed covered in pillows and stuffed animals. It looked like the room she should be living in, instead of the house in which she was currently surviving with a group of strangers. She deserved so much better than the hand she'd been currently dealt.

He had a flashback of the night he'd stood in the middle of his house, the moment before he'd set it on fire and burned it all down.

'You OK?' He didn't know what else to say.

She didn't turn as he approached her. Up close he could see her hands trembling. She stood a little straighter and walked over to the closet. 'I thought maybe I could pack a few things,' she said. 'You know. Take something back. A girl can always use some make-up, right? Would be nice to look good again. I'm sure some of my clothes will fit Clementine and Joy. Eve too, but she's a bit smaller than us. Too bad I didn't have a younger sister. Maybe we can find a way to get into some of the shops on Robson. I'm sure she'd like to go shopping with us.'

'You don't have to do this to yourself,' he said.

From inside the closet she pulled out a gym bag. Opening it, she dumped the contents on to the floor. Some old shoes. A pair of tracksuit bottoms. A bottle of liquid soap and a small travel towel. She began yanking clothes off the hangers, some of which she discarded on the floor, others went into the bag. There didn't seem to be any reasoning behind any of it.

'Aries.'

She ignored him. Went over to the dresser and pulled the drawer right out and on to the floor. Got down on her knees and started digging.

'Aries. Don't do this.'

The heel of a pair of boots got tangled up in a tank top. She yanked hard, tearing at the fabric until it ripped clean in half.

Mason got down on his knees and grabbed her arm. 'Stop it.'

'No!' She pulled back and away from him, smashing her back on the bedpost. There were tears in her eyes. They rolled down her cheeks and splattered on to the carpet. She looked at the torn tank top and turned it over in her hands before tossing it on the floor.

Mason sat on the floor beside her, leaning back against the blue-and-green bedspread.

'My parents are dead, aren't they.' It wasn't a question.

'I don't know.'

'The Baggers must have been here. They came in and cleaned up the mess.'

'Maybe.'

'Where do you think they're taking the bodies?'

'I don't know. Maybe they're burning them. Or burying them, but I think that would take too much time.'

'Yeah, probably.'

They waited in silence for a bit. Aries finally got up and opened the window. Fresh air immediately hit the room, but it wasn't enough to get rid of the scent of decay. If anything it made the stench worse. Aries walked back into the middle of the room where the gym bag sat on the floor. She kicked it with her foot. Picking the brush up off the ground, she came back and joined Mason again. Turning it round in her hands, she plucked some of the dead hairs from the bristles.

'I can't do this,' she said. 'Everyone thinks I'm strong but I'm not. They want me to lead them, but there's nowhere to go. What am I going to do? I'm going to get them all killed.'

Mason didn't say anything. How could he when he was constantly thinking the exact same thing?

'I'm sorry,' she said.

'What for?'

'For freaking out like that. I guess everything just got to me. You were right. I shouldn't have come back. I should have known it would mess me up like this. Those days are over. The big question is where do we go from here?'

'We survive I guess.'

'Yeah, I guess we do.' She got up off the floor and offered him her hand. 'We should get out of here. We've been long enough. They're probably waiting in the bushes to jump us as it is.'

Mason climbed to his feet and she threw her arms round him, hugging him hard. He almost pulled back at first, feeling his muscles tensing as her hands touched his back. He breathed deeply, trying to relax, forcing himself to bring his arms round her and complete the hug. Bits of hair pressed against his cheek and the warmth of her body burned into his. She pressed harder.

She smelt good in spite of the lack of hygiene these past few months.

And then it was over and she untangled herself from his grasp, lowering her chin as if she was embarrassed that she'd actually touched him. Moving past him, she returned to the window, closed and locked it. She pulled down the blinds and the room instantly grew darker.

'Do you ever think about it? Going back? Don't you

wonder what happened to your family? You've travelled a long way.'

His mother was probably still rotting away in her death bed at the hospital. His home was burned to the ground. His friends were dead and buried beneath the remains of his exploded high school.

'There's no going back,' he said. 'I've got nothing there.'

She nodded in agreement. 'We should go.'

He started to tell her they should search the rest of the house first and maybe take whatever supplies they could find. But she raced down the stairs so quickly he changed his mind. They were OK; the local stores still had stuff on their shelves, even if the stocks were dwindling. Aries made it clear she wanted nothing more to do with the place. He decided to honour her unspoken request. Besides, when the time came for them to start scavenging houses, he could always come back.

When they walked out into what remained of the afternoon light, she didn't look back. Mason completely understood. There was no point in going back. He'd tried to tell her that earlier before they'd even left the safe house. She didn't want to listen. But she'd learned.

It wasn't a good lesson.

CLEMENTINE

'WARNING. WARNING. THE CITY IS CLOSED . . .'

'Yes, yes, we hear you,' she muttered. 'We heard you the first five hundred times, so will you please shut up.'

The white van crawled down the street, the driver hidden behind the tinted glass. From twenty feet away, Clementine and Michael watched, hidden between an overgrown hydrangea bush and someone's front porch. It was moving slowly, barely more than a few miles per hour; obviously whoever was inside was scanning the area for signs of life. Clementine didn't want to imagine what might happen if they were spotted. Being shot on sight was one thing; who knew what might be lurking inside the van and where it might take them if they got caught.

'Dare you to run out there and flash the driver.'

Clementine punched Michael in the shoulder. Hard.

He chuckled and winked at her.

They both grew quieter as the mystery van passed within twenty feet of their hiding spot. Clementine held her breath as it cruised by, wondering what kind of heart attack she might have if it actually stopped.

But it didn't. A few minutes later it came to the end of the block and turned off towards Broadway. They both watched until the bumper and tail lights disappeared.

'How many of those things are there?' she asked, even though she knew Michael didn't know the answer. 'That's the third one we've seen.'

'How can you tell?' Michael said. 'They're all white.'

'The first one had a scuffed bumper,' she said. 'The second one was a Ford. That one's a GM. I may be a girl, Michael, but I know my cars. Or vans, as the case may be.'

'Yeah, well, I'm a boy and they're all white to me,' he said. 'Quit stereotyping – you're looking rather sexist. It's not very becoming.'

She rolled her eyes at him.

'Now I suggest we get out of here before they come back.'

'Still,' she said as she climbed to her feet and brushed off some of the dirt from her jeans. 'There are a lot of those cruising around. If they're here, they're probably all over the place. I sure hope Aries and Mason are OK. Didn't they say they were going out today?'

'Aries can take care of herself.' Michael reached forward and picked a leaf out of her hair. 'And Mason strikes me as someone good to have on your side. I'm sure they're fine.'

Clementine looked at him with both amazement and sarcasm. 'You got all that from him? Really? All I get is that he's some sort of silent brooding dude that always acts like he wants to be anywhere else but here.'

Michael laughed. 'Yeah, he's quiet. I'd say something bad happened to him, like something bad happened to all of us. But he does seem a little more haunted.'

'That would be an understatement.'

They both started walking back to where they'd abandoned their bicycles beside a parked car. They were good quality, fancy Rocky Mountains borrowed from a shop down on Broadway. Clementine didn't consider it stealing when the store windows were smashed in and most of the place had been looted.

'Let's get out of here,' Michael said as he picked up the closest bike and wheeled it over towards her. He was always doing little things like that. Michael was quite the gentleman. Not like Colin who'd pushed past her this morning to snag the last packet of instant mocha-flavoured coffee.

She climbed on the bike and they headed off along the empty street.

It didn't take long for them to reach the university. This would be their third trip out to the campus.

A few days ago they'd only explored around the outskirts. The University of British Columbia was huge. Built on a point, three sides of the campus were surrounded by ocean. There were only a few roads by which to enter, and they had to travel miles through a very large national park before they began to see buildings through the woods. The second day they began to explore the roads, leaving the bikes behind and sneaking across the campus on foot. Although the place was isolated, Michael and Clementine realized immediately they weren't alone. The white vans were out and they'd watched some Baggers going through the student-union building. They were carrying out bodies and loading them into the back of a flatbed truck. Many of the bodies were in early stages of decomposition. Even the Baggers wouldn't get too close to them without wearing face masks and protective clothing.

They'd also seen some regular people too. At least she assumed they were normal. Michael had his binoculars out and they'd watched the two girls sneaking from one building to another. They too were taking great care to hide from the Baggers. But they'd disappeared before she and Michael could actually cut across to talk to them.

Clementine realized that it would probably take several weeks to properly explore the campus. But she was determined. If her brother Heath was there, she'd find him. She'd search each and every building before she gave up.

She still had the letter he'd written to her, that she'd found back in his dorm room in Seattle when things had first kicked off. She kept it safe in the pocket of her jeans.

Dear Heath, I know you're there. I can feel it. You said you were coming here because you'd heard Vancouver was safe. I'm sure you've figured it out by now that it wasn't true but I hope you didn't go anywhere else. The university's large enough; I can't imagine how long it'll take me if I have to search all of Vancouver and Canada too. But if you left a message I'll find it. And I'll come for you. I'm not giving up, no matter how difficult it seems.

If only he'd make it easier for her. Maybe he could set off fireworks or set up a big neon sign with her name on it.

Until then she'd continue to talk to him inside her head as she'd been doing since this whole thing started. Before she'd met Michael and the others, he'd been the only person with whom she felt she could communicate. For some reason it made her feel safer and less alone. When she chatted with Heath in her thoughts, he was still alive.

When they arrived on campus, they immediately ditched their bicycles again in some bushes just off West Mall by the parking lot. Their goal that day was to search some of the buildings down the road. The girls they'd seen yesterday had headed off in that direction. If there were people holed up there, maybe they could find them.

Clementine looked up at the hundreds of windows as they passed the psychology building. Yesterday they'd tried going in but the doors were all locked. She made sure to mark that off on the tiny map they had. Each day they hoped to block off another section, noting to which places they'd gone and to which ones they'd have to come back.

'Do you think anyone's watching us right now?' she whispered.

'Maybe,' Michael said. 'Maybe there's some mutated psychology experiment gone bad checking us out with his dozen eyes.'

'Rage-infected monkeys,' she said, bringing a hand up to cover the giggle trying to escape.

'But you're right. It's like a ghost town within a ghost town,' Michael said. 'I can't imagine anyone hiding out here. What would they eat? Also look at all the garbage that's been blown up against the doors. No one's been in or out of there in a while.' He paused to study the windows for a few seconds and then looked back down at the map. 'Didn't Aries say there's a clothing-optional beach here? Maybe that's where everyone's hiding.'

'End of the world,' Clementine said. 'Might as well show it off.'

'Exactly.'

Joking aside, it still didn't change the feeling of eyes on the back of her neck as they walked along. She decided to take it as a good sign. The Baggers wouldn't just watch. They'd swoop in for the kill. If there were people inside, they were hiding too. That put them on the same playing team.

They cut across the park and on to Main Mall near, according to the map, the Koerner Library. They'd decided earlier that morning that it would be the building they wanted to search. It was a large place with several floors and plenty of places to hide. And it was close to a food-court area. It made sense that people might be staying there.

Tomorrow they planned to search the book store and the student-union building, as long as it looked like the Baggers were no longer ransacking it.

'Maybe we can find a store,' she said as she noticed a paper cup in the gutter. 'We're out of coffee and that just makes me cranky.'

'I'll buy you some more for Christmas,' he said. 'And one of those really fancy mugs that keeps your coffee nice and hot.'

'I keep forgetting,' she said. 'Christmas is right around the corner. My dad used to love saying that. Even in July. It seems so weird to me. It doesn't feel like December.'

'It's the lack of snow,' Michael said. 'I used to believe that all of Canada was snow-covered all year round. And then I came here. All this rain. It's changed my perspective on reality.'

She laughed. 'I miss the snow. And I miss the coloured lights. Christmas is supposed to be pretty and warm inside. Maybe that's why it's so surreal now.'

The doors to Koerner Library were wide open. Someone had started to spraypaint some sort of message. They didn't get to finish. The few words they might have written had obviously been painted over so the whole thing was an undistinguishable mess. On the ground were several cans of spraypaint and Clementine bent down and picked one up. Shaking it, she discovered it was still at least half full. She walked back to the main road, and shook the can several times to mix it up. Kneeling down on the ground, she began to write her own message. She sprayed the words carefully in big, jerky letters.

Heath. I'm here. Clementine.

When she was finished, she put the spraypaint can into her jacket pocket and walked back to the front of the library where Michael waited, leaning against the security rails.

'Not going to leave a number?' he asked.

'You're not funny.'

'Yeah, and that's not paint,' Michael said, pointing to a rusty Rorschach splotch on the ground. He looked back at the painted mess on the library doors. 'Wonder what *they* were trying to write? It must have been good for the Baggers to block it like that.'

'Maybe it was some sort of warning?'

They both stared into the blackness that was the library. The afternoon light only went so far and Clementine couldn't see anything beyond the information desk. The shadows swallowed everything up.

Clementine reached into her backpack and pulled out their flashlights, handing one over to Michael. Keeping their baseball bats raised and ready, they entered the building. The smell was bad and instantly assaulted her nostrils. There were bodies here. Coughing, she pulled her bandanna up to cover her face.

A building with the dead inside? How odd that she was prepared for such a thing? Even weirder was the fact that it was normal.

They moved past the main desks and towards the wooden doors that led into the actual library. Now that they were inside, neither would talk to the other unless it was absolutely necessary. Voices carried, especially in large places like this. A whisper could echo off the walls, and who knew who might be listening.

Michael pointed to the stairs and made a walking motion with his fingers. Clementine nodded. They should start at the top and work their way down.

The top levels were empty. Nothing but books and study rooms. Many of the books had been pulled off the shelves and journals littered the aisles. They found fresh blood in the bathroom on the top floor but no bodies. They wandered around carefully but turned up empty-handed.

It was on level three that they saw the light. Someone else was wandering around. Quickly they turned off their own flashlights and ducked into one of the study rooms. The stench of decay was stronger, Clementine had to breathe slowly through her mouth to keep from gagging. Small gasps.

Dear Heath, I read somewhere that when you smell something you're actually inhaling the particles. So that means I'm not just sniffing the dead – those itty bitty tiny specks are going down my throat and into my stomach. I'm eating them. And, if that's not enough to make me want to barf up my morning protein bar, I can't help but wonder if I'd recognize your decay if I smelt it. You'd better not be here, brother dearest. I don't want to think that I might have tasted you. That's just too creepy for words.

The light was coming from the back of the library. They couldn't see who was there but it didn't seem to be more than one person. Clementine watched the shadow moving around from behind the bookshelves. Too far away to tell what side they might be on. But he or she was making a lot of noise and that made Clementine wonder suspiciously just how careful this person felt they needed to be. She nodded at Michael and the two of them left the study room and slowly took the long way round towards the mystery person.

She tripped over the first body. One second she was moving carefully with one hand out against the wall to help her through the darkness, the next second she stumbled, knees collapsing. She couldn't really put her hands out to block her fall either; she didn't want to risk the noise the bat made when it hit the floor. Twisting her body sideways, she managed to land on her hip, keeping the metal weapon up in the air instead of having it bang into the tiling.

She came face to face with a blackened corpse. Opened her mouth to scream but Michael was there, pulling her up and into his arms.

The noisy mystery person stopped making a noise. The shadow stopped moving. Several terrifyingly long seconds went by before a scuffling noise ensued and the guy or girl went back to their job in progress.

Michael held her tightly until her heart slipped back down from her throat and into its rightful position.

Finally she nodded and waved with her hand to let him know she'd regained her composure, and he let go of her.

He mouthed, 'Are you OK?' at her, and she nodded.

Together they moved deeper into the building. When they rounded the last bookshelf, they could make out the mystery person from fifty feet away. He had his back to them but it didn't take long before he turned round and let them see his face.

He wasn't very old – mid twenties maybe. He'd probably been just another student at the university. His hair was short and curly; his jeans and shirt were clean. He didn't look like a Bagger; he was too jumpy and his eyes kept nervously darting between his job at hand and the empty darkness surrounding him. Like them, this guy was watching for what else lurked in the shadows.

He had good reason to be scared. Not just because of the Baggers. What he was doing wasn't exactly honest.

The light wasn't a flashlight. It was a small kerosene lamp with a little flame. He had it positioned on the floor beside him, tucked between several bodies. The guy was walking among the dead, reaching down to check their pockets. She watched as he pulled something from the front jeans pocket of a dead girl with long black hair. Keys. Studying the set, he tossed them aside and moved on.

Stealing from the dead!

Clementine was horrified. She'd seen a hell of a lot of

bad things over the past six weeks. She'd even done some of those unmentionables herself. But taking personal items from the dead . . . Well, that seemed wrong on levels she couldn't even begin to imagine.

Clementine didn't think. Red rage filled her vision, blocking her sight. What if Heath was in that pile? What if he'd left a letter for her and this guy had already stolen it? The anger surged forth, forcing her into action. Raising her baseball bat, she charged.

Vaguely she heard Michael call out her name but it wasn't enough to stop her. She ran straight for the guy. He was still hunched over another body, a decomposed body with blond hair that could very likely be her brother.

He saw her coming but tripped over his feet when he tried to stand. He fell backwards, his eyes wild with fear as she raised the bat.

Hands wrapped round her waist from behind, Michael yanking at her, fingers grabbing at the baseball bat as she tried to aim at the stranger's face. The weapon was pulled from her hands. It fell and hit the ground, bouncing and then rolling underneath a table.

'What the hell do you think you're doing?' Michael screamed. Their vow of silence broke. If there was anyone lurking, they'd have heard the scuffle.

'He's stealing from the bodies!' she said as she struggled. She elbowed Michael in the gut and he grunted. But he still managed to keep his arms tightly round her waist.

'He's not a Bagger.'

'He's a thief.'

'But he's not a Bagger. Think about it. He's not a killer.'

'It's just as bad.'

'Just chill out a second, will you!'

Clementine stopped struggling and all the rage inside her slowly began to drain out the bottom of her heels. Michael was right. It wasn't worth it. Suddenly she couldn't understand what had brought forth such anger in the first place. Whatever it was, it was gone now.

She was left feeling tired. All she wanted to do was sit down for a bit.

Michael let go of her and her knees buckled but she didn't fall. Instead she leaned up against the desk, trying to catch her breath.

The guy on the ground hadn't said a word through the whole scuffle. Once he realized it was unlikely Clementine was going to smash his head in, he scrambled to his feet and backed up until he smacked into a shelf. He yelped and looked around frantically in all directions for an escape route. But he was cornered.

'I'm not a thief,' he finally said with a strong English accent. 'I'm not. I wasn't stealing. I'm just looking for something. I need to find the keys. Just the keys. I didn't take anything. You can even look in my pockets.'

'What keys?' Michael didn't lower the bat. He kept it

pointed right at the stranger's chest.

The guy swallowed, his Adam's apple bouncing up and down in his throat. 'The Chemistry lab. I'm trying to find the keys to the lab.'

'Why?'

That seemed to stump him. His eyes widened and one eyebrow rose in the air as he thought. 'I'm a chem major. I belong there.'

Michael couldn't hide the grin at the corner of his mouth.

'Look,' the guy said as he inched forward. 'I'm not one of them. Baggers, right? I've heard that term before. It seems to be the name that's caught on. Anyway, I'm harmless, as you've probably figured out. Chem majors don't usually pack their own heat. I can't even bench press my own body weight.'

Michael nodded, lowering his bat. 'Yeah, you're cool.' He glanced over at Clementine and she gave him a half smile.

'Thanks.' The guy relaxed but still kept a good distance between them. 'Anyway, I'm just looking for keys. See that body there.' He pointed to an older Asian gentleman who was lying face down in a pool of blood. 'That's Professor Harvey Yuen. Brilliant man. I guess not any more. He's the head of Chemistry and I was hoping I'd be able to find something. Two days ago, back when he was alive, he had the keys in his trousers. Wouldn't let us go near the lab though. Said it was too dangerous. The lady beside him, the pretty girl, Carol, she is, I mean *was*, his assistant. We were all holed up together until yesterday.'

'What happened?' Clementine asked.

'I don't know. I woke up and they were gone. No note. Nothing. I'm assuming they went to try and find some food. We were running low. Why they didn't wake me or anyone else is beyond me. I would have come. I should be lying there too, with them.'

'I'm sorry,' Clementine said.

'Yeah, well, that doesn't bring them back,' he said. 'And I wasn't stealing from them. I'd never do such a thing. Never.'

A loud bang came from across the room. Michael immediately grabbed the kerosene lamp. The light flickered and then disappeared, pitching them straight into blackness.

Clementine's heart jumped into her throat. She reached around blindly in the dark until she found her baseball bat. Michael's hand found her shoulder and grabbed hold.

Something crashed and glass shattered. Someone had just broken the window of one of the study rooms. A voice shrieked and another voice matched it.

A quick burst of laughter.

'Is it them?' she whispered.

'We've got to get out of here and fast,' Michael said.

'Follow me,' the chem student said. 'I know a way out.'

She found Michael's hand in the darkness and wrapped her fingers around his warmth. He squeezed back. They were in mutual agreement.

'Let's do it,' Michael said.

ARIES

They arrived back near the house just before dusk. Mason didn't say much. He removed his helmet and dropped it on the ground. He was walking away before she even got off the bike herself. Rushing, she struggled with her own safety gear in order to catch up with him. When she finally matched his stride, they were already halfway down the street.

Because of safety reasons, they didn't actually park the motorcycle close by the hideout; instead they stopped several blocks away, hid it behind a bush and then took a complicated route through backyards and a high-school football field before arriving at their actual destination.

Better safe than sorry.

The hideout – she'd never be able to think of it any other way – was a big suburban house off King Edward Avenue. Whoever had lived there before must have been doing pretty darn good in the money department. Aries had always dreamed of living in a million-dollar mansion, she just never thought it would happen this particular way. The house comprised several bedrooms and just as many bathrooms. The kitchen was massive with big copper pots, and giant bay windows that let in the morning light. The fridge was big enough for someone to actually live in. There was a walk-in pantry that was now crammed full of as many canned goods as they were able to snag from the nearest Safeway, and the blinds were always pulled down so no one could look inside. There was no electricity or running water but they were all used to that by now.

It was a pretty decent hideout as far as these things went. It was big enough so that they could have some of their own space and comfortable enough so that no one actually wanted to move on. It's not like they'd ever be able to find absolute safety anyway. Compared to the last building with its caved-in roof and smelly blankets, this place was apocalyptic heaven.

That worried Aries. She knew it still wasn't safe and that one of these days they'd have to leave without warning. It was harder to walk away from this sort of luxury, especially when they'd had so little. Staying in one place for too long was never safe either. Everyone had pretty much agreed to that. But it had already made them a little reckless. They were sacrificing caution for comfort. Even Aries caught herself doing it.

And she didn't want to be trapped again. The last time was too terrifying. Sometimes she'd sit in the living room, staring blankly at the sixty-inch flat screen that didn't work and wondering when the flaming Molotov cocktail might fly from a Bagger's hand and crash through the front-room window.

When they came to the corner, Mason and Aries crouched between a front porch and some overgrown bushes desperately in need of a trim. They would spend at least five minutes studying the street before moving on. That was one of their top rules – standard operating procedure. She didn't want to be the one who might accidently lead the Baggers into their safety blanket.

'There's no one on watch,' Mason said with a frown. 'Who the hell isn't doing their job?' From their hiding spot they could see the monster black SUV, the secret place from where someone was constantly supposed to be watching the street. They had a schedule. The area was meant to be under twenty-four-hour surveillance.

But the vehicle was empty.

'Who else,' she said with a sigh. 'I believe it's Colin's turn.'

'That idiot's going to get us killed.'

She nodded. 'I'll talk with him.'

Mason shrugged. 'Don't even bother. I'm up for the next shift in a bit. Let me grab something to eat and then I'll get out there.'

'About earlier,' she began. Her eyes were still a little sore from crying and she wished she had a mirror to see if her cheeks were splotchy.

'Nothing happened,' Mason said without looking at her. 'We went in, we went out. A good time was had by all.'

She smiled. 'Thanks.'

'Any time. Shall we go?'

She brushed off some leaves and an ant that was making steady progress up her arm. 'Yup. Let's cruise before I get spiders in my hair or something equally disgusting.'

'Can't have that.'

It didn't take long to cut across a few lawns and head around to the back to jump a couple of fences, skirt past a leaf and bug-infested pool, and trample a rose bed. A few minutes later they were safe and at the back door. Aries knocked three times, paused and then three more. Their secret code. Someone peeked through the blinds, and Aries smiled and waved at Joy Woo, her high-school friend from their former lives.

'You're back,' Joy said as she opened the door. She was holding a spatula and wearing an apron that made some silly sexual reference to how golf and cooking really heated things up. Aries didn't quite get it but she wasn't a golfer or a chef. Must be an inside joke.

Mason nodded and mumbled a hello. He put his hand briefly on Aries's shoulder before pushing past Joy and into the kitchen. He tossed the motorcycle keys down on the table and headed through to the living room. She heard his feet on the stairs as he went straight for his bedroom. He was the only one besides Colin who preferred to sleep alone and away from the group.

'Anything good?' Joy's eyes searched her carefully.

'*Nada*,' Aries said. 'But it was expected.'

Joy nodded. Earlier that morning Aries had asked her if she wanted to take the trip back to her home too. Joy had declined the offer even though she had three brothers and a sister she hadn't seen since the night of the earthquakes. Her reasoning was simple although Aries had thought it was a bit cowardly. If they were dead, Joy didn't want to see their bodies.

'My sanity is better off not knowing. At least this way I can picture them still healthy and alive and not the other way around.'

There was a certain amount of intelligence in Joy's reasoning now that Aries had her answer. Would she have been better off not knowing?

No, if it gave her nightmares and the inability to sleep at night, she'd survive. She'd had her breakdown back in her bedroom. Although it had been hard, she still felt less heavy than she had this morning. She could move on now.

'So you found nothing?' Joy closed the door and locked the deadbolt in place.

'Yeah, pretty much,' Aries said. Her eyes burned and the tears threatened to come back. Blinking hard, she fought to keep them away. 'There was some blood though, so I'm going to say it's probably best to assume my parents are dead.'

'Oh, hon, I'm so sorry,' Joy said as she threw her arms around Aries.

'Don't be,' Aries said. 'It was to be expected. I just needed closure. Now I have it.' She forced a yawn. 'I'm beat. Gonna go lay down for a bit if you don't mind.'

'Not at all,' Joy said, waving her spatula. 'I'll call you when it's time to eat. Kinda doing a potluck-surprise thingie. We'll have to do a grocery trek soon. We've run out of everything decent. There are only so many things I can do with stewed tomatoes and macaroni noodles. And I'm running low on propane for the camping stove. If we don't find any soon, it'll be cold canned tomatoes and noodles. Bleh.'

'I hear ya, sister.'

She left Joy in the kitchen to finish preparing their canned meal of the evening, and decided to stick her head in the living room before going upstairs.

Nathan and his sister, Eve, were sitting on the couch. Colin sat in one of the big chairs, playing a video game on an ancient Game Boy Advance that ran on batteries. The theme music for Super Mario filled the room. Someone had found it a few days ago and everyone had got excited over it. In a new world where iPods, PlayStations, and Xboxes no longer worked, finding something that ran on regular batteries was a godsend.

In the middle of the room stood Brandi, an older woman who was hiding out in another home a few streets down. Since their arrival a few weeks ago, they'd discovered others taking refuge from the Baggers. Brandi ran a safe house with a bunch of people, mostly adults in their thirties and forties and a few children. Another group of survivors a few blocks down had Graham, a father in his forties who was lucky enough to have his entire family intact. He was taking care of his wife, his kid and his elderly mother and father, along with a few other people who had found him along the way.

Aries, Graham and Brandi went out of their way to visit each other every other day or so. It helped being in contact. And if one of them got some information they were able to pass it on.

'Good to see you, sweetie,' Brandi said when Aries entered the room. 'Just popped my head in to say hello.'

'Any news?' Aries asked.

'Got something, maybe,' Brandi said. 'I was telling it to Nathan and Eve here. Ran into another guy this morning. Bit flaky and didn't smell very good but that didn't seem to bother him. He's in a safe house over by the London Drugs on Forty-first. Said they've got a doctor. Can you believe it? A doctor! I'm dreaming. I'm going to try and head out there tomorrow. If I can find them, do you want me to see if he'll come and check out your friend Jack?'

'That would be wonderful,' Aries said.

'You've got it,' Brandi said. 'But I'm not going to hold my breath and I wouldn't either if I were you. Like I said, the guy was kinda odd. Smoked away too many brain cells if you ask me. Graham tends to believe most of the doctors have been rounded up already. I kinda agree with him.'

'Why do you think they're rounding up people like the doctors specifically?' Nathan asked as he unzipped his jacket halfway. Inside was just as cold as outside these days and winter coats had become the lounging norm for the living room.

'I don't know,' Brandi said. 'But they're not asking

people to go downtown for the good of their health, regardless of what that damn message says. I think they're looking for people with certain skills. If you've got it, you're good enough to live. Or not.'

'Clementine said something about that,' Aries agreed. 'When she was in Seattle, she ran into a guy at the university. He said that the Baggers came and rounded up a bunch of people. The rest they killed.'

'But what makes someone good enough to live?' Eve asked. 'I mean, what are the qualifications? I can't do anything. I'm pretty useless.'

'Don't say that, sweetie,' Brandi said. 'Everyone has their good points. I'll bet yours are better than most.'

Eve nodded, but Aries could tell she wasn't convinced.

'My guess is the younger you are the better your chances,' Brandi continued. 'Youth is easier to mould. Aside from Graham's kid, I haven't come across any young ones since this all started. That means something in my book.'

'Of course doctors would be useful,' Nathan said. 'And people with certain skills like electricians, welders, carpenters, stuff like that. If they're planning on fixing things. I'm sure it's just a matter of time before the Baggers decide to turn the power back on.'

'And get the phones and internet working,' Aries said, thinking of Clementine's brother, Heath, who was studying computer programming. 'Don't forget the hot water. I'm sure I'm not the only one who would kill to have a shower.'

'My father wanted me to be a plumber,' Brandi said. 'When he was drunk, he used to make cracks about how everyone would want to hire a gal named Brandi to fix their pipes.' She laughed when Colin looked up from his video game, a look of shock on his face. 'Yeah, he was a bit of a sexist pig.'

'Either way,' Aries said as she stifled a yawn, 'we can't make it easy for them. We can't let the Baggers find us.'

'Amen, sister,' Brandi said. 'And, on that note, I should head back. Don't want to turn into a pumpkin. The gals will get mad if I'm not back exactly when I said I would be. Say hello to the others. And you, my dear, should take a nap. You look exhausted.'

'Will do,' Aries said. She got up to follow Brandi to the back door, but the older woman shook her off.

'Don't need guest status,' she said. 'I can find my own way out.'

Aries hung out in the living room for a few more minutes but no one had anything new to report. Clementine and Michael were still at the university but they probably wouldn't be back for a few more hours. No need to worry just yet.

Finally excusing herself, she went upstairs to the bedroom where Jack sat alone in the dark.

'Hey,' she said from the door.

A few weeks ago, Jack had taken a baseball bat to the head during a Bagger fight. He'd been left blind and suffering from terrible migraines. No one knew if the blindness would last forever or if it was temporary.

There weren't exactly doctors around to give a proper diagnosis.

'Is that a beautiful woman I hear?' Jack said. 'I'd get up but I'd probably get lost trying to find you.'

She came over and sat down carefully beside him. Covered in blankets, her pale friend didn't look nearly as strong as he had a few weeks before. It was really hard. Jack was handling it well; he was the first to make all the dumb blind jokes. There was always a smile on his face but Aries could see how he was forcing the edges of his mouth to turn upward. His eyes were dull. They stared off into space, seeing only blackness. Sometimes he'd blink, squeezing the corners of his eyelids tightly as if trying to block out the pain. He'd always insist he was fine if Aries tried questioning him but, no matter how hard Jack tried to remain positive, Aries knew the reality of the situation wasn't lost on him. Having a blind person around made things that much harder. If the time came when they'd have to leave quickly, it wouldn't be that simple. Jack couldn't run.

Every time she looked at him, she couldn't help but feel it was her fault. She hadn't saved him. And she knew for certain she'd never be able to leave him, no matter the consequences.

'How are you feeling?'

He smiled. 'Good. Head hurts a bit but I'm used to that.'

'Do you want some pills?' On the bedside table was

an assortment of all sorts of painkillers. Tylenol. Advil. Aspirin. There were other brands with long unreadable names that packed more of a punch, courtesy of Nathan raiding a pharmacy a few weeks ago. None of them really worked well enough but Jack had tried them all just the same.

What Jack really needed was an MRI or an X-ray or some other sort of treatment that only came from a hospital.

'No pills,' Jack said. 'But you can tell me how your day went. And don't try to lie. I can hear your voice. I know you're hurting.'

'If it's just the same, I'd rather not talk about it right now,' she said. 'It was hard. I should have known better. Can we leave it at that?'

'Fair enough.'

That was the great thing about Jack. He never pushed or prodded. *He accepted what was.*

She stayed for a few minutes longer and then left for the bedroom she shared with Joy and Eve. They'd moved extra bedding from other rooms so the floor was wall to wall mattresses. Kicking off her shoes, she sat down on the bed and pulled a pillow close to her chest.

She had a new family now. But knowing for certain she'd lost the old one still hurt.

Closing her eyes, she waited for sleep.

When Aries woke up it was dark. No one had called her for dinner, or perhaps they had and she hadn't heard them. Rolling over, she checked the small alarm clock that was half hidden under the mattress. It was a little after ten. She'd slept just over four hours.

'Great,' she mumbled to herself.

She picked her hoody up off the floor and pulled it over her head before heading out into the hallway. She checked in on Jack and found him sleeping. Then she went down to where everyone was in the living room sitting around a small candle. The light flickered and shadows bounced off the walls. When they'd first moved into the safe house, they'd covered the back of the window blinds with blankets. From outside no one could tell the extra covering was there. This way they could have a minimal amount of light in the evening and still be safe.

'Why didn't you wake me?' she asked.

'Because you looked so cute,' Joy said. 'And no one could make themselves heard over that much snoring.' She giggled and ducked as if she thought Aries might take a swing at her. 'It's not like my meal was anything to write home about. There are some leftovers in the kitchen. Jack wasn't very hungry so he only ate a few bites. Probably cold by now but it can't be any worse than when it was warm.'

'You're the best cook here,' she said as she headed to the kitchen. 'We'd be lost without you and you know it.'

Mason was sitting alone on the counter in the dark and looking out of the window. Holding on to the little glass vial he always carried, he turned it round absently in his fingers a few times before stuffing it into his pocket. He picked up a can of soda and took a long drink.

'Going out tonight?' she asked.

He jumped, spilling Pepsi down his shirt. Cursing, he reached out and started wiping at the mess with his hand.

'Nervous?' she asked. There was a plate on the table with a napkin resting on top of it. She pulled it off, revealing some sort of pasta dish. Grabbing a fork she began to eat. It was cold but it still tasted good enough. Too bad there wasn't any bread left. A slice of garlic toast would be perfect.

'Clementine and Michael aren't back yet,' he said as he tore off a piece of paper towel and tried to soak up the soda from his shirt.

She stopped shovelling food into her mouth. 'Really?'

'Yeah.'

The all-too-common cold feeling crept along her spine and up into the roots of her hair. 'What time did they say they'd be back?' She glanced towards the living room, wondering why no one had bothered to tell her that a few minutes ago.

'No idea. I don't think the others are too worried,' he said. 'They've been late before.'

'But you're worried.'

He nodded. 'A little but I'm sure they're fine. Just because *you* think it's safer to travel after dark doesn't mean everyone wants to do it. They probably decided to spend the night. There'll be lots of good hiding spots on campus. Maybe they found other people. There could be a dozen reasons.'

'Maybe she found Heath.' But even as she said it, she knew just how doubtful it sounded. Vancouver was a huge city. The odds of Clementine finding her brother were slim. Even if he had made it all the way from Seattle, there was still the chance he might be dead. Although Clementine knew it, she was still determined to remain overly optimistic.

Aries often wished she shared her new friend's positivity.

'We can give them a day or two,' Mason said. 'Then everyone should consider moving on. If they've been caught by the Baggers, it's only a matter of time before they let them know we're here.'

'Clem and Mike would never rat us out.'

'They might if the Baggers use extreme measures,' he said. 'Even the strongest person might reveal anything to make the pain stop.'

'You think they'd torture them?'

'Yes. Without a doubt.'

She put the plate back down on the table. She wasn't hungry any more. Instead she zipped up her jacket, pulling up the hood and tucking her hair inside.

'Going out?' he said. There was a smile on his face she didn't much like.

She shrugged.

'Don't worry; I'll keep your secret. I'll tell them you've created a lab in the basement and you're breeding monster fighting rats or something.'

'Gee, thanks.'

Travelling at night *was* much easier than moving around in the day. There were more shadows to hide in. She bypassed Nathan who was doing the evening shift by sneaking round the back way. It didn't take long for her to walk down towards Kitsilano Beach. It was a nice enough night, not too cold and it wasn't raining. The sky was dark and she could see the moon was a half sliver hidden behind a few clouds.

The beach was empty. Gone were the days when couples walked hand in hand along the water. No one had time to be romantic any more.

She cut through the parking lot, her feet softly treading on the concrete. She went slowly, trying to avoid stepping in the piles of litter that were no longer being picked up by the city's sanitation crew. There was a lot of paper, mostly flyers and local newspapers that the wind scattered about. She came across the occasional food wrapper but there weren't many. The survivors had more important things to do than drop by the beach to eat their lunch. Even the rats weren't hanging out any more. They'd fled to the supermarkets and rotting fruit and vegetable stands where the pickings were better. Maybe that was one of the reasons the Baggers were burning the bodies instead of leaving them in their homes to rot.

She sat down on a bench close to the water and waited. She'd been here the past several nights. She'd close her eyes and listen. The ocean spoke to her, a steady sound of water crashing against the sand. For a few brief minutes she could forget everything and almost imagine the city the way it once was. Over the roar of the surf, she almost heard car horns, people talking, even ambulances and fire trucks as they blared their sirens. Every time she opened her eyes, there would be a jolt of disbelief when she looked across the bay and didn't see the lights from the thousands of condos, shops and office buildings.

Downtown Vancouver was now a dead zone, just like the rest of the world.

She could, however, see a soft shimmer of light from the Plaza of Nations where the Baggers were assembling the survivors. She figured they had to be running generators. But why? What were they doing to those poor people?

Further down on the beach, a few seagulls argued over something only birds could understand. She thought she saw a stray dog but it ran off before she got a better view. Could have been a coyote or a skunk; it was hard to tell in the darkness.

She saw him coming across the parking lot. Head down, face hidden by both a hoody and the lack of aforementioned street lights. Her stomach lurched out of fear and anticipation. Biting down on her cheek, she ignored the urge to run. There was always the chance the moving shadow might not be the person she expected. A few nights ago she had to run and hide under a picnic table while a few Baggers walked by sharing a bottle of whisky. Luckily for her, their inability to walk in a straight line saved her. But, as the figure approached and his face became visible in the moonlight, she relaxed.

'Hey.' Daniel stopped at the bench.

'You came.'

She was always surprised to see him although he hadn't missed a single day yet. For someone so determined to stay away from people, he didn't seem to want to stay away from her. It made her feel really good, yet it frustrated her that he still remained so vague about where he was staying and why he wanted to be alone.

It would be easier if he would give in and come to live with them. What exactly was she doing wrong to keep him always running away?

'You look tired,' he said as he sat down beside her. He held a Thermos in his hand. He twisted off the lid, and then passed it over. The smell of fresh coffee hit her nose. 'How did things go today? Did you get your answers?'

'The house was empty,' she said. She took a sip of the drink and the hot liquid immediately burned her tongue. Tightening the lid, she gave it back to him.

'That doesn't mean much. They could have found shelter elsewhere.'

She shook her head and told him about the blood. She even mentioned her breakdown and how there was now a half-packed gym bag of all her worldly goods lying on the floor of her bedroom. Once upon a time the bedroom and the items in it were the most important possessions in her world. If she'd been asked a few months ago what she couldn't live without, she'd have been hard pressed to give a single answer. Her books, computer, music, clothing – everything she owned had so much value back then. Now they meant nothing.

She'd left it all behind.

'Once I was there, all I wanted was to get out as quick as I could. I couldn't even bring myself to grab the ring my nana gave me. I used to love my things so much. I couldn't live without them. Today I looked at it all and I hated it.'

Daniel nodded.

'That was so selfish of me,' she continued. 'There were things we could have used as a group. I could have at least grabbed some toilet paper or shampoo. Does that make sense?'

Daniel nodded again. 'You can't take it with you. You may think you can, but you can't. The world's changed. You've changed. You're not the same girl I met back on the bus when the earthquakes happened. Back when it all started.'

'That was a million years ago. Just thinking about it makes me feel ancient.'

'I know,' he said. 'Some mornings I wake up an old

94

man. My back hurts and my body refuses to move the way it used to. I look down a stairwell and I think if I fall I'll break into a million pieces. And thinking hurts. My brain bangs against my skull. My stomach is hollow. Empty. It makes me wonder if it's all worth it sometimes.'

'You want to die? After all we've been through? You're giving up?'

'No.' Daniel looked away from her, his eyes drifting down to the shoreline. 'It's not like that at all. I can't expect you to understand.'

'Why not?' The anger was rising in her throat and she couldn't help it. Why did she keep hoping that he might change? He was doing it again, saying things and then refusing to embellish, forcing her away the second he gave up a bit of information that made her think he really was human and not some sort of weird emotional hermit.

'Isn't the ocean beautiful?'

'Huh?'

'The ocean,' Daniel said. 'Look at it. Not just the surface but picture down beneath. Twenty to a hundred feet below the surface. There's a lot of life in that dark water. Lots of death too. Right now everything is correcting itself. The oil rigs are no longer drilling, boats are no longer polluting, and the fishermen have long lost their daily quota.'

'So?'

Daniel shook his head. 'We're righting our wrongs. For centuries we've done nothing but pollute our skies, earth and water. We've killed off entire species of animals. The ocean was in trouble. We were overfishing it. Now that we're mostly gone, everything is being righted. The fish will repopulate. Within a few years the ocean will be full of life again.'

'You make it sound like the Baggers are some sort of radical environmentalists.'

Daniel laughed, his teeth shining in the moonlight.

'Or a deranged Mother Nature,' he said. 'Something's pulling the apron strings. What really made all the people go crazy? What created the Baggers?'

'It could be a disease,' she said. 'Some sort of mental disorder. Like a new form of schizophrenia. Or it could have been a government experiment. A bio-weapon of some sort. Created in a lab maybe.'

He shook his head. 'No, I don't believe humans could do this. I think it's something else. And we pissed it off. It's probably done it before too. Civilizations have been inexplicably destroyed in the past too.'

'It's possible,' she said. 'But what can we do? How do we kill a deranged Mother Nature? Does such a thing even have a body? Where would we find it?'

'Agreed,' Daniel said. 'But there are other, more-available options. Maybe we can't stop it but we can stop what it's doing.'

'You mean the Baggers? They're still crazy and hell-bent on killing all of us, no matter what lies they feed us. Are you suggesting we kill them all? Do we go to war?'

'What if some of them can come back?'

'You mean turn normal?'

'Yeah.'

She chewed absently on her lower lip for a bit. 'I think it's gone too far for that.'

'Maybe.' He smiled but his eyes looked very sad.

'Did someone close to you become a Bagger?' she asked.

There was a long pause while he twisted the Thermos lid in his hand. His fingers were long and graceful. She wanted to reach out and touch them but that seemed too personal. What if he pulled back?

'My mom,' he finally said. 'She tried to kill me.'

She sucked in air, a whooshing sound passing through her lips. 'Oh, Daniel, I'm so sorry. I've been very selfish.'

His eyes widened. 'How have you been selfish?'

'Because I've spent too much time talking about my own problems,' she said. 'I never bothered to ask about your family. When did you go back? After you left me at the school?'

He nodded.

'You said you can't go back. You spoke from experience.' This time she put her hand out and placed it gently on his leg. His body stiffened beneath her touch. But he didn't move away.

'You should head home,' he said.

Those were definitely not the words she wanted to hear.

'Walk with me?' she asked, knowing he'd say no. And he didn't surprise her. He shook his head. He probably wanted to spend time alone. She understood. Keeping something to yourself was one thing. When you spoke it out loud, it became that bit more real.

At least her parents were probably dead. To imagine them out there alive and killing innocents, that was more than she could stand.

She stood and brushed off her jeans. 'OK then,' she said. 'I'll see you tomorrow?'

'Maybe,' he said, which was his standard reply. But there was a hint of a smile on his face again and that made her know he'd be here. 'Be careful.'

Now it was her time to nod. 'You too. Stay alive.' Without waiting for a reply, she turned and headed off into the night.

MICHAEL

The strange guy made his way across campus with ease. He seemed to know all the shortcuts. He led them west past the Chan Centre for Performing Arts and through the parking lot. There were a lot of abandoned cars and a few of them even had bodies still inside them. The Baggers may have killed this far down, but they still hadn't been around to clean up. All four doors were open on an SUV and Michael turned away quickly when he saw a child seat along with a blanket and a purplish lump that might have been a foot. He checked to see if Clementine had noticed, but she was preoccupied with studying the back of the stranger's head.

'My name's Raj,' he said as they raced along.

'I'm Clementine and that's Michael.'

They came out at the bottom of the lot, beside the abandoned attendant booth, where they crossed the road to the Museum of Anthropology.

'We'll take cover there,' Raj said.

'Seriously?' Michael said. The building in front of them was bright and cheerful. Surrounded by trees, it was still noticeable from the main road and the structure had twice as many large windows than safe, sturdy brick or steel. 'Are you sure it's safe? That's a lot of glass. Kinda easy entrance. Hard to barricade. Shouldn't we be looking for a bomb shelter or something?'

Raj shook his head and grinned as if Michael had said the dumbest thing on the planet. 'It's called hiding in plain sight. We've been here since the beginning. They've crashed and burned all the dorms and totalled the Student Union Building. They tore apart the gymnasium brick by brick and you saw what they did to the library. But they haven't come here.'

'Right in the open where they'd never expect it,' Clementine said. 'Genius.'

Michael frowned.

'And there are good exits,' Raj said. 'Behind the museum is nothing but forest. It leads in many directions. Down to the water or around the university and back towards Vancouver. We've got stuff hidden in the woods. Food and water. All sorts of supplies. We've even got a boat. If we have to leave in a hurry, we can get out virtually undetected.'

'You keep saying *we*,' Michael said. 'How many people are there?'

Raj grinned. 'Sixty or so.'

'Is there a guy named Heath?'

Raj paused. 'Don't think so, but that doesn't mean much. We're pretty big. I don't know all the names. But you'll see for yourself.'

They walked right up to the front doors and Raj tapped several times on the glass. Raj pointed up towards the ceiling and waved.

'Security cameras,' he said. 'We've got them hooked up to a generator. Someone watching all the time. This ain't no shoddy operation.'

Finally someone appeared from the left. A girl with long hair down to her waist came over and unlocked the doors. She didn't look very happy. In her right hand she held something that looked like a taser. Michael couldn't tell for sure – he'd never seen one before except in the movies.

'What the hell, Raj?' she said. 'Where are Harvey and Carol? Didn't you find them? And who are these people? Are they safe?'

'They saved my life,' Raj said. 'Helped me get out. Got myself into a spot of trouble. Won't bore you with the details. Carol and the prof are dead. And I couldn't find the keys.'

The girl sighed. 'You're gonna have to tell Ryder yourself then. I'm not gonna be the bringer of that bad news.'

'I'll do it,' Raj said, 'but for the record it wasn't my fault. I wasn't the idiot that went out this morning without telling anyone.'

'No, but you're the idiot that brought back strangers,' the girl said. 'And you know Ryder's policy on that.'

'Relax, babes,' Raj said. 'It's all good. These kids are cool. They're just looking for someone. They'll chill here for a bit while it dies down outside.'

The girl locked the glass doors and sighed heavily. 'Come on then,' she said. 'Face the music.' She gave

Michael and Clementine a glance that seemed hardly worth her time. 'Follow me. I'll take you to the boss.'

Michael looked over at Raj, and the chem student nodded at both of them. 'She's right. If we don't go straight to Ryder, he'll just have some sort of hissy fit later. Best to get it over with. Come on, I'll introduce you to our just and fancy leader.'

There was no missing the sarcasm in his voice. Neither Raj nor the long-haired girl seemed to care much for this Ryder guy. Michael figured there was a good reason behind it and he was about to find out why.

They headed through the doors and into a huge room filled with impressive artefacts. There were half a dozen totem poles, all bearing animals that probably had some mythological story behind them. Giant stone carvings and wooden boats were on display. Too bad there was no one left to appreciate them. Taking a left, they went through another set of doors that opened to several more rooms filled with hundreds of glass cases containing all sorts of anthropological items.

Michael wondered where everyone was. Raj had said there were at least sixty people. They didn't see a single one as they walked along. Just how big was this building?

They moved through several more rooms before finally stopping in front of a door that had the word

OFFICE stencilled at the top. The girl turned and smiled wickedly at them.

'He's doing whatever it is he does,' she said. 'You're on your own from here on out.' Without waiting for a response, she knocked several times and then disappeared back down the corridor.

'She's polite,' Clementine said.

'She grows on you,' Raj said, and he gave Michael a wink. Opening the door, Raj leaned to the side and motioned with his hand for them to walk through.

Michael went first. The room was long and cast in shadows. Against the back wall, a man in his early twenties sat behind a desk. Beside him a small lamp burned. There were no windows in the room and no other doors. It must have been some sort of store room at one point.

The desk was filled with papers. The guy sitting behind it was scribbling something meticulously in a notebook. When he finally glanced up, his eyes met Michael's and there was no missing the jolt of surprise that forced him to straighten up and push his chair back a few inches.

'Raj?' The guy's voice was calm. 'What is this?'

'They're cool,' Raj said. He quickly explained the situation, starting with how they'd all met and ending with the death of Harvey and Carol. It didn't take very long.

'And you know these people are safe because . . .'

'Well, they haven't killed me yet. Or anyone else.'

The guy named Ryder stood up and walked out from behind his desk. He approached Clementine and grabbed her by the arm.

'Hey!' Michael grabbed Clementine's other arm and yanked her back towards him.

But the guy held firm. Reaching into his pocket, he pulled out a flashlight and brought it up to Clementine's face. Pointing the light right into her eyes, he studied them carefully. Once he'd finished he did the same thing to Michael.

Michael immediately understood. He was searching for black veins or a lack thereof. Proof that they were still human.

'You both need to leave this room,' Ryder said. Clicking the flashlight off, he placed it on the table behind him. 'Please wait outside. I want to have a chat with Raj alone.'

Michael stood his ground. He didn't like the way Ryder smiled. His lips may have been turned upward but his eyes were cold and deadly. He stepped closer to the guy in a way that forced Clementine behind him. Staring straight into Ryder's eyes, he waited.

'It's cool,' Raj said. 'Maybe better if we sort stuff out anyway. Gotta talk about the prof and how we're gonna find those keys. If you head towards the hall, you'll find Katarina. She'll take you to the cafeteria. Just tell her I said so.'

Clementine spoke directly into his ear. 'Come on.' He allowed her to take his hand and lead him out of the door. Ryder closed it behind them and there was a click as the deadbolt slid into place.

'That guy gives me the creeps,' Michael said as he stared at the door.

'He can't be that bad,' Clementine said, tugging gently on his arm. 'Especially if he's managed to keep all those people alive. He's smart enough to be checking our eyes. We should be doing that too. Come on, I could use a drink. And it gives me a chance to look for Heath. If Raj isn't back in half an hour, I'll let you break down the door and be a hero.'

Michael finally nodded and followed her. They walked through a few of the display rooms before they found Katarina. Clementine repeated what Raj had said. She didn't look very happy about the idea but she nodded and led them straight to the cafeteria.

There they found more survivors.

A bunch of them were hanging out. There must have been at least twenty faces. Most of them were drinking cups of coffee poured from a gigantic espresso machine. A few others were eating food that must have been prepared in the big kitchen. The food smelt warm and surprisingly appealing. Clementine squeezed Michael's hand as they walked past a girl eating a slice of pizza. Melted cheese fell in long strands from her lips.

Katarina ushered them over to the corner where there were some empty tables. 'You can sit here and wait,' she said. 'Raj will come for you when he's finished.'

Without waiting for their answer she turned and walked away, her heels clicking on the tiled floor.

'I want a generator,' Clementine whispered in his ear. They sat down together on the same side, their backs to the wall. 'These people are living like kings. I haven't had pizza in forever. Where do you think they got the cheese? Do you think they have a working freezer?'

'They must have,' Michael said. 'But this can't be safe. How is it they haven't been spotted? It makes no sense. It can't be this easy.' His eyes came to rest on a guy with flaming red hair. He had a large espresso on the table in front of him. He spooned in a generous amount of sugar. There wasn't any fresh cream, just powdered milk, but Michael could care less. His mouth started to water.

How unfair was this? Some people were living in hellholes without water and light and the monstrous Baggers still managed to find them and hunt them down. How was it that this incredibly large group managed to hide right out in the open and have luxuries like coffee and pizza? Not to mention a generator that most likely gave them an abundance of hot water. Looking around, Michael couldn't see a dirty face among the lot of them. And their clothing was fresh and probably smelt like detergent.

'Hey.' The red-haired guy finally noticed Michael studying him. 'Want some coffee, man?'

'Sure,' Clementine said, elbowing Michael in the

ribs before he could refuse. It was amazing how well she knew him.

The red-haired guy went over to the espresso machine and expertly prepared two cups for them. He dropped them off at the table and immediately left. That appeared to be the limit of his hospitality. The same went for the rest. Although they gave the occasional nod or smile, the group stayed as far away from Michael and Clementine as possible.

Michael took a sip of his hot drink, trying not to make a face. It was very strong and he couldn't even remember the last time he'd actually had real coffee. The red-haired guy hadn't offered them either sugar or powdered milk and he didn't want to get up from the table to get it himself. With all those eyes watching them, he didn't think it would be a good idea to make any sudden moves. Katarina had her taser. Who knew what the others might be concealing?

Clementine gave him a sharp nudge in the side. 'Do you think we should ask them about Heath?' she whispered.

Michael shook his head. 'Let's wait a bit. Once we clear everything with that Ryder guy, maybe then they'll be friendlier. Right now I think they'd rather toss us in front of one of those white vans.'

'Yeah,' she said. 'Good point.'

They waited.

Other people came in. They wandered over to tables where they sat with the others. Many of them whispered to each other, trying to pretend they weren't looking or paying attention to the new strangers. But no one came over.

Clementine sipped her coffee politely. Michael could feel her foot tapping nervously on the floor beside him.

The silence grew louder. The stares and whispers became more blatant. Finally, after an unbearable ten minutes, Raj walked into the room. He looked around until he spotted them, waved and then headed over to their table. He moved nonchalantly through the others, stopping to slap palms with the red-haired guy, and spoke a few words to the group of girls who were eating the pizza.

Raj pulled out a chair and sat down across from them.

There was a nice red mark on his face from where someone had hit him.

'Are you OK?' Clementine said. 'What did he do to you?'

'Ah, it's nothing, babes,' Raj said. 'Just a bit of a misunderstanding. But it's all cleared up now. You're both welcome to spend the night. It's probably too late for the two of you to be heading back. The scouts said the main roads are heavy with those crazies. They didn't like our little library escapade.'

Clementine looked at her watch and her eyes widened. 'You're right. I didn't realize it was so late.' She turned to Michael. 'Should we try and make it? We said we'd be back an hour ago.'

'What am I, a broken record?' Raj shook his head. 'I just said it's not safe. Can't let you leave, babes. Not with a clean conscience.'

'You don't understand,' Michael said. 'We've got others waiting for us. If we don't show up on time, they'll worry.'

'They'll understand,' Raj said. 'Anyone who's made it this far is bound to understand. You missed the bus. Couldn't find a taxi. It's not like you can call Mummy to come pick you up. Stay with us. You can return in the morning. Besides, you don't want to miss the show.'

'Show?'

'The rally.' Raj leaned forward until his chin was almost touching the table. 'Our plans for disorderly destruction. We have them every night. Keeps us angry. Keeps us aware.'

'Huh?' Michael put his coffee cup down.

Raj leaned back in his chair. 'It's simple. Revenge. It's our way of righting wrong. The Baggers took away a lot of things. We're taking it back.'

'How do you plan on doing that?' Clementine asked.

'Come to our meeting and you'll find out.'

They waited in the very back of a large exhibition room. The room was empty of furniture except for a bunch of folding chairs and a currently empty podium. But it was filled with people. Raj had told them there were at least sixty people living at the museum. They were all crammed into the small space. Michael figured they were mostly refugees of the university, students who had gathered together when the earthquakes and killings began. Most of the faces he saw were under the age of thirty. There were a few older ones, maybe former professors or staff. Michael had trouble believing that educated professionals would actually listen to someone like Ryder. But as he scanned the room he saw that most of the older people did look like they wanted to be there.

They'd arrived late because of Raj; he'd disappeared for a bit, leaving them to continue sitting in the cafeteria until the sun went down and darkness set in. Now they stood with their backs up against the wall because all the chairs were gone.

'He's not here,' Clementine said as she scanned the crowd for her missing brother. She studied the faces and heads of people walking past them. But she didn't venture off on her own. Michael could tell she preferred to keep close to him. She kept chewing on a thumbnail and ignoring the girl with long ponytails who'd taken it upon herself to make sure they didn't try to sneak off before the rally officially began.

'He's really amazing,' the girl said. 'He's got this way of talking. You can't help but fully believe everything that comes out of his mouth.'

'I seriously doubt that,' Clementine turned and whispered in Michael's ear.

He smiled.

'He's OK,' Raj said, but not loud enough for the

ponytailed girl to hear. 'He's got some ideas. Bit of an extremist but he has kept everyone alive. That counts for something in my book.'

The lights dimmed in the room. Music began to play over the speakers. The crowd came alive, cheering and stomping their feet.

All this for that guy? I so missed something earlier. You'd think he was a god or something.

'You are trapped.' A voice echoed over the PA system. Michael raised his head and looked around.

The crowd cheered louder.

'They have tried to steal your soul. They have chained down your life. Taken your family. Abused your mind. But we have a weapon too.'

The crowd went ballistic. Michael looked at Clementine, and she rolled her eyes and stuck out her tongue at him.

The lights in front of the podium went on, flashing red and blue as Ryder took the stage. He held a microphone in one hand, a judge's gavel in the other. The people in the front screamed harder and waved their hands at the dark-haired man. Someone lit a lighter.

'Kinda loud, isn't it?' Michael asked Raj. 'I mean, don't you worry about the sounds reaching the street?'

'Completely soundproof,' Raj shouted back. 'Can't hear a thing past the main lobby. Besides, we've got people guarding the place outside. We do this almost every night. Nothing bad has happened yet.'

111

Ryder puffed up his chest and raised the gavel into the air. 'This ends now! We will take back our world!' Slamming the gavel down on the podium, he grinned ravenously at his followers. 'We will not let these monsters keep us hidden. We need to rise out of the darkness. Take back the light. They try and give us warnings?'

'WARNING, WARNING, WARNING!' The crowd chanted, eyes alight. One of the girls in the front started crying and threw herself down at Ryder's feet. Her antics only made the crowd that much more crazy.

'We will give them hell!'

'WARNING, WARNING, WARNING!'

'We will give them pain!'

Clementine turned and stared at Raj. 'You believe this crap?'

Raj laughed, showing perfect white teeth. 'Never said that, babes. I said he's doing a good job keeping us safe. He's still a bloody chav. All bright lights and glam. Keeps the stoners interested though.'

'It's nothing but a light show,' Clementine said. 'We used to do the same tricks with cheerleading.'

'It's not so much the delivery but the entire message as a whole,' Raj said. 'Flashy lights aside, I do think we need to rise up and kick some Bagger arse. There are a lot of us hiding in this city. If we manage to organize ourselves better, we could actually take them on. It's all about the numbers.'

Michael watched the group of people whipping

themselves up into a frenzy. It was amazing. Ryder was a jerk. There was no denying that. He'd treated them terribly during their brief meeting and he'd even thrown some punches although he'd been careful to have no witnesses. Raj had told everyone he'd fallen against one of the displays and the others seemed to believe it.

But when Ryder talked the crowd listened. They heard his words and they cheered him on with all their hearts.

Michael wished people would listen to him like that. He missed being in charge of a group. He closed his eyes and a face flashed across his memory. A small sick boy. He remembered the child's mother. She'd fought so hard to keep her boy alive. Then there was Evans. The man who'd travelled with Michael for three weeks after the first initial Bagger attack. Evans had trusted him. And Michael had betrayed him.

He'd left them all behind to die during an attack.

No, it was better if he wasn't in charge. He'd only make a mess of things again.

But still.

Clementine nudged him with her shoulder. 'I think we should leave after this,' she leaned in close and shouted straight into his ear. 'We can sneak out or something. Heath isn't here. He wouldn't get involved with stuff like this. I'm game to head home tonight if you are.'

Michael nodded. 'Maybe,' he shouted back. 'Let's see what happens.'

She looked at him, raising a single eyebrow. 'Don't tell me you believe this crap? There are thousands of Baggers out there and less than a hundred untrained students here. What chance do they have?'

'It's probably the same chance whether they want to fight or hide,' Michael answered.

The girl with the ponytails started jumping on the spot, waving her hands about, and he ducked and moved closer to Clementine.

'We will fight,' Ryder screamed. 'We will kill them before they get the chance to take any more of us down.'

'WARNING, WARNING, WARNING!'

Michael turned his head, wondering where Raj had gone. He spotted him a few feet away, leaning against the wall and drinking from a bottle of rum. He caught Michael's gaze and winked.

'Enjoying the show, mate?' Raj offered up his half-empty bottle. Michael took a long drink.

He never got a chance to answer. A loud bang echoed through the exhibition room. Someone had thrown open the heavy doors. Katarina rushed in, blood pouring from a gash on her face. Everyone's vocal chords cut out at once.

Dead silence.

Katarina swayed back and forth as her eyes tried to focus on the people waiting.

'They're here,' she said.

Her knees buckled beneath her and she fell forward,

her face making a sickening squelching noise as it hit the floor.

The PA system hummed. No one moved.

Several seconds ticked by. Finally the girl with the ponytails opened her mouth and let out a very long scream.

People began to run. They rushed past each other, bodies slamming into bodies as they all tried to reach the exit at the exact same time. A girl went down, tumbling to the ground as others stomped over her, completely oblivious to her weak cries. Another guy, the red-haired one, grabbed a girl by the hair, pulled her aside to try to get closer to the door. The girl spun round and ended up punching the guy beside her.

Complete frenzy.

They'd have to try to follow the crowd if they were going to get out in one piece.

Michael grabbed hold of Clementine's hand and squeezed tightly. 'Don't let go of me,' he said.

'Not a chance.'

They tried to stick to the sides as they inched their way towards the door. Michael's foot stepped on something squishy and he jumped back, horrified to see a body beneath him. He couldn't see the face attached to it; there were too many legs rushing about. From somewhere down the hall, gunshots fired. People screamed louder. Some of them turned and tried pushing their way back into the room. A fist came out of nowhere, slamming into Michael's ear; tiny stars exploded across his vision. Clementine's hand was almost jerked out of his. An older man pulled her back by her blonde locks, trying to get past. Ignoring the pain in his ear, Michael raised an arm and tried to prise the guy's hands out of her hair. He managed to free her and the older man turned round in confused circles, several pieces of Clementine's hair tangled in his fingers.

'You did this.'

The voice hissed in his ear. A fist hammered down on Michael's skull, forcing his legs to jelly. Suddenly he was down on the floor and staring up at the ceiling lights. Clementine immediately knelt to help him up but Ryder grabbed her, pushing her aside, as he reached down to place his hand across Michael's throat. Bringing up his foot, he slammed the heel of his shoe straight into Michael's stomach.

'You did this,' Ryder repeated. 'You brought them here.'

'We didn't do anything.' Michael's voice gurgled under the pressure as Ryder's hand tightened.

'Leave him alone, man.' Raj had joined the circle. 'Look at him. There's no black veins. He's one of us.'

'He's one of them,' Ryder continued. 'He's managed to fool me. His eyes are normal but he's one of them. Maybe he's working for them.' Ryder forced up a good ball of spit and let it fly at Michael's face. 'Traitor.'

The light of the room was starting to grow dim around the edges. Everything started to slow down. Michael could see Clementine throwing herself on

Ryder's back, pounding at him with her fists. A bright halo of light flickered from the back of her head. Her blonde hair was glowing in the spotlights.

She was so beautiful. How come he hadn't noticed it properly before?

He did notice, however, that Raj had turned over his rum bottle and the liquid was draining out on to the floor.

Someone's going to slip, he thought.

Then Raj brought the bottle down along the side of Ryder's head.

The air rushed back and Michael took it in with great gasping whooshes. He started coughing, which brought the stars back with a vengeance. Ryder dropped down across his legs and Clementine quickly grabbed his arm and tried to prise Michael off him. Ryder was unconscious, blood trickling from a gash in the back of his head.

'Told you the guy's a bit dense,' Raj said. Reaching down, he grabbed Michael by the arm and helped him up to his feet. Clementine appeared on his other side, wrapping her small arms round his waist, trying to prop him up.

'I'm OK,' Michael finally mumbled. His throat burned when the words came out. So much pain. Everything had happened so quickly. It was a miracle the nut hadn't crushed his windpipe.

'Really, I'm OK,' he repeated but Clementine still refused to let go.

'We have to run,' she said. 'Can you do it?'

Michael nodded.

Raj paused and glanced down at the unconscious Ryder on the floor. More gunshots echoed through the halls. The majority of people had made it outside the exhibition room and their screams were distant as they rushed for the museum's exits.

'You are cool, right?' Raj asked. 'I didn't just waste my booze on that guy for nothing, right? Holy crap, I can't believe I clocked him like that.'

Michael stepped forward, trying to keep his knees from buckling. 'Yeah, we're cool. We had nothing to do with this. How could we?'

'I hate to admit it, but I think it is kind of your fault,' Raj said. 'Mine too. Too much of a coincidence. They must have followed us from the library.'

'You think?'

Raj nodded. 'I'll take full blame. I should have known better. Not too sure what to do now.'

'You can come stay with us,' Clementine said. 'And anyone else we can round up. We've got a safe house.'

'If we get out alive, babes,' Raj said. 'I guess you're following me again.'

He turned and headed into the darkness of the hall.

Michael twisted his body round in Clementine's hands until he was facing her. 'Hey,' he said, and when she looked into his eyes he leaned down and covered her lips with his. Time stopped for a brief moment.

'What was that for?' she said when he pulled away.

Her eyes shone brightly under the generator lights.

'Because you're beautiful.'

'You just discovered this now?' Her fingers wrapped around his. 'Let's get out of here,' she said. 'Plenty of time for that later.'

He smiled and limped after her.

NOTHING

There is nothing more thrilling than the hunt.

Nothing.

Not even the kill.

I am Nothing.

I live for the moment of breathtaking anticipation when I pinpoint my prey.

Stalking it.

Waiting for the right moment to jump.

I crave the surprise on their face, the dulling of the corneas as I bring my weapon down and slash their throat. The feeling of life as it leaves their body. I can feel it. It's both suffocating and invigorating. The air grows heavy as the mind starts to shut down. They greedily suck in that final breath. Then it's over in the blink of an eye. If they have a soul, I am the one who devours it.

It doesn't matter who they are. I will take them and I will consume them.

This is why we were drawn to each other. We both wanted the hunt. The reasons were different, but none of that mattered. We didn't even particularly like or trust each other. We were too much alike in that way.

But we'd still bonded.

We wanted the kill. We could taste it on our tongues.

The sweet sticky flavour of revenge. There would always be the desire to right the deaths for which we felt responsible. We weren't that different although he'd have been shocked if he knew it. He would have blamed me for turning him. Twisting his thoughts and making them my own.

I had nothing to do with it.

At least when I was hunting with him, I was still normal. Well, as normal as I could be.

Secrets.

We had them. They were different but at the same time I wouldn't have been surprised to hear they were the same.

Something made me stronger when I was part of a team, able to push the darkness deep down inside of me. I could control it.

But it was always hard.

I didn't want it.

I lied to myself, refused to listen to the voices when they called. Tried to block them out. I needed to be strong enough to keep my own mind.

But they called to me.

When they grew too powerful I'd get away.

Run. Run away.

Hide.

When they passed and I returned to normal, the guilt would eat me up.

And, believe me, there was guilt. Lots of it. I lived each moment as if a thousand pounds of molten lava crushed my chest. You may not think I felt pity for my victims by the way I talk, but I did. I felt sorry for each and every one I harmed. I remembered them all in secret. All that weight on my soul took its toll.

Scratch that. I don't have a soul. It's gone. I lost it a long time ago.

And when I closed my eyes I saw their faces etched on my corneas. Staring down at me. Accusing. Hating. Wishing me the same death. Demanding to take back what I'd stolen from them. They'd eventually find me and drag me down. After a while I stopped looking in mirrors. I didn't want to see what they saw.

They all haunted me.

Even when I killed my own kind.

MASON

They'd moved across town in the dark, sticking to the shadows, constantly searching for signs of life. They had their plan and it required careful movement. They'd been doing this for a few weeks now. Most nights after Aries said goodnight to Daniel, Mason would step out of the shadows and sit down next to the guy he didn't like. It wasn't a personal thing that kept him coming back. No, it went deeper.

The Baggers had noticed. They had to tread more carefully as the days went on; it would be bad for them to fall into a trap. But as they made their way across the Granville Bridge nothing waited for them.

Dead city all around him.

The streets were hushed.

Mason didn't believe it for a second. It was too calm.

'Why aren't there more of them?' he asked. They leaned against the concrete edge, peering out across the bridge and towards the darkness beneath them. There was no electricity and it was hard to tell if the ground was empty. There were too many shadows in which to hide. Too many abandoned cars and overgrown bushes. Plenty of places for psycho nutbars to crawl out from. From a distance he could see the sky lit up from where the Plaza of Nations stood hidden behind several street blocks. A soft glow seeped above the now-empty condos that were once considered the most luxurious places to live. At least the ones that were still standing. Several of the buildings had collapsed into themselves. All of those indoor pools, hot tubs and fitness rooms gone in the blink of an eye.

The Plaza of Nations was the place the white vans advertised as a safe haven. It was the only area in the downtown core that had electricity. Either they had powerful generators or someone had figured out how to turn on the juice for that section only. They were making the most of it. Sanctuary. All a person had to do, no matter how terrified or timid, was walk up to the gate and they'd welcome you in with open arms. No one would be harmed. It was supposed to be that simple. Mason didn't believe it for a second.

A single spotlight flashed straight up into the night sky. It cut across the bay and both boys ducked as it grew closer.

Daniel shrugged. 'Guards? Maybe one or two. Do you really think they expect someone to come down and try to break up the joint? Only an idiot would consider trying to attack the Plaza right now.'

'They know we're out here.'

Daniel snorted. 'We're not a big enough threat. Sure, we've taken a few of them down. But there's thousands more. I doubt we've even blipped on their radar.'

Last night they'd found a nest of Baggers down in Moberly Road. They'd quickly scouted the area, mapping it, planning how best to come back and destroy them. Then it had been a bit of a shock when dozens of the white vans arrived on the scene. Mason and Daniel realized they'd been discovered and had barely managed to get away.

The day before they'd killed four of them.

It wouldn't bring back the people they'd murdered, but at least it would keep them from claiming more. Daniel had become his partner in crime. It was the only thing so far that made him cool.

Something had happened several weeks ago when Daniel had first handed him the knife and they'd let Aries and the others run off to safety. It was the first time he'd actually felt in control since he'd got the fateful news that his mother was in the hospital just before everything broke loose. Before the darkness inside him that he'd fought so hard to ignore had taken control. The Baggers hadn't killed her directly, but they were still responsible. And he would make them pay.

Tonight they had a different plan. A nicer one. It was Daniel's idea and a good one.

The spotlight passed them by. Mason half expected to hear gunshots. Bullets tearing through his flesh as he tried to run between the shadows. He had these fantasies whenever he got too exposed. The Granville Bridge held no hiding spots. If the Baggers were to attack, their only way out would be to jump.

Of course Mason knew he'd never do that. He'd fight

instead. Even if it was hopeless. He'd just make sure to take as many of those monsters down with him as he could. It wouldn't bring Chickadee back. But the thought still made him smile.

Nothing happened. They reached the end of the bridge without great difficulty and set off through the darker parts of Yaletown. It was hard work. Most of the streets had been destroyed in the earthquake and several of the fallen buildings made it impossible to move in a straight line.

The stink of garbage was overwhelming. There were a lot of restaurants in the area and it smelt like every single one of them must have been overspilling with rancid food. Mason could see the rats too. Several of them moved in and out of the darkest corners as they searched for whatever it is rats search for.

'Even the cats stay away from those suckers,' Mason said when a particularly oversized white rat ran out in front of them with something dead clamped between its jaws. It glared at them with pink beady eyes before disappearing into a pile of rubbish.

'Cats are smarter than that,' Daniel replied. 'They'll stick to the mice and birds. Majority of them are probably feral by now. At least the ones that managed to get out of their human prisons. Must be cat heaven these days. No people. Lots of rodents. Cockroaches too. I used to live in a place over on Broadway that was infected with those little beasts. I used to have to shake my clothing out in the morning before I got dressed.

Did you know you can freeze them and they'll still come back to life?'

Mason had never seen a cockroach but he nodded anyway.

'Come on,' Daniel said, kicking at a pile of bricks, the remains of what was probably once a trendy clothing store. 'We're not going to get round this way. We should go back to Pacific. It'll be more open and that's probably where they're going to be standing guard but I guess we don't have much of a choice, do we?'

Pacific Avenue was better. There were still a lot of buildings standing, silent skyscrapers blocking out the moonlight. Most of the windows had broken in the earthquakes but there wasn't any shattered glass on the concrete. The Baggers had obviously already started cleaning up this area. Easier for all those poor unlucky souls to just walk on in. And Daniel and Mason were taking full advantage of it. But the landscape was more open and it didn't take long before they spotted the Baggers doing their patrol. They crouched down behind some cars and watched.

'Just a few guards, huh?' Mason said.

Daniel smirked. 'I only see two.'

'You failed to mention the weapons.'

Daniel shrugged. 'Stop focusing on the negative, Tourist Boy. It'll just give you wrinkles. What are those anyway? It's too damn dark out here. Are those machine guns?'

Mason peered into the darkness where, a hundred

feet away, a Bagger crossed the street, turned and started walking back towards the Plaza. Held firmly in his arms was a long dark shadow that did look like an automatic weapon.

'Where the hell did they find that?' Mason whispered. Up until now, the Baggers they'd attacked seemed limited in the brains and sanity department. The ones from two nights ago probably couldn't have held a cucumber properly, let alone a gun. Things were definitely changing with the Baggers these days. They were getting much more organized.

This was going to be a bit of a challenge.

'Probably raided the police stations,' Daniel said. 'Would make sense. I'm sure there are a few rabid Bagger cops out there. That would explain why we haven't been able to find anything. They beat us to the punch. You want to back off?' Daniel went on but Mason could tell he didn't mean it. No, Daniel wanted the chase as much as he did.

'We should get a little closer,' Mason said. 'I doubt we can take anyone out tonight. But maybe we can get a better idea of what's going on. Would be good to see inside that complex. I'd like to know how many people they're holding hostage.'

'Little recon,' Daniel said. 'I'm game.'

They jumped up from behind the car and scuttled forward in the dark. Sticking to the shadows wasn't that difficult. They stayed far enough behind the patrolling Baggers so that any noise they made wouldn't be heard.

When the giant spotlight swung in their direction, they took cover behind abandoned cars or oversized bushes. It was slow moving; after about an hour they'd only travelled two blocks. But they were that much closer.

The area was brighter now. The glow from the Plaza was seeping out on to the streets. The security was still slim but there was always the possibility that Baggers were on guard in the buildings above. Mason spent so much time looking into the shadows of the condo windows that he didn't notice the danger right in front of him. Luckily Daniel was paying attention. He grabbed Mason and yanked him sideways and behind an abandoned vehicle before Mason's brain even registered the threat.

Daniel opened the door to the SUV as quietly as possible. 'Get in,' he whispered.

They crawled into the cab while one of the Baggers backtracked towards them. Whoever owned the SUV had obviously never cleaned it. There were dozens of empty water and Gatorade bottles, crumpled bags of rancid-smelling takeout, and a lot of construction equipment. The interior smelt of old socks and sour food. Mason wrinkled his nose in disgust.

They crawled into the back where a pile of dirty clothes was draped over some tools and empty bottles of engine oil.

'This is cosy,' Daniel said.

'Shhhhh.' Mason elbowed Daniel in the side as the Bagger passed them just a few feet away. He was relieved to hear Daniel suck in his breath and hold it instead of continuing to blab. He tapped his fingers absently on his jeans but didn't say a word. They waited several minutes until they were positive the monster had passed them completely and headed off into the night.

Mason shook his head. 'You really are crazy.'

Daniel sat up and opened the side door. 'Crazy is good. Makes me feel alive. But don't worry – I'm not dumb. Let's not take chances. I don't fancy being caught and dragged into whatever hell they have set up there either.'

They climbed out of the vehicle. Mason was careful and closed the door as quietly as possible before they moved on.

The perimeter of the Plaza of Nations was cut off by thick chain-link fence and barbed wire. Just like a prison, there were spotlights and posts set up where Baggers stood guard with more automatic weapons. Beyond the fencing, Mason could see the courtyard where they'd pitched tents. There were no people walking around, but he could see shadows behind the canvas.

'We need to get a better look,' Daniel said.

Mason nodded but it was obvious that they weren't going to get any closer without being discovered. The grounds were brighter than a sunny day. They'd have to find another way if they were going to get a better look inside the compound.

'We should go up,' Daniel said, and he pointed to

the closest building. Beside them stood the remains of a silent skyscraper, once beautiful beachfront property, now nothing but piles of rebar and broken glass. But Daniel was right. If they could find a way up to the tenth floor or so, they'd have a perfect view.

'Think we can get inside?'

Daniel grinned. 'I can always find a way.'

Mason wasn't in the slightest surprised to hear that. Of course he'd figured out that Daniel was shady from the very start. It didn't faze him at all that Daniel knew how to break into buildings. A guy like him probably had a record sheet a mile long.

But they didn't have to break into anything. The front doors were completely shattered. All they had to do was walk right through and make sure they didn't cut themselves on the jagged glass. A small child could have done it. The foyer was dark and empty. A single suitcase stood in the middle of the floor by the elevators. The baggage lay tipped over on its side. Dried blood spread across the floor beside it. Someone with very large boots had left several footprints on the marble. A once sticky handprint was on the wall by the middle elevator. Someone had tried pressing the button but obviously their luck ran out shortly after.

'I hate taking the stairs,' Daniel said.

'Cheer up,' Mason said, giving him a slap on the back. 'It'll do you good to put some colour in those pasty cheeks of yours.'

'I can kick your ass anytime, Dowell.'

'If you still feel that way when we get to the top, I'm game.'

'Throw in a round of chess too,' Daniel said. 'We all know I'm smarter, might as well prove it.'

They walked past the elevators and into the back where they found the stairwell. The door was closed, but a set of keys was stuck in the lock. Mason reached out and twisted the key. It worked. Automatically they both reached into their pockets and pulled out flashlights. Mason's was small and metal and it always felt cold in his hands, even after he'd been holding it for a long time. It had become one of the most important things to carry these days, especially at night. That and the Swiss army knife he kept in the back pocket of his jeans.

Instant security.

They didn't talk. They just climbed. When they got to the sixth floor, they decided to stop and look around.

The hallway was long and empty. All the doors to the condos were open. They approached the closest one. They could see the cracks in the wood where someone had forced it open.

'They must have come in here and broken down each one,' Daniel said. He ran his fingers along the splintered wood. 'Looks like they used a crowbar or something. I wonder if it's like this on every floor.'

'Possible,' Mason said. 'They've been cleaning out the houses. I took Aries to her parents' house today. Someone had been there and removed the bodies.' He paused and glanced at Daniel. 'What's the matter? Didn't she tell you she was with me?'

Daniel looked over at him a bit too quickly. 'She told me.'

Mason grinned.

They moved further into the darkened condo. The air was musty. The leather couch was arranged perfectly in front of a worthless fifty-inch flatscreen. A mouldy plate of noodles and half a cup of spoilt wine rested on the expensive coffee table.

'A few months ago I would have killed for a TV like that,' Daniel said.

'Me too.'

They both moved past the undisturbed furniture and made their way over towards the windows. Below them was a perfect view of the compound. The place was as motionless as it had been when they were on the ground. But the view was a little better. Problem was there was nothing to see.

Daniel pressed his face against the window's clear surface, breathing heavily enough to fog the glass.

'I should have brought Michael's binoculars,' Mason said. 'Next time give me a heads up and—'

They both heard the noise.

A soft resonance as feet stepped through the doorway behind them.

Daniel turned his face, still pressed against the window, his eyes staring straight at Mason. 'Oh, that can't be good. Tell me it's not bad.'

Mason glanced over at the entrance. There were only two of them and the shadows crowding the door were a lot shorter than he would have expected. He raised an eyebrow and bit down on his tongue to keep from laughing.

'It's different,' he said.

Daniel slowly turned round and faced their new audience. The two shadows stepped further into the room, raising their arms so Mason and Daniel could see the kitchen knives in their hands.

They all stood their ground and stared each other down.

Daniel was the first to speak.

'Those are kids.'

'Pint-sized kids,' Mason agreed.

The smallest one opened his mouth and bared his teeth. The bigger one growled and moved inward until he was about ten feet away. Up close, Mason could get a better look at his face. The kid couldn't have been older than eight or ten. Out of habit, Mason held up the flashlight and directed the beam right into the child's eyes. Sure enough, from across the room, Mason could see the black veins.

Daniel burst into laughter. 'You've got to be kidding me.'

Mason grinned. Even with their weapons it was hard to see either of them as a threat. The small one couldn't weigh more than seventy pounds. He was waving the knife around in front of him, but it was obvious the kid didn't know a single thing about using the weapon.

'You want the one on the left or the one on the right?'

Mason opened his mouth to say 'piece of cake' but he never got the chance. The bigger kid screamed and suddenly flung himself forward, crossing the remaining distance at a remarkable speed. He crashed straight into Mason's stomach, knocking him backwards and against the window. Mason heard a cracking noise as his head bounced off the glass. He fell to his knees and the kid immediately jumped on top of him, bringing the knife slashing down. Mason brought his arm up just in time to block the blow.

The kid grunted hard and squirmed enough to get free and bring the weapon down again. Mason couldn't understand how something that tiny could be so fast. And heavy! The kid felt like a tank. It took him seconds to press Mason down by his shoulders, using his scrawny kid knees until Mason's back was on the floor. Keeping his arms up, he had to use all his strength to defent himself.

From the corner of his eye, Mason saw Daniel jump over the couch and crash against the dining-room table. The smaller kid was right behind Daniel, his own weapon raised above his head as he screamed and hooted. Daniel barely managed to grab a chair and use it to bat the child away. The kid smashed against the wall, but was racing back at Daniel the second his feet touched the floor.

Mason finally brought up his legs and bucked the small grunting child off him. The kid flew straight into the bedroom doorframe. Mason seized his chance while the boy was on the ground to reach out and grab the kid's wrist, using all his strength to slam the kid's hand against the floor. Grinding the delicate bones, he finally forced the child to drop the knife. He kicked it with his foot and the weapon disappeared under the couch.

'Gotcha, you little brat,' he said through gritted teeth.

The kid threw his hands at Mason's face and started scratching his skin.

He shoved the kid away from him a second time. Pulling himself to his feet, he swung hard, knocking the kid off balance and straight into the leather couch. When the kid tried to get up, he threw him back down again.

'Stay down,' he said. But he might as well have been talking to an untrained puppy.

Daniel tossed his kid against the kitchen table and the pint-sized monster slid across the soft wood and crashed into the counter.

'It's like fighting rabid runts,' Daniel said as he came over to join Mason.

They stood together as the children both climbed back to their feet.

Mason realized that if this continued the odds were very good that he and Daniel were going to kill the kids.

It was one thing to kill Baggers. But child Baggers? Could he really do it? Were they really that different from the full-grown ones?

The bigger kid growled again and crouched low to the ground. Mason prepared himself for the launch.

'No.'

The voice was loud and came from the front entrance. All four of them turned their heads at once. Several Baggers crowded into the room, two of whom held automatic weapons in their hands. They stepped to the side and let another one move forward. He was wearing a business suit and a pair of sunglasses. He walked over to the children and shook a finger at them.

'You will not harm them,' the Bagger said. He was wearing a dirty Santa Claus hat on top of his greasy head.

The child grunted twice. The smartly dressed Bagger beckoned and two of his partners grabbed the children by the shoulders and pulled them away, dragging them back by their clothing and out into the hall.

The Bagger in the suit smiled and adjusted his tie.

'Sorry for the inconvenience,' he said. 'Now, if you don't mind, you're coming with us.'

There was no room for negotiation.

'Shit,' Daniel said.

CLEMENTINE

They weren't going to get out of the Museum of Anthropology alive.

Hiding behind some ancient musical instruments, Clementine, Michael and Raj tried to assess the situation. Everything was in chaos. So many people were screaming, it was hard to tell where one voice ended and another began.

It was impossible to tell who were Baggers and who were normal.

The building was surrounded. They'd discovered that quickly enough. After the initial attack, Clementine and Michael followed Raj towards the front entrance. They'd turned the corner in time to see a group of Baggers literally tearing apart a few victims with their bare hands. Clementine recognized one of them as the girl who had cried and thrown herself at Ryder's feet. Now she was on the floor, her brain being beaten to a pulp by a female Bagger with long purple dreadlocks. Without thinking, Clementine stepped forward to try to do something, anything to get that poor girl to stop screaming, but Michael, still holding her hand, yanked her backwards and towards him.

'They'll kill you too,' he said.

Fortunately the screams cut off abruptly at that

moment, replaced by a steady gurgle.

'This way,' Raj said. 'We'll go around the back.' He turned and disappeared down the hall. They had no choice but to follow, yet even after they'd fled she could still hear the sound of baseball bat hitting brain. That noise would never leave her memory.

The problem was that now everyone was trying to make a break for the back exit. There were too many people crowding the hallway towards the emergency doors.

Even worse, when Raj squeezed his way through the manic crowd to get a better look, he returned a few minutes later, blood trickling down his face from where someone had elbowed him, saying, 'Doors blocked. We can't get out that way.' He started shouting at the others beside him, trying to make them understand that their stampede wasn't going to lead anywhere. But there was too much panic in the air. No one was listening.

'We have to keep moving,' Michael said. 'Are there any other exits?'

'Yeah, but my guess is they're blocked too,' Raj said. 'They're forcing us towards the front.'

Just like cows towards the slaughter. Clementine's class had once taken a tour of a slaughterhouse. When the cows got into line for the kill floor, they would howl and scream because they could sense what was coming next. She'd had nightmares for months.

'Come on,' Raj said. 'I've got an idea.'

They set off again. Michael was still holding her

hand, Clementine realized, and it was hard not to think about how warm and strong his skin felt. Comforting.

Dear Heath, If it hadn't been for the Baggers I'd never have met Michael. Isn't that one of those weird acts of fate that rocks the entire universe? I used to believe that if people were soul mates, nothing in the world could keep them apart. That if they were meant to meet and fall in love they'd find each other no matter what. But that seems trivial now. I can't believe I was ever that stupid. I think you'd like Michael. I know you didn't care much for Craig Strathmore. You always told me I could do better. Considering he tried to kill me, I guess you were right.

They moved through display rooms, only stopping occasionally to listen for where the screams were coming from. Twice they stopped to check on fallen bodies. Both times the person was dead. Once they had to turn round and race back towards the First Nations canoe display because their path became blocked by fighting. It was confusing and Clementine had trouble figuring out where they were. All the rooms looked alike as they passed through them at full speed. Even Raj seemed to get confused a few times. Twice they had to backtrack when faced with a dead end.

Finally Raj led them into a room and sighed in relief. There were several exits here, one of which led out to the bigger rooms at the front from where Clementine could see the darkness of night seeping in through the windows.

'We have two choices, mate,' Raj finally said. The

room was full of woven blankets. According to the display signs, the creators had been dead for hundreds of years.

'Yeah,' Michael said. 'Head for the front or hide. Both choices equally bad.'

'Yup.' Raj turned towards Clementine and nodded at her. 'Your call. What do you think? Fight, flight, or cower like babes under blankets?'

And that's how they ended up hidden behind the musical instruments. It wasn't a good hiding spot, but it had been the only place big enough for the three of them. Raj had smashed a display case a few rooms back and the three of them held ancient spears that would probably shatter when confronted with Bagger skin.

It didn't help that they could still hear the muffled cries of people dying from somewhere else in the building.

They only lasted a few minutes before Raj changed his mind.

'I can't do this,' he said. 'I can't listen to them die like that. They're no one to you but these people are my friends and it's probably my fault that all of this is happening. I'm no hero like Ryder but I'm not a wimp either. And I don't want to die here stuck behind some tribal drums. I'm sorry, but I've got to go.'

Michael and Clementine looked at each other.

'We do have these great spears,' Michael said.

'What do we have to do?' Clementine asked Raj. 'You said there were supplies in the woods? What kinds? How do we get everyone out?'

'I don't know,' Raj said. 'In all honesty, it never dawned on Ryder that they might block the exits. We used to do drills. But we always went out the back.'

'Then we have to gather them up,' Michael said. 'If we all make a break for the front at once, maybe we can overpower them. And we'd better do it fast.'

'Right,' Raj said.

'Because I smell smoke.'

Clementine inhaled deeply. Michael was right. The acrid smell filled her nostrils. Somewhere in the building, something was on fire.

'They're gonna burn us out?' Raj said. 'How could they do that? All the ancient artefacts too?'

'No offence,' Michael said. 'But I don't think they care much for human history. I'll bet the Louvre isn't doing so well these days either but you don't hear me bitching about that. And if we don't come up with a plan soon, all of us are going to be one of those things that no one remembers.'

Raj nodded.

Someone screamed. The red-haired guy ran into the room, the one who'd brought them coffee earlier when they were in the cafeteria. He passed by their hiding spot, tried to clear one of the displays but crashed into it with his hip. His whole body spun round, knocking him into a glass case of old clay pots.

His shirt was on fire.

Michael jumped forward, pulling his jacket off as he

moved. Using it, he began beating the red-haired guy to extinguish the flames. Clementine waited with her spear poised, alternating between watching Michael and staring at the exit where she could hear footsteps growing louder.

'Someone's coming,' she yelled.

'Hold 'em off,' Michael grunted. He continued to beat at the flames with his jacket. Clementine was relieved to see they were getting smaller. The red-haired boy wasn't screaming and his eyes were open. He wasn't dying.

She and Raj stood their ground as the footsteps grew louder. Just as Michael managed to extinguish the flames altogether, a group of people barged their way through the doors. At least a dozen of them rushed in, armed with baseball bats or kitchen knives. They weren't Baggers.

The initial panic seemed to be over. They were starting to fight back.

'Raj!' A small girl with a big voice stepped forward. She didn't even come close to reaching Clementine's shoulders. She wore huge glasses; one of the lens frames was bent slightly, which gave her a lopsided look. In her hands was a machete as big as her entire arm.

'Larisa,' Raj said. 'What's happening?'

'They've set fire to the cafeteria and the gift shop,' the girl squeaked. 'All the exits are blocked.'

Michael reached down and helped the red-haired guy up. His eyes were a little dazed and his back was blistered and bloody, but overall he didn't appear especially wounded. Michael gave him his own slightly smoking jacket which he put on, wincing slightly as the fake leather touched his skin. His legs looked a little wobbly but he managed to stand just the same.

'We need to get everyone together,' Raj said. He pointed in the direction of the main entrance.

The petite girl shook her head. 'They're all gone. Everyone. A few might have got out earlier, but the rest are dead. We're all that's left.'

Guilt. That was the look she saw on both Michael and Raj's faces.

No, she wasn't going to allow that. None of them were to blame for this even if they were the ones who had led the Baggers to the museum. It was still the Baggers' fault and no one else's.

Holding her spear high in the air, she turned to the short girl named Larisa and surveyed the survivors. 'All right then. There's a lot of us left. They can't get everyone at once. I say we rush them.'

From the corner of her eye, she saw Michael raise his head and look at her. She returned his gaze with what she hoped was a confident stare. She needed him to know that they could do this. They could lead this group and maybe save at least half of them.

'Rush them,' Raj said. 'Yeah, I think we've run out of other options. It's that or burn to death. Don't fancy that much.'

The others murmured agreement. There weren't a

lot of hopeful faces by this point.

They began marching to the front door. Faster now. There was no plan. Just run. Don't get caught. Don't get killed. Meet up in the woods afterwards, by the water. Michael and Clementine were to follow Raj.

Don't die.

Michael held her hand tightly. She squeezed it; amazed at how warm his skin felt when hers was so icy cold with fear.

Dear Heath, I can't die, right? I've come too far to end things now. I feel in my heart that I keep getting closer to you every day. I don't know if I believe in God any more. I've fought hard and worked each step of the way to make it to this moment. But please, if you're up there, don't let my story end here, OK? Talk to the big guy. Tell him that I'm not beneath a little holy intervention right about now. And, if you're still alive like I hope, then I'm just talking to myself like some crazy chick and need to stop wasting my brain on all these empty thoughts. I've had so much faith during this entire ordeal. Why am I doubting myself now?

They turned the corner and the front entrance was only about fifty feet away. Clementine sucked in her breath. Michael gripped her hand tighter.

Funny thing about doubt. It grows that much larger when the odds in your favour suddenly drop off the map.

The lobby was crawling with Baggers. The front doors were jammed open and more of them were coming in. Some of them carried dead bodies through the doors, victims that had made it outside only to die a quick death. One of them had the body of Katarina under his arm. He tossed her roughly on top of a pile of other remains in front of the gift shop. The back of the shop was steadily going up in flames. Gift cards and poster maps of Vancouver were quickly consumed and turned into hot ash.

Other Baggers had managed to capture some of the survivors, dragging them out and into the vans that waited by the kerb.

It didn't take long before the Baggers saw them.

'Don't think,' Michael whispered in her ear as if he could read her mind. 'Don't think about it. Just get ready to run.'

'Don't let go of my hand,' she whispered back.

'Never.'

The short girl screamed and they surged forward. Clementine fell into step right behind Michael, desperately clinging to his hand as other bodies bumped up against her. Suddenly she tripped over her spear, falling down on her knees. Michael kept going, yanking her forward as she tried to scramble to her feet. Her spear disappeared behind her and she saw the red-haired guy reach down for it. She turned her body, attempting to pull herself up, but couldn't get a good grip with her running shoes. Raj reached out and took her other hand, yanking her up hard like a toddler who had tripped over her shoelaces. He raced past her and jumped into step beside Michael. They formed a wall between her and the Baggers. Her knights in shining armour.

Time stopped.

She couldn't stop. Michael and Raj wouldn't let go of her. The Baggers turned and started running towards them, meeting them halfway between the doors and the information booth. Weapons swung through the air. A Bagger jumped in at her from the side, but the short girl with her machete cut him down instantly.

The front doors were so close. Someone slammed into her back, pushing her forward and into Michael and Raj. The three of them hit the window, her face pressing up against the glass. Michael's arm hit the frame and the force of the hit must have pinched a nerve because his fingers slipped away from hers. She could see his mouth open and close.

'Come on,' Raj said. He literally swung her out of the door with his arm.

Cold air hit her face.

She spun round just as another person raced through the door, screaming in terror, and they both tumbled to the floor. Blinding fire shot straight through her guts and along her spine. She gasped, but no air came in or out of her lungs for a few seconds. Waves of nausea washed over her as the endorphins rushed to do their job. The guy who'd body slammed her crawled up to his knees, coughing and wheezing, unable to catch his breath. A Bagger rushed him, catching him in a full tackle. Blood splashed the cement. She couldn't move.

If only she had her spear . . . instead all she could do was lie there as the Baggers descended on the boy.

Where was Michael? She daren't move to look for him. The most she could do right now was curl up into a foetal position and try to make herself as small as possible. As long as she lay on the ground, maybe they'd think she was dead or dying.

Stupid! Stupid! Stupid!

How could she let go of his hand?

'Clementine!'

She opened her eyes, hoping to see Michael, but it was Raj who came out of nowhere and punched the Bagger about to crouch down and finish her off with a wicked-looking carving knife. Bending down beside her, he pulled her upward and tight against his chest.

'Michael,' she gasped.

'Right behind us, babes,' he said. 'He's helping Larisa. He knows where to go. We'll meet him around back. Can you run?'

She was managing to stand by herself though her legs were still shaking but there wasn't enough time to sit and wait until her body stabilized and the crushing pain left her stomach.

With Raj's help, they managed to get round the back of the building. Through the enormous windows she could see the flames working their way through the totem poles and ancient canoes. There were dead bodies lying across the floor. She couldn't tell if she recognized them.

What about the girl with the blonde ponytails? Was she in there? Lying in a pool of blood or shattered pottery remnants? Why hadn't she bothered to learn the girl's name?

'Clementine?' Raj shook her gently.

'What?' she snapped.

'I've got to go back and get him.'

'Huh?' She finally turned all her attention to him. Raj was staring at her, his arms still on her shoulders. 'Where's Michael?'

'That's what I mean,' he said. 'He should have been here by now. I'm going back. I need you to head down to the beach. We've got boats waiting there. You'll be safe. I can give you directions.'

'No.' She pulled away from him. 'I'm coming.'

'You're hurt.'

She inhaled deeply, still feeling the sharp stabbing pains in her gut. 'So?'

'You'll just slow me down. The woods are safe.'

She started to disagree, determined to head back round to the front of the building but the endorphins gushing around in her body had other ideas. Suddenly everything inside her stomach lurched upward and she fell forward and vomited on to the concrete.

'Oh God,' she mumbled.

'Satisfied?' Raj quipped. This time he wasn't so quick to touch her but he did steady her slightly once she'd pulled herself up. 'Come on, let me show you the way. I'll bring him back, I promise.'

She spat twice, trying to get the foul taste out of her mouth. 'Fine. But you better both come back. If you don't show up, I'm coming to find you and when I do, I'll . . .' She paused. 'I'll . . . hell, I don't know what I'll do but you'll be sorry.'

'Fine, babes,' he said with a bit of a sad grin. 'Threat accepted. Now see that path over there? Follow it. It'll lead you down.'

Raj didn't wait. He turned and disappeared into the darkness. She stood there for a few unbearably long seconds, wondering if she should follow him, but her stomach cramped again, reminding her how useless she was at the moment. Turning, she started limping towards the path and into the woods.

Stupid! Stupid! Stupid!

The wooded area behind the museum was pitch black and it didn't take long for her to realize that she wasn't alone. Raj had been wrong. The Baggers were there. She could see them trampling through the bushes, flashlights in their hands as they searched for stray victims. And she didn't have her spear any more.

She checked her pockets and found the half-empty bottle of spraypaint she'd picked up back at the library. As far as weapons went, it was pretty useless, but she supposed it was better than nothing. It felt heavy in her hand anyway and just holding it made her feel a little bit more secure. She followed the path, picking up speed as the cramps slowly faded.

She should go back. More than anything else she

wanted to go back. She remembered the helplessness she'd felt the night her mother grabbed her arm and pushed her towards the front doors of the town hall to escape. Her mom who had that crazy knack for knowing when something bad was about to happen. She'd been right. How long had it been since she'd last thought about her? It seemed like a million years ago. She'd been so young back then somehow. But in reality it had only been about twelve weeks since the earthquakes.

Best not to think about the past. She'd learned that from Michael. She could see how he pushed away the dark thoughts that clouded across his brown eyes. He didn't think she noticed, but she did. Whatever happened to him must have been horrible.

The decline was steep and it was hard moving in the dark, but she slowly managed to work her way down to the water. She ducked a few times behind bushes when the Baggers got too close, and once she was positive she'd heard Michael's voice call out in the darkness, but she didn't dare call back. Not when so many of them were nearby.

There were boats tied to trees by the shore. They were canoes, but she also saw a few kayaks. Inside were supplies covered with tarps.

No one else was there and she didn't know how many boats had been there to begin with. Was it possible that a few others had managed to make an escape by sea?

Sitting on a rock, she waited. It was cold down by the water. She brought her hands close to her face and tried to blow warm air on to them. She shivered.

It wasn't long. She heard branches breaking and jumped to her feet, her can of spraypaint raised in front of her. She realized the nozzle was aimed at her face and she quickly turned it round. But not before someone crashed through the trees.

She yelped. Someone grabbed her arm and she shrieked louder, pulling backwards but refusing to let go of the can.

'Clementine, it's me.'

Michael.

She threw her arms round his neck, pulling him close. The instant heat of his body warmed her, comforting her, making her feel that everything was going to be all right.

When she tore herself away from him, she noticed that they weren't alone. Not only was Raj standing behind them, a big grin on his face, but there were a few others. Larisa was one, there was a sullen-faced boy with bright anger in his eyes and two other girls she didn't recognize. One of them was covered in blood from a gaping wound on her shoulder.

'That's OK, babes,' Raj said. 'We got about three minutes.'

Her cheeks instantly began to burn. She turned her attention to the wounded girl who was leaning against a tree. Her friend had taken off her jacket and had it pressed into her shoulder. The cloth was turning red at an alarming rate.

'We have to get her help,' Clementine said. 'Who else is wounded?'

Larisa had a gash on her forehead but it wasn't major. She was also walking with a severe limp. Blood pooled in her shoe, which made squishing noises when she moved. Already Raj was untying the canoes and preparing them to head offshore. It would be the quickest way out.

'If we can get her to our place she'll be OK,' Clementine kept saying to Raj as she helped him pull the paddles out of their hiding spot in the bushes. 'We've got some medical supplies there in case you need more. Stuff from the pharmacies.'

One of the girls jumped into the water then clambered into the boat, pulling her friend after her. Raj and Larisa followed. The sullen-faced boy grudgingly walked past Michael, slamming him with his shoulder as he passed. He was obviously blaming them for everything that had happened.

Michael reached out and touched Clementine's cheek. 'I told you not to let go.'

'Me?' she said. 'You're the one who let go.'

He laughed.

Branches snapped behind them and a Bagger appeared, running straight at them. Someone in the boats screamed. The monster reached out to grab hold of Michael's hair before he could turn his head round. Clementine didn't think. She raised the can of spraypaint and pushed down on the nozzle, sending a steady stream of inky paint right into those nasty black-veined eyes.

The Bagger screamed. He pulled his arms away from Michael, clawing at his eyes as he bent over in pain. Michael shoved him and he flew backwards and into the rocks, cracking his head against the stone.

It was over as quickly as it had begun.

Clementine was still pressing the nozzle button, but there was no more paint. She'd finished the can. Letting it drop, she turned and looked at Michael in astonishment.

'Nice,' he said.

The silence was short-lived. Someone started screaming for help off in the woods beyond them. Coherent pleads. Desperate.

Everyone else was in the boat.

'I have to go back,' Michael said suddenly.

The air inside her lungs was sucked out in an instant.

Michael put his hands on her shoulders. 'I need you to take them back to our place. Get them help. I'll be right behind. There are others out there. You . . . you know I can't leave them.'

He'd done it once before – he'd never do it again.

'But I need you.'

'And Raj and his friends need you. I won't be far behind, really. You won't even notice I'm gone.'

'You promise?'

'Swear to all that matters.' With that he led her over to the water and helped her into the boat. Her entire body was numb; she didn't resist although she wanted to. Someone handed her a paddle and Michael gave the two boats strong pushes to send them off.

She watched him disappear back into the woods. The sun was beginning to rise over the horizon. The air was thick with smoke from the destroyed museum and it made the morning light burn even redder in the pale sky.

'He'll be fine, babes,' Raj whispered.

She nodded. But would she?

ARIES

Bang!

A strange noise brought her up from a deep sleep. No dreams. She didn't seem to have them any more. Nothing but thoughtless darkness. It sure beat the horrible nightmares she kept having the first few weeks after the earthquakes. Dreams in which she was running down the dead-end streets as monsters popped out from the shadows. Quick jolting images of her family dissolving in front of her eyes while she was frozen in place and unable to help. Her mother silently mouthing her name and Aries screaming back.

But sleeping was better these days.

Bang!

Her whole body was heavy. She had sunk into the mattress and it had taken her hostage, almost refusing to let go. Struggling, she finally opened her eyes. Soft muted light fell across her face, the morning sun fighting its way through from behind the blinds.

'Aries?' Tapping on the door again.

Panic. What time was it? How long had she been asleep?

'Aries?'

'Yeah, I'm awake.'

The door opened and Nathan hesitantly walked in.

His forehead was full of frown lines and his lips were stretched in a tight grimace.

'What's wrong?' she asked. 'What time is it?'

'Ten a.m.'

She'd slept in. How could she? She was almost always the first one awake in the morning. There was so much to do. Sleeping in was a luxury she couldn't afford.

'Why didn't someone wake me?' she snapped. Unwrapping the sheets from around her legs, she managed to get up. The mattress was a tangle of blankets. Pillows were on the floor. A glass lay turned over on its side, whatever liquid it once held now absorbed into the beige carpet. She may not remember her dreams but obviously they were still there. She had been thrashing around like a wild woman. Night travelling.

'You were tired,' Nathan said. His face changed from worried to guilty. 'And I think we just kinda forgot. We've got some problems.'

'What problems?' She ran her fingers through her hair. Tangles. Lots and lots of them. She cringed as she felt the hair break between her fingers.

'Clementine and Michael are still missing in action.'

The last thing she thought about before falling into her dreamless sleep was what she'd do if morning came and they weren't back. She hadn't come up with an answer last night and she still didn't have one now.

'We'll figure something out,' she said.

'There's more. Mason's gone too.'

Now that surprised her. 'What do you mean *gone*?'

'He's not here.'

That made her pause. Why would Mason leave? He'd been there last night when she'd got back in from meeting Daniel. Right? She tried hard to remember if she'd seen his face with the others. 'Did he take off? Is his stuff gone?'

Nathan took a step backwards. 'I didn't check. I didn't think about it.'

She pushed past him and stormed down the hall to the last room, where Mason had shut himself off from the rest of the world. She stopped for a moment at the closed door but didn't bother knocking. Instead she turned the knob and walked right in.

His room was dark. He'd covered the windows with dark bed sheets. Squinting in the gloom, she scanned the room quickly. The bed was empty. Wrinkled and tangled blankets spilt off the mattress and on to the floor. For some reason she was relieved to see that Mason was obviously doing his own night travelling.

What did he dream about that made him run miles in his sleep?

She walked into the middle of the room, carefully stepping over a pile of checked shirts and wrinkled jeans. Nathan followed behind her. In the corner was a dresser, the drawers open, the mirror cracked from where it looked like he'd put his fist right through the glass.

'Guess he didn't like his new haircut,' Nathan

said with a heavy load of sarcasm.

'Or he just needed to hit something,' she said. 'I can honestly say I feel like that at least once a day.'

Aries went over to the closet and opened it. Inside was a mess of clothing, most of it the former occupant's. On the shelves, in pristine condition, were stacks of photo albums, yearbooks and other personal items that would never again be enjoyed by the person to whom they belonged. It didn't look like Mason had ever looked through them. She closed the door and walked back over to the bed.

'So do you think he took off?' Nathan bent over and started picking through some of the clothes. 'I always got the impression that he didn't want to stick around. Didn't talk much, did he?'

Aries took a deep breath and nudged a sock with her toe. 'No, he didn't leave.'

'How do you know?'

She moved over to the side of the bed where a small table was pushed against the wall. Reaching down she picked up a worn photograph. Turning it over, she read the inscription.

Stanley Park, Second Beach, Vancouver, BC.
Mason and Mom – enjoying the sun.

She handed the picture to Nathan. 'Because he wouldn't leave this behind. He never goes far without it.'

Nathan took it from her and studied the print. She

liked how young and happy Mason looked in it. She liked how big his smile was and the way the baseball cap covered his ears. A reminder of better times. Times they couldn't get back no matter how much they wished it. It would have been nice to have known him before the earthquakes. She liked to believe the two of them might have been good friends.

Nathan nodded. 'OK. What should we do?'

'Organize a search party,' she said. 'We've got to find them. Or at least figure out what happened. They deserve that much.'

She popped her head in to check on Jack on the way down. Joy was there with him. They were sitting together on the bed and she was reading a magazine article out loud. She stopped speaking and both of them looked up.

'I need you downstairs, Joy,' she said. 'In a few, OK?'

Joy nodded and the expression on Jack's face wasn't hard to read. He knew what was going on and was frustrated that he couldn't do anything to help. Even climbing down the stairs was a hard enough challenge.

'You feeling any better?' she asked.

'Just fine,' he said, but he gritted his teeth as the words popped out. The light banter was gone. 'Wish I wasn't so damn useless though.'

'Don't say that,' Joy said. 'You've done so much for us. It'll get easier.'

'No, it won't.'

Aries suppressed the urge to tell him to stop feeling

sorry for himself, especially when she couldn't really disagree with him. So she left the room. She'd sit down with him later once the others were found and discuss what they'd do in the future when he was able to get out of bed. There had to be something he could do so he'd feel like he was contributing to the group. Maybe Joy could teach him to cook?

As much as she loved Jack, this wasn't the time to have that conversation. Finding the others took priority. Aries hated to admit it but she was lost without Mason. For all his silence and mystery, he'd pretty much taken over Jack's role since the blinding, becoming her new confidant and helping her through the tough problems they faced as a group. They'd spent a lot of nights discussing things in the living room long after everyone else had gone to sleep. He always knew the right words to say to calm her down. Being a leader wasn't easy, especially when everyone was so lost and scared most of the time. She had to make sure people were organized and had something to do. She had to assign tasks and keep them busy. She had to keep them together. And if three of her friends disappeared she had to find them.

But where to begin? If only Mason was here. He'd be able to give her advice.

Or Daniel. But she wouldn't see him until later tonight. If the others weren't back by then, maybe he would know where to look.

Depending on Daniel, however . . . that was something she didn't care for much. She didn't want to owe him any favours. If only he was more reliable. If only he stayed with them instead of returning to whatever rock he crawled to every night. Why did he have to complicate things so much? What was wrong with her that he could only stand to be around her for a few hours each night?

'Stop it,' she snapped to herself. Daniel spent enough time in her thoughts. She didn't need him now. She needed to concentrate.

It didn't take long for everyone except Jack to assemble in the living room. Eve and Nathan, the rare brother-and-sister team who were so lucky to still have each other, sat on the couch and Joy was in the rocking chair by the fireplace. Colin sat in his usual seat, the Game Boy powered on in his hands, a stack of burnt-out batteries on the floor beneath him.

There were so few of them. How could she expect them to fix this?

She didn't sit down. Instead she stood in front of the darkened flat screen and addressed them all. 'We've got to pair up,' she said. 'I know it's dangerous but some of us have to search for Clementine and Michael, the others for Mason.'

'I agree,' Nathan said. 'We know Clem and Mike are off at UBC. So two of us should head out that way. But does anyone have any idea where Mason might have gone?'

Silence.

Aries shook her head. She knew Mason went off on

his own sometimes at night but she had no idea where. She assumed it was personal and didn't ask. He was always home before dawn; she often heard the creak of his door when he snuck back into his room.

'It's going to be harder with him,' she finally said. 'I hate to admit it but I don't even know where to start. Did he ever mention any places he liked to go?'

'You'd know over us,' Joy said. 'He only talked to you. He pretty much ignored the rest of us.'

Aries looked over at Nathan and Eve but they were both staring at her with blank expressions.

'He was cool when we used to pick up the food,' Nathan finally said. 'Except when I saw him talking with Daniel about a week ago. We ran into him at the Safeway. They acted like they didn't know each other very well but afterwards I saw them huddled over by the soup section. They seemed pretty heated up with each other. Kinda pissy.'

'Really?' Aries raised her eyebrow. Why hadn't anyone mentioned this to her?

'Yeah, that's pretty much it though.'

'How can we know so little about him?' Aries finally said. 'We've been living with him for a few months now. It's so strange.'

Joy shrugged. 'He told me he liked my stew one night,' she said. 'That was the longest conversation I had with him.'

There was a pause while everyone tried to think about what to do next.

'We have no proof that he's missing,' Colin said without looking up. Whatever game he was playing on the Game Boy had the most annoying theme music. 'How do you know they all just didn't find a new crowd? It's not like we really knew any of them. Even Clementine and Michael. Maybe they eloped or went back to Seattle. Either way, no great loss.'

'They wouldn't leave us,' Aries said. 'Even you know that.'

'Then they'll come back,' Colin said. 'Or they won't. I'm not risking my life to go after them.'

'Yeah, you don't like risking your life for anything,' Nathan snapped. 'You won't go get food. You won't help the people who do bring you food. You've always got an excuse. Half the time you don't bother going out to take watch, or you get bored and leave your post. These people have done so much for you and you refuse to return the favour. Remind me again, Colin. Why do we keep you around here?'

The words worked. Colin finally looked up from his game, a darkness crossing over his face. 'What the hell do you know about anything?' he said.

'He's right,' Joy said. 'You never pitch in or help.'

Aries bit her lip. These were the words she'd wanted to say for so long but, being the leader, she felt she couldn't say them without stepping on toes. Yes, Colin had been completely useless from the very beginning. He argued about every suggestion and refused to do anything that involved helping the group. But she'd even stuck up for him at certain points, mostly because she'd known him for a long time and because Sara had loved him. Sara, her best friend who'd died when the earthquakes started.

Besides, she'd never kick anyone out. No matter how annoying they were. It wasn't in her nature. She would protect everyone. If they threw Colin out for being such a pain, then what would stop them from wanting Jack out next because he was useless? Who after that? No, she couldn't allow it. This place, this group they'd all worked so hard to save, she couldn't pick and choose. Everyone was welcome. Everyone would be treated well. Even if they weren't equals.

It also didn't help that Colin had threatened them all about a month ago, though only she knew it.

It had been the exact same argument. They'd been in discussion about who would go pick up the canned goods for the week. Not exactly a dangerous job considering the Baggers weren't in the area. She and Mason had been watching and, as far as they could tell, the crazies were in the downtown core, building the fencing that would surround the Plaza of Nations. Back before the white vans had shown up and started advertising sanctuary there. As usual, Colin had refused to even consider the job, and he and Nathan had got into a heated argument.

Colin had stormed off into his room and Aries gave him an hour to calm down before venturing up to try to talk some sense into him.

'We all have to pitch in,' she said. He'd been sitting on the bed, leafing through an outdated health magazine and giving no clues as to whether he was listening. 'Everyone has to play his part, otherwise it's not fair to the others. Those are the rules.'

'That's the thing,' Colin said. 'You seem to think we're all this one big happy family. We're not. I never agreed to your so-called rules and I don't recall anyone asking my opinion. I'm not going to risk my life for people I don't care about.'

'So why should they risk their lives for you?'

Colin tossed the magazine on the floor and rolled over on his side. 'They want to toss me out? I'm sure even you know that's a bad idea.'

'Is it?' she asked.

'Yeah, it is. Who knows who I might go join then? I don't have the alliances you have. I might be willing to give up certain information if the price is right.'

'You'd give us up?'

'In a heartbeat. Now get out.'

She'd left the room and when she came back downstairs she'd told everyone that they should just let Colin be for now. She avoided the curious looks and refused to say anything more. If Mason found out he'd threatened them, he'd probably grab Colin and physically remove him. She couldn't take that chance. She knew Colin better than anyone else. The threat was real. Since then, she'd been putting in double effort to try to keep everyone peaceful.

It grew harder each day.

Now it looked like Nathan was ready for war.

'I've really had it with you,' Nathan growled. 'Maybe it's time for you to leave.'

'There's no need for that,' Aries said.

'Yes, there is.'

Colin slowly turned off the Game Boy. He got up off his chair and walked over to Nathan. For several extended seconds, the two stared each other down.

'It must suck being last,' Colin said. 'Even with me here, you're still last on her list.'

'What are you talking about?' Nathan said.

'I see the way you suck up to her, but she'd never take your word over Mason's either. With Jack a cripple and Mason gone, you must have been hoping if you kissed ass enough she'd actually turn to you.'

The room had grown deathly quiet. Aries had taken the few steps towards them but neither of them paid her any attention. Eve and Joy sat frozen on the couch with wide-eyed expressions.

'You don't want to be saying those words,' Nathan said.

'Funny enough, I already did.'

'It's not true.'

Colin snickered. 'Sure it is.' He turned to Aries. 'What do you think? Now that your boys are gone, are you going to actually listen to this wimp?'

Nathan threw the first punch. It hit Colin directly on the cheek, sending him backwards and on to the couch. Eve scrambled out of the way.

Colin was up in a flash. He crashed into Nathan and both boys flew across the floor and into the flatscreen television. Metal crunched against the wall and the glass cracked as everything fell over with a loud bang.

The three girls stared in disbelief while the two boys wrestled on the ground. Finally Aries managed to thaw and she reached down, trying to separate them while avoiding any stray blows.

'Enough!' she screamed.

But the boys weren't letting go. Finally, with Eve and Joy's help, she managed to pull them apart.

'This is not helping anything,' Aries snapped. 'Grow up. Both of you.'

Nathan didn't say anything as he moved back a few feet. His cheek was beginning to swell. He allowed Eve to gently drag him towards the couch but he wouldn't sit.

Colin didn't look much better. He'd taken a good hit to his eye and the skin was bright red. 'I guess the truth hurts,' he said with a cold smile.

Nathan jerked forward but Eve and Joy pushed him back.

'Stop it,' Eve said. 'He's not worth it.'

'Fine,' Nathan said. 'You're right. He should just leave. We'd all be better off.'

There was a noise behind them coming from the hallway. Aries spun round, half expecting to see a group of Baggers grinning at them, drawn by the sounds of their ridiculous drama. 'Wow,' Clementine said. 'We're gone for only a day and all hell breaks loose.'

Colin was up in his room and Eve had coerced Nathan into going with her to find some groceries for the evening meal. The house was silent. Aries and Clementine were in their bedroom while Joy and Raj stayed downstairs to try to figure out where the new guests were going to sleep.

'They're cool,' Clementine said. 'I mean, I can't really say it about all of them. But Raj really helped us out. One of the girls is Larisa and she's fine. I'm not actually sure about the others. Don't even know their names yet. That other guy, I think his name is Claude, well, he's a bit of a jerk and I don't trust him, but he's not a Bagger or anything. I think he was good friends with Ryder so he blames us for the attack.'

'Does that make him dangerous?' Aries asked, thinking of Colin and his threats.

'No, I don't think so,' Clementine said. She pulled one of the pillows into her lap and hugged it. 'He came willingly enough. I think he's just as lost as the rest. They put all that effort into keeping everyone safe. And the Baggers took them down in seconds. I don't think he was really aware of how quickly they can kill.'

'They're more than welcome here,' Aries said. 'We've got the space.'

Clementine nodded.

'What about Heath?' Aries asked. 'Anything?'

'No,' Clementine held the pillow tighter. 'But UBC's a big place. There's still plenty of other places he could be hiding. I'm not giving up that easily. Besides, I have to go back. What if Michael doesn't show?'

'He'll be here,' Aries said. 'He's a champion fighter.'

Clementine nodded.

Aries gave her a hug. 'I'm really glad you're back. I was worried. I think now we should have the radios with us at all times.'

'Yeah, good idea.'

'And that leaves Mason.'

'Why? What happened to Mason?'

Aries shrugged. 'He's gone. Last night.'

'He wouldn't just leave,' Clementine said. 'Something must have happened – like with us.'

Aries blinked several times to avoid the tears. It was good to know that someone else was so sure of Mason.

'We'll find him,' Clementine said. 'You and me will go out tonight, OK? We'll go see Daniel. Don't give me that shocked look. I know you meet him at night.'

Aries choked back a laugh. 'How do you know that? I've been so careful.'

Clementine smiled. 'Because you check your hair in the mirror before you sneak out,' she said. 'Just because you think we're all sleeping doesn't mean we actually are. I can't imagine you'd be concerned about your looks if you're just taking a walk through the park. Totally understandable. Daniel's hot.'

'I'm so glad you're back.'

*

It was raining when they headed out later that evening. Michael still wasn't back and Aries could see the doubt and fear in her friend's eyes. But Clementine wanted to come; she said it gave her something to do besides sit at home and go crazy with every passing second. At the last moment, Raj insisted on coming along too.

'It'll be good to have a strong chem trainspotter such as myself,' he said. 'Who else can you toss in their direction that might slow 'em down?'

Aries liked Raj instantly. He was light-hearted and enjoyed cracking jokes; it was a nice distraction in the severely stressed household. In less than a few hours, he'd already managed to make Jack smile properly twice, and that was something she'd been trying to achieve for weeks.

They'd decided to put the newcomers in the basement family room. It made sense because they all knew each other.

Hopefully Daniel would have heard something. He seemed to have a real ear for picking up rumours and secrets in the empty city streets.

They pulled their hoodies up over their heads and snuck out into the night. The rain wasn't heavy, but it was still cold enough to chill her to the bone. By the time they reached the beach, they were all soaked through. Maybe it was time to start investing in rain gear. Maybe they could hit up one of the survival stores and get some proper stuff.

'So this is where you've been going?' Clementine whispered with a giggle. 'I wish Michael was this romantic. I could use some beach-side snuggling.'

'It's not like that,' Aries said. She was glad it was dark out, because she could feel the warmth rising in her cheeks. 'We just come here to talk. Nothing else.'

Nothing at all. Not since the time on the beach when he'd kissed her. Back when they'd carved their names in the log. No hand holding. No exchanging loving words.

And no more kissing.

In a way it was better. It wasn't that she didn't want to, but it wasn't really the time and place to start a whirlwind romance. And Daniel wasn't exactly cold towards her; he just always seemed to be holding back in some way.

'There's always Mason,' Clementine said mischievously.

Aries shot her a glance. 'I'm not looking to hook up with anyone, so stop pushing, OK?'

'Just saying,' Clementine said, but thankfully she dropped it.

They waited by the bench, standing because it was too wet to sit. Eventually Raj went over to the shore and started tossing pebbles. The waves were wild and thrashing, and everything he tossed sank without so much as a splash.

'He should have been here by now,' Aries said as she double-checked her watch. It was getting closer to midnight and still there was no sign of Daniel.

'Is this normal?' Raj asked. 'Does he always show up?'

'Yeah, pretty much,' Aries admitted. 'It's not like we plan to meet every night. It just sorta happens. But this feels weird. There's something wrong here.'

'Maybe he's with Mason,' Clementine said.

'Doubtful,' she said. 'They hate each other. Nathan said they almost got into a fight at the Safeway the other day.'

They waited a little longer before even Aries had to admit it was best to head home. There was nothing moving on the beach except for the rain and the tide.

'We can try again tomorrow night,' Clementine suggested as they started back across the parking lot.

Would she do it? Come back every night like a jilted lover, waiting for her prince to appear and take her away from everything?

'No,' she finally said. 'Tomorrow we start looking for Mason. You don't give up on Heath and I'm not giving up on Mason. Like you said, until we see a body, there's always hope. And if Michael's not back tomorrow we start looking for him too. I've worked too hard to start losing people now.'

Raj pulled back his hoody, letting the rain splash down on his hair. 'I'm in, babes,' he said with his cheerful accent. 'I owe you guys that much for taking us in. Where do we start?'

Aries turned and pointed back across the bay where she could see the lone spotlight reflecting off the pregnant clouds. 'There. We go there.'

'The lion's den?' Raj said. 'You want to go to the one place we should be avoiding like the plague?'

Aries nodded. 'Mason's not here for a reason. He's being kept away. If the Baggers have him, they'll have taken him there.'

'We'll need better supplies,' Clementine said. 'Michael's binoculars aren't going to be enough.'

'We'll hit up something tomorrow,' Aries said.

Raj clapped his hands together. 'Wish I had the keys to the chem lab. Then we'd really be able to have some fun.'

Aries smiled. 'You know, that's not such a bad idea.'

They headed back to the house, talking about what sort of supplies they'd have to find. But no amount of conversation could change the gnawing feeling growing inside her stomach.

Aries was the leader. She'd kept them safe. How was she going to keep them alive if more of them went missing?

NOTHING

Black paint.

The sounds and the screams are silenced here, bouncing off the paint and being absorbed by its darkness. I'm a frozen shadow. A puppet. My strings have been reeled back in.

Help me.

Voices. Voices whispering through the walls. They caress my skin and when I open my mouth, the voices slip down inside my throat and drop into my stomach cavity. They slosh against the walls, crawling along my spleen like a thousand baby mice. My stomach is crammed full of rodents. There's fine dining to be had on my spleen.

They came, they saw, they conquered. They came to take me away. They're determined to climb further inside my head. They want to talk. The voices warned me that this would happen. If I smash my head against the wall enough times, I might be able to stop them. But I can't bring myself to touch the wall. The darkness will consume me. Not that way. I can't go that way.

Help me.

I'm not strong.

MASON

Cages.

An entire room filled with cages.

The fluorescent lights burned bright above him. A never-ending day. It was strange seeing electricity again. It scalded his eyes and made him want to blink a lot. Intense. Like being on display in the middle of the sun.

Nowhere to hide in all that brightness.

They were in the remains of the Edgewater Casino. It had been a bit of a surreal experience earlier when the Baggers had escorted Daniel and Mason through the doors and underneath the gigantic darkened neon CASINO sign. How often could someone say they were ushered into a gambling establishment at gunpoint? Once upon a time that would have been well worth a tweet or a Facebook update.

The Baggers had obviously been doing a lot of remodelling because the inside was completely unrecognizable. Weren't most casinos cheerful in a tacky sort of way? Mason had never been there before so he couldn't quite tell what kind of room it used to be but it had clearly been gutted, everything removed in order to put in the cages. The walls had been painted black. In the furthest corner of the room, he could see a stack of Blackjack tables and electronic slot machines piled against each other.

Mason sat on the ground in his cage. His back leaned against the edge of his five-by-five cell. The walls were ten feet high of fencing that ended with more chain link and barbed wire over the top as a makeshift ceiling. There were a few gaps between wall and ceiling but they were narrow. Even if he tried to climb his way out, he'd either slice his skin trying to slip through the gap or be stopped by the guards who paced the floors at regular intervals. They carried guns and various other weapons. Mason still had his jacket. They'd gone through his pockets and removed his Swiss army knife. They'd taken his wallet and the few dollars he had left, not that money meant anything. But they hadn't checked his shirt pocket where the tiny vial of sand still pressed against his chest. It was now the only thing he had left in the world. He wanted to take it out and hold it in his hands but he was afraid someone might notice. So it remained hidden away, his lucky charm.

Some charm.

It was strange having his proof of identity gone. It wasn't like he could order up a new set. His back pocket felt empty against his bum. What if something was to happen to him now and there was no one to recognize his body? He'd die without a name. Had Chickadee been carrying a wallet when he'd buried her? Would someone come along in the future and unearth her body? Would it matter if they read her name off her decaying driver's licence?

Mason shook his head slightly. This wasn't the time for ridiculous thoughts. He needed to focus. Figuring out how to get free would be a good start.

But even if he managed to scale the fence and get outside, they'd bring him down in a second.

There wasn't really a door to his cell. They'd just pulled back the mesh to reveal a two-foot opening and shoved him inside. He'd been locked in with a combination padlock. It was one of the cheap ones he used to buy at the discount store. Two bucks or not, it was still strong enough to keep him trapped. He double-checked his empty pockets again, but there wasn't anything useful to try to pick the lock.

There was nothing to do except wait, for now at least.

There were a lot of other people in the room. The majority of the cages were filled. Someone was crying in the far corner. It might have been a woman's voice but it was hard to tell. He'd tried to spot them but they were too far away and there was too much fencing. All he could see was a darkened lump curled into a foetal position. A small shadowy figure lay on the floor in the adjoining cage. They'd pushed their hands through the wire to try to reach the sobbing person.

No one spoke to anyone. A few people glanced in Mason's direction every now and then. But no voices. They didn't have to speak. It didn't take a genius to know what every single person was thinking.

The fluorescent bulb above him kept flickering on

and off. It made a loud humming noise that hurt his ears.

'This is just peachy.'

The voice came from his right.

Daniel was two cages down from him. Between them was an elderly man that might have been dead or just sleeping – neither of them could tell. The man had been lying face down on the floor, his features half covered by his jacket. He hadn't moved since they'd arrived. Mason thought his leg might have twitched at least once but he couldn't say for sure.

The air was cool and Mason exhaled several times to see if he could actually see his breath. Negative. Stuffing his hands inside his pockets, he leaned his head back against the fencing.

'Whose bright idea was this again?' Although he spoke quietly, his voice sounded like a shotgun echoing through the silent room.

'Yours, I believe,' Daniel said. He was leaning against the wall too, only about seven feet away. He tapped his foot against the concrete absently. 'Of course, I do recall saying we shouldn't get caught.'

'Glad to see you're so casual about this.'

'I'm shaking to death on the inside. Trust me – shivers, conniptions, the whole shebang.' Daniel leaned his head over and took a long look at Mason. He held up his hand in front of his face and made his fingers shake slightly. 'Seriously, all jokes aside, you know they're not going to just let us go, right?'

Mason turned away from Daniel and the first pair of eyes he found was that of a young teenage girl. Her hair was long and matted and her glasses askew. Although her face was covered in grime, he could tell that once upon a time she had been quite pretty. He probably would have noticed her if she'd walked down the hall at school. Now her cheeks were sunken and there were shadows under her eyes, which were big and frightened. Had she been captured or had she listened to the white vans and walked willingly into the Baggers' grasp? It wouldn't have been difficult. She was probably scared, tired of hiding and slowly starving to death. It wouldn't have been hard to convince herself that the Baggers meant everything they said about safety. Mason opened his mouth, maybe to say something to her, but he couldn't think of a single word that wouldn't sound fake or condescending. Besides, she was several cages away; he didn't even know if she'd be able to hear him.

'So what do we do then?' Mason swallowed. The insides of his mouth were dry.

'Keep quiet,' Daniel said. 'We can't tell them anything. Especially about the others. If they find out where Aries lives, they'll kill her. They'll kill all of them or worse.'

'You really think I'd do something so stupid?'

'Yes.'

Mason's cheeks burned. He clenched his hand tightly into a fist. 'I'd never do anything to hurt Aries, and you know it. At least I have the decency to stick around. You can't even bother to be there when she needs you.'

From two cages away, Mason watched Daniel's eyes narrow and harden.

'You have no idea,' Daniel said. 'I stay away to protect her.'

'Protect her?' It was impossible to keep his voice from rising. 'From what? How?'

'You'll see.'

There was a long pause as the two of them refused to acknowledge each other. Mason focused on his chain-link ceiling. It was easier than looking at the other hopeless people. He didn't know how much longer he could continue to keep his face from breaking.

'It won't matter,' Daniel finally said. 'If they want the information, they'll find it. There's nothing you and I can do about it. They have ways of getting inside your head.'

The sound of shoes slapping the casino carpet made him pay attention. Four Baggers, all carrying police batons, moved along the aisle. Mason knew immediately they were coming for him and Daniel. He wasn't disappointed when they stopped at his cage. The smaller one shoved a key in the lock and opened the gate.

'Come,' he said.

Mason didn't move.

Two of the bigger ones stepped into the cage and reached down, yanking Mason up by the arms and pulling him out. It happened so quickly he didn't have time to react. Besides, even he wasn't stupid enough to pick a fight. All four of them looked like they'd personally love it if he tried to cause a scene. One of them held on to his baton so tightly that his white knuckles glowed under the fluorescent lights.

They slammed Mason up against the cage of his neighbour, the still-unmoving clump of a person who might or might not be dead. A foot twitched slightly but it might have been a muscle spasm. He didn't have time to go in for a closer look. The largest Bagger grabbed Mason's arm, pulling it painfully back, and slapped handcuffs round his wrist. Mason's face pressed tightly up against the fencing and he managed to twist his head a little to where he could see Daniel back against the wall. His arms were crossed over his chest, pulling his jacket tight against his skin.

Daniel's eyes were big.

Mason opened his mouth again but the Baggers were already dragging him away.

They took him to a room with no windows. Inside were a couple of chairs and a desk. A filing cabinet stood against the wall, covered in dust, a mouldy Burger King sandwich wrapper resting on the top.

The Baggers shoved him into the chair closest to the desk and then vacated the room. Still in the handcuffs, he managed to wrestle himself up on to his feet. He turned round and tried to open the handle behind his back. The door was locked. Looking around the room, he focused on the desk. There might be something useful if he could get inside it. There were two drawers, both on the right side. It was a little trickier; he had to bend his knees in order to reach the first one. He managed to get it open but found it empty. No pens or paper clips, nothing he could use to try to pick the lock on his cuffs. There wasn't even so much as an envelope. The second drawer was even harder to reach. He had to manoeuvre himself down on his knees, which was no easy feat. Moving around with his hands locked behind his back was nearly impossible. They always made it look so easy in the movies. After balancing himself on one knee, his fingers closed round the metal handle and he pulled.

Drawer two was empty too.

Leaning against the desk, he pulled himself back up to a standing position. Frustrated, he kicked the drawer closed with his foot.

He didn't have any better luck with the filing cabinet. The drawers were locked.

There was nothing to do but wait.

He refused to sit back down. That seemed too vulnerable a position. Instead, he leaned against the wall awkwardly, ignoring the tingling sensation in his hands from where the blood was being cut off by the handcuffs. When he looked up, he saw there was a small security camera in the corner by the door. Were they watching him? Laughing at his helplessness?

If his hands hadn't been cuffed behind his back, he would have given the camera the finger. It was suddenly a lot harder to maintain a certain level of coolness.

It didn't take long before he heard the key in the lock.

The Bagger that walked through the door wasn't particularly terrifying. He wasn't big and menacing. There wasn't blood dripping off his hands or clothing. In fact, he was rather normal. He wore a nice dress shirt and a pair of jeans with shoes that were polished to a high gloss. There was a blue silk tie round his neck but it was loose and not tied properly. His hair was stylishly trimmed and he was cleanshaven. Laugh lines were at the corners of his eyes. He looked like he was ready to go out for a casual night on the town, not the killer he actually was.

Even monsters can sometimes hide what they are.

The man walked over towards the desk and pulled out the chair there. He sat down and leaned back casually as if settling in for a nice chat with a good friend. Mason half expected him to put his feet up on the wooden surface. Maybe kick off his shoes and offer him a cup of coffee or a glass of something old and expensive.

The man motioned towards the other remaining chair across from the desk. 'Have a seat. No?'

Mason didn't move.

'This isn't a choice,' the man said. 'Either sit down of your own free will, or I'll call in a few of those nice boys to forcibly bend you into it.'

It wasn't worth the fight and they both knew it.

Slowly Mason walked over to the desk and eased his way into the chair. It took him a few seconds longer than normal to get situated because his balance was off. He ended up with his hands pinned uncomfortably between the metal and his back. Leaning forward, he tried his best to look like he wasn't feeling the handcuffs biting deeply into his wrists.

The man nodded his head approvingly.

'Hello, Mason.' The man studied Mason's expression for a few seconds and smiled, showing a row of fresh, white teeth. 'You can call me Mr Leon. You're perplexed that I know your name?' He folded his hands across his lap and smiled politely. He waited for Mason to speak.

The room was deadly silent. If there had been a clock, it would have been ticking insanely loudly. The man continued to smile, but as the seconds wore on the grin stopped looking friendly.

Finally Mason opened his mouth. 'You have my wallet. My ID's in there.'

The man laughed. His chest rose and fell. His cheeks flushed and his eyes sparkled. 'Very good. Very, very good. You're a clever boy.'

'I tie my own shoelaces and everything.'

'I doubt you would have survived this long if you couldn't.' Mr Leon continued his never-ending grin. Mason could just see the black veins twisting around the edge of his irises. They made his expression darker somehow. 'But that's not the right answer. You've been on our radar for a while now. We know you've travelled a long way to come to Vancouver. We know that you had some interesting run-ins along the way too.'

Mason shrugged.

'You're not surprised we know all that?'

He was but he'd never admit it. He thought it over for a moment before coming up with an answer. 'You've got my ID,' he finally said. 'You know where I'm from. The rest is all a guessing game. It would be impossible to make it halfway across the country without having to deal with one or two of you idiots.' He pictured Twiggy, the one-legged Bagger who had tried to kill him back in Calgary. There was also the redneck in Hope who had bothered him when he was trying to dig Chickadee's grave.

The Bagger laughed long and hard. It was a forced laugh and Mason knew he was doing it to try to get under his skin. He was determined not to let this jerk Bagger get away with it. He would maintain his cool and not give anything up. Aries and the others were depending on it, whether they knew it or not.

'How's Chickadee?'

Mason jerked up in his chair. The man leaned forward, his brown eyes focused intently on Mason.

'We know all about you, Mr Dowell,' Leon said. 'We know about your mother and your friends. It was a car accident that killed your mother, right? What a shame but probably for the best. And the school bombing that you luckily avoided. We especially know about Chickadee and that she's buried in a shallow grave out by Hope. Diabetic coma took her, right? You have no secrets you can keep from us.'

Mason's heart banged against his chest and he could feel his own pulse beating rapidly in his temple. All thoughts of remaining calm washed out of the window. 'How?' he finally asked.

The man smiled. 'Isn't it obvious? We hear your thoughts. They come across us in the night like radio waves flying through the atmosphere.'

No. It wasn't possible. He had chosen his own path. There was no way these creatures were inside his head. That would make him one of them, and he wasn't.

He couldn't be.

He'd know if he was. Right?

Suddenly he found himself trying desperately to wipe all thought of Aries and the others from his mind. If they were in his head, he wouldn't make it easy for them.

Mr Leon stood up and placed his chair neatly back under the desk. He walked round the room until he was standing right behind Mason. Placing his hands on Mason's shoulders, he dug in deeply with his fingers.

'She was a very special girl, wasn't she?' The fingers tightened, digging into his nerves, sending shooting pain along his arms and into his neck. 'I'm sure you did everything you could to save her. Such a shame. We knew there would be accidental deaths like this. It was impossible to fix them all. A small price to pay for the great future of mankind. A world in which the strong will prevail and the weak will perish. There is no humanity to be found in prolonging the lives of those who weaken the gene pool.'

Chickadee with her diabetes. Weak genetics. Mason closed his eyes and tried to block out the voice in his ear.

'You must understand that we wouldn't want to lose someone we felt had potential. Especially if that person could help us sway the opinions of someone like you. I do wish she had lived. Even with her damaged genes, she would have been a great team member. We need new recruits. People like yourself that will offer something to the new world.'

'She never would have helped you.'

Mr Leon paused his weird painful massage. 'You'd be amazed what people will do when they're given the right opportunity.'

'Then what are you offering me?' Mason asked, trying to keep his voice from cracking. 'Because there isn't a single thing in the world that I want. There's nothing you can give me that would make me join your . . . team.'

Mr Leon leaned in until his mouth was right against Mason's ear. 'And that's exactly what I want to hear. Do you really think I expect you to be willing? Oh no. That would be too easy.' He paused, his breath hot against Mason's cheek. 'It would be disappointing. I expect more from you. And you will give it to me.'

Mason yanked forward in his seat but the man

tightened his grasp again and pulled him back. If only he didn't have the cuffs on. He'd at least have a chance to pop the guy one in the mouth.

'Let go of me,' he growled.

'Not until I'm finished,' Mr Leon said.

He yanked again, twisting Mason's body until he bit down on his lip to keep from yelling out. It was as if his arms were being pulled right out of their sockets.

'There is darkness inside you, boy,' Leon said. 'There's no disputing it. It oozes out of your pores. The interesting thing is we're not sure whose darkness it is.'

'You're lying,' Mason said through clenched teeth.

'Am I? Are you denying the dark thoughts inside your mind? I can read them, remember. All that hate has so much potential. Either way, we've got plenty of time to figure this out. You're not going anywhere. And we will be talking about your friends too. I'm most curious to know more about the girl named Aries. You'll be telling me all about her.'

Mason worked hard to keep his face empty of shocked emotion. 'I don't know anyone named Aries.'

'Oh, come now, you're just embarrassing yourself.' Mr Leon leaned in. 'We can play this game, but you're going to lose. We know everything. This is our world now so you'd better get used to it. All you have to do is look out of the window to see the greatness we've accomplished. There is no way that you or your petty little friends can change this. You'll do what we ask and you won't complain. Don't worry about resisting. You will. But it won't last long. We have ways of bringing you round.'

'Go ahead and try.'

'We've already begun.' He reached out and brought his thumbs up to Mason's face, resting his fingers on Mason's temples. Pausing, he waited, his grip tight and unmoving. Then he brought his thumbs down until they were less than an inch from Mason's eyelashes. 'All I have to do is give a small push. It's about pressure, not strength. How much pressure would it take to pop your eyes like balloons?'

Mason held his breath and waited for the pain. He wouldn't scream. No matter how much they tortured him, he wouldn't give them the satisfaction. At least he hoped he'd be as strong as necessary.

Mr Leon suddenly let go of Mason, chuckling to himself, and then headed to the door. He opened it, and another Bagger handed something over to him. He sauntered back to Mason.

'This, my friend, is an ankle monitor,' he said as he held up the small device. 'Fantastic little gem. It will tell us where you are at all times.' Bending down, he pulled off Mason's shoe and sock in quick jerking movements.

It took all the willpower in the world to keep Mason from kicking him in the face. The other Bagger stood in the doorway and his expression suggested he'd love it if Mason tried pulling something.

'You can't tamper with it,' the head Bagger said. 'You can't remove it. And if you try to escape we'll know exactly where you are. We'll come and retrieve you, along with anyone else you contact. See? You're that special to us.'

The small bracelet clicked into place. It felt heavy against Mason's skin.

'There. I do hope you try to run. You'll make it so much easier for us if you do.' Mr Leon stood up and readjusted his tie. 'Someone will come and lead you to the yard. They'll tell you what to do. I suggest you follow their orders.' He went back to the door and paused. 'I must admit I'm disappointed. I expected so much more of you.'

It was Mason's turn to smile. 'Sorry.'

'I'm just surprised you haven't figured it out,' the man said. 'But you're a clever boy – I'm sure you'll get it eventually.'

'Get what?' Mason's arms were burning and he shifted in his seat to try to ease the pain.

'Ask your friend, Daniel. He knows all about it.'

The door closed behind him, leaving Mason to try to think above his pain.

A short while later, he was uncuffed and shoved unceremoniously into the yard.

An extension of the casino, the yard was a large area that used to be an outdoor theatre for the Plaza of Nations. Now it was nothing but a pile of garbage surrounded by more chain-link fencing with coils of barbed wire to keep everyone in. Just like a real prison, there were towers in each corner, poorly constructed, and Baggers stood guard with automatic weapons.

The theatre was off to the side. Once it had been a great place for bands but smashed stage lights and twisted metal now covered the stage.

A few weeks ago, Mason and Aries had gone over to the Army and Navy on Hastings to rummage through the camping goods for supplies. It had been a wasted trip. They'd found the shelves mysteriously empty. Now Mason knew why. The camp was literally that, a collection of dozens of tents and canvases providing shelter from the constant rain that Vancouver seemed to love so much. There were several communal spots where giant umbrellas were set up around dirty plastic lawn chairs. In another area were portable outhouses and basins for people to wash in. Over in the corner, fresh laundry swayed gently on the lines. There was even a tent where a red cross had been painted over the canvas.

There were prisoners everywhere. They were crouched around small fires, warming their hands. They huddled in the entrances to their tents, kneeling on the hard cement. In the middle of the camp, a few women were surrounded by a group of children, all seemingly under or around the age of ten. The children didn't run or play. They sat, sombre, in a circle and stared at each other. They didn't even dare to cry.

The number of survivors rounded up here was overwhelming. Mason guessed there had to be at least two hundred. They all looked exhausted. Dozens of people sat in the dirty lawn chairs or on the ground and talked quietly with one another, their eyes occasionally darting in the direction of the armed Baggers. He noticed that some of them were looking in his direction too. No one spoke to him.

Mason didn't know what to do. He stood where he'd been dropped off, unsure of where to go. He moved a few steps and then paused, wondering if he should wait to see if anyone came to talk to him. There had to be somebody leading this group. They would tell him where to go. Let him know which tent would be his.

Finally he decided to approach the closest gathering. Several men were sitting around a small fire by the stage, mumbling to one another. Some of them were covered in bruises, dark black and yellow marks on their skin. A few had their hands wrapped in dirty bloodstained cloth. One of the men closest to Mason looked like his fingers had been broken in several places. His eye was swollen shut and there was a huge scab on his face. But as Mason moved closer to them they broke up, scattering in different directions, refusing to look his way.

'They don't trust you.'

'Huh?' Mason looked at the man who had mysteriously appeared by his side: a muscular guy in his late thirties wearing a baseball cap and one of those blue Gore-Tex jackets that cyclists often wore.

'The people,' the man said. He had a friendly face and he gave Mason a weak smile. 'They don't know what to make of you and that other fellow you came in with. This is a small place and lots of gossip goes round. They've heard you're both bad news, and that sort of thing only causes trouble here.'

'How are we bad news?'

The man shrugged. 'I ain't one for gossip so I try to close my ears to the negativity. I'd ban it if I could. But I'll say this. There's some questionable talk about which side you're on, you and your friend. Someone said you killed a girl. Of course some of the Baggers said you've been killing them too. No one knows who to believe. It's not the first time they've planted spies. People get weird. Don't know who to trust.'

Mason shrugged. 'I'm not one of them and I never killed a girl.' It didn't sound as positively reaffirming as he wished. 'Neither is Daniel.' He quickly scanned the grounds. 'Is he here?'

The man shook his head. '*Nada*. He's still locked away inside. But if they brought you out I'm sure it's just a matter of time for him.'

'Why do they do that? Keep some in cages like that?'

'Some people need special motivation. There's a lady inside that used to be a neurologist. She got caught trying to go over the fence a few weeks ago. Normally that would be a death sentence but doctors are too useful. Another girl in there is supposed to be a computer genius or something. University graduate by the time she was sixteen. Employed by the government. They got some guy who used to work with the power company too. They've been pushing him to get things running again.'

'How do the Baggers know all this about them?'

'They have ways of making you talk,' he said. 'Lying doesn't get anyone far around here. The Baggers always find out.'

'So they throw them in there because they won't cooperate?'

'Not just that. Some of 'em are plain too valuable to keep outside. That of course leads to the gossip. Most people who go into the casino don't come out. They're not too sure what to make of you.'

'So what am I supposed to do?'

'Lay low. Don't draw any attention to yourself.' The man nodded in the direction of the closest guard tower. Two Baggers moved across the grounds, armed with automatic weapons. 'Especially with them. You don't want them noticing you.'

Mason nodded. He watched as the Baggers stopped at a group of people. They spoke to the crowd and a few men stepped forward. A fourth man refused to move. He was rewarded with a sharp blow to the head. When he hit the ground, the closest Bagger kicked him several times.

Mason took a step in their direction but his guide pulled him back. 'I wouldn't do that if I were you.'

'What's happening?' Mason asked angrily. 'Why isn't anyone doing anything to help?'

'What can they do?' the man asked. 'Fight back?

There's no more fight inside these people.'

'They could do something?'

'That would only get them shot,' he said. 'That guy who got punched? He should have known better. You do as you're told here and that's how you stay alive. The second the Baggers think you're useless, you're dead. Dumb idiot must have a death wish.'

'Where are they taking them?' Mason watched the group move across the yard and towards the front of the compound.

'Clean-up crew from the looks of it,' he said. 'Lots of work to be done. They just started sending out people every day to work the streets. Body removal and whatnot. Someone's gotta clean up the mess they made. Those earthquakes did a hell of a job too. They been sending groups up to the power plant as well to get the juice working again. Every day they load up about twenty or so. You'll find out soon enough. Pretty much everyone here has a job assigned to them. Some better than others.'

'What's to keep them from running once they're outside?'

'Fear's a pretty good motivation. Some of them have loved ones that are here too.'

Not ankle monitors then. Mason looked down at the guy's feet. His ankles were bare. So he was the only one with a tracking device. Why him? It made Mason glad that his was covered by his jeans.

'The only way to survive here is to be useful,' the

man said again. 'So you'd better hope you've got something they want.'

Mason nodded his head absently. Yeah, the Baggers wanted him. Leon had made that very clear.

'Come on,' the man said. 'Let's find you somewhere to sleep. Not quite the Holiday Inn but I'm sure you've done worse this past bit. We all have. Got a few tents although not as many as I'd like. More and more people coming in every day. But we can get you something that'll keep the rain off your head.'

'Thanks.'

'I'm Chaplin,' the man said, and he extended his hand.

'Mason.'

They walked past a group of women spreading soil in an area where all the concrete had been torn up. There were bags of fertilizer stacked against the metal fencing. Beside them were piles of gardening gear: hoes, seeds, watering cans and various other items. The women worked hard, carrying the bags across the manmade field. Their faces were dirt-smudged, and their hands were sliced up and covered in makeshift bandages. None of them looked happy; most kept their eyes to the ground, occasionally glancing up and towards the guard towers.

'Nice thing about Vancouver is we can garden almost all year round,' Chaplin said sarcastically as he noticed where Mason's attention lay. 'Probably won't do much growing till the spring but that doesn't stop the Baggers from getting everything nice and ready now.'

There was a pile of sleeping bags under a canvas by the casino door. Chaplin went over and picked one up, then tossed it at Mason.

He began to walk through the camp. As they moved along, he pointed in various directions. 'Toilets there. We've got some stuff laid out if you want to try to clean up a bit. Everyone's entitled to use it but don't take anything back to your tent. We don't tolerate hoarders. We share everything.' He pointed to the only area where there were tables, a long row of them surrounded by what looked like a makeshift kitchen area. 'Dinner's around six. Nothing fancy, just basic stuff. But it'll keep you healthy to a degree. Never enough to go around though. I'd suggest you come later, let the others eat first. That's our rule of thumb. Let the children and women eat first. Let me tell ya, that really annoys a few of the feminists here.' Chaplin laughed hard. 'And if you're as cool as you claim, well, the others will figure it out soon enough.'

Mason nodded.

'But I'd still sleep with one eye open if I was you,' Chaplin said. 'We're not Baggers here, but we're not really human any more either. Dark days. They change a man. They've changed all of us.'

They finally came to a stop outside an empty tent in the corner. It was a small two-person contraption that had seen better days. The zipper was broken and the door flap had a hole in the canvas from where it looked as if someone had burned it with a candle.

'This is the best I can do,' Chaplin said. 'I'll send that friend of yours over if he ever comes out. Good luck.'

Mason watched Chaplin disappear back into a group of people by one of the fires. He spoke quietly to them but it was obvious what his topic of conversation was. Several men didn't bother to hide the fact that they were discussing Mason, glaring at him openly.

Determined to ignore them, Mason tossed his sleeping bag inside the tent and climbed in after it. The canvas was heavy and the air inside damp. He sat down on the ground and unravelled his new bedding. There was no mattress pad to protect his back from the hard ground. No pillow to place beneath his head.

Traitor? Really? Him?

There was darkness inside him. Leon had said he could see it. If he was truthful, even Mason knew it was there just below the surface. Daniel told him once that he had that potential. How did Daniel even know that?

Had he really given the others away because of this, without even knowing it? No. He would continue to fight until there wasn't anything else left to do. After that, well, he didn't want to think about what came next.

He looked around at the green walls, taking in his surroundings. He tried not to think about how claustrophobic the dim light made him feel. The walls were so thin, so easily penetrable.

Easy target.

What was he going to do now?

He reached down and examined the ankle monitor attached to his leg. It was a slim device, definitely something that looked impossible to remove on his own.

His mind wandered. Was Aries even aware that he was missing? Had they checked his room? Would the others simply assume he'd just taken off? Would they look?

Aries would know immediately he hadn't just taken off. Right? At least he hoped she would. They'd spent a lot of the past few weeks talking. She was the only one he felt even slightly comfortable being around. She knew him well enough to know he wouldn't split without at least saying goodbye to her. But would she be able to convince the others?

What if they refused to help? It wasn't like he'd gone out of his way to be friendly towards them. And even if they did look, even if they found him, what could they do to get him out? Should he even let them? Did he deserve it?

He'd been through so much in the past few months but this was the first time he'd ever had to force back the tears that burned in the corners of his eyes.

MICHAEL

It would be easier if the woods were dark or if it was raining. At least then they'd have extra camouflage. But, no, the sun was bright and the forest twinkled as sheets of brilliant light warmed their bodies. They could have gigantic I AM HERE signs above their heads and they still wouldn't be any less obvious.

They were hiding out by the dorms. Somehow they'd managed to work their way through the woods in the early hours and cross the road back into the main campus area. There they'd taken refuge in the wooded area near some of the student housing. The trees weren't as densely packed here as by the museum but it was still better than nothing.

Michael glanced over at Ryder who crouched in the dirt next to a slightly bent-looking pine tree. Ryder ignored him, a giant scowl on his face. His ankle was swollen and bruised, an injury that he'd incurred while running through the dark last night. It was a bad sprain; Michael didn't have to be a doctor to understand that. It slowed them down and that was a major worry.

There were only the three of them left, and the girl was fading fast. Michael had laid her out on top of the soft moss to make her more comfortable but it was a worthless gesture. Most of the time she stared up at the sky, her expression dazed, but a few times she focused on him, her eyes wide and clear.

'Don't leave me,' she whispered.

'I won't,' he said. Michael held her hand as she inhaled in short panicky gasps.

'I'm so cold. Don't leave me.'

Ryder covered his ears with his hands.

She tugged at the end of Michael's shirt, trying to keep him close. Each time she breathed out, more blood seeped from the wounds in her stomach.

'You're better off putting her out of her misery,' Ryder said.

Michael gritted his teeth. They'd been having this running conversation since they stopped to take a break. 'I told you before. I won't do that.'

The girl wheezed and gurgled, trying to get air past the blood pooling up inside her lungs.

'Then let me do it.'

'No.'

Ryder rubbed his ankle and retied his shoes. 'You're only making things worse. You know she doesn't stand a chance. You'd put down a dog that was suffering, right? What's the difference?'

'Shut up.'

The girl moaned.

'This is war, loser,' Ryder said. 'You can't be going all soft and sweet at a time like this. The strong survive. Sitting around and waiting for her to die, that's just going to get us killed. Have mercy. Send her to heaven.'

The girl coughed. Blood splattered across her lips and cheeks.

Ryder continued. 'Do you think those monsters have soft spots? Hell, no. I've seen them work. They'll just as easily kill their own to get to their goals. That's why they kicked our asses. They have their objective and they stick to it.'

'We're not Baggers,' Michael said. 'The moment we become like them, then we really have lost.'

'We've already lost. All we can do now is play out the rest of the game. Go out with a bang. Take as many of them with us for the ride as we can.'

The girl's breathing was slowing down. Her chest was still rising but not nearly as high or as continuously as before.

'That's not what you said last night,' Michael said. 'You had them all worked up. Talking about victory and taking back what's ours.'

Ryder shrugged. 'I'm a general. A commander. I'll tell them what they need to hear to get motivated.'

'So you'll lie?'

'Isn't that better than telling the truth? Hey, you. All of you. You're all going to die and it's going to be painful.'

'Still doesn't make it right.'

'Doesn't make it wrong either.'

The girl gurgled and sighed, and her hand went limp. Michael didn't have to check for a pulse to know she was gone. He gazed at her sadly for a moment and then brushed her eyelids closed with his fingers. He slowly moved his body away from hers and stood up. Knees screamed in protest. He'd been sitting still for over an hour.

'Look,' Ryder said, 'you can think of me as a monster all you want. I'm just being a realist. Decisions have to be made and someone has to make them. Ask the person who leads your group and they'll tell you the same thing.'

Michael instantly pictured Aries. She had a completely different approach, always trying to remain positive and focus on the remaining good things in life. He couldn't imagine her being so cold, not for a second.

'Come on,' Michael said. 'We need to get out of here.'

'It's all gone,' Ryder said, more to himself than Michael as he stumbled after him. 'I brought them together and now it's gone. I knew we weren't ready but I never thought they'd go down so quickly.' Ryder's eyes narrowed suddenly. He looked at Michael with renewed hatred. Michael knew what he was thinking. He still blamed Michael for bringing the Baggers. As far as he was concerned, they'd been safe until he and Clementine had shown up.

That's why he'd attacked Michael from behind. A completely cowardly action.

But none of it mattered now. Ryder could shoot death looks at Michael all he wanted. It didn't change a thing. With his injury, he needed Michael.

And Michael had saved his life.

Last night, after parting with Clementine, Michael had raced back through the woods and towards the sounds of people crying. He'd got there too late to save the group of girls. Two Baggers had lined them up against the wall of the museum and executed them one by one. Ryder was the last in line. Lying on the ground and sobbing, he'd covered his head with his hands and was waiting for the fatal blow.

But somehow Michael had managed to get in there first. He'd taken out the closest Bagger with his spear before anyone even noticed he was there.

The second Bagger had almost killed him but he'd prevailed. As the Bagger turned his weapon towards him, Michael had managed to knock the gun out of his hands with the tail end of his spear before he could pull the trigger. Then he'd speared him too and stumbled over to Ryder.

'Come on,' he said, and he held out his hand.

Ryder refused his gesture. But he'd wiped the tears from his eyes and followed Michael back into the woods.

Now, after spending the entire night hiding out, it was obvious to Michael that he and Ryder would never be friends. Michael could live with that. But they weren't going to last much longer if they didn't find a better place to hide.

'We could take cover in the dorms,' Michael said. They'd been watching the buildings for the last forty minutes and no one had gone in or out. They appeared empty but of course that didn't mean anything.

'Not a good idea,' Ryder said. 'They haven't been in there to clean up yet. Lots of dead bodies. It'll be one of the first places they check.'

'Fine,' Michael said. So far Ryder had vetoed all his suggestions. 'You pick then. Where should we go?'

'The First Nations Longhouse.'

'Are you joking?' Michael asked as he pictured the big public building they'd passed earlier on their way to the dorms. 'That place is wide open. All the windows are broken. We can't even barricade ourselves in. We'd be sitting ducks.'

'When are you going to learn that the most obvious hiding spot is usually the safest?' Ryder said. 'It's called hiding in plain sight. That's why I chose the museum.'

It was on the tip of his tongue to point out just how well that had worked for him but Michael kept silent. According to Raj it had been their fault the Baggers had found them. Getting into a huge fight wouldn't be a good strategy right now.

'OK,' Michael said. 'Let's do it. But as soon as you're good enough to walk we're heading back to Clementine and the others. I'm not staying here any longer than I have to.'

The Longhouse wasn't that far away but because of Ryder's ankle it took them half an hour to creep across the parking lot and round the side where they crawled through one of the broken windows and into the auditorium.

Aside from all the shards of glass scattering the floor, the place was in decent shape. The main room was huge, designed to look like a wooden cabin. There were a few chairs piled up in the corner and an overturned garbage bin but the rest of the place looked untouched. There were no signs of life. If anyone was hiding here, they were doing a fine job of keeping invisible.

They made it halfway across the auditorium before Ryder's ankle gave out on him. Collapsing to the ground, he cried out, and started swearing loudly as he rubbed his leg.

'Let me see,' Michael said. Kneeling down, he waited as Ryder pulled up his jeans and showed his wound. The bruising was darker, black and red designs spreading out from his ankle and all the way down his foot towards his toes. 'That's really not good. We've got to get you somewhere you can lie down for a bit. You shouldn't be walking.'

'I have no choice,' Ryder said. 'We can't stay right here.'

'Agreed,' Michael said. He glanced around the large bare room with all its broken windows. If anyone were to walk across the lawn right now, they'd spot them in a heartbeat. 'I'm going to have to carry you.'

'You're not touching me.'

'Fine. You need to wait here then. Stay right in the open.' He glanced over at the stage with the PA and other electronic gear. 'Maybe we can give you a microphone and you can make your whereabouts even more obvious. That speech you gave last night was breathtaking. Think you can do another?'

Ryder grunted. 'You're not helping me.'

'At least haul yourself over to the stage then, where you can kind of hide yourself.'

Ryder nodded in agreement. He had to half crawl, half drag himself but he managed to get over to the corner of the stage where there were some stacked chairs to hide behind.

'I'll scout ahead and see if there's a spot where we can rest,' he said. 'If you need me, holler. I'm sure I'll hear you and come running.'

Ryder gave him the finger.

Michael went over to the doors beside the stage and tried to open them as quietly as possible. Beyond them, a long hallway waited, that branched out in both directions. He stepped into the hall and the door closed behind him with a bang. The noise echoed, bouncing off the walls and he flinched involuntarily.

He paused, waiting for the sound of footfalls as the Baggers came for him but nothing happened. No Baggers.

That didn't mean the building was empty or safe though. Not by a long shot.

He decided to head right past a set of bathrooms and payphones. This brought him to a reception area with several entrances. One led towards the front lawn, which was thankfully empty. The glass windows were broken here too and a soft breeze scattered the leftover junk-food wrappers and paper into the corners. The other door was locked. It led out down a path along the back that faced one of the covered parking lots. He'd have to try to find a set of keys if they were going to stay here. They would need an escape route.

Beyond the reception desk he found an office area. Darkened computers and printers rested on desks, covered in dust and bird droppings. Obviously the animals had decided to make this building their home. He found two dead birds in the corner along with empty water bottles and an open bag of crisps. He picked out one of the crisps and snapped it with his fingers. Still fresh.

When he looked up, he saw a handprint on the table. The dust was smudged and disturbed. It looked recent.

Michael knew he wasn't a professional tracker by any means but he was positive about one thing. Someone had been here recently. Opened bags of crisps grew stale and softer within a day if not closed back up.

But who? Could it have been someone from the museum? It seemed unlikely. There was a lot of discarded litter. He couldn't imagine that someone had eaten that much in less than a day.

Either way, they were gone now. Michael had left his weapon buried in the chest of the last Bagger he'd killed. They'd have to find something with which to arm themselves if they were going to stay here. Michael looked around the office quickly but the most he could find was a roll of tape and a heavy hole punch – better than nothing. He put both items in his hoody pocket.

For the next half hour Michael went through every desk looking for a set of keys that would open the back door. Eventually he found them after prising open a filing cabinet with a letter opener. He plucked out the ring with dozens of keys attached. It took several tries but on the tenth key, the back-door lock clicked and fresh air hit his face.

He pulled out the tape and wrapped it round the key so he'd be able to identify it at speed in case they had to get out in a hurry.

When he went back to the reception area, there were people walking across the front lawn. Quickly he ducked behind the desk, his heart hammering in his chest. Pulling out the dust-covered office chair, he crawled under, tugging the chair back in so he was partially covered. His hand closed round the hole punch, and the whole concept seemed ridiculous. What had he been thinking? It was the most useless weapon of all time. He discarded it on the floor, realizing the letter opener would have been a better choice. Too late now.

He waited, and soon enough he heard shoes treading on broken glass as the people approached the window.

He couldn't tell if they were Baggers or not. He hadn't got a good enough look. But he couldn't take the chance. Pressing his back against the wooden desk, he tried to will himself invisible. If they walked through the doors, it wouldn't take long to find him.

It wouldn't take long to find Ryder either.

Sitting ducks.

Time stopped. Michael's ears strained as he waited for the sound of the front door scraping on the cement as they opened it.

Nothing happened.

The air burned in his lungs. He'd been completely unaware he was holding his breath. He exhaled as quietly as possible. Knees screamed in pain from sitting scrunched up and still.

The door scraped. The two strangers entered the building.

They didn't speak. Feet crunched on more glass and one of them put something down on the table right above his head. Michael covered his mouth with his hand to try to silence his breathing.

He couldn't see much from his hiding spot behind his chair so he only caught a glimpse of their legs as they moved past the desk and into the office area. As soon as their shoes disappeared, Michael shoved the chair aside and crawled out. He moved as silently as possible, jumping over the desk and racing down the hall towards the auditorium. He didn't dare look back to see if he'd been noticed or not.

Ryder was still in the same spot.

'Come on,' Michael said. 'We've got to get out of here now. They're here.'

Ryder didn't move.

Michael grabbed his arm. 'Now!'

'Leave me. I'll only slow you down.'

Michael wasn't about to show any pity. Not for this guy. He yanked Ryder to his feet, forcing the injured guy to put his arm round his shoulders.

But where to go?

'Come on,' Michael said. 'I've got keys. There has to be somewhere we can hide.'

Ryder dragging his leg, they moved slowly out into the hallway. Turning left, Michael led the way along the narrow corridor. He immediately rejected hiding in the bathroom. If they locked the doors, the Baggers would instantly know someone was hiding there. They needed to find a storage place, a locked door that wouldn't arouse suspicion.

The next set of doors on the left were big and heavy. He fumbled with the keys while Ryder kept watch, then unlocked it on the third try. He didn't even bother to search the area first. Instead, he shoved Ryder unceremoniously through the opening and quickly closed the door behind them, locking them in. Once inside, he reached around in the dark until he pulled the flashlight out of his back pocket.

They were in a large kitchen.

He quickly scanned the room but it was empty. There was another set of doors and he checked them out. They led outside to a loading bay. Excellent! Always good to have another exit.

They waited. No one came and banged on the door. No footsteps echoed down the hall. Michael was positive that they'd managed to get inside without the Baggers noticing.

They were safe for the time being. There was little chance the Baggers would break down those doors so, unless there were other keys lying around, they should be OK. Ryder slouched against the wall while Michael looked around for weapons again. There wasn't much to work with, not even a knife or two. Most of the cupboards were locked and he didn't seem to have keys that worked on them. He didn't want to risk the noise of trying to break them open.

Some kitchen.

The refrigerator smelt mouldy. It was empty except for some expired coffee creamers. The freezer only had a few ice-cube trays filled with tepid water.

'This sucks,' he finally said. 'We're safe but there's nothing here. We can't stay. We won't last more than a day or two without supplies.' He tried twisting the water tap. It remained dry. 'We don't even have water.'

Ryder nodded.

'Maybe later I can try slipping out and looking for something,' Michael said. 'The student housing has to have a vending machine or two.'

'If it did, we probably raided it,' Ryder said. 'Most of the food on campus was brought over to the museum.'

'You couldn't have got all of it.'

'My people were pretty thorough.'

'Then I guess we get to sit back and starve,' Michael said. 'Because you're not going anywhere with that ankle and I can't exactly leave you behind.'

'I would.'

'Would what?'

'Leave you behind.'

Michael leaned against the fridge and sank down to the floor. 'That's the difference between you and me,' he said with a sigh. 'You let people die. You leave them behind. I actually try to do something about it.'

'You really have no clue,' Ryder said.

'We'll just have to agree to disagree on that one.'

And they did. There was nothing else to do but sit on the cold tiled floor in silence.

He'd been sleeping. Dreaming about something but the picture slipped away from his brain the second he heard the key turning in the lock.

Michael was up off the floor in a heartbeat. He fumbled around, searching for the flashlight that had slipped out of his hands while he'd slept. How could he have fallen asleep? He should have spent more time searching for weapons, tearing the kitchen apart piece by piece until he found something. Why on earth had he discarded that hole punch? He moved around in the dark until he found the countertop. Crouching down, he blindly groped the cupboards beneath, trying to find something useful. His hands wrapped round a hand blender. Not exactly a weapon of choice but it would have to do.

In the blackness he heard metal jiggle in the lock

again and then stop. A slight pause. A rattle as someone searched for another key. There was a second set of master keys and this person had found it.

'Get behind the door,' Ryder whispered. 'Get the upper hand.'

'We don't know how many there are,' Michael whispered back. But he felt his way around in the darkness until he found the door. Stepping behind it, he waited with his hand blender held high, feeling absolutely ridiculous. Good thing the lights were out because Ryder would probably burst into laughter if he could see him.

The person on the other side tried another key. This time Michael heard the sound as the lock clicked. His whole body tensed.

The door opened cautiously. Someone took a step into the room. Michael waited. He couldn't strike until the person or people came in a few feet further.

A hand fumbled with a flashlight.

Brightness filled the room, forcing Michael to blink several times in pain. He jumped forward blindly, ready to bring the blender hurling down but paused in mid strike.

A blond-haired guy froze, his hand still attached to the door handle.

'Holy crap!' the stranger said. 'Don't! I'm cool. I'm cool!' He covered his head and dropped to the floor. The flashlight rolled off into a corner where it continued to give off light.

Michael kept the blender raised but he couldn't get past the visual of stopping to mix up this guy a smoothie. All he needed to do was arm Ryder with a cutting board or food processor and they'd be in business.

'Don't hurt me,' the guy said. He'd completely covered his head with his hands. 'I'm cool.'

'You already said that,' Michael said. But he lowered the blender and hid it behind his back.

From the corner, Ryder was watching Michael with a look of amusement on his face. Before he could help himself, a wave of hysterical laughter burst out of Michael's chest.

'Don't just stand there,' Ryder said. 'Get inside and close the damn door behind you.' 'Yeah,' Michael said through the giggles. 'What were you, born in a barn? Don't let the heat get out.'

CLEMENTINE

This was one of those nights that would end without Clementine getting any sleep. Nothing new there. She was getting really good at functioning in a sleep-deprived state. As long as she didn't wake up by the side of a road again, like she had once in the early days, she could deal with it.

They'd returned home last night to discover that one of the university girls was running a high fever and the Tylenol Larisa had been dumping down her throat didn't appear to be working.

The girl's name was Emma. A good chunk of her arm had been torn off. The skin around the gash was hot to the touch and there were red streaks crawling up to her shoulder and down towards her elbow. Larisa had explained that this was a major sign of infection along with her 103° temperature. Her friend Janelle wasn't doing well either. She'd taken a knife to the stomach and had started vomiting blood about an hour ago. Although Clementine was no expert, she was pretty positive there was internal bleeding. Without proper medical care, they both might not make it.

'I don't know what to do,' Larisa said. She was busy hopping around on her good foot, ignoring Joy's attempts to get her to sit down and take a break. 'I'm not trained enough to deal with this. I was only in my first year of nursing school. We haven't learned anything yet.'

'Joy's right,' Aries said. 'You need to take a breather. You're bleeding through your bandages. Let us take over.'

Larisa finally agreed to sit down and Nathan helped her to the living room where he attempted to change her bandages under her direction. Joy tried to help out but retreated to her bedroom after growing pale and muttering something about the sight of so much blood.

The main-floor bedroom had become a hospital ward. It had been empty until now. Everyone was doing their best to help out, except Colin obviously. Even Claude, the sour-faced guy who'd shoved Michael, was trying to pitch in. Colin of course had to be difficult. The only appearance he'd put in so far was to pass them all on his way to the kitchen to find a warm bottle of Gatorade.

Clementine checked the girl's temperature by placing her hand on Emma's forehead. Boiling hot. Not an understatement. She could probably cook an egg on her skull. Maybe fry up some hash browns to go with it. She turned to Aries who was pouring bottled water on to a face cloth. It was a real shame they didn't have any ice. Weren't you supposed to dunk people in the shower if they got too hot? She tried to remember if she knew anything else but came up blank. She'd never been much of a caregiver. That was more Mom's field. Then again, it wasn't like anyone she knew ever got that sick.

Dear Heath, Do you remember the time you tried jumping the kerb on your bike and your foot got tangled up in the chain? You hit the pavement really hard and there was dirt and gravel stuck in the palms of your hand. Your knee was bleeding and your jeans were sliced to bits. I remember how brave you were — you didn't cry once, even when the doctor stitched your palm back up. You walked funny for several weeks while we waited for the scab to fall off. I wish I'd paid attention now to all those times we gave Mom and Dad heart attacks by jumping off the rafters in the barn or skateboarding in the town park. I'm a lousy nurse. Can't even figure out what to do for a fever. What's the old saying? Feed a cold, starve a fever? Or is it the other way around? Either way, breaking out the Doritos isn't going to help in this situation.

'I don't know what to do,' she muttered.

'Me neither,' Aries said, and she placed the cloth against the girl's forehead. Clementine waited to hear if the water would sizzle under all that heat.

The girl just moaned but didn't open her eyes.

'We need to find help,' Aries said. 'It's fantastic that we have Larisa but she's right: one year of nursing school isn't enough. Brandi was here yesterday. She said they'd run into someone who had a doctor in their group. She was going to go check it out. Maybe we should send someone over there to see.'

'I'll go,' Raj said from the door. He'd been standing around with his hands stuffed into his pockets. His dark face was quite pale, even with all the shadows in the room.

'We'll both go,' Clementine said. 'Brandi's place is well hidden. And they'd probably shoot you on sight. They're not kind to strangers.'

'Fair enough,' Raj said. 'Let's go do this, babes. I can't stand here feeling so helpless.'

Clementine looked at Aries. 'Will you be OK?'

Aries nodded. 'I've got Nathan and Joy. They can give me a hand until you get back. We'll survive.'

Clementine glanced down at the girl one last time before standing. 'OK,' she said to Raj. 'Let's go get some weapons from the garage.'

The sun was a faint glimmer in the eastern sky when they started out. The clouds were trying to push it back down. The morning was cold and drizzling. It seemed so strange to be in the middle of December without snow. Clementine would much rather put up with the white stuff, even if it did make it harder to cover their tracks.

Dear Heath, No White Christmas for me. Remember how we always knew the holidays were round the corner because Dad used to hum that song all the time? I swear, it was the only Christmas carol he knew. He drove Mom completely crazy last year. I thought for sure she was going to toss him in the barn for the night.

The rain was worse. It made her depressed when the clouds took over the sun for days on end. She was always cold too. Not the kind of cold she could fight by slipping on an extra pair of socks or a sweater. No, this was something different. This got into her bones and no amount of extra clothing could chase it away.

Clementine had the two-way radio tucked away in the bottom of her backpack. She'd worked out a deal with Nathan to check in every half hour or so. Not using the radios was what had got them into this whole situation in the first place.

How she wished she could turn on the radio and hear Michael's voice right about now. Just to know he was OK and still alive.

Brandi's safe house was located just off Granville Street. It wasn't far – if they cut through the backyards of houses on the way, they could get there in about ten minutes.

'WARNING, WARNING! THE CITY IS CLOSED. NO ONE IS ALLOWED IN OR OUT.'

They ducked round an old two-storey house to avoid the white van patrolling the street.

'Every time I hear that message, I don't know whether to cringe or laugh hysterically,' Raj muttered as they crawled underneath a back porch.

'I know what you mean,' Clementine said, ducking to avoid a web with a juicy brown spider in the middle of it. 'We better be careful. The Baggers are close.'

They managed to reach Brandi's block without any major run-ins. The white van headed off in the direction of downtown and the warning message grew progressively weaker as the minutes dragged on.

'This is weird,' Clementine said. They'd reached the beginning of the block. She could see the white-and-green trimmed house a few doors down. She'd been here twice before. Brandi's team of survivors was efficient. There were always two or three guards hiding out on the street. Normally there was one positioned right where they were standing, hiding behind a barricade that wasn't noticeable from the street. Brandi herself often sat there for hours on end.

The area was empty. The only signs of recent life were a couple of empty cans and a half-eaten package of trail mix.

'We'd better be careful,' Raj said. Rain dripped from his curly hair and he breathed warm air into his hands.

She nodded. Her own hair was stuck to her scalp. In another world she could have been sporting a bright red umbrella, maybe even with polka dots. Instead her blonde locks felt like icicles against her ears. Jumping up and down a few times, she tried to bring some feeling back into her toes.

They continued along the street, keeping to the shadows of the houses. Many of the buildings were closed up tightly and locked. Several of them had the blinds drawn. Was it possible there were other stray stragglers hidden behind those walls? Or had Brandi and her group gone from house to house, closing everything up so their own safe house wouldn't stick out among the others?

Eenie, meenie, minie, moe. Catch some survivors by the toe. If they holler, kill them on the spot.

So quiet.

In all her years, she'd never noticed how truly quiet a place can become until after the Bagger invasion. And she was used to quiet, considering she grew up on a farm. The townsfolk of Glenmore weren't the rowdy types. More than seventy per cent of the town was over the age of sixty. Women who sat around playing Bridge all day didn't really kick up their heels and party all night long. Even the roads were quiet and hardly ever used. Clementine used to take her books into the fields as a little girl and hide out in the tall wheat. She'd listen to the crickets and close her eyes as the wind gently swayed through the grain. She enjoyed the solitude and took it for granted.

Quiet used to mean calm and peaceful. Now it was deadly. The ominous feeling pressed down around her, making her that much more aware of little things like her quickened breathing or the way the birds were no longer chirping away above them.

'Should we go round to the back?' Raj asked. His voice sounded weird in the midst of all that silence. They were one stop away from the safe house and Clementine couldn't tell if anyone was watching their movements. If Brandi and her group were inside, they'd be fully aware that Clementine and Raj were outside. Last time she'd come with Aries, they'd approached the front door and someone had opened it before they'd even put their feet on the first porch step. So going round the back seemed too sneaky, especially since they were welcome. Everyone in Brandi's group knew who they were.

'No,' she said. 'We can go round the front. The street's empty. It's safe for us, I think.'

No one opened the door when she and Raj climbed up the steps towards the porch. Now she was at a loss. What was she supposed to do? Knock? Hello, would you like to buy some Girl Scout cookies? She glanced over at Raj but he looked as clueless as she felt.

She tapped on the door softly with her knuckles. The sound seemed shockingly loud. Stepping back, she turned and glanced both ways down the street. Nothing out of place. Just rain, rain and more rain. A set of wind chimes echoed from the house next door, the sound came across as lonely as the cry of a loon.

'You know that creepy feeling you get when something is about to go dreadfully wrong?' Raj asked. 'It's like a thousand snakes are trotting around in your stomach?'

'Snakes don't trot.'

'Slither, crawl, gallop – same stuff, different pile. Well, I'm getting that right about now, babes.'

She nodded. 'Me too.'

They both faced the door. A glass window with the curtains drawn looked back at them. There was no way to tell if anyone or anything was waiting for them.

'We should check it out,' Clementine said. She

gripped her baseball bat tightly in her soaked fingers. Rain dripped from the wood, pooling on the welcome mat beneath her feet.

'Yup, we should.'

Neither of them moved.

'Even if the Baggers got them, someone might still be alive.'

'Yup.'

Still no movement.

She reached out with her fingers and grasped the handle. Slowly she turned it, careful to make as little noise as possible. It was unlocked. She pushed gently, and the door opened, creaking loud enough to make her cringe.

The smell of blood assaulted her nostrils immediately.

Oh, this was bad.

Raj gagged and stepped backwards, just managing to rush over to the side of the porch where he vomited into the bushes. Clementine held her breath, refusing to let the smell into her nose and mouth. She stood at the door, straining her ears for the sounds or lack of them coming from inside the darkened house. But all she could hear was Raj spitting several times as he tried to clear his throat.

'Sorry, babes,' he whispered when he finally returned to the door. 'Much better. Never was good with the stomach. Smells. They overpower me. Make me all weak in the knees. But there's nothing left in the stomach now so I should be OK.'

'You talk too much when you're nervous,' she whispered back.

'That too.'

She opened her mouth and took a series of small little breaths. 'OK,' she said as she raised her bat. 'Let's do this.'

They stepped through the door.

A putrid smell of copper and overripe bathroom hit her face. Clementine gasped, her eyes watering as she pulled her shirt up over her mouth. Behind her, Raj made a choking sound in his throat.

'Are you OK?' She didn't dare look at him. Misery loves company and she was afraid that if she took even a small glance at his face she might end up joining him in a visit to the bushes to throw up.

'I'll live,' Raj said. His voice was muffled as if he was talking through his shirt too. 'I think the worst is over.'

The first body was lying on the stairs. Clementine didn't recognize him: an older man, his arm sticking through the banister at an awkward angle. A pool of blood lay sticky beneath his head while his eyes stared up at a black-and-white photo of seashells. Clementine bent down to double check. There was a big gaping hole in the middle of his forehead. The expression on his face was more bewilderment than horror. He might have been the first to go. They must have surprised him when he came down the stairs.

Dear Heath, Am I going to die like that? A pile of cold flesh left to rot in an abandoned house. What —

No! She wasn't going to delve into self-pity. She straightened up. This man might be dead but she was alive. And there might be others inside the house that were too. Feeling sorry for everyone and everything wasn't going to get the job done. It might make things worse. She had gone this long without imagining what her final death scene would look like. She wasn't going to start now.

From further inside the house, there was a loud crash, as if someone was being thrown against the wall. Clementine stepped back and bumped into Raj. He steadied her, dropping his baseball bat in the process.

They shouldn't have come here. They should have realized from the moment they opened the door that there was nothing but death waiting for them.

Stupid! Stupid! Stupid!

Raj bent down to retrieve his weapon. 'Let's get out of here,' he whispered. 'If we leave now, we might make it back alive.'

'No.' YES! 'We can't,' she whispered back. The noise was coming from the kitchen area. It sounded like someone was digging through all the pots and pans to find a clean spoon. 'There were others here. We have to make sure. If any of them are still alive –'

Her hands were shaking and she couldn't find the will power to make them stop.

'OK, babes,' Raj said, giving her a nudge forward. 'Let's do it.'

The smell lessened as they moved further into the

house. Or maybe it was because they were getting more accustomed to it. Dust particles floated through the murky light. The air had a hazy feel to it, trapped underneath all those blankets that covered the windows. More bodies waited for them at the edge of the living room. A woman. Not Brandi. Clementine recognized her immediately. She was one of the older women, a beautiful hippy-type lady who had braids in her hair and always wore a patchwork skirt. She had grown up on a farm too; a few weeks ago she and Clementine had talked about it.

She was dead now.

There were two more bodies in the dining room. Both men. Blood was splattered all over the walls and the fifties-style table. They'd really put up a fight. One of them was missing his hand. She actually found herself looking around for it, and spotted it under one of the chairs. There was a hysterical moment when she almost thought about picking it up and trying to reattach it to his arm.

She heard Raj move towards her but she waved him back. 'No, get away,' she managed through a garbled voice. He complied. She dropped to her knees, closed her eyes, swaying back and forth, listening to the sounds of the air going harshly in and out of her lungs.

'*Clementine.*'

Her mother's voice. Clear as a bell. Right inside her head. Her mother who used to wear pretty summer dresses with flower patterns and did all the stereotypical things that small-town mothers did. The smell of bread and freshly baked cookies in the kitchen when she came home starving from school. Her hair used to smell like strawberries and, even though Clementine used the exact same shampoo, she could never get her own blonde locks to smell as good or look as fresh.

'*Clem. You need to leave. Get up.*'

Those had been the last words she'd ever spoken to Clementine, right before – well, right before the bottom of her world collapsed and the Baggers destroyed everything she knew and loved.

Had it been like this for Mom and Dad? All that blood? Yes. They'd attacked the entire town hall. Locked the doors and blown away the hundreds of people trapped inside.

No, she couldn't think about that. Not right now. She was going to go crazy. And if she left her mind on the floor of the dining room next to that severed hand she and Raj would be in even more trouble.

No, this was one cheerleader that wasn't going to cower in the corner and wait for the man with the hockey mask to come and hunt her down.

'Come on,' she said, hoping her voice sounded as strong as she wanted it to be. She led them over to the kitchen and with a strong shove, pushed open the door.

A Bagger crouched next to the refrigerator. He let out a sharp shriek and jumped up to his feet. 'Oh, aren't you a pretty thing,' he said.

'I can still kick your ass,' she said, trying to look tougher than she felt.

'Too bad the others left,' the Bagger continued. 'They already took the useful ones away. You'd be a good one to bring in. Pretty girls like yourself are hard to find. We'd make good use of you.'

'What about me?' Raj said. 'Aren't I good-looking enough?'

Tucking his head down, the Bagger barrelled straight into them. Clementine didn't think. With one arm, she shoved Raj back into the dining room while she raised the bat with her other hand. Swinging hard, wood hit head with a sickening thump, and the Bagger dropped to the floor like a stone.

It happened so quickly. It wasn't until the Bagger lay there twitching on the floor that she remembered to breathe.

'Well done, babes!' Raj said, re-entering the room. 'Where'd you learn to hit like that?'

She stepped past the body on the floor, giving it a good shove with her heel. 'Little League Baseball,' she replied. 'I was a pitcher for six years.'

'You must have hit a lot of home runs.'

She smiled. 'Actually I sucked. Never could keep my eye on the ball. At least that's what Coach said. I struck out more than I hit.'

'Not when it matters, babes,' Raj said.

Someone over by the refrigerator groaned. Clementine raised her bloody bat so quickly she actually knocked herself in the forehead. So much for looking smooth. Rubbing her head, she moved over towards the sound.

Brandi lay on the granite floor, her chest rising and falling rapidly as the blood pooled underneath her. Clementine dropped to her side, reaching out to cradle the older woman's head in her lap.

'You're gonna be fine,' she heard herself say.

Brandi tried to laugh, a combination of wheezing and red-tinged spittle.

'Raj,' Clementine said, 'I need paper towels, whatever you can find.'

He had already crossed the room and was pulling out drawers. Yanking a pile of hand towels out from beside the kitchen sink, he tossed them over. Clementine grabbed one and immediately shoved it into the area on Brandi's chest that appeared to have the most blood gushing out of it.

Brandi just sighed as if she knew it was a wasted effort. She grabbed hold of Clementine's hand. Her grip was still strong.

'I didn't tell them about you,' she wheezed. 'They tried to make me but I didn't do it. I wasn't gonna let anyone hurt you.' She coughed several times, spraying red liquid against Clementine's hoody. 'I didn't tell. But –'

Clementine waited while the woman beneath her swallowed several times. The breathing was slowing down but still steady.

'G-G-Graham,' she stuttered. 'Someone told about Graham. I heard them.' Her eyes squeezed tightly together, trying to hold back the pain and tears. 'Don't be mad. He couldn't help it. They cut him open and started removing his insides.'

'It's OK,' Clementine said. 'We'll get you help and then go there next. We'll help Graham.'

'No.' Brandi shook her head violently. Her eyes grew a little clearer as she tugged on Clementine's arm. She pulled herself up towards Clementine's face. 'I'm not real any more, sweetie. I'm already dead and so is everyone else that was here.' Two harsh coughs. 'It's over. Don't waste your time on me.'

'But—'

'Nope,' Brandi said. Even though she was dying, she was taking control one last time. No wonder she was such a good leader. 'You go after that child,' she said. 'You hear me? You promise me.'

'OK,' Clementine said. 'You have my word.'

Brandi sighed. 'Now I can leave this world. I'm ready.' She leaned her head back and closed her eyes. 'Well? What are you waiting for? Get out of here.'

Clementine tried to lower Brandi's head to the floor as gently as possible. Standing up, she swallowed tears, nodded at Raj and the two of them bolted from the house. Once outside, she paused, heavily breathing in the fresh air.

'Where do we go?' Raj asked. He also inhaled deeply.

'We go get Aries and the others,' she said, brushing

away his look of surprise with her hand. 'Graham's house is on the other side of ours. It's going to take us twenty minutes to get there. We have no idea where the Baggers are. I say we get back-up.' She waved the baseball bat absently. 'And better weapons.'

Raj nodded.

'Let's go.'

They ran hard.

NOTHING

There are three sides to every story.

Yours.

Mine.

What really happened: the truth.

The truth is we all have a dark side. Every single one of us. The truth is we all have bad thoughts at one point or another. We've all done things that were mean and awful, and we almost always regret it when we act on these dark desires.

Almost.

There isn't a single brother who hasn't thought about killing his sister at least once in his lifetime. There isn't a single parent who hasn't thought about smacking their screaming child. Everyone has thought about breaking the law. We all think about cheating. Stealing. Revenge.

Some religions claim the thought is just as bad as the actual sin. So if you think it you're creating it out of nothing. You're sinning.

Philosophers have spent generation after generation wondering why we have morals. Why aren't we more animalistic? Why do we think?

Why do we live?

I am what I am. I'm not what they are. I am not like anyone.

I am Nothing.

Is it easier for them? The ability to forget or discard everything they once were? No conscience. They've forgotten all the little things that revolved around love and happiness. Enjoying a latte on a rainy day. Reading a book in front of the fireplace. Cuddling with the special person in their life.

Love. They've forgotten about love.

Desire.

Hope.

If I'm going to continue along this path, I'd like to forget. I can't take responsibility for my actions. I need to believe that my behaviour is a product of *their* environment and not mine. The voices in my head are not mine. I am NOT responsible. I kill because they make me.

I am their puppet.

I kill.

The Baggers have expectations of me. They don't say but I can tell what they expect. I am the perfect spy. I will destroy the light that my friends still cling to. I am the most logical choice to flush them out.

And I will do it.

A frog is sitting on the edge of a river, doing all those interesting things that frogs do, when a scorpion comes up to him and starts chatting.

'Yo, frog, dude,' the scorpion says. 'Can I hitch a ride on your back to get across the river?'

'I dunno,' the frog says. 'How do I know you're not

gonna kill me? I've heard about how crazy you scorpions are.'

The scorpion shrugs. 'That would be really stupid of me, dude. If I stung you, we'd both end up dying. I can't swim. I'd drown. Do you really think I'm dumb enough to kill myself?'

The frog nods because that's what frogs do and he agrees to give his arthropod friend a lift. But halfway across the river the scorpion lifts his giant ass up in the air and brings down that homeboy stinger. The frog is instantly poisoned.

'What the hell?' the frog says with his last dying breath. 'I was totally hooking you up.'

The scorpion shrugs as he slips off the frog's back and into the raging river to drown. 'It's in my nature.'

I will betray them. There is no solution to this problem. It is in my nature and we can't change that. No one can change the evil inside us.

I am dark inside. Black. Decayed.

It is my nature.

ARIES

'Th-they're all dead.'

Clementine couldn't seem to get the words out properly. She was breathing heavily; both she and Raj must have run the entire way back at full speed.

'It's true,' Raj said, leaning against the door frame while trying to recover. 'It's a bloody bloodbath. Just like the museum. They got them all.'

'We've got to warn Graham. They're heading there next.' Clementine filled them in on all that had happened.

Everything was a mess. Aries didn't know what to do. She'd been running around like an insane chicken, trying to fix everything. Janelle was dead. She'd died shortly before Clementine and Raj had returned. Larisa was with Joy, wrapping the body in a sheet so they could sneak it out after dark and find a place to dump it. Hopefully they'd be able to find a place where a discarded corpse wouldn't look unusual. It's not like they could take the time to bury her. And she certainly couldn't stay there.

'I don't think we should go.'

Clementine's mouth opened into a perfect circle of surprise.

'Think about it.' Aries tried to keep her voice calm

and steady. 'It's probably too late by now. If the Baggers attacked, it'll be over. I think it's a wiser choice to protect ourselves. Brandi may not have told them about us but who knows what Graham might say? What if they threaten his kid?'

'We can't do that,' Clementine said. 'I can't leave those people to die.'

'But you'll run off and get the rest of us killed?' Aries snapped. 'We need to protect ourselves first. We have to come first.'

'She's right,' Nathan said. He'd been hanging out in the doorway but now he stepped into the room. 'We should be more concerned about maybe evacuating ourselves. We've got hurt people here. What about Jack? He can't exactly make a run for it. And that Emma girl is pretty messed up. We've got to try and protect them first.'

'But they might not be at Graham's place yet,' Clementine said. 'What about that? If they're still alive and we don't warn them—'

'If someone in Brandi's group blabbed, they'll have already torn the place to shreds,' Aries said. 'And if they torture Graham they'll be here next.' Ignoring Clementine's protests, she turned to Nathan. 'We all know what to do, right?'

Nathan nodded. 'I'll tell the others we're on high alert. Eve's out on watch. I'll go grab her and we'll do a street search. Keep your radio on. First sign of danger and we scramble.'

Aries nodded, thankful for all the sleepless nights when they'd sat around and planned their escape routes. After almost being defeated back in Gastown, they weren't going to make the same mistake again. They had multiple escape routes, all memorized by the entire group. Even Michael and Mason, who were AWOL, knew the routine. They knew where to go.

No one would ever be separated by accident. Funny, all that planning and they were still missing half their group. Everyone knew what to do if the safe house was attacked but no one knew what to do if someone simply didn't come home one day.

What about Daniel? That was simple. He didn't count. Aries knew that he'd manage to find her no matter where she went. He always seemed to know her next move, even before she made it.

Protect the group. Maintain focus. She liked Graham and his family but she had her own family to worry about. And Graham was six feet of pure muscle. He was also one of the rare people to have a gun. He could take care of himself. At least she hoped he could.

Meanwhile, she had a blind guy and a girl who was bleeding profusely and not a single person with enough medical knowhow to do anything.

'I need you to go and help Larisa,' Aries said to Clementine. 'You have to tell her to get ready. We may have to leave in a hurry.'

'That's it?' Clementine stamped her foot down hard on the tiled flooring. 'I don't get a say in this?

I just do what you tell me?'

Aries sighed. 'No, that's not it,' she said. 'Of course you have a say, but we have to be level-headed about this—'

'Oh right, I'm just the stupid blonde cheerleader – what the hell do I know.'

'That's not fair,' Aries said. 'You know I don't think you're dumb.'

Clementine stormed across the room until she was just inches away. Aries actually stepped backwards, unsure of her friend's next move. She heard Raj suck in his breath.

'We are letting a man die,' Clementine said. 'And his family. And you're just going to let it happen because the rest of us are oh-so-more important.'

Aries opened her mouth to retort but Clementine shouted at her. 'No, let me finish! You're in charge. Perfect Aries whom all the boys love. But what have you done to actually deserve this?'

'Excuse me?' Aries said. 'I've done just as much as everyone else. I've kept this group together. I've kept us all alive.'

Clementine's face was growing steadily pinker. 'But you've done nothing. You haven't watched your parents die. You haven't had to hide out while the boy you thought you loved stalked you, and tried to kill you. You didn't stab someone in the gut and feel his blood pour out on to your shirt.'

'I saw my best friend die and I kept everyone in the

school back then safe. I protected them.'

'Protected them?' Clementine snorted. 'That's the biggest lie of all. All you've done is hide. You've barely stepped outside since all this happened. Lucky you. You haven't even killed anyone yet.'

'That has nothing to do with this,' Aries said. She looked over towards Raj for help but the British guy had magically disappeared from the conversation. He must have retreated to the living room during all the accusations.

'It has everything to do with it,' Clementine said, refusing to stop. 'You play it safe – I get that. But you have no idea what it's really like out there. You're so bloody clueless.'

Aries stared at the anger in her friend's eyes and couldn't quite understand how this conversation had grown so dangerous. Clementine was her friend. At least she'd thought she was.

'And what about Mason?' Clementine asked. 'Or Daniel. Are you really going to rush to their defence if it compromises the group? You said last night you think Mason might be captured and down at the compound. What are you going to do if you find out that's true? Are you going to risk everyone's life to try and get him out? Doubtful. You'll probably say it's too dangerous and turn your back on him.'

'I'd never do that,' Aries said.

'What about Michael?' There was no stopping Clementine. Tears began to fall down her cheeks. She furiously wiped them away with the palm of her hand. 'Are you going to leave him out at UBC to die? Is he too risky? He might be dead as it is. Best to leave him and focus on more important things.'

'Of course not.'

'But you'll leave Graham and his family?'

'They're probably dead,' Aries shouted. She was getting tired of all these accusations. Clementine was trying to make her out to be a monster. How could she do this to her?

'You don't know that,' Clementine said.

'Yes,' Aries whispered. Her own tears were wet on her cheeks. 'I do know that. Because, regardless of what you believe, I know the Baggers. If they found out about Graham, they've already gone there and killed them. And we're wasting time here arguing about a dead man. For all we know, we're next.'

'How can you be so . . . so cold?' Clementine didn't wait for an answer. She turned and ran out of the room.

Aries listened for the door but she heard Clementine's feet on the stairs instead. She retreated to her bedroom and the muffled sound of the door slamming vibrated against the walls.

Aries stood in the middle of the kitchen, completely unsure what to do next. Eventually she grabbed some paper towel to wipe away the tears. It wouldn't do any good to have the others see her that way.

More than anything else in the world, she wished Mason were with her. He'd know what to say to make everything right. He'd find a way to calm Clementine down. Sure he didn't speak much, but when he did the others listened. They respected him. That was something that Aries suddenly discovered she was severely lacking.

Respect.

Colin laughed at her. He refused to do anything she asked and threatened her when she pushed.

Now Clementine was basically calling her a coward. How dare she.

Aries stormed up the stairs but stopped when she got to the top. She wanted to confront Clementine again, scream and yell at her, but she didn't have a clue what to actually say. Stopping at Jack's door, she thought about going to him for comfort but paused when she heard Joy's voice. Joy had been spending a lot of time with Jack lately.

She turned away and went back downstairs.

At the front door, she paused. Pulling the radio out, she turned it over in her hands. Maybe it was best to go check on Graham. It wouldn't take long, just a few minutes to run on over. Then she could go back to Clementine and prove that she wasn't the bad guy after all.

'Nathan, are you there?' Her breath made a scratchy sound when she breathed into the radio.

'Yeah, it's all clear out here.'

'OK,' she said. 'Meet me at the end of the block. I need you to come with me. We're gonna take a trip. Just you and me.'

'OK,' his voice said, sounding far away.

They'd only be a few minutes. Just enough time to determine the situation. If everyone was dead, she'd be able to relax knowing she was right. If they were alive, she'd be able to warn them and be the hero a leader needed to be.

Either way she couldn't lose.

She looked forward to hearing Clementine's apology.

Graham's safe house was on the corner of what used to be a very busy intersection. Gone were the long lines of cars, the honking horns, the impatient drivers who wanted to get home after a long day at work.

Aside from a few abandoned vehicles, Granville Street was empty.

Aries and Nathan sat crouched behind a monster Hummer. One of its tyres was flat, and its passenger door was open. There was dried blood on the dashboard and cracks in the glass. It rested halfway up on the pavement, the front bumper embedded in a stone gate. Whoever had been driving must have been speeding and not wearing their seatbelt.

Safety first.

'Do you see anything?' Nathan peered round the front of the Hummer. His baseball bat rested between his knees.

They both studied the darkened house.

'No,' Aries said. 'But that doesn't mean anything, right? We're too far back to tell. The doors are closed.'

Nathan frowned. 'I don't know. There's no one on guard. It's exactly the same as Clementine said about Brandi's place. I think maybe we should go back.'

Aries stood up. Clementine's accusations were still running through her mind. Her cheeks burned as she remembered the words. Clementine had called her a coward. A lousy leader. Well, maybe not in those exact words but the implications were there. Aries couldn't let it go. She needed to prove that she was more than just a clever girl who was really good at hiding.

'We can't,' she said. 'I'm not leaving until I know for sure.'

Nathan sighed. 'You're the boss. But, for the record, I don't like it. How do we know they're not on their way to our place right now?'

'We would have seen them,' she snapped. 'There's only one direct route to our place from here and we took it. The Baggers aren't going to sneak along the side streets. They have no reason to be cautious.'

'I've still got a bad feeling about this.'

Aries didn't. She felt exhilarated. The adrenaline coursed through her veins. If there were Baggers inside, she'd kill each and every one of them. That would prove to Clementine that she was strong enough to lead the group. It might even make Colin respect her a little bit.

'She didn't mean to hurt you,' Nathan said. 'Really, Aries. You should let this one go.'

She shook her head. 'Come on.' Without waiting for a response, she moved round the Hummer and headed across the street. Nathan's footsteps slapped the concrete behind her.

She knew she was being reckless but she couldn't seem to stop herself. Clementine was right; she'd spent too much time refusing to take any chances. And there was still a chance that Graham and his family were safe behind those walls. The more she thought about it, the more positive she felt. She was going to warn them, become the hero and save the day.

Leaders took risks. They made dangerous decisions that sometimes cost people their lives. This was war and the Baggers were the ones making the rules. She needed to learn to play their game.

The front door was slightly open when they approached.

She didn't stop to think about it. She ignored the little voice in the back of her head screaming at her to stop being such an idiot.

Bringing her kitchen knife higher up against her chest, she pushed open the door and stepped inside.

The door opened only halfway. Something blocked it. Putting her entire weight against it, she shoved on the wood until the mystery thing behind it shifted. A body made a squishing noise as it rolled back towards the stairs. The smell hit her face and Aries involuntarily stepped backwards and into Nathan, gagging.

Clementine was right – she really was too sheltered. She'd been around dead bodies lately; even the smell of decay at her parents' house was still etched in her mind.

But this was the first time she'd ever been up close and personal to something so fresh.

So wet.

'It's Graham's wife,' Nathan said in a small voice. 'I can't remember her name.'

'Me neither,' she said, and that angered her even more.

'Think anyone's still alive?'

She straightened her back and took a deep breath. She could do this. She was strong, no matter what others thought. 'Let's find out, but be quick. We need to get back and make sure the others are safe.'

She turned up the volume on her two-way radio but it remained silent. Aries knew that Eve, Joy and Jack were on the other end and it made her feel a little better. If something had happened, they would have contacted her by now.

Aries stepped past Graham's wife, nothing she could do about her now. Trying not to notice how the woman's chest was ripped open, she headed up the stairs first. They checked the bedrooms quickly but there were no signs of death on the second floor.

Graham was in the living room, face down on the carpet. Someone had shot him in the back of the head. He'd crashed into the bookshelf on the way down; dozens of books and DVD movies were scattered around him.

'There are three bodies in the kitchen,' Nathan said as he came through the dining room. 'Elderly people. There are no signs of the kid.'

Aries nodded. There hadn't been a single clue to suggest that Graham's little girl was still here. 'They must have taken her.'

'Were there any others?'

'Yeah, another girl in her twenties. They probably took her too.'

Nathan grimaced. Obviously he was thinking the exact same thing as her. The Baggers had killed the old and the men and taken the little girl and the young woman. It didn't get much creepier than that.

'We should leave,' Nathan said. 'Aries?'

She didn't get a chance to respond.

Nathan didn't even see it coming but she had a full view. The dining-room door was open and the Bagger slipped through without making a sound. He crossed the few steps towards Nathan before she could even open her mouth in surprise. She didn't even have time to gasp.

Nathan looked at her, a puzzled expression on his face. His eyes widened when the Bagger grabbed him by the face.

One violent twist.

A loud cracking noise. Nathan dropping to the floor, the surprised look etched on his face forever.

She might have screamed, she wasn't sure – she couldn't hear anything but at the same time the world had grown extremely loud. Lifting her knife, she jumped forward, throwing herself on the

Bagger before Nathan's body even finished hitting the ground.

The Bagger tried to swat her away but she was too quick. Adrenaline pounding through her veins, she raised her knife and pushed it straight into the Bagger's chest. Blood squirted out in all directions, spraying her face, soaking her shirt.

This time she did scream, a long sickening wail that surprised her. It wasn't even her voice. It belonged to someone else – it had to, she wasn't capable of making such a noise.

She shoved the Bagger backwards, leaving him to clutch at his chest, trying to remove the kitchen knife that stuck straight out of his body, while gagging on his own blood as he crashed into the dining-room table. Dropping down on her knees, she grabbed at Nathan, pulling him against her body, trying to will her own life into his.

'Don't be dead. Oh, dear God, don't be dead,' she whispered. Her throat was already sore and when she swallowed it was like she'd eaten glass.

His blue eyes stared up at her in surprise.

But there was no light in them.

She wasn't overly surprised when the pair of dirty running shoes stepped out in front of her. Looking up, she saw another Bagger staring down at her. He was smiling, a ragged Santa hat perched on top of his filthy hair. In his hands was one of the largest guns she'd ever seen in her life. Behind him was a second Bagger, a woman with bleached blonde hair and two inches of brown roots.

'Merry Christmas,' the first one said.

She had no weapon. It was still sticking out of the Bagger rolling around on the floor past her reach.

She closed her eyes.

MASON

They brought Daniel to him around eight in the evening. The Baggers unceremoniously opened the tent flap and dropped him on the ground by Mason's feet. One of the Baggers smiled, his teeth crooked and rotting. The decay on his breath instantly permeated the tent. Before he left, he gave Daniel one final kick in the side.

Daniel looked bad.

'Jesus, man,' Mason said as he bent down over his friend. 'What the hell did they do to you?'

'Invited me to dinner,' Daniel said. 'Got a little pissy when I declined. Apparently I lack in the table-manners department.'

Mason bit back laughter.

Daniel's nose was bleeding and his cheek was puffy but aside from that his face was untouched. He groaned and brought his arms in to cradle his stomach when he slowly raised himself into a sitting position. His dark eyes glazed over slightly as he winced in pain. Mason noticed that his ankles were bare.

'Here,' Mason said. He tossed a roll of toilet paper at Daniel. Chaplin had come by earlier and grudgingly given him some supplies. A ratty blanket covered in dead leaves and dust. A bowl. A cup. A roll of toilet paper. Everything he needed to survive. Apparently.

'They're hired goons,' Daniel said as he ripped off a few sheets of toilet roll and dabbed at the blood on his cheek. 'Just like some bad movie. Dark room. Tied down to a chair. All that was missing was the single light bulb burning right above my head. Did some massive sculpting on my chest but left my pretty face. I guess they figure I still need the ladies. Don't think I'll be running that triathlon any time soon.'

'You're a real comedian,' Mason said.

'Only with you,' Daniel said as he looked around the tent. 'Did you know that, Tourist Boy? I never kid with Aries. She thinks I'm the most serious guy in the world. I wonder why that is. Could be I have multiple personalities.'

Mason frowned. Maybe they'd smacked Daniel around a few times in the skull department. It was a little hard to tell.

There was a long pause while Daniel studied Mason's expression.

'You like her, don't you,' Daniel continued.

'Who?'

'Aries, you dolt.'

Mason didn't say anything. He didn't see any point in continuing the conversation. Aries wasn't someone he wanted to talk about, especially not with Daniel.

'It's obvious,' Daniel said. 'You sometimes get this really stupid expression on your face when I mention her name. Probably a good thing too. You'd be a hell of a better guy for her than me. You're a decent man, Dowell.'

Mason grabbed his plate and cup, and stood up. 'I'm going to get some food. Want me to bring you something back?'

'No, I'm cool,' Daniel said, and he winced again. Lying back down on the ground, he reached for the dirty towel and shoved it beneath his head. 'Doubt I'd be able to keep anything down. Think I'll just have a bit of a nap instead.'

Mason shrugged and headed out into the night.

Almost everyone had left their tents and gone over towards the kitchen area where it seemed a few of the camp residents had managed to scrape something together that might be vaguely edible. A giant pot was simmering over an open fire and a woman with long hair was doling out a small amount of what looked like cabbage soup. Another person stood beside her, handing out pieces of bread. There was nothing else. Not even salt and pepper. Over by the big tables, there was a bucket filled with water and people could dip their mugs in to get a drink.

Most of the women and children were already sitting down with bowls of food. Because of the lack of silverware, they resorted to lifting their bowls to their lips or using their fingers and bits of bread to scoop out the scraps of cabbage. The only people left in the queue were men and Mason lined up behind them. He saw Chaplin but the older man was too far ahead, chatting with a group of people, his back to Mason.

Then Mason saw someone else.

Every little bit of civility left his body in a single second.

He was barely aware that he had dropped his cup and bowl, unaware that he'd pushed past several people in the queue, but he was wide awake when he stopped in front of the insanely tall guy he'd spotted, raised his fist and popped him right in the mouth with all his strength.

Shouts came at him from all directions. Men surged both forward and away from him at the same time. Someone grabbed him from behind but Mason shrugged them off.

'You bastard!' Mason's voice was hoarse and filled with sorrow.

The tall guy blinked twice. He didn't say anything. Instead, he stepped forward and put his arms behind his back.

'Hit me again,' he said.

Mason did. He hit him several times before the other prisoners finally managed to pull him away kicking and screaming.

There was no ice at the camp but someone had been nice enough to wrap his hand with a cold wet cloth. His broken fingers burned with pain but he tried to ignore it. Not his brightest moment, hitting someone when his bones were already broken. He'd probably done yet more damage. It sure felt like it.

He's gone. He left me. Us.

The words of a ghost echoed in the back of his brain. Paul.

The overly tall First Nations guy sat silently across the table from him. The other prisoners had given them some space to talk, but the men remained close enough, just in case Mason went ballistic again.

But he wouldn't. The blinding anger had already left his body. Now he sat, calmly rubbing his good fingers round the vial of sand in his pocket. The last conversation they'd shared was back in Banff when Paul had told the story about the Indian Warrior who left behind the only woman he ever loved. Then, without a word to anyone, Paul had snuck out into the night, leaving Chickadee alone. Well, with Mason, but without her closest childhood friend.

'When did she die?'

'Not long after you left,' Mason said. 'We made it to Hope.'

'She really liked Hope,' Paul said. 'She had a great story about the campground there. Something involving the biggest spider she'd ever seen and being stuck in her sleeping bag while it crawled across her pillow.'

They were both silent for a while. In the corner of the camp, the last remaining stragglers washed their dinner plates.

'Was it quick?'

Mason nodded. 'Quick for her. Slow as hell for me.'

'I'm sorry,' Paul said. 'I hope you buried her.'

'Of course I did,' Mason snapped. 'I wasn't the one who left her.'

He remembered the blisters on his hands and how the sun had been shining so brightly in the sky that morning. He'd wrapped her body carefully in the hotel sheets, plain white with a cigarette burn in the corner. Then he'd had the conversation with the stupid Bagger. He couldn't forget how the guy had terrified him.

You ain't figured it out yet. You belong on our side, boy. You're just the kind of human they like.

When he'd looked in the mirror, he'd believed he'd see the black veins staring back at him. He'd expected to see the monster inside. He still did.

'Why'd you do it? Why'd you leave her?'

'Don't you remember my story?' Paul looked at him carefully. 'The Indian Warrior? He couldn't stand to watch the love of his life die, so he left.'

Chaplin came over with mugs of hot coffee and put them on the table. He gave Mason a curious glance but didn't ask any questions. He was probably worried that the rumours were right and Mason's eyes were turning blacker than a moonless night. Mason gave him a look back that he hoped said he wasn't going to start any more trouble. Chaplin nodded and rejoined the circle of onlookers.

'And that makes everything OK?' Mason finally asked.

Paul absently turned his coffee mug round in his

hands. 'No, but it explains my actions.'

'Yeah, but this wasn't a story,' Mason said. 'And Chickadee wasn't a fictional character. You killed her.'

Paul's eyes flashed anger. 'The disease killed her.'

'Your running away didn't help.'

They stared at each other. Out of the corner of his eye, Mason watched the crowd of hovering men tense in anticipation.

'All actions have consequences,' Paul finally said. 'The warrior in the story turned to stone for all his selfishness. Don't think for a second that I walked away without losing a bit of my soul.'

'Don't you dare,' Mason said. His voice was unnaturally low and calm. 'You aren't allowed to feel pity. And you can't grieve for her. You took the coward's way out. Turning you to stone would only be rewarding you.'

Mason stood up and started walking away. The group of men parted as he moved towards them. Everyone was silent.

'For the record, I'm glad it was you,' Paul called out to him. 'She really liked you.'

Mason wanted to point out that Chickadee deserved to die surrounded by her entire family and all the friends in her life. She shouldn't have spent her last few hours locked away in a dusty hotel room with only Mason there to helplessly hold her hand.

Better yet, she should have died an old woman,

surrounded by her children and grandchildren. She should have been a legend.

Someone should have given her the world.

But she was dead. Buried in a shallow grave where only Mason would be able to mourn her properly.

He could have told all of this to Paul but he didn't. He didn't see the point.

Wishing wouldn't bring her back. And guilt was the biggest regret. He'd seen Paul's eyes. He wouldn't feel sorry for him, but he understood.

Daniel was asleep when he got back to the tent. Someone had dropped off another blanket, a bright pink one with a horrific flowered pattern, and Mason carefully covered him up. Daniel stirred a bit, stuck in his own dark dreams judging by the stressed expression on his face. Mind you, no one dreamed of puppies and kittens these days. Too wired to lie down, Mason instead went back into the main compound area and started walking aimlessly around the camp.

Thankfully it wasn't raining but the night was cold. He could see his breath when he exhaled, a white cloud of mist disappearing into the atmosphere. He wished he had a better jacket; his hoody didn't do much to keep out the chill. His entire body was in a constant state of dampness. But there were a lot of people worse off. He'd seen several men and women who had only thin shirts. A few of them walked around wrapped in blankets and he'd seen a woman in nothing but a very sheer summer dress.

The Baggers had promised sanctuary to all those who came. They'd promised food and shelter and a safe place to rest one's head. But obviously no one had been allowed to pack overnight bags and the limited amount of supplies was a downright joke.

And, according to what he'd seen, the working conditions were abysmal. The saying 'worked to death' was beginning to take on new meaning. The Baggers obviously had their plans for how they wanted the world to be now, and they were putting them into action, with or without willing normal-human help. Who knew what would happen after that? Mason had a strong suspicion that it wouldn't be good for the non-Baggers.

Stopping along the fence line, he stared out at the water, ignoring the Bagger guard who watched him from several feet away, his finger lazily resting on the machine gun's trigger.

From his position, he could see the boats floating in False Creek. They bobbed gently on the waves, empty vessels haunting the harbour. Wouldn't it be nice to board one and sail off to nowhere?

He didn't want to think about Chickadee any more so he imagined Aries standing at the bow, wearing a sundress, her hair catching in the breeze. No land in sight, nothing but miles of sparkling blue waves. She'd turn and smile at him, the sunlight warming her skin. He'd be wearing something summery and stupid, a pair of Bermuda shorts and a straw hat. She'd smile as he approached her, maybe he'd be holding some sunscreen lotion or tropical drinks. She'd reach out and take his hand in hers.

No, he didn't deserve this daydream. Aries was a good person and she didn't need someone like him. He was better off doing what he always did. So much easier to live within the walls he'd built up around himself. Safer. For everyone.

The sound of a vehicle approaching made him turn his attention reluctantly back to the camp. A few of the white vans were returning. Mason's guard stopped paying attention to him and moved with the other Baggers towards the gate to let them in. Several of the prisoners popped out of their tents to come over and watch from a distance.

The first van came to a complete stop. Two Baggers jumped out and went round and opened the side door. Inside, the back of the van was packed full of people. They were roughly herded out and led over to the stage where other Baggers started forcing them to line up.

Mason moved alongside Chaplin who stood close to the stage, a tight-lipped frown on his face.

'What's happening?' Mason asked.

'Bad things,' Chaplin said. 'You may not want to watch. Not everyone can handle it. Just pray that no one you know is in that group.'

Mason waited. When the Baggers finished, there were about fifteen people on the stage. A collection of survivors stood nervously, mostly women and a few men, their eyes moving from the Baggers to the group of prisoners who waited tensely.

A woman in the crowd began screaming; she had recognized someone. The man on the stage stepped forward when he heard her cries, but was stopped by a Bagger savagely using his machine gun as a baseball bat. The man's kneecap popped under the force of the metal. He fell to the ground in a heap.

The woman continued screaming and finally some of the other prisoners forcibly carried her away to the back of the crowd.

Mason's eyes were diverted back to the stage. There was a little girl standing at the end of the line. Her face was downcast as she played with the zipper on her dirty pink-and-purple jacket. He recognized her immediately. He quickly scanned the rest of the group but Graham and his wife weren't among the crowd. His stomach churned uneasily. If they'd found Graham's safe house, did that mean they'd found Aries and the others?

'I know that girl,' he said.

'Which one?' Chaplin asked. 'The child?'

Mason nodded.

'Better pray you get reunited with her.'

'What's that supposed to—'

He didn't get a chance to finish. The closest Bagger raised his rifle up to the sky and fired off a shot. The uneasy crowd grew instantly quiet.

The Baggers began moving across the stage, stopping

at each prisoner to study them. They poked some people to check for injuries and even forced one man to take off his shirt so they could check out his chest. They asked questions but the words couldn't be heard over the murmuring of the crowd. Some of the prisoners onstage were picked out and pushed back against the wall. Others were pulled forward and shoved off the stage where someone from the crowd would dart forward and lead them back to safety.

Mason began to understand. The fallen man with the broken kneecap was dragged back against the wall and the woman in the crowd began shrieking like a crazed banshee. One of the Baggers turned his machine gun on the crowd, pointing it warningly. Several men grabbed the woman and dragged her away from the scene. They carried her off into one of the tents but her cries could still be heard although everyone pretended to ignore them.

The Baggers finally approached Graham's little girl and Mason held his breath. Relief swept over him as one of the monsters yanked her forward, tossing her off the stage. Mason broke away from the crowd, reaching her first. He put his arms around her, picking her up in a quick sweep.

'Hey,' he said as cheerfully as possible. 'You remember me, right?'

The little girl rubbed her fingers against her teary eyes and nodded shyly.

'I'm going to take care of you,' Mason said. 'No one

is going to hurt you. You're safe with me.'

The little girl, her name was Casey if Mason remembered correctly, dug her tiny fingers into the fabric of his hoody and held on with all her might.

He turned, ready to walk away from the crowd, but the show wasn't over. The guards had gone into the gathered crowd and were searching for someone. They pushed prisoners aside, hitting them with baseball bats and the butt end of their guns until they finally grabbed someone. As they pulled him up to the stage, Mason recognized Paul. People began murmuring and there were some angry shouts from the men at the back.

'It's because of you,' Chaplin said beside him.

'Me? What did I do?'

'They don't like fighting.' Chaplin turned and spat on the ground. 'They want us docile. Subdued. If we fight among ourselves, it's only a matter of time before the uprising begins.'

'Why aren't they coming for me then?' Mason scanned the crowd. The Baggers weren't even close. They were returning to the stage without so much as a glance in his direction.

'No idea. Maybe what the others say is true. Maybe you are a spy. But it's not too late. You might be able to stop it.'

Mason stepped back towards the stage, completely unsure of what he could say or do. The child in his arms grew suddenly heavy and he shifted her fragile body to try to distribute her weight more evenly. The Baggers paused, their guns positioned in their arms. They were obviously amused, eager to listen to Mason beg for the other man's life.

Then Paul's eyes met his.

And Mason understood.

There was pain there. Pain and regret and a soul that couldn't be repaired. A warrior who'd spent thousands of years as a stone statue. Now he was waiting for his destiny to appear.

Paul didn't want Mason to save him.

Mason nodded.

The taller guy gave him a slight smile before looking away.

Mason walked back towards Chaplin, ignoring the angry cries and protests that burst from the crowd. He'd done the unthinkable. No one was going to forgive him for this. No one except the person standing on the stage.

Casey leaned her head against Mason's chest. He could see the tiny little pink-and-blue hair clip hidden in the mess of tangles at the back of her neck. He could feel her breath on his skin and the softness of her fingers on his arm. There was only one thing left to do. Mason needed to get Casey out of there before the bullets started flying.

'Where can I take her?'

'Come on,' Chaplin said. 'We've got a bit of a daycare set up over by the toilets. Lots of other kids there. It'll be the best place for her.'

Mason nodded. He allowed Chaplin to lead him through the crowd. Someone spat on him as he walked past. Other people hissed obscenities under their breath. Another voice said they wished he'd die.

The Baggers finished thinning out the line on the stage. They brought their guns down on the remaining few while the audience watched helplessly.

I will not flinch. I will not flinch. I will not flinch.

Mason's hands clenched tighter against Casey's jacket and he pressed her head down into his shoulder. There were several long seconds of silence before the guns finally fired.

MICHAEL

It took a bit of coaxing before the blond stranger finally stopped rolling around on the floor and covering his head with his hands. It took even longer to get him to stop pleading for his life. When he finally looked up, his face held a mixture of embarrassment and contempt, not overly impressed with Michael and Ryder's laughing spell.

'I'm so sorry, man,' Michael said between hiccups. 'It's just too funny. Not you, dude, me.' He waved his hand blender around before chucking it into the corner by an empty trash bin. 'Seriously? I'm standing in the middle of a kitchen, which is probably full of knives and cast-iron frying pans, and all I could pick up was that?'

Michael had his flashlight turned on and a small amount of light bounced off the ceiling. His batteries were beginning to die. Not good. Now if only he could stop laughing he might be able to think about their next step.

He went over to the closed door and opened it, glancing carefully down the hallway of the Longhouse. It was dark now so he wouldn't be able to head out and search for supplies.

'I've got candles,' the blond said, reading his mind.

He yanked his backpack off his shoulders and rummaged around until he produced a few long white sticks. 'I've got food too,' he added. 'Mostly crisps and chocolate bars. Got a few bottles of water and some Pepsi. Been living off the vending machines in the student buildings. Not much but better than nothing. You're welcome to whatever I have.'

'Amen to that, brother,' Michael said. His stomach had been grumbling for most of the afternoon. He hadn't eaten anything since forever. Vaguely he remembered someone giving him a stale Twinkie at the museum but that had been over twenty-four hours ago. 'We've got nothing.'

Ryder gave him a discreet kick with his shoe. Right. They still didn't know anything about this guy. Best not to look so eager.

With the door firmly locked, the three of them sat down on the floor. Flickering light reflected off the refrigerator, giving the room a slightly cheerful atmosphere. Anything was better than nothing. The blond tossed Michael a small bag of crisps and a can of Pepsi.

'No thanks,' Ryder said when he was offered some Doritos. 'Not hungry.'

'Really?' Michael studied him, wondering if he was really going to be that stubborn or if there was actually something wrong with him. Ryder was looking quite pale, even with all the shadows half covering his face. But with his wrecked ankle, he was going to need every ounce of strength, even if that meant forcing down a chocolate bar or two.

'What I really need are drugs,' Ryder said, gently stretching his foot up and down. 'It's getting worse.'

'Wish I could say I was a doctor,' the blond said. 'But I'm just a computer techie wannabe, and a lousy one at that. Unless you've got a hard drive that needs debugging, I'm pretty much useless in this new world. Can't even chop wood.'

'You've made it this long,' Ryder said with a grimace. 'That's got to count for something. Don't sell yourself short.'

The guy nodded. 'I had a lot of help. A good friend of mine kept me safe. He had a much better head for this sort of thing. But he's gone. Happened right after the nut jobs came on campus. He just disappeared one day.'

'So you've been here a while then?' Ryder asked.

The blond nodded. 'A little over a month I think.' He shrugged. 'I haven't seen a calendar in ages. Can't be certain. Why do you ask?'

'Just surprised we haven't crossed paths,' Ryder said. 'I've been running a group here. We've been pulling people off campus and giving them a safe place to hang. At least until last night.' He gave Michael a snide glance. 'We've made several sweeps of the grounds. Thought we'd pretty much found everyone there was to find.'

'Guess not,' the blond said.

'Yeah,' Ryder said. 'Guess not.'

The tone in Ryder's voice was unmistakable. But then again, considering he'd also accused Michael of being a Bagger, his radar was clearly a little damaged. It was obvious he didn't trust the new guy but Michael didn't think there was reason to worry. No one could fake that kind of panic and the guy had literally almost peed his pants at the sight of that hand blender.

But, just to double-check, Michael started playing with his almost dead flashlight, pretending to accidently draw the beam of light across the stranger's face. A pair of blue eyes winced at the direct contact. Blue eyes. No black veins.

Nothing to worry about.

'Do you think there's a bathroom here?' the blond suddenly asked. 'When I saw those crazies, I grabbed the keys and tried the first door I found. No time for a toilet break.'

'There's one across the hallway,' Michael said, remembering seeing the washroom signs from earlier. 'Not sure if it's safe though. I didn't spot anyone a few minutes ago but that doesn't mean the Baggers aren't still around.'

'Baggers?' The guy grinned. 'Interesting name. Haven't heard that one before.' He climbed to his feet. 'I'll take my chances.'

'Leave your keys,' Ryder said.

The blond gave them both a puzzled look.

'You can knock when you're done,' Ryder said. 'Leave them. I'm not taking any chances.'

The guy pulled the set of keys out of his pocket and dropped them on the counter without a second thought.

Michael waited till he disappeared through the door. 'What the hell?' he asked. 'What's your problem? He's not one of them. Didn't you see his eyes?'

'Just because his eyes aren't black doesn't mean he's not working for them, or even one of them,' Ryder exclaimed. 'Some of them can hide it. I don't understand how you're not dead in a ditch somewhere. You can't trust anyone. How do you not get that?'

'Not everyone is the enemy.'

'Everyone is my enemy,' Ryder said, leaning forward, pulling up the leg of his jeans to check his ankle. 'How do you think they managed to pull this off? Do you not think about that? Within a matter of weeks, these monsters managed to kill almost the entire population. Not just here but across the whole world. Why? Because we were too stupid and we trusted them. We ignored warning signs. We ignored everything! And you're sitting here pretending like none of this happened and it's perfectly all right to become best friends with the first stranger that comes through the doors? And why? Because he screams like a girl?'

'That's not it at all,' Michael said, feeling the heat rising in his cheeks.

'You're an idiot and it's a miracle you're not dead.'

Michael stood up, bits of discarded crisps falling from his shirt. 'You're really beginning to annoy me. I don't know how on earth you managed to lead a big group like you did, especially when it was obvious that no one actually liked you.'

'They didn't need to like me,' Ryder said. 'They respected me and listened because I kept them alive. I didn't take chances, except with you and your girlfriend. Look where that put us.'

'I'm not a Bagger,' Michael said as his fists clenched involuntarily at his side.

'You're no leader either.'

That hit below the belt. Ryder couldn't possibly have known about what had happened back at the cottage. He didn't know that Michael had taken the cowardly way out and run away, leaving his friends to die.

Evans.

Billy.

The woman with the sick child.

Michael had tried to lead them to safety. But at the first sign of real trouble he'd run away while his entire group was slaughtered.

Ryder couldn't possibly know about them.

But he sure knew the truth. Michael was no leader. And he was right, no matter how much Michael wished it wasn't so.

A soft knock at the door announced the return of the blond-haired stranger. Michael didn't even bother to wait for Ryder's response. He went over and opened the door with a wide, swooping motion.

The blond was alone.

No Baggers.

Trying hard not to give Ryder an 'I told you so' look, he returned to his place beside the candles and plopped down on the floor.

'Thanks,' the stranger said. 'I tried keeping my ears open. I don't think any of them are still in the building. It sounds pretty empty. Of course it's pitch black out there. Almost couldn't find the toilet to pee in.'

'We'll have to wait until morning,' Michael said. 'I can't stay here longer.' He suddenly didn't care so much about Ryder and his ankle. 'I've got people waiting for me. I should have been back ages ago as it is.'

The stranger sat back down on the floor and began rummaging through his backpack. 'I didn't get your names,' he said as he pulled out a Snickers bar. 'I'm Heath.'

'Heath?' Michael perked his head up. 'As in, Heath White?'

The chocolate bar paused halfway to the stranger's lips. 'Yeah. How did you know that?'

An excited jolt tore through Michael's stomach. 'You're Clementine's brother.'

Heath's eyes grew wide. 'You know Clem? How is that possible?'

Michael jumped up; he couldn't contain his excitement level sitting around. 'Oh man, oh man, you have no idea how happy she's going to be. We've been searching for you forever. We travelled from Montana, where I met her. We were at your dorm in Seattle. It was your letter that led us here.'

'She read my letter?' Heath jumped up to join him. 'I can't believe it. I never expected . . . well, I hoped she was still alive, but I never expected her to come.'

Ryder stayed on the ground, slowly shaking his head in disbelief.

'This is amazing,' Michael said. He couldn't help himself. The biggest grin grew on his face. He wanted to grab Heath and give him a bear hug. Then they could dance around the room together. He couldn't wait to tell Clementine. Hell, he couldn't wait to show her!

'What about my parents?' Heath's eyes were excited and full of hope. 'Did they make it too?'

'No,' Michael paused. 'Sorry. They died back in Glenmore. Clementine will tell you more about it.'

Heath nodded but the joyful expression never left his face. 'Yeah, I can't be greedy, can I? But I've got my sister and that's really all that matters. When can we go see her?'

Michael glanced back at Ryder. The safe house was a long way off for someone who couldn't walk. But there had to be a way to get them home safely without being hunted down by the Baggers.

'I'll get us back,' he said. 'I'm just not sure how yet.'

'We can drive,' Heath said.

Michael shook his head. 'Too risky. The Baggers are really set up around the area. Those crappy white vans. If we try to start a car, they'll hear us and come running. We'd only end up leading them right back to our place. There has to be another way.'

Heath grinned, his eyes sparkling in the candlelight. 'I think I know what we can do. I've got a great plan.'

They'd left Ryder back in the locked kitchen with the candles while he and Heath snuck out into the late night. It was a crazy idea but still a really good one, the more Michael thought about it.

It amazed him how peaceful the campus looked at night. With all the shadows covering everything up, the damage the earthquakes had left behind seemed secondary. The broken glass wasn't as depressing and the damaged buildings were more artistic than devastating.

They came across Clementine's message scrawled in spray paint outside the library. Heath got down on his knees and touched the cement.

'It's real,' he said. 'I mean, I know you told me, but I don't think it's fully sunk in yet. To see this though, her words, her writing, it's real.'

Michael nodded. He wondered what he would have felt like if he'd known his sister had travelled across the country to try and find him. Even though he and his sister didn't get along well (she was three years younger and way too crazy about boys in his opinion), he knew that he'd still have felt an insane amount of joy and relief. It would have been beautiful. To discover that anyone loved you enough to travel thousands of miles to find you in this new world was incredible.

Could it be possible that his family was still out there

and alive? OK? Mom and Kathy, his sister, were in New York when the earthquakes hit. Dad had been in Colorado on business. His parents had divorced when Michael was eight, Mom leaving for the big city because of a job offer of all things. They'd tried to keep things going for a while but it was too hard. As the years went by, the phone calls slowed and the holidays became more of a chore than a reunion.

He'd give anything to see them again now.

Michael had thought, several times during his journey west with Clementine, that his father might have actually made it back to Whitefish, Montana, where they shared a small apartment. Mentally, he'd kicked himself repeatedly for not leaving behind a note to say he was OK and where he was going. He should have done it. Heath's letter to Clementine had been the one thing that kept her going after they'd found his Seattle dorm empty. Why hadn't he thought to do that for his own father?

'We've been searching the university for a while now,' Michael finally said. 'Clementine never gave up hope. She kept pushing even though she knew the odds were not good. She really had faith in you being alive.'

'Amazing,' Heath said. 'I don't know if I could have done that. I can't wait to see her. It's going to be incredible.'

As dawn broke across the horizon, they found what they were looking for. A single white van, parked across from the Psychology building. There were two Baggers outside the building, one of them drinking a can of Sprite while the other used a crowbar to smash open the glass doors.

'We'll wait until they both go in,' Heath whispered. 'Then we'll take the van.'

'What if they have the keys?' Michael asked. 'I don't know about you but they didn't teach me hotwiring in high school.'

Heath grinned. 'They won't take the keys. There's no reason to. Do you really think they'll expect us cowardly normals to steal their ride? They're too arrogant for that.'

'They might have radios. They'll be able to let the others know the van is gone.'

'Not a chance,' Heath said. 'I've seen them up close. They're not using anything of the sort. This is going to be like taking candy from a baby.'

Michael wished he had Heath's confidence but he knew better than to expect things to be that easy. But it was still a good plan if they moved fast enough. Steal a white van, load up Ryder and head back to the safe house. Drop everyone off and then go toss the van somewhere a few blocks away where the Baggers wouldn't find it. Simple and easy. None of the Baggers would stop to chase down their own white van, especially if they could get that annoying message to start playing. It might give everyone at the safe house a bit of a scare when they heard the 'WARNING, WARNING' but all would be forgiven once they had the reunion.

Clementine was going to be so excited. Michael got goose bumps just thinking about it.

A loud shattering noise filled the morning air and the Sprite-drinking Bagger went to help his partner remove the remaining glass from the door. A few moments later, both of them disappeared into the building and it was time to jump into action.

'Keep low,' Michael warned, and they dodged round the side of a Toyota and headed for the van.

The inside was empty. Relief poured over Michael but it was momentary. They still had a long way to go. He jumped into the driver's seat.

Heath had been right. The keys were in the ignition.

'Unbelievable,' Michael muttered to himself.

The van started on the first try. Michael half expected the Baggers to come running out into the street, brought back by the sound of the engine. But as he put the vehicle into drive and pulled away nothing chased after them. They made it to the end of the block and turned the corner without any problems.

'Done and done,' Heath said. 'Let's go get your friend. And then let's go get my sister.'

'I can't believe how easy that was,' Michael said. 'If I had known, I would have done it ages ago. So much better than riding our bikes everywhere.'

Although he sounded happy on the outside, a nagging voice kept pushing its way up from the back of his mind. It was easy. Too easy. Michael knew from experience that nothing in this new world ever went that smoothly. But he forced the voice back down. It was always wise to be cautious but also to appreciate having a bit of good luck now and then.

Maybe finding Heath was the beginning of a long overdue run and things were going to be easier for a bit now.

It was a good morning. No rain in the sky and Michael was about to reunite the girl he loved with her brother.

Things were looking up.

CLEMENTINE

This wasn't the first time her temper had got her into trouble. Normally Clementine was easy-going – there were plenty of dead people back in Glenmore who could endorse that statement. She was the nicest, friendliest cheerleader that ever cheered the Goblins on to victory. But when she got mad she lost control. Every logical bone in her body went into serious hibernation.

She never should have had the fight with Aries. It had been utterly unfair; she shouldn't have allowed herself to take out her pain and frustration on her friend. She should have gone into a corner and counted to ten, or done anything that might have sent her blood pressure back down to a normal rate. Instead she'd allowed her anger to take control and she'd behaved like an absolute jerk. Aries was her friend. She didn't deserve to be treated that way.

Stupid! Stupid! Stupid!

And heartless, don't forget heartless.

Clementine also knew everything she said had been a lie. Well, maybe not all of it but she was wrong to say it the way she had. She'd been right when she said Aries had been comparatively lucky but that wasn't fair. True, Aries didn't wake in the middle of the night, sweating, from dreaming about the man she'd stabbed through the stomach with a letter opener. Unlike Clementine, she hadn't walked through a sea of hanging bodies in the small town she'd passed through just before she'd met Michael. But that didn't make Aries less of a hero. It didn't mean that her caution didn't, in fact, make her the perfect leader for the group.

But there was no time to apologize.

She'd followed Aries and Nathan over to Graham's house after Eve came running to find her.

'I couldn't stop them,' Eve said. 'Aries nearly took my head off when I said it was a bad idea. Do you think she's mad at me? She didn't tell me not to tell you.'

Clementine went to find Raj and told him to come with her.

The worst part was that Aries was right. Clementine had been enraged, beyond angry, ready to kill anyone who tried to tell her otherwise. But she'd calmed down quickly and once she'd thought it through logically she'd realized going to Graham's house when Brandi had specifically told them the Baggers were heading there was a bad idea. Child or no child, promise or no promise. Staying at the house and preparing for evacuation was the smarter thing to do.

There were sacrifices in war. The fewer casualties the better. But no matter how good their intentions people were going to die and there wasn't a damn thing anyone could do to stop it.

That sucked. Boy, did it suck. But no one ever said life was fair.

Aries was right. They couldn't save them all. But now Aries was trying to because Clementine had opened her big mouth and said the wrong thing.

Dear Heath, I've screwed up yet again. They should put that on my grave. Here lies Clementine – she screwed up a lot. But I can fix this, right? Right?

She didn't have an answer. All she could do was convince Raj to come with her to try to find Aries. Hopefully it wouldn't be too late.

The worst part was that even after all that a tiny voice in the back of her mind tried to convince her that Aries was doing this deliberately to steal her thunder. Aries was going to be the hero. She'd be the saviour of Graham's family, not Clementine.

Stop it. Look at me, Heath. I'm still that competitive. Remember how upset I was when I thought Imogene was going to make head cheerleader over me? I pouted for a week and you finally slapped me upside the head and told me to stop being so greedy. Give others a chance. Be the best I can be and give others a chance to do the same. Yadda yadda yadda. Am I really this shallow?

They weren't going to last long in this new world if they continued with all this petty bickering. No, they had to work together on everything. She knew this. Aries knew this. It was like Michael and Ryder too. She saw the way Michael both resented and admired the new guy's leadership skills.

They were falling apart. Was Clementine the only one who saw this? With some of them missing and others bickering, it was only a matter of time before the Baggers managed to break them down.

But Clementine wasn't going to go out without a bang.

She'd bring them all back together if it killed her.

Clementine froze at the kitchen door, unnoticed by both the Baggers and Aries. Raj was with her, his body pressed against hers, weapon poised and ready. She could feel the tenseness of his muscles as he waited for her to react.

When the Bagger raised his gun, the bells on top of his filthy Santa Claus hat jingled. She wanted to grab that hat and shove it down his ugly throat.

'Merry Christmas,' he said. 'Such a pretty present. Get up. I'm going to deliver you. I'll wrap you up with lots of bows. Leon will be pleased.'

Aries lay on the ground, her eyes glazed and staring at the unmoving body beside her. A small scream nearly burst through Clementine's gritted teeth when she realized who it was.

Nathan.

No time to mourn.

'So you're the infamous Aries,' the Bagger said. He was grinning from ear to ear. He pointed with the gun to Nathan lying on the floor. 'That's what he called you, right?'

'What do you mean?' Aries asked.

'Come on,' the Bagger said. He pressed the automatic

weapon against Aries's arm. 'Get up. You'll be joining your friends in no time. That ought to make a perfect Christmas for everyone.'

'Kill me,' Aries said. There were tears spilling from her eyes.

Clementine's heart stopped. No, she couldn't be giving up. Not after all she'd been through. Clementine wasn't going to allow that. Without thinking, she jumped forward, raising the taser she'd taken from Katarina.

She shoved past the female Bagger, knocking her into the wall and thrust the tiny machine right up against Christmas Hat's neck, pressing the button.

The filthy man jolted as his body went into convulsions. There was no noise. Just complete overwhelming silence as he did his death dance. The smell of burning flesh wafted up into her nostrils. Then the gun dropped from the Bagger's hands and Clementine finally let go. His body slumped to the floor, head cracking on the table as he went down. She pressed the machine into his still body one last time just to make sure.

'Damn,' Raj said from behind her. He bent down and picked up the machine gun, pointing it in the direction of the female Bagger who was cowering in the corner. 'I knew Ryder had some engineering guys juice those tasers up, but that's really something.'

'Aries.' Clementine was down on the ground beside her friend in seconds. 'I'm so sorry. I'm such a jerk. I take back everything I said. You were right. I was being stubborn and stupid. I was frustrated. I never meant for any of this to happen.'

'Nathan,' Aries said. Her eyes were glued to the still form on the floor. 'I can't. I didn't mean . . . It was so fast.'

Beside her, Raj knelt down to examine Nathan. Without taking his eyes off the remaining Bagger, he carefully turned the body over to check for a pulse. Maybe he wasn't dead. Maybe he was just unconscious. Optimism surged through her, but it was short-lived. Raj shook his head gently and looked at her momentarily. There was no hope in his eyes.

'How am I going to explain this to Eve?' Aries asked. Her voice was flat and unmoving. 'I killed him.'

'There's nothing to explain,' Clementine said. 'We'll just tell the truth. Eve will understand. You had nothing to do with it. You didn't kill him.'

'I brought him here,' she said.

'Only because I was too big-headed to realize you were right. If anyone should be held responsible for his death, it's me.' Clementine tried putting her arms round the other girl but Aries shoved her away. The three of them sat there on the floor, surrounded by the smell of death and blood, the house quiet and empty.

'How could I let this happen?' Aries finally asked. 'I've tried so hard. All I wanted was to keep everyone safe. I'm such a failure.'

'You're not a failure,' Clementine said. 'Without you

and your mad skills, we'd be lost. Can't you see how important you are?'

'I still killed him.'

Raj finally spoke. 'Actually, the Baggers killed him. Not us. We're just here. We're just surviving.' He raised the gun up a few inches as the female Bagger blew him a kiss. It took all of Clementine's will power not to go over and slap her hard.

'That's the biggest load of crap I ever heard,' Aries snapped. The anger in her eyes came burning through like wildfire, consuming her self-pity. 'I'm a complete idiot. Don't ever try to say it's not my fault. You were right, Clem, and I needed to hear it. I really have been lucky. I've done everything I can to avoid . . . everything. I'm nothing but a coward. And what happened when I tried to fix that? I got someone killed. Nathan's dead. What else is new? Others died in my group before. Back when we were hiding out at the theatre, I couldn't save them all. But I should have done something. I need to get better! Nathan was a good person. He didn't deserve this.'

Aries stood up and faced the nearest wall. There were family photographs, framed and assembled tastefully, all over it. Pictures of Graham's family doing various things. A day at the beach. Positioned around a Christmas tree. Meeting Belle from *Beauty and the Beast*.

Aries punched the wall with all her strength.

Clementine gasped when the first picture fell, hitting

the table below with a small thud.

Aries punched the wall again. And again. Her fists beat a steady rhythm as they cracked the plaster, leaving a white dust on her knuckles. Blood dripped and smeared both her skin and the white walls.

Raj stepped forward to stop her but Clementine grabbed his arm. Aries needed to get the pain out, and if this was the only way she wasn't about to stop it.

The punching went on for a good minute. When she finally stopped, her hand was already beginning to swell. It looked like Mason's hand from when the Baggers fractured his fingers back in Gastown.

'Now what do we do with this one?' Aries snapped as she turned her attention to their captive on the ground.

But the Bagger was no longer grinning in the corner.

She was rocking back and forth, her eyes wild and confused, talking to herself. 'No,' she said. 'Not true. Not true. I didn't mean to do it.'

'Do what?' Aries asked.

But the Bagger didn't hear her. 'So cold,' she whispered. 'Sleeping. I've been sleeping.'

'She's mad,' Raj said.

The Bagger suddenly jumped up and pushed forward, knocking Raj backwards. The gun went flying from his hand. Clementine rushed to retrieve it. The Bagger threw her arms round Aries and pulled her into an awkward kind of hug and then bolted out of the room before anyone could recover.

Raj was the first to speak. 'What the hell was that?'

'She was crying,' Aries said. 'It's almost like she was . . . normal for a second.'

'Or she just found a brilliant way to escape without any of us managing to shoot her,' Raj said. 'Should we go after her?'

'Let her go,' Aries said. 'I doubt she'll come back.'

Clementine went to Aries, put her arms round her and held her tightly. 'I'm such a tool,' she whispered. 'Can you forgive me?'

'No,' Aries said. 'I can't. I won't forgive myself either. But we can move on.'

Clementine nodded.

'First things first,' Aries said. 'We have to find the others. And we have to find Graham's little girl too. She's not here. The monsters took her. I will do whatever I can to get her back. I owe Graham that much. And I owe Nathan.'

'That's easy enough,' Clementine said. 'We know where Mason is now. And I'll bet that the little girl is with him.'

Aries's eyes widened. 'You know where Mason is? How?'

Clementine pointed to the dead Bagger on the floor. 'He told us. When he was pointing the gun at you. He recognized your name.'

'So?' She frowned.

'Then he said he wasn't going to kill you but take you to be reunited with your friends,' Clementine said. 'That can only mean one thing. Mason's at the compound at the Plaza of Nations. Maybe he gave them your name. They . . . could have tortured him. Or maybe they found out another way. Let's go rescue him and find out. You know what we have to do next.'

Raj smiled. 'Prison break, babes?'

Clementine raised her taser. 'As my father used to say – darn tooting!'

They took Nathan's body back.

'I'll dig the hole myself if I have to,' Aries said. 'I want to bury him in the garden by the wild flowers.'

'I'll help,' Clementine said. 'I'm sure we can find some shovels in the garage. If not, I'll go down to the Home Depot and get some.'

'We'll all help,' Raj said.

Raj didn't even have to be asked. He picked Nathan's body up and carried him the several blocks to the house. Aries and Clementine didn't want Eve to see him until they managed to talk to her first.

Luckily for them, Eve wasn't in the kitchen when they snuck in through the back door.

Joy came rushing over. 'Oh God,' she said.

'Help us,' Clementine said. 'Let's get him into the bedroom. We don't need the others to see just yet.'

They took the body upstairs and laid him down on the bed. Raj immediately headed out into the garage to look for shovels.

'What are we going to tell Eve?' Joy asked. There

were tears in her eyes, flowing down her cheeks and dripping off her chin.

'We'll figure something out,' Clementine said.

Aries went to open her mouth but Colin came into the room, a strange look on his annoying face. He was still holding that annoying Game Boy, the noise of Super Mario bouncing off the walls.

'One down,' Colin said in a soft voice. 'Your fan group is failing, Aries.'

Clementine stepped forward, fists clenched at her side but Joy suddenly pushed past her, rushing towards the door and Colin. The boy actually flinched, dropped the game system in an attempt to cover his face.

But Joy just pushed on past him and raced down the hall, slamming the door to the bathroom.

'You know what?' Clementine said. 'You're despicable. And not worth my time.' She pushed past him too, shoving him against the door with her shoulder. From down the hall, she could hear Joy throwing up. Hopefully into the garbage bin and not the toilet. Nothing flushed any more.

Aries broke the news to Eve, and Clementine was angry because she felt relieved at not having to be a part of it. Instead she went outside and helped Raj dig the grave. The work was hard and within minutes, her back felt like it was going to snap in two. But she refused to feel sorry for herself. Instead, she worked harder, savouring the blisters as they formed on her hands.

They worked in silence.

It gave her time to think. To prepare. Evacuation was on the back burner. They had to go get Mason now. If he was being tortured by the Baggers, unbearable as the thought was, it might only be a matter of time before he told them about this place. She would go on the assumption he hadn't said anything yet since the Baggers weren't already breaking down their door. But who knew how long he could last? Getting Mason out was going to be complicated though – they needed a solid plan.

As for Michael, she refused to allow herself to worry about him. He was safe. She would keep telling herself that. She would make herself believe it. And when they had Mason and Graham's little girl back she would head over to UBC and go through each and every building to find him. Even if she had to do it alone.

'We're going to need supplies. Weapons and other things,' she said to Raj once they'd dug a hole about four feet deep. It would have to do; neither of them had the strength to go any further. They'd wrap Nathan in blankets and maybe she could pick some flowers from the garden to cover him.

'We can get those,' he said.

'You don't have to come along,' she said. 'You don't even know Mason. You don't have to risk your neck. Everyone will understand.'

Raj snorted. 'You obviously don't know me, babes. Beneath this skinny chem student exterior is a hero at heart. And you're going to need me. I can do one thing that the rest of you can't.'

'What's that?'

Raj grinned. 'I can make things explode.'

NOTHING

She dances through the night air. With each step, lightning flashes from her eyes like diamonds, and thunder rages like a heart beating in love. Her feet move with an agility and grace that can never be replicated. The flowers float beneath her, raising their petals up towards her being. All things good and beautiful want to feel the warmth of her aura.

She's beautiful and I sit back and watch her dance. She's a light I can't touch. Her brilliance blinds my eyes but I still can't look away.

She's a song that I can't remember. The melody slips past my ears before I can memorize the progressions. She's the ending of a book I lost before reaching the final pages. She's everything good that can never be replaced and I don't think I can stand the feeling that makes me want to love her more and more with each passing moment.

She is a goddess.

She can't cure me.

I dream of her but my dreams are dark, and she's always one step out of reach. I want to find her but there are too many trees and I get lost easily. I'm left standing out in the rain, water pooling in my sneakers as she dances away in a sunlight that only shines over her beautiful hair and face.

She is not and can never be mine.

My darkness can't ever break through her charms. I must be strong and keep away. I don't want to make her wilt.

She is a song written for someone else.

MASON

Morning came, cold and clear, the sun a pale yellow and bleak as it pressed against the horizon.

Mason's arm was screaming as he shook his head to clear it of his strange dreams. He'd fallen asleep with his body curled around Casey, trying to keep her warm. She had one arm around him too, pressing her head against his shoulder while she sucked her thumb. The lack of mobility had caused his entire right side to prickle and burn. But he was afraid to move now, wanting to allow the child a little bit more sleep. At least this way she didn't have to deal with the pain.

Last night, after he'd dropped her off with the daycare workers, Casey had refused to let go of his jacket. Clenching tightly to him, she screamed as they tried to prise her fingers loose. So he'd had no choice but to sit down with her until she closed her eyes. Although some of the ladies offered to help free him once she finally fell asleep, he decided to stay there instead. He felt sorry for the tiny girl. Now a nerve in his lower back was pinched and his arm continued to scream but he still didn't move.

He was worried about the child's sudden attachment to him. He wasn't the best person for the job. She needed someone better, someone who could be . . .

trusted. Someone not wearing a tracker device.

Casey showing up at the camp alone meant only one thing. Graham and the rest of his group were obviously dead. Had they tortured the older man, trying to get information on Aries and the rest of them? As far as he knew, the Baggers hadn't brought anyone new in last night. He'd have to keep watch and hope that Graham had died a quick and silent death.

Through the morning shadows, a woman approached. She was a grandmotherly type, her hair in a loose bun, and she carried a cup of coffee in her hand.

'Here,' she said, lowering the drink towards him.

'Thanks.'

He took a sip and the warm liquid soothed his throat. Blinking several times, he drank again, trying to ward off the exhaustion wracking his body. How long had it been since he'd had some proper shut-eye? He couldn't even remember.

'You need to get some rest,' the woman said. 'The child is safe. I can promise you that. They don't bother with us. They never come in here. But you are going to be no good to her in your condition. I'll keep her safe until you return.'

Mason started to shake his head but paused. She was right. He needed at least a few hours. Putting the coffee cup down on the floor, he allowed the woman to help him lift Casey up and off his numbed arm. Together they carried the little girl over to the empty bed the woman had prepared.

Casey turned on to her side, still asleep, thumb still in her mouth.

'She's a lucky girl to have you,' the woman said. 'Rumours or not – I don't care what others say – you're a good boy. Being here tonight proves it.'

'Thanks,' Mason said. 'Tell her I'll be back in a few hours. If she wakes up scared, come get me. I don't mind.'

The woman smiled and gently nudged him in the direction of the door.

The morning air was sharp on his face. Breathing in, he watched his breath exhale in a puff of white mist. A few others were up, mostly women with children; they studied him carefully as he crossed the grounds towards his tent.

By the time he reached his destination, his feet dragged so badly that he stumbled trying to get through the tent flap.

Daniel was still asleep. Mason pulled one of the blankets off him, and tried to cover himself as best as possible.

'Good night?' Daniel's voice was quiet and muffled against the dirty towel.

'Yeah, thrilling,' Mason said.

'Get some sleep,' Daniel mumbled. He said a few more words but Mason didn't hear him. He was already too far gone.

Sleep took him hard.

*

He woke up to the Baggers standing over him, grabbing him by the arms and yanking him off the floor. Confused and half asleep, he didn't even try and fight as they dragged him across the grounds and into the casino.

He saw Daniel just before the casino doors closed. Standing alone, watching everything. The look of fear was strong on his face.

Mason wondered why Daniel was afraid. It wasn't him they were taking back into the casino. If anything, he should be relieved.

They returned him to the same room and cuffed his hands behind his back once more. Mason didn't even bother this time. He sat down in the chair and waited for Mr Leon.

Ten minutes passed. Finally the door opened and the head Bagger came in. He wasn't alone this time. He had another Bagger with him. This one wore a doctor's white lab coat and she was carrying a black bag. Mason was about to get a house call.

'Good morning, Mason,' Mr Leon said, his voice overly cheerful. 'Can I presume that you slept well?'

Mason had to keep himself from cringing. There was something in that voice that reminded him of fingers being raked down a blackboard.

'No?' Mr Leon went over to the desk and sat down on the edge. 'I heard you caused quite a commotion last night. Got one of your buddies killed. Of course rumour has it you beat the crap out of him first. Now is that any way to treat a friend?'

'That's how you knew about Chickadee,' Mason said. 'At least some of it. Paul told you, didn't he?'

Mr Leon flashed a perfect white-toothed smile. 'I'd rather say a little bird told me but that would be clichéd, now, wouldn't it?'

Mason shrugged.

'You don't get it?' Leon leaned in until he was inches away from Mason's face. 'Little bird? Chickadee? The thought alone is so cute. It brings joy and laughter to my soul.'

'Things like you have no soul.'

Mr Leon laughed. 'I do like the way you bring personality to a room, Mr Dowell,' he said. 'But, no, your friend Paul didn't give away your secret. I'm not about to tell you who or what did either. I do need to maintain my air of mystique. Remember, I can read your mind. How else am I to keep you cowering at my feet?' He turned and nodded to the doctor Bagger who came over and placed her medical bag on the desk, pressing the latches simultaneously.

'Of course,' Leon said, 'she's going to help too. She's here to make you sing. Just like a little bird.'

Now it was Mason's turn to grin. 'Never gonna happen.'

Mr Leon wasn't fazed in the slightest. 'Never say never, Mr Dowell. And I can guarantee you won't be so cheerful once you hear my news.'

The room grew silent while Mr Leon waited for Mason to take the bait. But Mason wasn't playing the game. Beside the head Bagger, the doctor began to unpack her bag. She started by pulling out a long scalpel, holding it admiringly up to the light. Next came a hand-held device. Long and thin with an electrical box on one end, metal tips on the other. Mason recognized it immediately from spending summers at his grandparents' farm in southern Saskatchewan.

A cattle prod.

Mason's body betrayed him, going completely against his mind. He straightened up in his chair and strained back against the wood, his feet pressed firmly into the ground. He couldn't take his eyes away from the instrument.

Mr Leon smiled even wider. 'You know what that is? I'm not surprised. You are a country boy. Raised in the big ol' farming community? How many cows have you tipped?'

Mason ignored him, angry at his own inability to keep his eyes off the doctor.

The doctor Bagger came round the table, holding the cattle prod. She placed the metal tip against the desk and pressed the button. A buzzing noise filled the room and sparks shot out of the end of the prod. Mr Leon backed away from Mason's face, allowing the woman to close in.

'This may hurt,' Mr Leon said. 'Of course, all you have to do is talk to me. Quite simple really. Tell me what I want to hear.'

The cattle prod sparked again, the electrical hum filling the room.

'Fine,' Mason said. 'What do you want to know?'

'There was an incident last night,' Leon started. 'We had a bit of an encounter with a few of your friends. That girl of yours, so feisty. I can see why you and Daniel are both fighting for her attention. There are so many things I'd like to do to her.'

Mason's hands clenched, pulling against the cuffs behind his back.

'But I digress,' Leon said. 'Where was I? Oh yes, the incident. She's still alive. But the other, not so good.'

'Who?' Mason asked.

Mr Leon smiled.

'Who?' Mason started to raise himself out of the chair but was pushed back down. 'Who'd you kill?'

'That I'm not gonna say,' Leon said, his hand pressing firmly down on Mason's shoulder. 'Where's the fun in that?'

Aries was alive. Leon had said so and the thought filled Mason with relief. But who was dead? Michael? Joy? Nathan? Momentarily, it occurred to Mason that the Bagger might be lying to him, trying to provoke him into losing control.

But there was no faking the snarkiness in the older man's face. He was happy. Overjoyed. That kind of delight couldn't be fabricated.

Something snapped in the back of his brain. Some sort of poison dripped through the cracks, filling his mind with all sorts of dark thoughts.

'I'm going to kill you,' he said.

Mr Leon laughed. 'Patience, boy. Patience. We've only just begun.' He turned and nodded at the doctor Bagger who moved forward, the cattle prod raised in her hand. 'We've got all day for name calling. Now tell me more about where I can find Aries.'

The electronic device pressed down.

They brought him back, tossing him inelegantly on the floor of the tent the way they had with Daniel. His head bounced off the thin vinyl covering, cracking hard on the cement beneath. He didn't even have the strength to protect his face, so he lay there with his cheek pressed on the hard ground. The blood on the back of his shirt had cooled, and he could feel it dripping down his skin.

Daniel was beside him in an instant, grabbing his shoulders and turning him over. He winced; the worst of the burns covered his back and the skin stuck to his clothing.

'You OK?'

He nodded, or at least tried to nod.

'What did they tell you?'

There was panic in Daniel's voice. He could hear it loud and clear and he knew if he opened his eyes he'd see the same intense look of fear on Daniel's face. But he didn't want to look. He wanted to sleep. If he was lucky, he could disappear into a dreamless state of unconsciousness and not have to deal with the burns and bruises that covered his entire body.

But Daniel wouldn't let up. 'What did they tell you?' He shook Mason slightly, not enough to hurt, but enough to make him open his eyes uncomfortably.

'Aren't you more concerned about what I might have told them?'

'Fine. What did you tell them?'

A slight moan escaped his lips. His back was on fire. 'Nothing.'

'Then what did they tell you?'

'They told me they shot Kennedy.'

Daniel let out a choked spurt of laughter. 'You're a real comedian, Tourist Boy.'

'Try my hardest.'

Daniel tossed him the towel for a pillow and he winced as he slid it beneath his neck. But there was no getting comfortable and he was pretty certain that he wouldn't be getting any sleep in his condition, not unless he managed to give himself a good shot to the head.

'They asked me a lot of questions about Aries,' Mason said as he stared at Daniel intently. 'How do they know so much about her?'

'No idea,' Daniel said.

He's lying.

'You know something.' Mason thought back to his first conversation with Leon. 'In fact, they said you did.'

'I know better than to open my mouth,' Daniel said. 'If you told them where she is . . .'

'I didn't say a word either,' Mason said. 'Why do you think I look this way? Do you think I asked for this? They stuck me with a cattle prod. Do you have any idea how much that hurts?'

'Yes.'

They watched each other for a while, the sounds of the camp drifting through the thin walls of the tent.

'I know what to do now,' Mason finally said.

'What's that?'

'I'm going to kill them,' he said. 'Whatever it takes. No matter how much it costs me.'

Daniel leaned in. 'Be careful what you say there, Tourist Boy.'

Mason closed his eyes. 'Do you really think I care if they're listening? Let them hear me. I'm not afraid.'

'That's not what I mean. Some things you can't take back. Some things take you further into the darkness.'

Mason paused. 'Maybe I want darkness.'

Daniel rubbed his eyes for a long time. 'You have no idea what you're saying. That's fine and dandy with some things but listen to me when I say this, Dowell. You think it's OK to go off and fight a few Baggers and declare yourself some kind of hero for mankind. That's fine. You've got a purpose. A great and sacred cause. But now that they've gone and taken away your toys and given you a spanking, you think you're going to get revenge? Kill Baggers before they kill you? Fine. Get revenge because they pissed you off? That'll change you. Open yourself up to the darkness? There's no coming back.'

'Are you suggesting I'll turn into a Bagger?' Mason sat up, leaning on his elbow. 'Because the last time I checked there were no black veins in my eyes. You said yourself, no one can just turn into one. I either am a Bagger, or I'm not.'

'And you think I'm right?' Daniel's voice rose an octave. 'Since when did you proclaim me the king of all wisdom? I don't know how this stuff works any more than you.'

Mason smiled. 'You're such a hypocrite, you know that? What about back in the department store when we killed those Baggers? Aren't you the one who told me I had "potential"? You said some crazy crap about me feeling the darkness. You put the knife in my hand and told me to embrace it. Now, because I agree with you, you're making a big deal about it? Telling me to go towards the light?'

Daniel shrugged. 'Maybe I was wrong.'

'You weren't.'

'Everything we do takes us one step closer to where we want or don't want to go,' Daniel said. 'The journey is up to you. Listen to me when I say this. Don't go where you're going. You have a choice. The Baggers don't.'

'Now you're feeling sorry for those monsters?'

'Maybe.' Daniel turned and moved over to the front of the tent. A shadow had formed on the other side. He unzipped the door and one of the daycare ladies looked surprised to see him.

'Um,' she said. She looked straight at Mason. 'The little girl from last night. She's awake now and she wants you. She's refusing to talk to anyone. Can you come?'

No, he didn't want to go. He wanted to lie down and try to forget everything, even if just for a few minutes. Why couldn't everyone just leave him alone for a bit? Instead he nodded and pulled himself up without screaming out in pain. Pushing past Daniel, he gave him a sharp shove in the side as he climbed out of the tent.

He saw Daniel open his mouth to speak again, but he moved on quickly before the guy managed to get any more words out.

The little girl, Casey, ran straight into his arms the second he stepped into the daycare area, hugging him tightly, forcing the pain in his back to flare and send waves of nausea across his stomach. Clenching his teeth, he held her back, wondering how much pain a person could take before falling apart.

The daycare worker must have seen the blood on his shirt and rushed over, trying to prise Casey's fingers from him. It only made her hold on tighter but Mason eventually managed to coax her into sitting down on the bed beside him.

'Here,' he said, taking the bowl of porridge the daycare lady handed him. 'You need to eat some of this.'

'I don't wanna.'

'I don't blame you,' he said, 'but you need to eat to stay strong. We can't have you weak. You might fade away to nothing.'

She giggled. But she opened her mouth when he put some of the porridge on the spoon. At least they had utensils here. It made his job easier.

Job? Was this what he had now? Was this little girl going to continue refusing to allow anyone else to take care of her? He didn't mind helping her out now and then. But a full-time job? No, he didn't need that. Especially not any more. He had other plans now. Leon had made sure of that. He had Baggers to kill. Someone else was going to have to take care of her.

'Now listen to me,' he said when she'd finished all the porridge, 'these are good people here and they're going to help. I'm going to visit lots but you've got to make friends with them too.'

'But I don't wanna.' She immediately flung her arms round him again, clinging on with all her might.

Two Baggers stepped into the daycare tent, looking around, their eyes falling on Mason. The lady beside him tensed, her fingers shaking as she tried to keep hold of the empty porridge dish. The first Bagger nodded in Mason's direction and motioned for Mason to follow.

Again? What now?

Mason gently unwrapped Casey's fingers from his arm. 'See those kids there?' He pointed over in the corner where some other children were playing with a few scattered toys. Most of the items looked broken and shabby. 'You should go make friends with them.'

'OK,' she said reluctantly. He waited as she walked over slowly and sat down next to a little boy about her age. The boy smiled and handed her one of his broken Hot Wheels cars. When Mason was sure she was fully distracted, he stood up and walked slowly over to the Baggers, using the last of his strength to try to maintain his dignity by not wobbling.

'Come on,' the Bagger said, a smile on his face when he noticed that Mason's legs were shaking. 'Time to put you to work.'

Work turned out to be cleaning duty. They herded Mason into the back of a white van with a few others. They were not given anything for protection. No gloves. No coveralls to keep them clean. No disinfectant. No masks to keep from breathing in tainted air.

Instead, they were driven several blocks to Burrard Street and dropped off at one of the large buildings that used to specialize in waterfront property that overlooked English Bay.

'Here's your job,' the Bagger said. 'You go in and get the bodies. Bring 'em out and dump 'em on the street. When the truck comes, you load the bodies up for removal. Nice and simple. No talking. No making friends. *Comprende?*'

'And I so wanted to get to know you,' a girl whispered sarcastically behind him. Mason found himself grinning for the first time that day. He couldn't help but think she'd fit in well with Aries and the others.

'You know the rules,' the Bagger continued. 'We do a headcount when we're done. If any of you are missing, the entire group dies.'

'Have they ever followed through on that?' Mason asked the girl behind him quietly.

'Two groups so far,' she whispered. 'Brought back to camp and shot in front of everyone to prove their point. Both times they found the deserters too. You don't want to know what they did to them. It wasn't pretty.'

Several hours later, Mason stood on the seventh floor, covered in sweat and smelling like rancid flesh. The window in front of him was gone, lost in the earthquake. Nothing but an open hole, where a small breeze did very little to fix the smell permeating the carpets and furniture.

The toes of his sneakers stuck out over the ledge. Looking down, he could see the white van, tiny in the distance, and two of the prisoners carrying out a badly decomposed body.

He could jump.

Would it be that easy?

Yes, it would. He knew that he could solve all his problems in one quick step forward. There would be no more pain. No more hiding. No more having to deal with the darkness that kept drifting across his mind, no matter how hard he tried to push it aside.

No more self-loathing.

But then there would be nothing.

And he wasn't ready for that.

The sun was going down and he had a perfect view of the bright yellow ball as it slowly sank into the ocean. In the distance he could see one of the offshore islands, a small dark glimpse of land at the edge of the horizon.

If he could get out of this, he might try to convince Aries and the others to head for the islands. Joy had told him the coast was full of them, the biggest being Vancouver Island. If they headed far enough north, they might even be able to find ones that hadn't been touched by the Bagger nightmare. They might find people. They could start a new civilization.

He could picture them living in a small cottage, one that had to be heated by firewood in the winter, and in the summer they'd have a garden. They could learn to survive in this new world; both Michael and Clementine had grown up farming and hunting. Mind you, Mason had never shot a deer and he wondered if he'd be able to do it.

Nice thoughts.

Unreal as they were, they were more than enough to keep him from going over the edge.

Besides, if he did that, then the Baggers won. Mr Leon would smile that big grin, knowing that he'd managed to get under Mason's skin. And everything he'd done since burying Chickadee would be a waste.

Turning away from the window, he stepped back into the room, his back to the brilliant sunset. His nose wrinkled at the smell; the bodies spread out on the floor before him had been there for a long time. There wasn't much left that made them recognizable. It was better that way.

He went into the bedroom and stripped the sheets off the bed. It took extra time but he wasn't about to touch the corpses without some sort of protection. Once he'd wrapped them up, another prisoner appeared and helped him carry the first body down the stairs.

Once upon a time, elevators used to make everyone's lives so much easier.

The street was steadily growing dim and the shadows lengthened as the remaining daylight came to an end. They tossed the body in the street, piling it up against the others.

On the first floor they found seven people. Two were children.

On the second floor they found ten. They also found two dogs and a hamster in a cage.

The third floor brought sixteen.

And so on.

The pile grew.

The Baggers weren't in sight so Mason decided to take a break. 'I'm going to use the toilet,' he said to his partner.

'Your death wish,' the other guy said before heading back into the building. 'Just don't make it mine too. You'd better come back.'

He went round the corner, wondering how far he

could walk before the device on his leg started to make noise. Would it be loud like a siren or silent? Probably not a good idea to try to find out.

He did his business next to a garbage bin and zipped up his pants. Only then did he notice the movement out of the corner of his eyes.

He looked up, catching a quick glimpse of blonde hair.

Blushing, he quickly ran his hands along his pants to make sure everything was closed. How long had Clementine been watching him?

She was too far away to talk to and he couldn't risk calling out to her. But she was looking right at him and she waved quickly to let him know she'd seen him. He glanced around to make sure no Baggers were sneaking up on him and waved back. She didn't stick around. Turning a corner, she disappeared into the shadows.

It was hard to ignore the warmth growing in his stomach. Clementine would tell Aries and she would come for him. It was dangerous to feel this happy, especially when he knew they'd be risking their lives for nothing.

The good news was he wasn't alone.

The bad news was he wouldn't be able to go back with them.

ARIES

The funeral was brief. They stood in a circle in the backyard, everyone silent and lost in their own thoughts. Even Jack was there, brought out and supported by Joy, who stuck to him like glue. His useless eyes stared up at the sky, a dark frown etched on his face as he stared at something he could no longer see.

Colin of course refused to go. 'You're all a bunch of hypocrites,' he said. 'Those other girls died and all you did was toss them in the dumpster.'

Aries and Clementine had returned to discover that both Emma and Janelle had died while they were gone. Larisa and Claude had removed the bodies from the house by themselves without saying a word.

But Colin's comment had really brought out the anger in her. Larisa actually went over and smacked him upside the head. 'Don't you dare,' she said. 'You didn't know them. I did and it was my decision. And we didn't dump them in the trash, we merely transported them to a place where we know the Baggers will come and collect them. If Aries and the others want to bury Nathan, I'm all for it. You were friends. But don't you dare criticize me for my decisions.'

They stood in the garden, the hole beneath them, Nathan's body wrapped in blankets found on the second floor. The yard was silent except for the sobs from Eve.

Aries couldn't cry any more. Her eyes were dry. She wanted to try to explain it to Eve, but she couldn't find the right words. It didn't help that when Eve looked at her there was nothing but hatred in her eyes. Aries had felt she needed to be honest when she told Eve. She'd only be damning herself further if she'd lied.

Her fault.

And she was as dry as a bone.

'Maybe someone should say something?' Joy said.

No one spoke.

'I'll do it,' Jack said. He stepped forward, carefully escorted by Joy. Everyone turned to him, waiting for the right words to make the funeral real.

Eve sniffled and blew her nose with a tissue.

'I didn't know Nathan for a long time,' Jack said. 'In fact, I'm kind of sorry I ever got to meet him at all.' He turned and faced Eve, drawn to the sound of the sniffling. 'Because if none of this had happened, we wouldn't have met both of you. And I still lie in bed and try and wish this new world away. All those "what ifs" and "if onlys".

'But we're here, and now one of us is gone,' he continued. 'And I guess in a way we should be thankful that we've lasted this long without more deaths.'

Joy reached out and took his hand.

Aries nodded. 'We've done the best we could.'

'We have,' Jack agreed. 'At least that's what I keep telling myself. But this isn't about us. It's about Nathan.'

He turned and stared blindly at the grave. 'Nathan and I had some great talks but it's only now that I realize I didn't know anything about him. I never knew his favourite band. Or what he was studying in school. I never knew if he had a girlfriend.'

'He did,' Eve said. 'But she was a bitch.'

Joy covered her mouth to hide her smile.

'So in honour of Nathan, who I hardly knew but still liked,' Jack said, 'I suggest we get everyone "home" and make this our one and only casualty from here on in.'

'Hear, hear,' Aries said.

They lined up and hugged Eve, and Aries tried to pretend that she didn't believe the younger girl had given up, even though her embraces were weak and she refused to look anyone in the eye. When it came to Aries's turn, Eve turned her back and moved away.

'She'll get over it,' Joy whispered in Aries's ear. 'You'll see. She just needs time.'

'No, she won't,' Aries said. 'But that's OK. I wouldn't forgive me either.'

One by one they took turns with the shovel until Nathan was buried.

'I found Mason!'

Clementine burst into the room, followed by an eager Raj, both their arms filled with bags of goods taken from both the liquor and hardware store.

'Really? Where?'

'He was part of a cleaning crew just over the bridge,'

Clementine said. 'They're making him and a bunch of others bring out the bodies from the condos.'

'Others? Was Daniel there? What about Graham's little girl?'

Clementine shook her head. 'Sorry, I looked but I didn't see either of them. That doesn't mean anything though.'

Aries nodded.

'Meanwhile, we've got lots of work to do if we're gonna pull this thing off,' Raj said as he began grabbing liquor bottles out of the bag. 'We've got two options. I can waste these fine bottles or I can mix up a bunch of the cleaning supplies we snagged from Canadian Tire. Either way, we're gonna have lots of flames on our hands.'

'Cleaning supplies,' Clementine said. 'Wasting booze on Baggers seems wrong to me.'

'Yup,' Aries said. 'No booze wastage. That's just sacrilegious.'

'Done and done,' Raj said. 'Now let's get to work.'

Jack was back in his room when she knocked softly on the door about an hour later. Joy was with him, sitting on the bed, and they were talking in hushed whispers. She stood up when Aries entered, brushed off her shirt and ran a hand through her hair.

'I'll let you guys be,' Joy said. 'Should be starting with dinner, I suppose. Not much to work with tonight. The Safeway is starting to get a little sparse.'

'We'll have to go further out,' Aries said. 'I promise you, once we get Mason back, we'll take a chance and hit up a Superstore or Costco.'

Joy nodded and headed out. Jack waited till he heard the door click and her footsteps echo down the stairs.

'Eventually we're going to run out of food,' he said. 'The grocery stores can't support us forever. What isn't hoarded by the Baggers and remaining survivors is only going to get eaten by the wildlife. Mason told me he saw deer a few days ago wandering down Granville Street.'

'Yeah,' she said as she sat down beside him. 'The raccoons and skunks have all pretty much realized they run this town. The last time I was at Safeway, the cereal aisle and all the crackers were demolished.'

'Racoon heaven.'

She choked back a sob.

'Hey.' Jack's voice was soft as he reached out with his hand to touch her face. He missed and brushed her ear instead. Her sob turned into a half-giggle, a noise that didn't sound happy in the slightest.

'What am I going to do?' she asked. The tears were falling again. Now that they'd started, it felt like they weren't ever going to end. 'If I hadn't been so pig-headed, none of this would have happened. I killed Nathan. And now I'm falling apart and I can't let anyone see.'

'Why not?'

'Because someone has to lead this group. Someone

has to keep everyone safe. And what good am I going to be if I'm having a mental breakdown? How on earth am I going to lead them all into battle? I'm breaking down, Jack, and I can't tell anyone.'

'You're doing a good job telling me.'

She let out the half-sob, half-giggle again. 'Yeah, I guess I am.'

'Do you feel better?'

She kicked at the bedpost with her heel. 'Maybe.'

'Let's make this easy then,' Jack said, reaching out and taking her hand. 'You messed up. You know it. I know it. Everyone knows it although they keep telling you otherwise. You know why? They believe in you. Yeah, you screwed up. So have they. We all have. But you've managed to last the longest. Everyone looks up to you, Aries. Just because you made one mistake, it doesn't turn you into a monster. It makes you human.'

He pulled her close and wrapped his arms round her. 'Come on, even leaders need a good hug now and then.'

She fell into his embrace, holding him tight. Jack was like the brother she'd never had. He always managed to make her feel safe. They stayed together for a while, him holding her while the tears rolled down her face.

'It seems like I'm crying all the time these days,' she said after a while. 'I bawled on Mason's shoulder when we were back at my old house. Now you. I can't control myself.'

'Me neither,' he said. 'I guess we've all been wrapped up in our own problems. I've been feeling rather sorry for myself. I guess I should have paid a little more attention to you.'

'Don't be ridiculous,' she said.

Jack paused. 'I need to ask you something and I don't want you to say no.'

She pulled away from the hug and sat up. 'You sound serious.'

'I am.'

'OK.'

Jack rubbed his forehead and winced, the frown lines digging deeply into his skin. 'This is something I've been thinking a lot about,' he said. 'If something happens, like as in we have to leave the house in a hurry, I'm not coming.'

'What? Why not?'

'It's my choice, Aries,' he said.

'You're talking about suicide.'

'Oh, come on, you know it's not that,' he said with a forced chuckle. 'I just don't want to slow the rest of you down. And don't make that face – I may not be able to see you, but I can hear the frown forming on your lips.'

'I'm not frowning.'

'Yes, you are. What kind of friend do you think I am? I've only known you since forever. And that's why I know you're going to give me your word.'

She sighed. 'I can't lose you, Jack. I can't.'

'Then let's hope you won't. But you still have to make the promise.'

'Fine. But it's not gonna happen so there's no point

in this discussion anyway,' she lied.

'Exactly,' Jack said. 'Now can you hand me some of the Tylenol on the counter? My head's about to explode.'

She fiddled with the childproof cap until she finally managed to get a few of the pills into his outstretched hand.

A few hours later Aries, Clementine, Raj and Joy dressed themselves completely in black. They carried backpacks filled with handmade Molotov cocktails that Raj had cooked up in the bathroom.

'So we stick to the plan,' Aries said. 'If things become too hard, we get out. No questions asked. Be careful. We can't lose anyone, especially not so soon after . . .'

Joy nodded. She pulled up her sleeve, checking the digital watch taken from the hardware store. They were each wearing one, all set to the same time. 'Do you think Eve is going to be OK staying with Jack? Larisa and Claude are here but they don't really know her well enough if she breaks down again. Do you think it's enough? Maybe one of us should stay too?'

'No,' Aries said. 'Give Eve more credit than that. She's strong. And, besides, she's got Colin.'

Joy snorted and Aries grinned at her.

'Then let's get out of here,' Clementine said. 'And, Aries, you know that tomorrow we're doing the exact same thing for Michael.'

Raj groaned. 'How on earth did I get into the rescue business? All I did was follow a few of you home and now you've got me going all *Mission Impossible*. I should start charging you for my time.'

Clementine smacked him in the arm.

'Tomorrow we get Michael,' Aries agreed, shaking her heavy backpack and listening to the bottles clink together. 'Let's just hope his rescue doesn't involve as much firepower.'

NOTHING

Jingle bells. Jingle bells.

It's beginning to look a lot like Christmas.

I'm dreaming of a white Christmas.

Fa la la la la la la

la

la.

OK, I'm lying. It's so not beginning to look like the holidays in any way, shape, or form. That warm fuzzy feeling people normally get when they drink too much eggnog? It's extinct.

This year the city really went downhill with decorations. Gone are the big Christmas trees, the fancy shop windows and the ice rink in Robson Square. Gone are the hot-chestnut vendors and the people rushing through the night, umbrellas in hand, last-minute packages in the other. Gone are the multitude of bright lights, miscellaneous chocolate and candy canes that taste like peppermint.

No staff parties this year. No mistletoe or drunken binges that may or may not end with someone throwing up in the parking lot.

Gone but not forgotten.

Everyone remembers. I can see the tension on their faces. They know what day is coming. But no one wants to say it out loud.

Can it still be Christmas if no one believes? If I gave you a gift, would you treasure it always? Or would you fret because you didn't get me anything in return? Wouldn't it be nice if I could gift my curse to you, package it up in a nice bundle and place a silver ribbon over my life? I would give it away to you in a heartbeat.

Of course you would probably just return it the next day.

I wish I had a tree. If I could, I would sneak off into the mountains and wander until I found the perfect pine. I wouldn't chop it down – that would be too cruel. I'd just like to sit there and stare at it, enjoying the smell and the beauty that is all around me. I might never want to come back.

Does anyone know what I want this year?

No, don't bother guessing. You'll be wrong.

And I wouldn't want to embarrass you by pointing it out.

CHRISTMAS EVE

MICHAEL

The Longhouse kitchen was empty.

Michael stood in the middle of the room where only a short while ago Ryder had leaned against the counter and cradled his sprained ankle. The spot was empty.

'There's no sign of a struggle,' Heath said, 'and the door's intact. The crazies would have smashed through it if they came for him.'

'I don't get it,' Michael said. 'Why would he leave? How would he? He couldn't even walk. He would have had to crawl away.'

'Do you think one of his friends might have found him?' Heath went over to the other set of doors and opened them. It led out into the alley but there wasn't anything there except for the stolen white van.

'I guess it's possible.'

'It's not as if he really liked you,' Heath said. 'I got the vibe that there was some bad mojo going on between the two of you. He seemed like kind of a dick.'

Michael nodded. 'Yeah, he had issues but I still don't see how he could have just got up and walked away. I had to drag him in here and, trust me, he would rather have died than ask for my help.'

'Then let's search for him,' Heath said. 'But we'd better be quick. We don't want to stick around too long with a stolen truck. They're probably already looking for us.'

They headed back to the reception area but there was no sign of the other guy. Ryder had simply vanished into thin air. Nothing. Michael was confused. He replayed some of their conversations in his head but he couldn't think of anything that Ryder might have said to suggest that he wanted to head off on his own. Yes, he didn't trust Michael but at the same time he'd made it clear he wanted to get back to the safe house and find Larisa and any others who might still be alive. So why would he go off on his own?

It made no sense.

There was blood on the glass by the front door but Michael couldn't remember if it had been there earlier. He studied it, ignoring the tingling iciness along the back of his spine. Was it Ryder's? He knelt down and ran his finger along the glass. Only a few drops, but it was fresh. Someone could have just nicked themselves on the way out.

'Come on, man,' Heath said. 'I'm nervous. I think we need to move on.'

Climbing to his feet, Michael took one last look at the reception area. 'Yeah,' he said. 'We should go. Clementine is probably worrying herself to death right about now. I can't wait to see her face when I show up with you.'

Heath smiled. 'It's going to be amazing.'

MASON

He'd never been so tired in his entire life. Never. Not even the one summer he'd worked at the golf course, getting up at 4 a.m. to plant flowers and cut the grass to save up money for his car. Early wake-up calls were not something he was good at. The first few weeks had been torturous; it seemed forever before he was able to climb out of bed each morning without feeling a hundred years old. He remembered complaining good-naturedly to Mom about how his back hurt from bending over to plant millions of flower beds with posies and yellow mums. She'd laughed and told him he was too young to be complaining of old-man problems.

Suck it up, buttercup.

He'd give anything to feel like that again. A little back pain was nothing now. At least he'd had the sun and the way the air smelt when he left the house each morning. He'd liked the feeling of knowing the rest of the world was still asleep. The world was still fresh, untouched by the exhaust fumes and other stagnant smells that would start filling up the atmosphere once everyone had had their morning coffees and headed out the door to work.

Mason yawned. The smart thing would be to retreat to his tent and lie down but he was afraid if he did that he wouldn't be able to get back up again. Daniel was nowhere in sight and he didn't have the strength to look for him either. So he limped over to the corner by the stage and stood there, using all his will power to keep his eyes open and scan the surrounding area outside the compound for signs of rescue.

They would come for him tonight. He was positive about that. Of course that didn't mean much. He couldn't follow.

Spasms raked his back and he bent over, trying to relieve the pain, but it was pointless. Nothing short of a needle to the spine would fix him. How many bodies had he picked up today? Too many to count. The burns from the cattle prod didn't help either. Every time he glanced over at the inlet, an overwhelming desire to jump into the water grew more prominent. Of course the salt water would sting beyond belief but it would also cool his burning skin.

What he wouldn't give for a bathtub.

Or a hot tub. Yeah, a hot tub would be fantastic.

Mr Leon was trying to wear him down, bit by bit. Mason hated to admit it but it was working. Would he still be able to stay strong after a few weeks of this? Or would he fold, babbling away his secrets in the confinement of that small office room? If he was lucky, his inner demons might explode, hopefully taking down as many Baggers as possible along the way.

How many of them could he take down before they overcame him?

'You don't look so good.'

Daniel's voice came from behind him.

'Yeah, had a long day. Spent it riding the roller coaster at Playland. Ate too many hotdogs so I had to sit down for a while. Good times were had by all.' He turned to look at Daniel and immediately the sarcasm left his voice. 'Holy God, what happened to you?'

If Mason had been hit by a car, then Daniel must have got in the way of a herd of wild horses. He limped the last few feet towards the fence, coming into the light, and his face was a mess of bruises and dried blood from a gash in his forehead.

'Leon,' Daniel said. 'We had a fantastic debate today. Had a good argument but his was stronger. Doesn't matter. Could be worse. At least I'm still standing. At one point he threatened to remove one of my legs.'

'So what did you tell him?'

Daniel managed a small laugh. 'Please, Dowell, do yourself a favour and give it up. You managed to get through all that without spouting off your big mouth. I'm stronger than you. I said nothing.'

'Why us?' Mason asked. 'I mean, I don't see them torturing the crap out of the other people here.'

'We've got information they want,' Daniel said, nodding in the direction of the casino. 'I guess we should be thankful that they keep giving us all this fresh air. Those people inside aren't as lucky.'

A small thought formed in the back of Mason's head,

turning his stomach to ice. 'Do you think they're using us as bait?'

Daniel frowned. 'It's possible. Never considered that.'

'I saw Clementine today. They know we're here. I think they might be coming tonight. Do you—'

A loud explosion interrupted his words. The far guard tower burst into flames. People screamed and rushed out of their tents in confusion.

'Hold that thought,' Daniel said. 'Something bad is about to go down.'

CLEMENTINE

The fire was brilliant. She'd tossed the bottle over the fence, completely unaware of exactly how loud the explosion would be. She let out a little chirp of excitement when the bottle smashed against the silver box beneath the guard tower, eyes lighting up in amazement when the flames engulfed everything at once.

The explosion was an extra bonus.

'You hit a generator,' Raj said excitedly behind her. 'On your first throw. You are amazing.'

'No time to roast marshmallows,' Clementine said. 'Come on.' Using a lighter, she fired up another Molotov cocktail and sent it flying out into the night. It hit one of the tents and she hoped no one was inside. Most of the prisoners had evacuated into the middle of the compound, grouping together in confusion, trying to keep safe.

'Time to move,' Aries said. 'We've been spotted.'

Sure enough, two Baggers were running towards them, guns raised and ready to fire.

They ran. Aries and Clementine headed off towards the water, leaving Raj and Joy to disappear in the direction of the casino. There were more generators there and Raj had suggested they hit them first. Without light and power, they'd have a better shot at chaos.

Clementine lit another bottle and hurled it behind her without looking. Hopefully that would be enough of a diversion.

All they had to do was keep the Baggers distracted long enough for them to find a way through the fence. Hopefully they'd track down Mason quickly. If they were super lucky, they might come across Graham's daughter too. They hadn't actually discussed what they'd do if Mason wasn't in sight. In fact, the thought hadn't even crossed her mind until now. It wasn't much of a plan but it was better than nothing.

As for the other prisoners, they couldn't exactly take them all back with them to the safe house. But, if they made enough holes in the fence, hopefully those healthy enough to run would escape into the city. Even those who'd once listened to the white vans and come down voluntarily wouldn't be fooled a second time, surely.

Mason tonight. Michael tomorrow. She couldn't wait to see him again. The memory of his kiss was still fresh on her lips. And she would find him. If she'd been determined enough to travel across the country to find Heath, she'd find Michael too. God wasn't about to be that cruel to her.

Heath, this is it. The Baggers started it when they declared war on the world. Now we're declaring war on them. I guess that makes me a soldier. I used to be so against war, thinking that solutions could be fixed by negotiation and not killing. I'm beginning to understand now that the world just doesn't work that way. I feel so grown up. Mom used to say I'd understand things better when I got older. I get it now. Bring it on. World War Three has been declared and I'm going to kick as much Bagger ass as I can find.

She tried to remain this positive in her thoughts. But the little realities weren't easy to ignore.

There would be no funerals if they failed. Their bodies would be left behind. End of discussion.

From the other side of the compound, flames exploded as Joy and Raj started tossing their own cocktails.

Bullets whizzed past her ear and she dropped to the ground, landing hard, the wind knocked out of her. Refusing to give in to the burning in her chest, she turned over, rolling towards the fence, pulling herself up and rushing for cover. Aries had escaped in the other direction and she watched as her auburn hair disappeared behind an abandoned car.

A Bagger stepped out in front of her, leering down with a big grin on his face. She smiled back, reaching into her pocket and pulling out the taser. As he brought his gun down towards her face, she quickly leaned in, jabbing the small weapon right into his foot. He screamed, flew back through the air a good five feet, hitting the fence and dropping to the ground. She jumped up and went in for the kill, stabbing him again with the taser until he stopped moving.

When it was over, Aries came over and joined her. They grabbed what they needed.

Now they had a gun.

Of course neither of them knew how to use it but Clementine was pretty sure they'd both learn fast given the opportunity.

'You take it,' she said, and she held up the taser. 'I'm really beginning to love this thing.'

Aries smiled and picked up the machine gun. Her auburn hair had come loose from her pony tail, and long wisps trailed over her face. 'Better hope you have extra batteries. We've got more company and I'll probably just end up shooting myself in the foot if I try using this.'

Another Bagger came running through the black smoke. He froze when he saw Aries with her gun; he didn't seem to have a weapon of his own. He turned and dived behind the parked car. Clementine reached into her bag and pulled out another cocktail. She lit it and tossed it, right on target, sending the Bagger screaming down the pavement, arms flailing wildly as he tried to beat out the flames.

A small part of her felt sorry for him. What a terrible way to go. But it was only fair, right?

'Come on,' Aries said. She rifled through her backpack until she pulled out the wire cutters. 'Let's get this fence open.'

Clementine stood guard while Aries began snipping the fence. They were clear; the Baggers had headed off in the other direction, where Raj and Joy had managed to take out another generator. Most of the prison camp had been reduced to darkness. She could make out the forms of people running around, but she could no longer tell who was who. Somewhere in the distance she could hear a child crying and a woman screaming for someone named Henry.

So much chaos. But the prisoners were beginning to get organized. Through the dim light she saw a Bagger brought down, bodies piling against him as he tried to fire on the crowd. Once the Bagger was subdued, another man took his weapon and raised it up into the air with a victory cry.

More shots were fired, sending the man to his knees. Someone else took his weapon and scurried off into the darkness.

'Done,' Aries said. She'd clipped the last wire, stood up, and revealed a hole about three feet wide.

'Let's do this,' Clementine said. 'You rock, by the way. Have I told you that lately?'

Aries grinned sheepishly.

No matter what words had been spoken, Clementine knew she'd been wrong. Aries was a fighter – it was clear to her now.

There was no one else she'd rather have on her side.

She dropped to her knees and crawled under the fence.

MASON

Frenzy.

After a quick discussion, Mason and Daniel agreed to split up and try to help Aries and the others.

'We need to get as many people out as possible,' Mason said. Funny, this was almost like when they did their sweeps of the Bagger hideouts, only this time they were trying to save lives instead of take them away.

'OK, you hit up the daycare and I'll take the casino,' Daniel said. 'They're gonna need the most help.'

'Meet me back in the middle?' Mason asked. 'And if you find Aries before me . . .'

'I'm going to give her one hell of a lecture,' Daniel said with a grin. 'Seriously? All this for us? Girl needs to sort out her priorities. I'm starting to feel like a movie star.'

'Get over it,' Mason said. 'And be careful.'

There seemed to be a lot of indecision and confusion in the yard. Some people were running around, trying to get others to follow them towards the gates and out of the line of fire. Others stood there stupidly, looking up in the air as if they thought the fire had come down from the heavens. Mason ducked as another Molotov cocktail hit one of the tents a few feet away from him.

'Come on,' he said, grabbing the arm of a bewildered onlooker and dragging him towards the middle of the camp. 'People need help. Do what you can.'

The man looked at him and finally nodded. When Mason let go of his arm, he headed off in the right direction, only to be gunned down seconds later.

One of the generators had caught fire and several Baggers had managed to round up a few people, forcing them to beat at the flames with sleeping bags. When one of the people caught fire, the Bagger simply shot him.

There was another explosion to his left and Mason looked, just in time to see a Bagger raising his gun towards him. Diving behind a tent, he rolled along the ground, ignoring the blinding pain in his back from where they'd tortured him. Stars popped into his vision and for a second he thought he might either faint or throw up. But it passed. When he finally scrambled to his knees, he discovered that a few others had managed to attack the Bagger, stealing his gun and rendering him unconscious.

A man wearing a John Deere baseball cap jogged over to him. 'Chaplin says I can trust you,' he said.

Mason nodded.

'Good to know. We need to organize better,' he said. 'They're tearing down a hole in the south fence. Try to send as many people as you can over there. They can't kill us all if we fight back!'

'I will,' Mason said. 'And thanks.'

The man just looked Mason up and down before nodding and taking off in the opposite direction.

The daycare tent was on fire. Mason stopped, repelled by the intense heat as fire ate through the canvas. It was like getting punched in the chest. Ignoring the lack of oxygen, he tried to move in to get a better look, but the heat blistered his skin, forcing him back.

If anyone was inside, they were no longer alive.

'They're OK,' a woman shouted at him. She was holding a package of diapers in her arm. 'We got them out. They're over at the casino.'

Gunshots brought the woman down the second the words escaped her mouth. She hit the ground with a thud; her body sprawled out, the bag of Pampers bouncing off her arm.

He froze, standing in the middle of the nightmare, watching people stumble and fall as the Baggers exacted their revenge. It was like being in a movie, with him sitting in the front row, watching but unable to participate. His legs no longer listened. He wanted to move, find cover at least, but he couldn't. Everything grew silent; his ears throbbed but sound became diluted, as if he was underwater. Someone fell at his feet, another woman, her eyes wide and staring up at him. She had a nose ring. The gleam of silver caught his attention and he couldn't look away.

A Bagger came up from behind, grabbing him by the hair and yanking him backwards. The pain in his back exploded and the edge of his vision went all blurry.

Struggling, he twisted his body round. Ignoring the blinding pain, he managed to throw a punch, forcing the Bagger to let go. Mason hit him again.

Two other men jumped in. One of them was Chaplin. They pinned the Bagger down, bringing him to his knees, then they kicked him until he stopped moving.

'Your kid is safe,' Chaplin said. 'They've ripped the fence down. Some of the others are getting them out. Now give us a hand and let's get *everyone* out.'

Mason nodded, ignoring the tight feeling of the bracelet on his ankle. He'd worry about that later.

He couldn't run but at least he could walk again. He moved through the crowd, which was beginning to thin. The smoke assaulted his eyes, forcing them to water, and he wiped at his face several times to try to clear his vision.

Then he saw her.

She was holding a gun but not properly. No, she had it up in the air like a baseball bat, which almost made him laugh out loud. Her auburn hair blew around her face, covering her eyes and she tucked it back behind her ears as she ducked behind one of the tents. His legs instantly began to move in her direction.

'Aries!'

She came to him, throwing her arms around him, pinching the nerves in his back but none of that mattered. He held her tight, breathing in the scent of her hair, feeling the softness of her skin.

'You have no idea how happy I am to see you,' she said.

There was something new in her eyes. Darkness. He knew instantly that something had happened.

Anger.

At herself?

At him?

'We have to get you out of here,' he said, taking her arm and pulling her away from the fire. 'Come with me.'

'The others,' Aries said. 'They're here somewhere. I can't find them. Have you seen Graham's daughter? They killed everyone off but we think she might be here.'

'She is. But she's with the others. They've broken down the fence on the south side. I hear they've taken the children there and are getting them out.'

'Good.'

They fled to the edge of the compound where the fighting was less intense. There were big gaping holes in the fence now and people were crawling through them, heading off in all directions. He saw a man wearing nothing but boxer shorts trip over the body of someone lying face down on the pavement.

'Listen to me,' he said. 'You have to find Daniel. He's over at the casino. You can go get him. We'll meet back here in a bit.'

'What about you?'

Mason paused and looked back into the middle of

the camp where people were fighting for their lives. More than anything else in the world, he wanted to grab Aries by the arm and lead her to safety. They'd leave it all behind, find their island, and spend the rest of their lives in hidden peace.

Mason wanted to be left alone. That was all he'd wanted since this whole thing happened. But he was beginning to admit it just wasn't on the cards.

He smiled to himself. The darkness wasn't going to win tonight. Mason Dowell wasn't a monster yet.

'I have to help the others,' he said.

ARIES

She didn't want to leave Mason but he waved at her to go. Already he was running into the crowd where a group of men and women were fighting to keep the Baggers from opening fire on them.

'Just get Daniel and meet me back here,' Mason yelled over his shoulder again. 'Be quick.'

She turned and the doors of the casino beckoned. It took her a while to get there; people kept pushing into her as they raced past. She stopped to check the pulse of a woman lying on the ground by the stage, but she was gone. After that, she stepped over the bodies of both Baggers and normal people, ignoring the urge to try to help them.

Anyone on the ground was pretty much past helping.

The casino doors were closed. In the windows, she could see the reflections of the fires that ravaged the compound. She looked up at the darkened neon sign above her head and tried to ignore the cold creeping sensation that ran up her spine.

She didn't want to go inside.

There was something awful in there. She couldn't explain it but she could feel it. Something dark. Horrible.

But Daniel was in there too.

She walked up to the doors and pushed one open. Keeping the gun raised, she stepped inside. The smell hit her face – sweat and fear. Aries gasped and bit down on her lip at the same time.

The place was brightly lit and she blinked several times to adjust to the sudden change. Moving across the foyer, she entered the main room. Inside were cages, row after row of custom-made prisons. The majority of them had people inside.

She heard a noise coming from the back and she raised the gun higher, wondering if she could even fire it. Taking a deep breath, she stepped forward, moving along the sides of the cages closest to her.

Someone reached out and grabbed her sleeve. A girl, maybe a few years older than her, with greasy braids and torn jeans.

'Are you one of them?' the girl asked.

Aries pushed her gun through the bars. 'I wouldn't do this if I was,' she said. The girl held on to the machine gun for a few seconds before handing it back to Aries.

'What's happening outside?' the girl asked.

'Prison break,' Aries said. She put her hand through the bar and their fingers touched reassuringly. 'Have you seen a guy come in? Dark hair?'

'Down at the end. He's helping people escape,' the girl replied. 'But he's not moving fast enough. He's trying to pick the locks but he doesn't know how.'

Aries shook her head. It had to be Daniel but she wasn't about to scream out his name just in case. 'Here,'

Aries said. She pulled her backpack off her shoulders and dug around until she found the pair of wire cutters. 'We used these to get inside the fence,' she said. 'I've got more than one pair. Free yourself and then help the others.'

The girl grabbed the tool and silently began to cut through the metal fencing. Aries slipped past her and continued along the row. A lot of people looked up at her, eyes wide and mistrusting. She couldn't blame them, especially when she was carrying a gun. For all they knew she might be a Bagger.

A loud explosion from outside shook the walls, and from about fifty feet away she heard someone swear.

'Daniel?'

A pause.

'Aries?'

Suddenly he was right in front of her. He looked terrible, swollen and beaten, not at all like the healthy boy she'd seen just a few days ago.

'What happened to you?' She reached up to touch his face but he brushed her away.

'Nothing I can't handle,' he said. 'But you can help me. I'm trying to open the cages but I'm kind of crappy at it.' He held up his hand and she saw the blood trickling down his fingers. 'Cut myself trying to pick a lock.'

'Here,' she said, handing him a pair of wire cutters.

'Perfect!'

Daniel turned and disappeared back down another

row. She went back and checked on the girl who had not only freed herself but was in the process of cutting through the cage of the person beside her.

She turned the corner again just as Daniel managed to free an older man. Climbing out of the small prison, the man turned and smiled at Aries.

'Why were they keeping you in here?' she couldn't help asking.

'They caught me a few days ago trying to get into the city. I travelled all the way up from Edmonton. A bunch of us came in as a group.'

'Why?' Aries asked. 'What's happening there?'

'Nothing. It's just a ghost world. Most of the prairies are dead or heading west or south. The snow hit hard this year. Lots of people came here to keep from freezing to death. I heard out in Ontario some communities have managed to get the electricity running again but that makes them easy targets. I thought it might be easier here.'

Aries's heart sank – there was nowhere better to run to.

'Why were they keeping you in here? Why in the casino and not with everyone else?' Daniel asked.

'I'm a doctor,' the man said. 'And I refused to help one of them. I guess they didn't like my negative attitude.'

They worked hard for the next quarter of an hour. The girl at the front moved the quickest and within minutes she had nearly all the people freed from her entire row. There were no more explosions from outside and Aries began to get antsy. If things were winding down, it was only a matter of time before the Baggers came into the casino to check on their key prisoners.

They didn't bother opening the cages of the people who were unconscious or non-responding. It killed her that they were going to leave them behind, but Aries knew there was no point.

They couldn't save them all.

'We've cut open a hole in the south fence,' Aries said once they were ready to make their exit. 'But you've got the wire cutters so look for another route if you can't get through that way.'

'Thanks,' the girl said.

'When you get outside,' Aries said, 'run. Look for shelter. Anything. Just get away.'

A loud crash boomed through the casino. Several people screamed in surprise.

'They're here,' Daniel said.

Aries turned round, raising her gun up towards the front doors. She hoped she looked tougher than she felt. 'Let's fight.'

CLEMENTINE

There was fire everywhere.

She ducked behind a tent and then raced straight out across the grounds towards the cooking area. There a group of people were actually managing to fight by throwing pots and pans at the Baggers. When they ran out of supplies, they started tossing vegetables. A tomato hit a Bagger right in the eye and he fell backwards, tripping over his own feet, and smashing his head against one of the tables.

'Brilliant,' Joy shouted at her as she came running round the corner. She was breathing heavily, her face flushed, but other than that she seemed unhurt. Raj came up behind her, his nose dripping blood.

'Have you found the bloke you're looking for yet?' Raj asked. Using his sleeve, he tried to wipe some of the blood off his face.

'Not yet,' Clementine said. 'But maybe Aries had better luck.' She looked at her watch. 'Either way, we have to abandon fort in the next ten minutes.'

'I tried looking for Graham's girl,' Joy said. 'No luck. I heard a bunch of kids got through the fence though. No idea where the Baggers are taking the ones they've managed to round back up. I can't see a damn thing any more. Too much smoke.'

'Yeah,' Raj said. 'I've got to agree, babes. Can't see a bloody thing. Some idiot keeps setting things on fire.'

Clementine snorted and started coughing at the same time.

'This is good though,' Joy said. 'We've done well, right? All these people. We've managed to save at least some of them. And look at the way they're fighting back.' She pointed to where a few feet away two Baggers lay dead in the dirt. 'We should have been doing this from the beginning.'

'Ryder used to talk about this all the time,' Raj said. 'How we were supposed to stand up and take back our city. But we never did anything. I have to admit it; it feels great. Scary as hell but good nonetheless.'

Gunshots echoed through the camp and Clementine felt something whiz by her ear. Ducking, she turned to see Joy yelp and drop to the ground. Screaming out her friend's name, she crawled along in the dirt until she reached her.

'I'm fine. The bullet just grazed my shoulder.' Joy wrapped her good arm protectively round her stomach. 'Don't mind me if I barf though. Bit queasy suddenly.'

'It's time to go,' Raj said. 'While we still can. What's the saying? Those who run live to fight another day?'

'Works for me,' Clementine said. 'Let's go.'

Raj helped Joy up to her feet and they half dragged, half carried her behind the back of the closest tent.

Carefully, under the camouflage of smoke, they started making their way towards the fence.

Dear Heath, We're on to something here. A war is starting and somehow I've managed to get right in the middle of it. And you know what? It feels good. We do need to fight. Join together as a group. There will be more deaths but we're ready for that. Either way, I think we've just declared war on the Baggers and we've won the first round. Now if only we can stay alive long enough to celebrate it.

She paused at the edge of the fence and turned back to look at the compound. It was almost empty now; the majority of people were either gone or dead. Outside the fence, she could still hear the sounds of people fighting for their lives.

She spotted Mason over by the casino but he didn't see her. He wasn't moving. Just standing there as if he was waiting for someone.

He looked so lost.

'You guys go on ahead,' Clementine said. 'There's Mason. I'm going to go get him.'

'Are you sure?' Joy asked. She was holding on to her arm, trying to stop the bleeding. Her skin looked pale under the flickering of the fire.

'Yeah.'

Turning, Clementine headed back into the camp.

ARIES

The Baggers piled into the room. There were at least five of them and they looked haphazard and angry. Behind the first few, she recognized the female from Graham's house, the one who'd started crying and babbling for no reason. She must have made a full recovery because she was carrying a machete dripping in blood.

Someone behind her began sobbing heavily. Another person, an older man with fine wisps of white hair on his chin, dropped to his knees and started praying. Aries looked at them all, the hope and light disappearing from their faces.

So unfair.

No one deserved to be treated this way.

She didn't think. Raising the machine gun, she pointed it in the direction of the Baggers and pulled the trigger.

The recoil of the gun immediately sent her backwards. Bullets sprayed across the room and up into the ceiling as she fell hard on her back, making her tailbone scream in agony. One of the Baggers dropped to the floor, the others scattered, ducking behind the rows of cages and out of reach of her crappy aim.

'Nice job, sharpshooter,' Daniel said, reaching down, offering her his hand.

A loud noise came from the main entrance. Suddenly more people started filing into the casino, prisoners armed with weapons. Some of them had guns, others had taken the more primitive route, arming themselves with frying pans, cutlery, knives and whatever else they'd managed to find that was heavy or sharp.

The outside group turned on the Baggers, attacking them at full force. Beside her, the girl with the bolt cutters gave out a long primal screech and ran straight towards the commotion. Another person followed. And another. Slowly, steadily, some limping, others wincing in pain, the group of people too important to be allowed outside joined the scrimmage.

The screams of terror that followed were not from any of the prisoners.

Aries watched in horror until Daniel tugged on her shoulder. 'Come with me. There are rooms in the back. We should check them quickly.'

Daniel didn't even give her the chance to argue. His fingers tightened round hers and together they ran towards an exit sign that glowed brightly above a heavy black door.

Behind the exit was a long hallway with lots of closed doors. As they moved along, Daniel turned the handles but the majority of them were locked. A few opened but there didn't seem to be anyone there. The area was abandoned.

'There's another exit at the end,' Daniel said. 'It'll take us outside.'

'How do you know this?' she asked.

'I spent some time here. This is where they tortured me,' he said, and he banged on one of the doors as they passed.

She looked at his face, repressing the urge to reach out and tenderly touch his bruises.

Daniel smiled at her as if reading her thoughts. 'Really, I'm OK. There are far worse things than getting a few smacks to the head.'

She wondered if the Baggers had done those 'worse things' too, and if Daniel would ever admit to any of it.

As they rounded the first corner, they realized they weren't alone. Someone had found them.

A hand reached out and shoved her hard. Aries hit the wall, knocking the air right out of her lungs and she dropped to the ground. Daniel was there in a second, arms reaching around her, pulling her back up.

She couldn't breathe. Her feet wouldn't support her. The gun in her hand was suddenly too heavy and it slipped past her fingers and on to the floor.

Daniel didn't hesitate. He turned and stabbed the attacker with the wire cutters. The Bagger screamed and went down. Opening the door closest to them, Daniel shoved Aries inside. Then he grabbed the gun off the floor and dived into the room behind her. Turning the handle, he pushed down on the button, locking the door and sealing them inside.

'We're in luck,' he said as he surveyed the room. 'Look, a window. We can climb out.'

Someone slammed against the door from the outside. Again. It was only a matter of time till they got in.

Aries looked around the room. There wasn't any furniture except for a single chair in the middle of the floor. Chains were attached to the chair. Although it was dark, she was positive the stains beneath it were blood.

'Come on,' Daniel said, grabbing her arm. 'You don't want to think about this. It'll just drive you crazy.'

The window was small but big enough for the two of them to squeeze their way through. Outside, the camp was clouded in smoke, and they made their way back to where Mason said he'd be waiting for them.

He was there by the fence, just like he promised.

Daniel stopped about fifty feet before they reached Mason. 'Hurry up,' he said. 'I think he wants to talk to you alone.'

'We don't have time for this.'

Daniel shrugged. 'Yeah, you do. Now go.'

MASON

When he saw Aries, he couldn't tell if he was happy or sad. Yes, he was relieved that she was OK; he'd been worried when time moved on and they hadn't returned from the casino. What if she'd found Daniel and run off with him, leaving Mason behind.

No, wait. That's what he wanted.

Then why did it hurt so much?

'I can't go.' The words escaped his lips the moment she stopped in front of him.

'What?' Anger and confusion flashed through her eyes. 'What do you mean?'

He bent down carefully and pulled up the hem of his jeans, showing her the electronic bracelet sticking frustratingly to his ankle. 'If I leave with you, they will follow. And I can't have that.'

He'd heard that they could be removed if someone knew what they were doing, but he wasn't one of those people and he doubted anyone else in the group had extensive experience with such things. If he ran, how far could he get before they came and dragged him back? He was nothing but bait. Now that he knew that, there was no way he'd ever leave.

'But you can't stay here,' she said. 'We came to rescue you.'

He gave her a smile, hoping it looked braver than he felt. 'It's OK. I'll be fine. I have a feeling they're not going to kill me.' Reaching into his pocket, his fingers curled round the small bottle of sand. He'd carried it such a long way. It was time now to pass it on. He pressed it into her hand. 'I want you to have this. Merry Christmas.'

She took the bottle and turned it over, studying the contents. 'What is it?'

'The ocean,' he said. 'It's from when I felt the ocean.'

'I have nothing for you,' she said.

'Then get home safe,' he said. 'That'll be the best present ever.'

He reached up and touched her face, feeling the softness of her skin beneath the dirt and charcoal smudges. Leaning in, he gave her a gentle kiss. He kept his eyes open but she closed hers, and he liked the way her eyelashes brushed against her cheeks.

'Come on,' he said. Taking her by the hand, they headed back over to where Daniel was waiting with a sheepish look on his face.

'Take her,' Mason said. 'Get her home.'

Daniel nodded respectfully.

Mason let go of her hand but it didn't really matter anyway. The way she looked at Daniel, a sharp twinge of jealousy wrapped its fingers round Mason's stomach.

She preferred Daniel.

He'd just have to live with that.

Aries finally turned back to Mason. She opened

her mouth but no words came out.

'I'll be fine,' he said. 'Now get going.'

Clementine joined the group, a taser sparking in her hand. 'Right about now is a good time to abandon ship,' she said, and she flashed Mason and Daniel a grin. 'Good to see you again. Hope you don't mind my rudeness but this isn't the time and place to have a personal chat.'

'Good to see you too, Clementine,' Mason said.

'Just one second,' Daniel said. He nodded solemnly at Mason.

'Are you sure you want to do this?' Daniel asked. 'There might be another way. If we try, maybe at least one of us can get that thing off your leg.'

'I'm positive,' Mason said. 'We can't take the chance. Besides, this is where I need to be right now.'

Daniel nodded. 'OK then. You be careful, Tourist Boy.'

'We're not going to forget about you,' Aries said. 'I give you my word. We'll find a way to get you back.'

'Huh?' Clementine looked around at all of them. 'What's going on?'

But there was no time to explain. Mason turned and walked away. When he got halfway across the compound, he looked back but the rest of them had already crawled under the fence and disappeared into the night.

ARIES

They ran along the ocean path towards Yaletown. People rushed past them, confused and heading in all directions. Some jumped into the bay and started swimming for Olympic Village on the other side. A woman was pushed in the commotion, falling into the water where she splashed around, screaming that she didn't know how to swim. Aries swerved in her direction but someone beat her to it and jumped in to rescue her.

The crowd started to dissipate as they hit George Wainborn Park and headed towards the Granville Bridge.

'That was amazing,' Clementine shouted as they ran. 'Did you see all that? There must have been a few hundred people in there and we freed them!'

'Except we didn't save Mason. Or Casey.'

'What the hell happened back there?' Clementine asked. 'Why wouldn't Mason come?'

Aries closed her hand tightly round the glass vial of sand that Mason had given her. Her breathing was heavy and she inhaled deeply before answering. 'I'll explain later,' she said. 'But we're not leaving him there for good. We're going back.'

Daniel held her hand tightly and squeezed, a bit harder than she liked. He was faster than her and pulling her along. It was hard keeping her feet moving in the right direction. She stumbled over some debris, almost falling to her knees.

'Can we slow down?' she said. 'I think we're safe.'

Finally Daniel slowed enough to stop her lungs from exploding. On a corner, they came to a halt and Aries bent down to put her hands on her knees, breathing in deeply, trying to keep herself from hyperventilating.

'I need a safer hobby,' she said between gasps. 'Like quilting.'

Clementine laughed.

'What about the others?' Aries said when she finally managed to bring herself back to an upright position. The ocean was still and silent to their left. 'Do you think they made it?'

'I sure hope so,' Clementine said. 'We've got to get to the bridge. They're going to meet us there, remember.'

'Aries?'

She turned towards Daniel. He was standing very still, his hands at his side, and there were too many shadows covering his face to read his expression. She stepped forward with a smile on her face. Seeing him again meant everything was OK with the world. She decided that she was going to do whatever it took to make sure he came back with them. No more of this sneaking around. They'd been through so much. Didn't he realize this? They needed to be together. They would be stronger as a team. She could do anything with him there. She could go back and get Mason. She could face

Eve and her intense guilt over Nathan's death.

She could . . .

Daniel was shaking.

'What's wrong?'

'Aries,' he said again, 'you need to listen to me and not fight. OK?'

She stepped forward again, trying to bring his face into the light. 'What's wrong?'

'Stop. Stop dammit!'

She paused, one foot in front of the other. So much anger in his voice. What the hell?

'You need to run,' he said. 'Get away from here now. I can't explain but you have to leave me.'

'I can't do that,' she said. She reached out to take his hand. 'You have to come back with us. No more of this running away. I'm tired of it. I want to be with you.'

Daniel let out a shout and dropped to his knees. She immediately crossed the gap, bending down to help him up.

Then he looked at her.

And this time she was close enough to see.

The intense look in his eyes.

The black veins.

'No,' she said. 'No, no, no, no, no.'

'Run,' he whispered.

Clementine was faster than her. She grabbed Aries by the arm, pulling her backwards. Aries fought against her, struggling to return to Daniel's side but he no longer seemed to realize she was there. His body shook with convulsions, hair covering his eyes.

Oh God, his eyes.

Her heart had stopped beating. That had to be the problem. She couldn't feel anything any more. Except pain. And it crashed through her body, tearing at her insides, turning everything to mush.

Daniel looked up at her one last time. She saw the pain in his eyes, the shame of being discovered. A secret he'd tried for so long to hide. Suddenly everything was crystal clear. The refusal to stay with her. The nights of meeting at the beach because he couldn't reveal his dark desires.

He'd betrayed her.

He'd been the one who'd given her name to the Baggers.

'No,' she said again, firmer this time. She broke away from Clementine and rushed towards him, hitting him with the palms of her hands. Again and again. How could he do this to her? She'd trusted him.

Screaming, he suddenly struck back at her, clawing at her face, tangling her hair between his fingers. She went flying backwards with him on top of her, his hands grabbing at her face and neck. She could hear Clementine screaming out his name and the growling noises coming from his mouth. Fingers tightened round her throat. Squeezing. Her vision exploded into a million white stars, and his eyes, with all their blackness, bore holes into her forehead.

There was no recognition on his face. Daniel no longer knew her.

Scrabbling about on the ground, her fingers closed round the machine gun that had slipped off her shoulder in the commotion. She gasped for breath but no air came. Clementine continued to shout but the words were foggy, further away. She could hear her heartbeat pounding inside her, louder and faster than anything she could have thought possible. Daniel was trying to take it away from her. Remove her heart and leave her a husk.

No.

She brought the gun up, smashing the end piece into his face with all her strength. He grunted and his hands loosened enough for her to pull away. Fire burned in her throat and she started coughing – too much. He came for her again and she was too busy hacking up a lung.

She brought the gun round again and swung it like a baseball bat. A loud cracking noise as the metal met his skull.

Daniel dropped to the ground. He twitched twice, shuddering, but his eyes remained closed.

She hit him again and again. His body jolted under each strike but he wasn't going anywhere. Crumpled on the ground. Unconscious. Blood dripped from his mouth, small splotches hitting the cement beneath him.

She hit him again for good measure.

Clementine managed to wrap her arms round her, pulling her back, slapping her in the face to try to snap her out of it. The tears began to flow; again, she brushed them away.

'I hate you,' she screamed. 'I hate you!'

But Clementine was pulling again and finally she allowed it. She turned to her friend, nodded, and squeezed her eyes closed tightly.

She realized she was still holding the machine gun in her hands. All this pain. All this death. Designed and used for the sole purpose of killing everything in sight. She no longer wanted to be a part of it. Disgusted, she turned and threw it straight into the water, where it landed with a loud splash.

'Let's go,' she said, a hardness in her voice she'd never heard before.

They left him on the cement.

She didn't look back.

CLEMENTINE

She couldn't look at Aries.

The pain the girl must be feeling. It was too much for her to even comprehend.

Luckily Raj and Joy were waiting for them back at the bridge. No other casualties. If the others hadn't been OK, Clementine wondered if Aries would have snapped under the guilt and pressure.

But she also knew her friend was stronger than she could ever have imagined before.

'That. Was. Amazing!' Joy squeaked. She was breathing heavily, full of adrenaline, and bleeding from the gash in her arm. Raj didn't look much better. His nose was swelling from where he must have taken a good hit. Noticing the dark red and black patches forming under his eyes, she guessed it was broken.

But they were all alive.

'Never seen anything like it,' Raj wheezed. 'It was like the bloody Running of the Bulls in Spain. Rampage! Brilliant!'

'Baggers flying everywhere,' Joy said. 'I saw a bunch of prison people chasing after them with wooden spoons and frying pans. It was beautiful! And to think we started that!'

'Wonder how many of them will get rounded back up again?' Raj asked.

'Who cares!' Joy covered her mouth with her hand when she realized how loud and excited her words were. 'We'll just go back and save them again, right?' She finally noticed that Aries was shaking something awful. 'Hey, what happened?' she asked.

'Did you not find them, babes?' Raj asked.

'We'll tell you about it later,' Clementine said. 'Let's get home safe first.'

Joy looked at Aries and then back at Clementine. Clementine tried to give her a 'trust me, you don't want to hear it' look.

'OK,' Raj said. 'Let's go.'

Everything was going to be OK when they got back. She kept telling herself that. She tried to concentrate on putting one foot in front of the other, but the image of Daniel's black-veined eyes kept creeping up on her.

She couldn't understand how they'd been betrayed. It was a terrifying thought. If the Baggers were capable of having spies such as Daniel, it meant that any of the others in their group might be playing on the opposite side of the game too. She thought about each person, even Michael, wondering if any of them could possibly have such darkness inside them. But, in the end, she couldn't believe that the friends she'd grown to trust could be Baggers. Even Colin with his obnoxious behaviour didn't strike her as being that twisted. No, he was too much of a coward.

But Michael. Now that made her shudder. She knew that Aries had kissed Daniel. She'd seen it back when they'd been on the beach. It must be killing Aries inside, knowing that the boy she'd kissed and loved was nothing but a cold-blooded murderer.

How would she react if it was Michael?

No. She shook her head as she jogged along. Michael was on their team. They all were. Daniel in his own way had been trying to protect Aries. It was so clear. That's why he'd always refused to come by the house or even let Aries tell him where they were living. It made no sense though. If he was a Bagger, eager to kill them, why did he go to such lengths to keep himself away?

There must have been a thousand chances for Daniel to kill Aries in the past few months; hundreds of times when he could have followed her back from the beach and then sent out for back-up to attack them while they slept.

So why hadn't he done it?

She glanced over at her friend and from her pained expression realized that Aries was thinking the exact same thing.

Daniel was a Bagger. But he was still different compared to the others.

The questions remained unanswered.

The street was dark when they finally arrived home. It had to be very late, maybe around two thirty, three in the morning, but Clementine was too weary even to check her watch. Strange how time used to be so important. She had to be on time for school, for cheerleading, she even had to be on time coming home or else her parents would ground her. But time was now meaningless.

They still existed but time passed them by without stopping to say hello.

'Oh man,' Joy said when the safe house came into view. 'I've never been so happy to see this place in my life. I'm going to sleep for a week.'

They all nodded in agreement. Even Aries looked like she'd be dead to the world once her head hit the pillow. Clementine hoped so. She didn't want her friend up the entire night, the millions of unanswered questions keeping her awake. Hopefully she'd have a dream-free night and the horrors lurking in her subconscious would stay away for now.

They entered through the kitchen and all was quiet. In the living room, Larisa sat in the shadows, reading a book by candlelight. Her face fell when she saw how straggled and wiped everyone was.

'I'm sorry,' Larisa said, automatically assuming they'd found nothing. 'No luck?'

'It was eventful,' Clementine said. 'Just not in the way you might think.' She began to explain and Aries jumped in too, telling them about Mason's ankle monitor.

'They can be removed,' Raj said. 'I've heard stories of people getting them off. Hmmm, there's got to be some info out there somewhere. How I wish the internet still existed – I could find out tonight.' He tenderly rubbed the bridge of his swollen nose. 'Man, I miss technology.'

'We're going back for him as soon as possible,' Aries said as she sat down on the couch. 'I'm not leaving Mason to rot in that hellhole. We need to find a way to remove the device.'

'I'll help best I can, babes,' Raj said. 'I guess we can hit up a library. Might find something there.'

'Me too,' Clementine added. Getting Mason back would be the best thing in the world for Aries. She would need the positive distraction and Clementine had seen the way they looked at each other, Daniel or no Daniel.

'But I should go stand watch,' Larisa said, pulling herself up off the chair. 'Eve is asleep. I gave her a sleeping pill; she was pretty distraught. Claude offered to sit with her but he's not happy. I don't think he's going to stick around much longer. And of course that Colin guy is more than useless.'

'I can do it,' Clementine said.

'Not a chance,' Larisa said with a wink. 'You need some beauty sleep for when you go searching for your boy tomorrow. And I'm more than wide awake.' She picked up the two-way radio on the table. 'I'll holler if anything happens, but as long as you weren't followed I doubt we'll have any surprises tonight.'

No sooner had the words escaped her lips than they all felt the draught. A cool breeze wafted in from the kitchen. The click of the latch as someone closed the door behind themself.

They all stood in unison. Clementine tightened her grip on the taser. There were several long agonizing seconds until someone walked through the door. She gasped in surprise.

It was Michael.

MICHAEL

He remembered it was Christmas morning just as Clementine threw herself into his arms. He couldn't think of a better gift. Not even a brand-new Les Paul guitar could have made him happier.

And he'd come bearing presents.

Clementine held him tightly for several seconds. Aries smiled at him, her eyes dark and lost. He knew immediately something bad had happened to her.

'I missed you,' he whispered into Clementine's hair. 'But look at what I brought back.'

She gazed up at him and then noticed Heath for the first time standing behind him. And . . . something was wrong. There was no recognition in her eyes. No jumping up and down. No screams of joy.

'Clementine?'

Heath began to laugh.

Michael suddenly understood he'd done a very stupid thing.

'You sure are gullible,' Heath said. 'You should have listened to your dead friend. He suspected me from the very beginning. But, no, you were too stupid to figure it out. Too eager to get back to your pretty girlfriend. You didn't even see when I dropped the key on the floor for the others to claim him while we were out nabbing the van.

Michael's teeth clamped down tightly, his fingers curling into fists at his sides.

'I mean, even I can't believe how easily you fell for that.' Heath's voice changed to a higher octave. 'Clementine? You've seen her? My dear, sweet baby sister. Oh, I'm the luckiest brother in the entire world. I can't wait to join her. We can bake cookies and pies. It'll be so delightful.'

Clementine jolted as if she'd been hit by lightning.

'How is that possible,' Raj asked, taking a step forward and looking right in fake Heath's face. 'There's nothing wrong with your eyes. I've never seen one of you without the black veins.'

'When it gets to be too much, it shows,' fake Heath said. 'The eyes are the window to the soul. But some of us have learned to push it back down. Keep it hidden. Sure as hell fooled you all. Who are you gonna trust now?'

'Everyone in this room except you,' Clementine said. 'Isn't that why you took Mason? Isn't that why you lied to Michael? You had no idea where we were until tonight. I trust everyone here. They've never let me down.'

The fake Heath moved quickly, shoving Michael aside and grabbing Clementine by the arm.

'They're gonna let you down now, sweetie,' he hissed. 'Not a single one of them can save you now.'

Raj jumped in but fake Heath slammed him back

and into the advancing Aries. Michael took advantage of the distraction and punched the fake Heath as hard as he could. It barely made a dent, but he let go of Clementine and shoved her into the pile of her friends.

'Oh, come on,' he said. 'You can do better than that.'

Michael nodded, raising his fist again. 'You're right, I can.'

He faked a left jab, punching with his right when Heath blocked. His fist smashed against the side of the Bagger's face, hitting his ear with all his might. The Bagger let out an *oomph* noise, and then punched back, sending Michael into the wall.

Michael didn't pause at all. Instead he ducked his head in, pushed forward and body slammed the fake Heath, knocking him back against the already broken flat-screen television. Jagged glass sliced Michael's arm but he barely registered the burning pain. Instead, he twisted his body round until he was on top of the other boy, and began sending blow after blow into the Bagger's face and upper body.

When he was finished, the fake Heath's face was mulched. He smiled up at Michael through bloodstained teeth.

'You do realize you're just helping me stall, right?' He turned and spat blood on the wall. 'They're on their way here. Any second now they'll burst through your security. Can you fight us all off? Nope, don't think so.'

'Come on, Michael.' Clementine grabbed his arms

and pulled him back. 'He's right. We have to get out of here.'

'Get the others,' Aries snapped.

'I'll get Eve,' Larisa said. She turned and headed up the stairs with Joy right behind her.

Fake Heath laughed again, a low throaty chuckle. Pulling himself up to his feet, he swayed unevenly as he tried to maintain his balance. 'I know who you are; I recognize you. I hope they get you last,' he said, looking directly at Aries. 'I hope they force you to watch them tear your friends apart piece by piece. And only then will they turn on you.'

Michael spun back towards him again, the rage turning his vision bloody red. But Clementine was on him at once, whispering into his ear with her soft beautiful voice.

'He's not worth it,' she said. 'Let it go. Let them all go. Don't leave me.'

And he didn't. 'You're not worth it,' he said to Heath. 'But she is.'

Turning his back on the Bagger, he gave Clementine a tender kiss. 'I love you,' he said. 'Now let's get everyone to safety.'

She nodded.

MASON

He sat on a bench down by the water and waited for the Baggers to come and get him. It didn't take long.

'All that work for such a poor result,' a voice came from behind him. 'An entire rescue effort for nothing. You're still here. I'll bet your friends were very disappointed in you.'

He didn't move or acknowledge the voice. If they were going to kill him, he wouldn't give them the satisfaction of getting a rise out of him first. No, he was done with all that. He'd accepted it; whatever they wanted to do to him was fine.

'Do you think you've won?' the voice continued. The Bagger stepped into view. It was Leon of course, surrounded by a few of his lackeys. He didn't look as impressive any more. His shirt was undone at the waist, and there was a sizable black smudge on his cheek.

Mason shrugged. 'It's not about winning.'

'Oh, but it is,' Leon said. He sat down on the bench beside Mason and pulled a small flask from his pocket. Twisting the cap off, he took a drink, and then offered it to Mason. 'Winning. Losing. It's all about how you play the game, right?'

Mason took the flask and sniffed it. A strong alcoholic scent hit his nose. He took a sip, enjoying the instant warmth as it slipped down his throat and into his stomach.

'I play the game very well, Mr Dowell,' Leon said. 'Better than anyone else. Why do you think they chose me to run this place? That is one thing I think you've greatly underappreciated about me. I like to win. And you may not know it yet, but I've won. Should I tell you how?'

He handed back the flask and looked out at the water. The crowds had dispersed; the majority of the prisoners had escaped into the dark city. The remains of the unlucky ones littered the pavement, but the casualties weren't as bad as he'd feared. The surviving Baggers were out hunting now, trying to round up whatever people they could find. Every few minutes he'd hear a scream or a shout as someone was torn from their hiding place. He hoped that Casey had got out but he probably wouldn't know for sure until everything settled back down.

'Most of the people in this camp were useless,' Leon said. 'We were using them to help clean the streets but they really meant little in terms of our future. Even the ones inside the casino – they're all expendable. Small fish. The important people are kept elsewhere. So it doesn't matter to us that a few escaped. Besides, we'll round them back up eventually.'

'You won't get them all. That's enough for me.'

Leon crossed his legs casually and stared out at the water. 'You are a fool, Mr Dowell.'

'Oh yeah? How do you figure that?'

'You could have run. You could have kept them safe. Instead, you destroyed everything that you hold dear. In one brief, shining, moment, you signed her death warrant.'

'I kept her safe by not running,' Mason snapped. 'Why else do I have this stupid thing on my leg? You would have just hunted me down. And her.'

Leon chuckled. 'If you had run, she would have stood a chance. At least for a short period of time. You might have been able to protect her.'

'She does a good job of protecting herself in case you hadn't noticed,' he said. A seagull dropped in from the sky to attack a piece of litter on the ground in front of them. He inhaled deeply, smelling the sulphur and smoke from the smouldering buildings behind them. 'They managed to do all this damage and still get away. Do you really think I worry about her safety? She's stronger than all of us put together.'

'She has her Achilles' heel, just like you have yours.' Leon took another drink from the flask and the Baggers standing guard behind him smiled knowingly. 'And you just tossed her right into the arms of her biggest weakness.'

Mason paused.

'She likes pretty boys, doesn't she?' Leon continued. 'She likes you but there is one other that she can't resist. You must hate that. Being second fiddle. Knowing that, no matter what you do or say to impress her, you will never hold the first position in her heart.'

'She can do whatever she wants with Daniel,' Mason said as casually as he could manage. 'It's her decision, not mine.'

'Is she better than Chickadee? You never did get the chance with that pretty little bird either. She was too busy dying.'

'That's none of your business.' The anger was strong in his voice. He tried to hold it back but it was getting harder.

Leon stood up slowly, brushing out the creases in his trousers. 'Ask yourself this,' he said with a grin. 'Do you really think I didn't have this all planned out? Did you think your friend's puny attack wasn't on my radar? I knew it would happen probably before you did. Of course I admit I didn't think your friends would end up doing quite so much damage. I might have underestimated that a little. Who knew those gutless wonders in my camp would fight back too.' He looked around at all the dead bodies on the ground.

'You're telling me you set all this up to trap Aries?'

'No.' Leon took another drink from his flask. 'We set all this up because we want to take everyone down. There are still people hiding out there and we're going to find them. This was a good location. It will be rebuilt and we'll continue to bring people here to work.'

'But why Aries? Just because she's managed to evade you for so long?'

'Like you, there's something inside her that peaks

our curiosity. A strength of sorts, perhaps. And, like you again, soon we'll have the chance to ask her about it. Do you think she'll like the cattle prod? Not strong enough? How about battery acid on that pretty face of hers?'

'You'll never get her,' Mason said, the grin appearing on his lips before he could stop it. 'She's too smart for you. She keeps proving that.'

'We'll get her. It's only a matter of time.'

Leon passed the flask over and Mason took another drink. Might as well; it wasn't like he had anywhere else to be.

'Your friend, Daniel, doesn't he seem odd to you? Always so secretive? Sneaking off in the dead of night, never spending more than a few hours with you at a time? He's been your ally all along, hasn't he? Or maybe he's lying. Perhaps he's only doing all that because someone asked him to do it.'

Mason's stomach turned to ice. Suddenly all Leon's hints made sense. Everything he knew about them . . .

'You just sent her off into the arms of one of us,' Leon said. 'And the best part is you were too stupid to notice.'

'No.'

Mr Leon brushed off his trousers one last time and then turned towards the other Baggers. 'Take him back.'

ARIES

At least they were prepared this time.

She raced up the stairs towards the bedrooms where Larisa, Claude and Joy were trying to get Eve out of her bed. She was still under the influence of the sleeping pills and couldn't seem to focus enough to know what was going on. Colin appeared from behind them, his face pale and terrified.

'Come on,' Aries said. 'You know where to go! Let's get there now!'

'Can you fetch Jack?' Joy asked.

A twinge of pain shot through her stomach. How was she going to explain all this once they were safe at the abandoned house they'd already marked a few weeks ago as their escape location?

She'd have to worry about it then. Right now there were more important factors to face.

'I'm on it,' she said.

Joy smiled in relief.

She left them in the room and raced down the hall, stopping to pick up a discarded baseball bat that had been left haphazardly on the floor by the bathroom. For a moment she regretted her decision to toss the machine gun but it was too late for regrets now.

Suddenly the image of Daniel looking up at her, the

black veins shadowing his beautiful brown eyes, hit her so hard she had to steady herself by leaning against the wall. A painful emptiness spread through her stomach like wildfire, making her want to curl up into a small ball and drop to the floor.

No! She wasn't going to think about it. Not now.

Not with so little time.

Pushing herself away from the wall, she stumbled down the hall, stopping at the next bedroom door. She didn't knock, but turned the handle with sweat-drenched hands and went inside.

'Jack.'

The boy on the bed was sitting up, his back against the headboard.

'Go away, Aries.'

Her mouth opened, a small sob escaped her.

'No,' Jack said. The expression on his face was serene. 'We made this decision. You and I. We're not going to go back on it now. Consider this our goodbye.'

'I can't –' She paused, inhaling deeply. 'I can't do it.'

He waved her over to the bed and she went to him. Wrapping his arms round her, he stared blindly at the wall. 'You can and you will. I'm cool with it. I want this. Respect my wishes.'

She stayed with him for a few more seconds before he gently pushed her away. Standing, she nodded, and then felt stupid because he couldn't see.

'I'll miss you,' she said, tucking in the blankets

around his body so he wouldn't get cold. 'You've been a good friend.'

'Me too.'

She stood, listening to the sounds of the others rushing through the house in a mad panic. Walking over to the door, she paused one last time. 'Merry Christmas.' The words sounded so sad that she regretted saying them instantly. She should be sounding more positive, more leader-like.

'Say goodbye for me,' Jack said. 'They'll understand.'

'I love you.'

'I love you too.'

Somehow everyone managed to get out of the house. As they ran into the dark cover of the football field, she heard the white vans, engines screaming, turn the corner and slam on the brakes.

They didn't look back. Moving at a decent pace, Raj carried the half-asleep Eve as he'd carried Nathan earlier.

Joy was waiting for them round the side of the high-school building.

'Where's Jack?'

Aries pursed her lips together tightly. She had hoped they'd be further away before the question came up. It was going to be hard to convince them all not to go back at this point.

'He doesn't want to come,' she finally said. 'It was his choice. We have to respect his wishes.'

Joy instantly began to cry. Michael and Clementine exchanged looks.

'We can't do that to him,' Joy said between huge sobs. 'We have to go back.'

Aries went over to her, tried to put her arm round Joy's shoulder, but her friend pushed her away. 'We've done everything we can,' Aries said. 'We can't go back. Do you see how many of them there are? They'll kill us all.'

'But we have to,' Joy said. The tears were slowing down, replaced by anger. 'He doesn't get to make that decision. I won't allow it.'

She broke free from the group but Michael was too fast. Grabbing hold of her arms, he held on tightly. She fought him like a madwoman, kicking and screaming. Panic welled up inside Aries; the Baggers were going to hear them.

'We have to get her out of here,' she snapped. 'Or we're all dead.'

Michael nodded, trying to pull Joy back, even lifting her up off the ground, but she continued to fight, scratching his face with her nails.

'He doesn't get to make this choice,' Joy screamed again. 'He doesn't know!'

'Know what?'

'That I'm pregnant.'

Michael let go of her instantly.

Joy dropped to the ground, landing on her knees, and every single one of them flinched in shock. She picked herself up, wiping the tears from her cheeks and neck, and walked straight up to Aries.

'I'm pregnant.' She was out of breath, panting from the struggle. 'And he needs to know. He'll change his mind if you tell him.'

'Are you sure?'

Joy nodded. 'I nicked one of those home-pregnancy tests last week while getting supplies. It was positive.'

Aries nodded. 'You're right then.' She thought about the white vans that were probably piled up in the driveway by now and how the Baggers were most likely in the house and running up the stairs to the second floor as they spoke. 'You all head on. Don't stop till you reach safety. You know the address. I'll get him.'

'Are you sure, babes?' Raj asked. 'The place is swarming with 'em. It might already be too late.'

'I can still try.'

Michael caught her by the arm. 'This is a bad idea,' he said.

She shook her head. 'No, this is the only idea.'

'Then I'm coming with you.'

JACK

He had told himself he'd be brave when it happened. There would be no begging or pleading for his life. He wouldn't give them the satisfaction.

It sounded like a herd of elephants tearing through the house. It was only a matter of time before they came up the stairs and opened his bedroom door.

Breathing deeply, he tried to control the panicky feeling in his chest. He'd chosen this. He needed to be strong.

Would it hurt? Dying?

Jack didn't believe in heaven. The thought of an afterlife where everything was calm and peaceful didn't make much sense to him. Dying, he believed, was like going to sleep and never waking up, and in the long run that didn't sound so bad. He enjoyed sleeping. At least there would be no pain.

I'll sleep when I'm dead.

His brain continuously banged against his skull. Some days were better than others. But although he tried to play it down, the pain of the migraines was immeasurable. He'd never experienced such agony. He didn't think such agony was even possible. On the bad days he couldn't even get a basic thought out. No amount of drugs could lessen the burden.

Sometimes the insides of his worthless eyes flashed bright white as the pain hit, knocking him back, making him useless. When it got this bad, he couldn't do anything except wish he was dead.

He hadn't told anyone that. Not even Joy, who pretty much knew everything about him these days. She'd only worry and he didn't want that.

Sleep sounded good.

When he heard the door handle turn, his body involuntarily froze. Breathing deeply, he pulled himself up till he was sitting as straight as possible. His ears perked, waiting.

Footsteps entered the room.

Silence.

'I'm not afraid of you,' he said as bravely as he possibly could.

Silence. The sound of someone breathing softly.

'Come on,' Jack said. 'Let's get this over with. I'm tired.'

The footsteps moved in closer until Jack could feel the Bagger standing beside him at the bed.

He closed his eyes and waited.

MICHAEL

They moved carefully back across the football field, bent low to the ground, trying to be as invisible as possible. Michael thought about the situation as they walked. Between them, they each had a baseball bat and Aries was carrying Clementine's taser. Three weapons. Two of them. Not nearly enough for an ambush.

And if by some miracle they managed to get back inside the house, how on earth were they going to walk out with a blind boy leaning on their shoulders?

It was suicide.

'We could always tell them we tried and it was too late,' he whispered to Aries as they approached the back lane. 'They don't need to know. That's a secret I don't mind taking to the grave.'

'I'm not backing out,' Aries said.

It suddenly dawned on Michael that they were missing a group member. He hadn't seen Nathan since they'd got back. And Eve, who was obviously drugged, couldn't even get sober enough to run.

Something had happened.

Was this some sort of rescue mission based on guilt? Had something happened to Nathan, and Aries hadn't been able to save him? Suddenly everything made a bit more sense and he mentally reminded himself to ask

Clementine about it when they were alone.

If he got the opportunity.

They paused at the back gate, ducking behind the white boards, their knees sinking into the ground. From their spot, they had a clear view of the house. The door was open and they could see the Baggers moving around inside the kitchen. Michael caught a glimpse of the fake Heath. He had a dishtowel pressed against his head and was being screamed at by another Bagger. Michael couldn't help but smile to see the bastard's discomfort.

There were a lot of them.

'I don't know what to do,' Aries whispered. She was clearly distraught, chewing on a fingernail, mesmerized as the monsters tore through the house. 'There's no way we can get in there.'

'This is pointless,' he said. 'We should go back.'

'Just a few more minutes. Let's wait and see if they bring him out. They captured Mason and –' She paused. 'Daniel. They might take Jack too.'

Michael thought about pointing out the low odds of that. The Baggers wouldn't want to keep Jack around, being blind and all. He was as useless in this new world as a three-dollar bill at a 7-Eleven.

But if Aries didn't know what to do Michael realized he was going to have to be the one to lead her back to safety.

'Let's go,' he said. 'Even if they do bring him out, there's nothing we can do. We need to get back to the others. Clementine and Raj are under enough stress as it is with Joy and Eve. And Colin's so bloody useless.'

Aries shook her head.

'Listen to me, Aries.' Michael grabbed her arm and forced her to look at him. 'They are the ones who need us. Not Jack. We look to you for leadership.' He spoke the words, wondering how long that would remain true. She looked like she might crack any minute. 'So you have to lead. Back at UBC I met a guy named Ryder who said something to me. Leaders lead. They make decisions that aren't always easy. You need to stop feeling sorry for the people you can't help, and kick some ass for the ones you can. You can't keep second guessing yourself or you're just going to go crazy. Get it?'

She nodded.

'Then let's go.'

They stood up together and turned, Michael almost didn't see the Bagger until it was too late. A woman, dressed in dirty clothes and carrying a huge kitchen knife, had snuck up behind them. A few more steps and it would have been over for at least one of them.

The woman opened her mouth, letting out a loud shriek as she raised the knife.

Michael tackled her, sending her flying backwards into a recycling dumpster. They both crashed to the ground, rolling around as he tried to get the knife out of her grasp. She continued to scream, and he half covered her mouth with his hand while fighting for control of the knife. She bit down hard on his wrist, sending hot pain up his arm.

'Shut up!' he grunted.

Aries swooped down, holding the taser up against the Bagger's body and pressing the button. Nothing happened. Michael could see the bewildered expression on Aries's face, so comical it almost made him want to laugh.

Yeah, hysterical.

Pulling back, he managed to free his hand but not before the Bagger swiped at him with her knife. He felt the blade scratch against his chest, tearing a ragged hole in his shirt, but enough adrenaline raced through his veins that he barely registered the pain. He punched her twice, blood flying from the gash in his wrist; he managed to push away from her enough to grab the baseball bat.

He hit her squarely on the second try. The Bagger dropped to the ground instantly, unmoving except for a few sporadic twitches.

The other Baggers were piling out into the yard. Of course they'd been heard.

'Time to go,' Aries said.

Michael couldn't agree more.

They raced across the football field with the Baggers in pursuit. If they could make it to the other side, the tangle of abandoned houses might give them better shelter. Footsteps stomped behind him and his shirt pulled tight as one of them grabbed hold. Michael swung the bat round, making contact, and heard a loud grunting noise as the Bagger tripped over his own feet. Michael didn't even pause to look back. He didn't want to know how close the others were.

By some miracle, they made it across the field and managed to escape between two houses and into a yard where a mouldy pool waited in the darkness. Several months' worth of dead leaves and garbage seemed to occupy the space where the chlorine blue water should have been.

'Come on,' Michael said. 'We need to hide.'

Aries understood and they both raced down the steps into the pool's shallow end. Michael's sneakers instantly became soaked. There was at least a foot of rainwater underneath all those dead leaves. Ignoring the freezing shock blasting through his body, he moved in further until he was waist deep.

From between the houses, they could hear the shouts of the Baggers. Not much time now.

Michael took a deep breath. Plunging his head under, the shock of icy rainwater tore into his system, and it took all the strength he had not to burst back to the surface, gasping for air.

He held his breath until he couldn't bear it any longer. Raising himself up a bit, he tilted his face just out of the wet debris and inhaled lightly. It meant swallowing dirt and bits of mouldy leaves along with his oxygen; but at least he remained hidden under all that mess.

He could hear the muffled shouts of the Baggers but

it didn't last long. The voices faded as the Baggers moved on, oblivious to the two of them hiding beneath the pool surface.

He waited until his fingers were numb and he could no longer feel most of his limbs. So cold. Finally, when he couldn't take it any more, he poked his head up a little higher, wiping the leaves and junk from his eyelashes, and took a quick peek.

The yard was empty.

Yanking on Aries, he brought her up too. She was shivering like crazy. Rubbing her hands against her body to try and keep warm. Leaves and twigs tangled in her hair.

'Next time I get to pick the hiding spot,' she said as her teeth chattered.

Carefully, making as little noise as possible, they climbed out of the abandoned pool and stood on the tiles, listening to the night and for any sounds of impending danger.

They could hear shouts from halfway down the block as the Baggers continued their search.

'Come on,' Aries said, breathing on her hands to try to send the numbness away. 'Let's go. If I get pneumonia, I'm coming back to haunt you.'

He took her fingers and rubbed them between his own. 'If we get out of here alive, I'm buying you the biggest, hottest cup of coffee you've ever seen.'

She smiled. 'You're on.'

CLEMENTINE

They waited in the new safe house, sitting in the living room, weapons close by just in case. Claude had agreed to stand first watch and she wondered if he would bother coming back. She had yet to hear him say more than a few words since he'd arrived with Larissa.

Eve was asleep again, her head in Raj's lap, drooling enough to soak a coin-sized spot on his leg.

An hour passed.

She went through the cupboards for something to do and was rewarded with some warm cans of Coke. After helping Clementine to pass them out, Raj drank his in a few gulps while Joy placed hers on the table and just stared at it sullenly.

No one talked. There wasn't anything left to say.

Even Colin looked lost without his Game Boy.

Poor Michael. How must he be feeling right now, knowing that he'd brought the Baggers right into their hiding spot? How dare one of them pretend to be her brother, Heath. Even weirder, how on earth did they know about Heath to begin with?

Daniel must have been feeding them information all this time.

The revelation hit her like a slap to the face. How were they supposed to trust anyone? Baggers or not, who's to say they wouldn't all turn into betrayers if they were given no other way out?

What if one of them had already done something? She studied Colin for a while, watching the way he crunched his empty Coke can between his hands. She didn't trust him, never had, but she still didn't think he'd go out of his way to rat them out.

Trust.

They'd have to learn it all over again.

And it was going to be hard. But still completely necessary.

A soft knock at the door broke her concentration. Flying out of her chair, she grabbed hold of her baseball bat, wishing for the millionth time she hadn't given Aries her taser.

Raj beat her to the door. Pulling back the window curtain slightly, his shoulders instantly relaxed. He unlocked the deadbolt and let them in.

Both Michael and Aries were soaked. Water dripped from their hair, which was covered with leaves and clumps of dirt. They looked like soggy water monsters.

The short burst of laughter escaped her lips before she could even think about it.

'Are you suggesting I'm not my usual hot self?' Michael said through chattering teeth. He came straight for her, wrapping his freezing arms round her, embracing her in a bear hug before she could even think to try to stop him.

'You're getting me soaked,' she protested.

'Misery loves company,' he said, refusing to let go.

Even though the cold dampness transferred to her own clothing, she was still filled with a warm glow of happiness. She wanted to hold on tight to him and never let go. But that feeling went away quickly enough when she realized Aries and Michael had arrived alone, and what their embrace must be doing to Joy. She pulled back, smiling at him, but firmly enough that he let her go.

Joy had stood up, waiting in the middle of the room, a strange look on her face.

'I'm sorry,' Aries said. 'We tried but there were too many of them.'

Joy nodded. The tears were thick in her eyes. 'Thanks,' she said with a soft voice. 'You did your best.'

Aries opened her mouth to say something more but didn't. Clementine went over to her friend and tried to put her arm round her but Joy shrugged her off.

'Do you think it's safe enough here to spend the night?' she asked in a hollow voice.

'Yeah, safe enough,' Michael said. 'They didn't follow us. We doubled back and forth a few times to make sure. I'm probably going to be sick as hell the next few days but it was worth it. Besides, I've always got Clem to be my nurse.'

Clementine made a tssking noise with her teeth. 'I'm not going near you if you're sick.'

He grinned at her wickedly.

'Then I'm going to go lie down for a bit,' Joy said.

'No offence, but I kinda want to be alone.'

They all nodded. They understood.

'And I need to find some dry clothes,' Aries said. 'I've never been so cold in my life.'

'Hope they have some good brand names in the closet,' Michael said. 'I won't cover my frozen skin with anything less than Louis Vuitton.'

'That's a bag, dumb ass,' Clementine said.

'Wow,' Michael said as he put his arms around her again. 'My girlfriend knows both cars and clothing. She's a dream come true.'

She laughed. It was a good sound and it made her feel warm inside, despite the icy fingers on her waist.

'It's good to have you back,' she said.

ARIES

She waited until they were all asleep before scribbling a quick note and sneaking out into the darkness. There were still a few hours to go before light and she wanted to get down to the water before it might be too late.

It was a stupid idea and she knew it. But she had to know for sure.

She'd managed to find something else to wear. Nothing nice, just a pair of men's tracksuit bottoms and an oversized hoody, but it was warm. The shoes she wore were a few sizes too big and she had to stuff some tissues in the toes but they were dry. She wasn't about to start being choosy at this point. They could always find new clothes. There was an abundance of stores from which to pick.

She rubbed her fingers against the glass vial of sand in her pocket. It soothed her, making the anxiety a little less painful.

Kitsilano Beach was quiet. Even the waves didn't seem to be making much noise. She walked through a pile of litter, kicking at a discarded Sprite can as she headed towards the park bench, keeping her guard up just in case.

She needed to know.

Ahead of her, she could see the figure waiting. She

approached him cautiously, the baseball bat tight between her clenched fingers. As she drew closer, she recognized the shape of his back, and her shoulders tightened. He didn't turn round, even when she stopped a few feet away.

'Who are you?'

'I'm Daniel,' he said. The waves washed quietly against the shore, and in the distance she heard a seagull cry.

'What does that mean?' she asked.

Daniel turned slowly to face her. She raised the bat, prepared for the worst but it was only his brown eyes looking back at her.

'How could you do this to me?' She could feel the tears burning, threatening to fall, and she blinked them back furiously. No, she wouldn't cry over him.

'Do you want an explanation? Would that make everything better?'

'No, but it's a start.'

He nodded his head slightly, gesturing for her to sit down. 'Don't worry, I won't bite. I'm normal enough for now.'

There was so much pain and misery in his eyes that she believed him. She sat cautiously on the edge of the bench.

He didn't say anything for a while and the silence was too much. Finally the word blurted from her lips. 'Why?'

'Did you know they tortured me back at the camp?

They're torturing Mason too, probably as we speak.'

'Why?'

'They want Mason to give up information,' Daniel said. 'As for me, they're mad that I've been avoiding them. I'd managed to stay away from them for too long. It was punishment because I've been behaving badly.'

'You betrayed us.'

'Not me. Never me. The monster inside me did it.' The anger rose in his voice and she flinched a bit, gripping her weapon tighter.

'Explain it,' she said. 'You tell me.'

'It started right before the earthquakes,' he said. 'I was having blackouts. Periods of time where I couldn't remember a damn thing. Often when I woke up I'd find myself in situations. I'd done something terrible. I beat the living crap out of some guy at school. I woke up in the park with blood on my face and hands. I had no idea why. Everything was a great big blur. Do you have any idea what that's like?'

She didn't say anything.

'After the earthquakes, everything started to make a bit more sense,' he said. 'I started putting bits of the puzzle together. They came for me and tried to make me join them but I ran away. I couldn't understand why they didn't try to kill me. But by then I was in too deep, I guess.

'And after a while I started remembering things,' he continued. 'Little flashbacks and small memories that invaded my mind. I was doing terrible things. I was killing people and I couldn't do anything to stop it. Part of me didn't want to stop either. It was like something primitive had taken over my brain and I enjoyed it. And the voices in my head, always whispering at me. Telling me that I craved it. I needed it. They get inside my brain and stir things around. I don't know which way is up or down.'

'Are they all like that?' she asked. She thought back to when Nathan died and the female Bagger that had started crying and mumbling about being sorry. 'I mean the Baggers. Do they all have moments of being . . . human again?'

He shook his head. 'I don't know. Most of them, they're stuck in their world, they don't have a conscience like me. At least, if they do, I've never seen it. I'm the only one who seems to be trapped between both worlds. But, if it makes you feel any better, you help me sometimes. You seem to keep me sane.'

'Me?'

'Yeah,' Daniel said. 'When I'm around you, I feel cleaner. I can last longer without changing. I think that's why the Baggers are so interested in you. In us.' Daniel reached out and gently pressed a finger on her shoulder. 'There's something special in you. But you have to be careful. The Baggers have you on their list and they'll do anything to stop you now. Not only did Leon fail at getting you, you made him look stupid. He's not going to be happy about that. He's someone you have to watch out for.'

'Then we need to figure out how to stop this,' she said. 'And you can help. Tell me more about the Baggers. What makes them crazy?'

'Something big,' Daniel said, and his voice quivered. 'Something evil. Remember what I talked about before – a deranged sort of Mother Nature? That's really what it's like. It's been here since the beginning of time. It has no name; it existed before words had meaning. You can't destroy it; it would be like unmaking the earth.'

'But why try to kill us?'

'This probably isn't the first time it's tried to destroy mankind. There are cultures in the past that have apparently self-destructed. Look at the history books; it's all there in black and white. It lies dormant for a long period of time and then it awakens. It looks at the way people misuse the earth and it gets pissed.' Daniel looked down at his hands. 'It finds ways to get inside human minds and make us turn against each other. It started the earthquakes. It wants us to get things right this time.'

'Get things right? It killed everyone off.'

'That's the idea. Fewer people means less damage to the world. More balance. No more pollution. No more animals being driven to extinction. Of course the execution is a little flawed. Killing almost everyone off and then putting the last of normal mankind into slavery isn't a great way to start over.'

'But what gives it the right to do this?' Aries snapped.

'Who said it could make all the decisions on who gets to live and who gets to die?'

'I don't know,' Daniel said. 'I'm just the messenger and even I don't have all the details. All I have is what the voices tell me. And when I'm in Bagger mode it all makes perfect sense.'

'How do we stop it?'

He shrugged. 'I have no idea. It speaks to me, to all of us. The voices we hear. It tells us plenty of things but not how to stop it.'

'Yeah, I guess that would be too easy, wouldn't it.'

'But I do know this,' Daniel said. 'The Baggers will continue to make themselves comfortable, and won't stop killing anyone who gets in their way. Eventually there will be no one left to remember how things were before the world ended. We'll have an entire culture built up around a new world order that they control. Sure, the Baggers won't last forever either. They'll die off too.'

'But will there be anyone healthy left alive by then? Mankind will be finished and the world left in peace!' Aries gasped.

'Maybe people will get tired of it and fight back before then,' Daniel replied. 'Maybe there will be enough survivors to take them down. But I doubt it. What's happening in Vancouver is happening all over the world. And they're far more organized than we are.'

'So we're just supposed to sit back and survive for a

few generations and hope that eventually everyone will be good again? Maybe.'

'You can't do anything to change them, Aries. The best you can do is wait it out.'

She paused, thinking about his words and their meaning.

'But maybe they could all "come back" instead,' she said. 'Maybe we could stop it. What if we can find a way to get this thing out of your head permanently? Out of everyone's heads.'

'Seriously?' Daniel asked. 'This isn't like turning a light switch on or off. I can't get rid of the darkness. It won't go away. You can't just smack some sense into me. No matter how much you manage to help me, you're just not strong enough to keep me sane all the time.'

'But you're *good*,' she said, desperately clinging to whatever hope she could find. 'I know you, Daniel. You're not bad. That thing that happened, that change, you weren't you. You're not responsible. If we could find a way to get rid of it . . .'

'Then what?' Daniel said. 'We'd ride off into the sunset? I've got news for you. There is no Happily Ever After. The Baggers' new world order will continue to rule this earth long after all of us are gone. It's not going to go away.'

'We can fight.'

'You can try.'

Her eyes narrowed. 'So that's it? You're going to give up just like that?'

Daniel stood, smiling softly at her. 'I wish I had your confidence,' he said. 'I wish I had your faith in love and I wish I knew the answers to make this all go away. But this isn't a fairy tale and there's no way to kiss away the beast buried inside me. I'm sorry, Aries, but I can't come back. I can't live in both worlds. I can't be in love with you knowing that I might end up killing you.'

'Stay with me,' she begged. 'We'll find a way.'

'No,' he said, and she could actually see the tears in his eyes, catching the light of the moon. 'Stay away from me and I'll stay away from you. That's how things have to be from now on.'

She stood up and put her arms around him, ignoring the warning thoughts in the back of her mind. If he changed now, so be it. She'd rather die than not try to take away his pain.

He allowed the embrace. His body was warm, on fire, and she wanted nothing more than to spend the rest of her life in that comfortable heat.

When she looked up at him, he leaned down and kissed her gently. Butterflies swished around in her stomach and she had to shift positions to keep on her feet. But when they finally drew apart, she could see that he hadn't changed his mind about anything.

'I wish I could explain how important you are to me,' Daniel said, reaching out and taking her hand. 'You make me feel like I'm really here.'

'Will I see you again?' she asked.

'No. Not if I can help it.'

'Well, I'm not giving up,' she said. 'And I'm never going to quit fighting for you or any of us. I'm going to find a way to bring you back.'

He smiled but his hand slipped from hers. 'I believe you. If anyone can do it, you can.'

Turning, he began to walk away, his shoulders heavy and slouched. He paused, about twenty feet away. 'I've left you a present a little way down. Just a few benches over. Be sure to go get it before it gets cold. Merry Christmas.'

'I didn't get you anything,' she called back.

'Yes, you did.'

She watched him fade away into the darkness, resisting the urge to chase after him. Finally she turned, heading along the water's edge, to find the bench, curious to see what waited for her.

'Jack?'

The boy on the bench perked his head up. Wrapped in a blanket, he stared out at the sea, unable to see its beauty.

She ran, stumbling in the sand, falling to her knees but pulling herself up at once. Throwing her arms round her friend, she held him tightly.

'I can't believe it,' she babbled. 'I thought you were dead.'

'It's good to hear your voice,' he said. 'And you can blame your crazy friend for all of that. He refused to listen to reason.'

'Let's get you home,' she said. Helping him to his

feet, she wrapped her arms around him and led him away from the water. 'Someone's got some good news for you.'

She would concentrate on getting him home. One step at a time. She'd worry about everything else later.

It would be a good Christmas after all.

MASON

It was New Year's Eve. He knew this because one of the Baggers kept screaming it at the top of his lungs as if it actually meant something.

Mason grinned to himself. Too bad there wasn't going to be anyone around to kiss when the clock reached midnight.

He stood off to the side of the Plaza of Nations in the corner spot he'd come to think of as his own personal space. He'd pitched his new tent here and, although it was away from the others, the Baggers hadn't made him move. He liked the little bit of privacy, although he didn't really need it any more. There was plenty of space these days. The Baggers had managed to round up a few of the escapees but the numbers were down. Way down. And, although the others were friendly towards him now, he still preferred to keep to the sidelines. As usual, he wanted to be solitary. It helped him think better.

It was a warm evening. No clouds in the sky and the constant dampness seemed to have lessened a bit. His bones didn't feel like they were going to snap from all the icy coldness any more. Turning his head, he looked off into the darkness of the water, straining his ears for a repeat of the sound he'd heard a few minutes ago.

A soft call. The sound of a bird's forlorn cry.

But there were no loons in Vancouver.

A small movement in the darkness confirmed his beliefs. A quick wave. A flash of what might have been auburn hair.

His fingers automatically reached into his pocket, feeling the crumpled note he'd found by the fence yesterday.

We will get you out. I promise.

A

He didn't know how they'd do it but he had faith and that was all that mattered.

There had been several days of darkness after Leon told him about Daniel. At first he didn't want to believe it but it was impossible not to realize the signs had been there all along.

Daniel had told him that there was darkness inside him. He knew better than all of the others and now Mason didn't have any reason to doubt him. It was probably true.

But Mason also knew for sure now that he wasn't a Bagger. Not him. Daniel.

So maybe there was something different inside him, something darker than anything the Baggers could ever imagine. But Mason had control of it.

He would stay in control as long as he could. And he'd use it to survive.

There was some relief knowing that Daniel was the one who'd been spying on them, passing information about the group on to the Baggers. It explained how Leon knew so much.

'Mason!'

Casey ran between the tents, and he knelt down and opened his arms to catch her. Hauling her up above his shoulders, he tossed her gently into the air, enjoying the happy screams and giggles that escaped her mouth.

'Play with me!'

At first his heart had nearly broken when he'd realized she hadn't escaped. But in the past week she'd become invaluable to him, keeping him sane. He pulled her into him and gave her a big hug.

'We should go get some supper. Are you hungry?'

She nodded vigorously. 'But no cabbage. OK? You promise? I don't like it. Yuck!'

'I'll see what I can do,' he said. Placing her gently on the ground, he took her hand in his and allowed her to drag him off to where the others waited for their evening meal.

He looked back and smiled before being pulled away into the light.

Knowing she was out there, alive, that was all that mattered.

They would meet again. That much he knew for certain.

ACKNOWLEDGMENTS

Thanks to Alison Acheson and Mimi Thebo for all their great advice and help during these past years. You've both been there so much for me. I can't thank you enough.

To my editors, Ruth Alltimes at Macmillan and David Gale at Simon & Schuster. Your skills are invaluable.

To my agents Julia Churchilll and Sarah Davis. You have both been inspirational and always willing to listen and offer advice.

To the Insomniacs: Andrea, Shannon, Laura, Marissa, Morgan, Ash, Ryan and everyone else. You've all been with me since the start. I can't begin to tell you how great you all are. You're my friends around the world and one day I plan to meet every single one of you.

To Evie, because you always make me smile.

And finally to my mother, Peggy. You are an amazing woman and I can't begin to say how much I love and respect you. You've helped me grow to be the person I am today.

D4RK INSIDE

JEYN ROBERTS

EARThQUAKES ShUDDER ACROSS
ThE WORLD

SOMETHING IS RELEASED

TRUST NO ONE – NOT EVEN YOURSELF

1

ThE KILLING GAME hAS BEGUN . . .

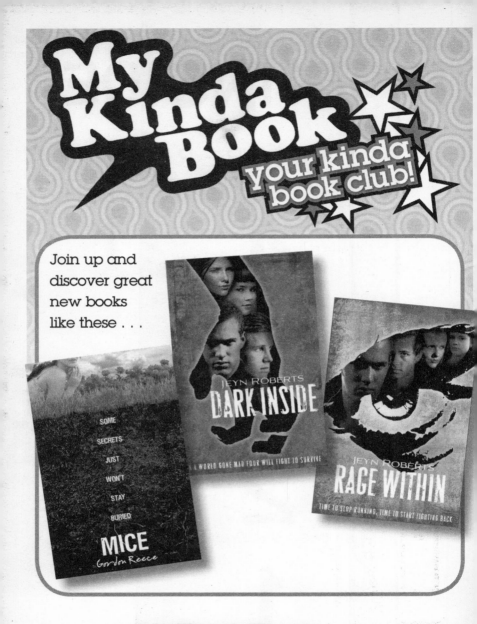